Chapter 1 - Sylvia

IT WAS TOO BRIGHT. WAY, way too bright! I tried throwing the pillow over my head but that just caused the throbbing to start. Why did I let Kai-ying talk me into the shots? Damn evil little sprite and her "just one more and if you don't meet someone we'll go home." I lost count of 'one mores' after four and that was on top of a couple mixed drinks. How the hell her little body could handle that much alcohol was beyond me. The morning sun filtered through the curtains and I had to get up and get the day started with the hangover from hell.

I laid in bed awhile longer thinking over the previous night. My happy go lucky best friend, Kai-ying had insisted that I go out with her and our third musketeer, Kerri. She claimed she had a good feeling that I was going to find my *Mr. Right* very soon and no one argues with Kai and her freaky future feelings. I went along even though I knew I was not going to find *Mr. Right* when I already lost him four years ago. Recently here had only been *Mr. Never Calls Back* and *Mr. Please Be Gone By Morning*.

Kerri's boyfriend Reed sealed my fate when he bought a new game for the play station. Reed and Kai's boyfriend Sloane wanted uninterrupted playing time, thus freeing Kai and Kerri for the evening. So the three of us dressed up and headed out to the bar.

I didn't even know why I bothered trying to look good when I'm out with Kai and Kerri. All eyes are on them no matter how I look. Kai-ying Adams is every boy's wet dream. She was a petite little Asian girl who was cute as a button. Kai was eye catching with her ever-changing streaks of color in her short black hair. Her love of bright colors often extended beyond clothes to the colored contacts she wore, often making her look like a Manga character. Her personality was as bright and bubbly as her appearance. She's the complete opposite of Kerri.

Kerrington Shaw was the definition of elegant sophistication. She was tall with long black wavy hair and violet eyes. Her bone structure was per-

1

fect, her cheek bones, high and fine, with dainty brows and a straight slim nose. More than once she'd been told that she looks like a young Elizabeth Taylor. Like Kai, Kerri knew she was beautiful. She had been told it all her life. She used that beauty to her advantage, yet often forgot that sometimes one needs to be nice and not just beautiful. Kerri can indeed come off as a bit of a bitch but that just seems to add to her appeal.

Then there was me. I was nothing but your average, everyday girl. My Irish descent was clearly evident in my naturally curly light red hair and green eyes. Nothing could be done about my hair. If it wasn't frizzy it was tangled in knots. My checks were dotted with freckles and my lips were puffier than I would have liked. I know celebrities pay big bucks to have lips like mine but to me they just seem too big for my face. Add all that with my small stature and I was really not much to look at.

It didn't really matter to me that Kerri and Kai were so much more interesting than I was. I loved them like sisters and going out with them was always an adventure. We had this little ritual we did when we went out. It started with getting a mixed drink, scoping the place out, doing a shot together and then dancing. That little ritual was exactly how we started the night. When we weren't dancing we spent most of the night at a back corner table with Kai and Kerri pointing out every guy in the place. Most nights none of them appealed to me but that night there was one that I couldn't take my eyes off.

I first noticed him standing at the bar smoking. In general, I don't like smokers but when they look like sex on fire I'll make an exception. He was the epitome of the classic bad boy, all wrapped up in a leather jacket and dirty Levis. Not my normal type at all but maybe it was a good time for change. Of course being me I couldn't just go up to him and guys like that don't seek average girls like me out, so I sat and watched him. He spoke with the bartender for a bit before scanning the room. He took a long look at Kerri. I'm sure had she noticed she would have led him along only to tell him about Reed in the end, that was if Reed didn't just show up. Reed is a big guy, intimidating to most until you get to know him. From all appearance he looks to be a big tough guy. He's loud and crass and doesn't like others looking at his Kerri. When you get to know him you know he's nothing more than a giant teddy bear. Reed was always joking around and more often than not those jokes were aimed in my direction. He said it's because he never had a little sister and if he did I would be exactly the one he would want.

ACROSS THE HALL

nm facile

central avenue publishing

2012

For my family,
For only the love and support that a family provides.

A special thank you to Corrina for answering each and every text and phone call, no matter how trivial. Thanks to Michael for his patience. Lastly, thank you to all the LTR girls for their encouragement and support.

ACROSS the HALL

Needless to say, it surprised the hell out of me when the bad boy from the bar came up to me and started dancing with me. He pulled me tight up to him and moved with me. I could smell the smoke and alcohol on him but I found it to be more of a turn on. The smooth leather of his black jacket was broken by little silver studs and rings. I could feel each little bump on his jacket the closer he danced to me. After a few songs he led me off the floor and back to the table Kai, Kerri and I had been at before. I probably would have gone home with him if it hadn't been for Kerri. She decided that it was time to go and she was going to make sure I got home safely. I knew I spent some time talking to him but for the life of me I couldn't remember his name in the morning. It was something like Bob or Brian or Bill. Hell, I couldn't remember. I would have to call Kai and ask her.

I looked over at my alarm clock, it was just after ten. I had to get moving if I was going to be into work by noon. I wasn't like Kai and Kerri, who came from wealthy families and didn't have to work while in school. Even though my education was paid for I still had rent and life expenses to cover. My part time job at the campus book store barely helped keep me afloat but the schedule was flexible and close to the apartment which was great since my car finally died the past spring and I didn't have enough to get a new one yet.

I got up and headed to the fridge for a pop and then the cupboard to grab the Tylenol. I twisted the lid to match up the little arrows but couldn't seem to get the damn thing to pop off. I finally tried using my teeth which only sent fresh waves of pain coursing through my already sensitive head. Frustrated I threw the bottle at the wall and headed to the bathroom for a long hot shower.

The combination of the caffeine and the shower had me almost feeling human again as I headed out for work. I pulled the apartment door shut behind me and paused for a second to fish my sunglasses out of my purse. The large window over the stairs was letting way more light in than I could handle at that moment. I put them on and let my head fall back against my door, that's when I noticed the door across the hall was propped open.

That place had been vacant since May. I knew from Kai that it had been rented in May but the new tenant wasn't moving in until the end of summer. I had been wondering for the past week when my new neighbor would show up. I'm sure Kai would know all about the person by the end of the day. It had been killing her all summer not knowing anything about the renter of apartment 304. She knew everyone else in the building. Of course that wasn't hard, there were only twelve apartments in our building and I was in 303, Reed and Kerri were in 203 and Sloane and Kai were in 201.

There was a moving truck in the parking lot. I gave it a fleeting glance and saw a shadow on the ground behind the truck. I would just have to meet my new neighbor later. I had to go the opposite direction to work.

Work sucked. I hated this time of year. All the lost freshmen stumbling around looking for their books just got old after awhile. By four o'clock my patience was long gone and my headache was back in full force. I stepped in the back room just to get off the sales floor and take a breath. I pulled out my cell and checked the missed calls. Three from Kai and one from a number I didn't recognize. I skipped over Kai's and went right for the mystery number. It was from a guy named Beau Dalton. Apparently Beau was the name of the man from the bar the night before. I was close. At least I had the B right. I hadn't recalled giving him my number, but then I didn't exactly remember his name either. He wanted to know if I was free for a late dinner. I called him back and we settled on eight and gave him directions to pick me up. I smiled inwardly as I realized I had something to talk about with Kai when I called her back. But that had to wait until after work. I took a deep breath and headed back into the chaos for a couple more hours.

I called Kai back on my way home. "Sylvia, you have to get back here. Your neighbor moved in across the hall today and Reed and Sloane met him and they said that..." she was talking so fast. I knew I wouldn't be able to interrupt her until she had it all out so I let her continue. "He lives alone and he's in med school and he was really nice. When you get here we need to go see him and say hi. It's the neighborly thing to do, you know."

"Sure, but aren't we doing this to satisfy your curiosity?" I teased.

"That too. Aren't you curious?"

"No. I have other things to keep my mind occupied. Beau called and asked me to dinner tonight."

The squeal she let out was like an ice pick to my head. "Oh, Sylvia see I told you I had a good feeling it was time for you to meet someone. You will have to invite him to the picnic this Saturday. And..."

I cut her off. "Stop now. I just met him. And yes, I am going out with him tonight but that doesn't mean he will be around by Saturday." My track record with guys staying around longer than a week wasn't good.

There had only been three or four boys that I'd dated for longer than a month since high school. I broke it off with all of them. Mostly I settled for one night stands. If I didn't get attached to anyone it wouldn't hurt when they left. The quick turnover rate was starting to wear on me and lately I found myself watching my friends in loving relationships and wanting one for myself.

"I'll come up to help you get ready. Then we can go see Quinn before he..."

"Quinn? Who is Quinn?" I felt the air rush out of me as pain over took my chest.

"Oh, that's what Reed said the new guy's name is." I stood frozen. It couldn't be. "We can stop and say hi..."

"Kai I have to go." I hung up while she was still talking. The panic came back bringing a hallow feeling with it. It's not him. It's just a name. There are lots of people named Quinn. I'm being ridiculous to even entertain the idea that it's him. I took a few deep breaths to calm myself down. Yet it still all came back.

"Sylvia it's not working." Quinn was looking over my shoulder. He couldn't even look me in the eye.

"What's not working?" My body went instantly cold with fear. I knew where he was going but I couldn't believe it.

"Us. I thought it would, but this is not what I want. I'm ready for a change and I need to be free for that to happen."

The pain was ripping into me. The lump in my throat had me choking on my words "but...but...I love you. You love me." The tears were falling and I just wanted him to wrap me in his arms and tell me he didn't mean it. "What about the last four years? Are you throwing that all away?"

Quinn pinched the bridge of his nose and closed his eyes. When he finally did look at me I could see the pain in his deep brown eyes too. "No, but it's time to end it. I want to move on. I have plans for my life and you don't fit into them anymore." I tried to take his hand but he pulled away. "Sylvia I have to go." He leaned over and kissed my forehead and turned to walk away. I tried to grab on to him but he just shrugged me off and kept on going. I just stood there numbly watching my love walk away as my world shattered.

I took another deep breath, I was past this. It was not Quinn. He was living the life he wanted. He was not here. With that thought I started back home. I turned my mind to tonight and Beau.

As I walked down the hall to my apartment I could hear the strains of the Stones coming from across the hall. My breath hitched and my heart ached in memory of Quinn listening to them. I repeated 'it's not him' over and over until I had myself believing it. I couldn't live through Quinn Lobato again.

"OH MY GOD! Syl, you seriously aren't wearing that." Kai was staring at me wide-eyed.

"I knew it would get a reaction out of you, but I didn't think it was THAT bad. I mean you bought me the shirt." I motioned to the length of my torso at the knotted-strap, black, silk cami.

"It's not the shirt that's the problem. It's what you're wearing with it." I looked at my faded, skintight jean crops and down to the worn, black cowboy boots I'd bought at a thrift store on a whim while shopping with Sloane.

I shrugged. "Yeah, well you saw how he was dressed last night. Like he's going to take me somewhere where I would need to be dressed in that." I said pointing at the little silver dress Kai was holding up.

She looked at the dress and then back at me before letting out a heavy sigh. "You're probably right. Well, you at least need to do something about that hair and put some makeup on." She pushed past me and headed toward the bathroom. "Aren't you coming? We have a lot of work to do to make up for that outfit."

I rolled my eyes at her and turned to follow her down the hall.

"Okay I think that's it," Kai muttered as she stepped back to inspect the lip gloss she just finished putting on me. "Now let's go over and meet your new neighbor."

"Um. I don't think I have enough time." Please, please let it be about eight. I just couldn't deal with that now. Not when just hearing the name Quinn could cause me a mini anxiety attack. I stood up and walked out of the bathroom and looked at the clock on my night stand. 7:35. This could be close.

"Sylvia, it isn't even a quarter to eight. We'll just stop over and say hi and you'll be back here before Beau even gets to the parking lot." Kai was giving me her big puppy eyes, this time she didn't have any contacts in and the deep brown pools almost had me. I wasn't going to let her puppy eyes fool me this time.

"No, Kai. What if he comes early and I'm walking out of some guy's apartment?"

"How will he know it isn't mine? Please, what if he's hot? You could be living next door to an Italian super model and you want to wait to meet him later? What if he had a spell put on him to marry and live happily ever after with the next girl to knock on his door?"

"If that's the case you go knock on his door now and I'll just take Sloane while you're off living in fairy tale land." I smirked at her hoping this would put a stop to her nonsense.

She slapped at my arm, "I saw Sloane first so I have dibs. If you would have come out of your room that first week of school for times other than class, you would have seen him first and then you could have had him. But noooo, you were holed up in your room alone. Now you don't get to complain because you didn't find the best guys first."

This had been a long running joke with the three of us -- that if I had seen Sloane or Reed before her or Kerri I would be with one of them. I loved both Reed and Sloane, but in big brother kind of way, just like I felt about Jason, my best friend from home. While all three were good guys, none of them were right for me. None of them had brown eyes. No, that wasn't it. I shook my head to lose that thought. None of them were what I was looking for. Yeah, a crooked smile and mahogany hair. Stop now! Even my own mind wouldn't let it rest tonight.

I laughed at Kai and tried a new tactic. "Okay, let's say I am the one he's supposed to be with forever. What is he going to think when another guy comes to pick me up?" Ha! I had her there.

Kai-ying scrunched up her nose and stuck her tongue out at me. "Fine, but we ARE going to meet him tomorrow." With that there was a knock at my door. "Wow, he's like fifteen minutes early he must really want to see you."

I gave her a dirty look as I opened the door. Standing there was a vision of hotness. He was all sandy blond hair hanging to his chin, sparkling green eyes and a dimple that all but made a girl week in the knees. Unfortunately it wasn't the right hot guy standing on the other side of it. "Hey Sloane." I opened the door wider for him to come in.

"I was just trying to get Sylvia here to go over and meet the new guy. But she's being difficult," Kai whined like a spoiled child.

Sloane gave me an apologetic smile and drawled out, "Sorry Syl, I'll get her home so she quits bugging you about that. Let's go, darlin'. Reed and Kerri are ready to watch that movie."

"They can wait. I'm going to stay with Sylvia until Beau comes."

"No, I don't think I can let ya." With that, Sloane picked her up and threw her over his shoulder. "Kerri said to get you out of here however I had to before he gets here. Night, Sylvia. Have a good time." Sloane carried the protesting Kai out of the apartment and down the stairs.

They must have been to their door when Kai called out, "Call me when you get home!" Kai always wanted the details when I got home. She said she was living vicariously through me, since Sloane is the only boy she ever dated.

When she was ten, Kai's parents took her to a carnival. There a palm reader told her she had a gift and with that gift she would know love at first sight. From then on, she ignored every boy that crossed her path because none of them were it. Then, her second day at the University of Minnesota, she was heading out of her dorm when the door opened and she looked up into shining green eyes. She stopped in front of him, and he looked at her surprised. "It's about damn time." She said with a smile on her face. Sloane didn't even question her. He just flashed his dimple at her. They've been inseparable ever since.

I shut my door and paced nervously around the room. I stopped in front of a small decorative mirror and rechecked my hair. Kai had done wonders with it. This time she had it parted in the middle and left it to fall in tight waves down past my shoulders. Just as I was about to recheck my purse to see if I had everything I needed, there was a knock at the door.

Beau was leaning against the left side of the door frame when I opened the door. I grinned in appreciation at him. His shiny black hair hung straight down to his shoulders framing his face, drawing attention to his sapphire blue eyes. Those eyes swept over me like I was his next meal and he hadn't eaten all day. Even though I felt myself blush from such a predatory gaze, I still felt a shiver of excitement race through me. He let out a low whistle. "Damn girl. Are you ready to go?"

"Yeah, I think so." I followed him down the stairs and out the door, admiring the view in front of me. He was dressed casually, too -- which proved me right in not wearing Kai's dress. A faded black Jack Daniels t-shirt was stretched across his broad shoulders and clung around his biceps. He had on jeans even more worn than my own. The right back pocket was ripped away at the bottom and starting to fray, but it just drew me to his amazing ass. I caught myself admiring it and totally missed what he was saying to me.

"I'm sorry, what was that?" I looked up at him and blushed all over again when I saw his smug smile, as if he knew exactly what I was thinking.

"I said I brought my bike tonight since it's such a nice night. Have you ever been on a motorcycle before?"

"Yeah, I've been on one. A friend had one and let me drive it a few times." He looked at me with disbelief. "It was more of a dirt bike than a full on motorcycle. But they're basically the same right?"

"Well then, do you want to drive?" I could hear in the tone of his voice that he didn't really want me driving.

As if I'd give up the chance to wrap my arms around him anyway. "Actually I'd rather just climb on back and hold on tight."

He smiled at me and stopped in front of a nice, big, black bike. I still can't tell one type from another so I had no idea what kind it was. Beau handed me the only helmet. "You wear this. I only have the one." I pulled it on. He brushed the hair from my eyes and put the shield down.

Once he was on the bike, he reached out for me. I took his hand and swung up behind him. He pulled my arms around him. "Hold on tight." And I did. I was pressed up tight enough against him that my nipples reacted to feeling his taut back muscles moving with every turn. It was already an abnormally hot night and the thin layers of my silk shirt and his thin t-shirt did not help.

I was so distracted with the scenarios my imagination was playing out for me from the closeness of his body that I didn't notice at first just how far we had gone. I started to look around but didn't recognize where we were. I had been living in Twin Cities area for the better part of four years, and I'd visited often before that. I thought I had known the area fairly well but I knew I had never been in a neighborhood like this. This was one of those areas in a big city that parents warn you to lock your car doors and not stop for anything if you ever get lost in it. The houses were small, and most had unkempt yards with older vehicles on the streets out front. The stores were all small and lumped on top of one another, many in need of a paint job. The diverse population of residents seemed to all be outside either sitting on porches or standing around in clusters on the sidewalks.

I wondered if I should be worried. I decided I should just act like this was normal. I was with him. I was sure it couldn't be that bad. He was probably just testing me, wanting a reaction from me.

We finally stopped outside of a, well, a fifties-style diner - and not one recreated for nostalgia. It was a dull silver color with spots of rust and several dents in the exterior. The paint around the windows was peeling and from the look of the shavings it had been painted several different shades in its lifetime.

After I took the helmet off, I looked at Beau curiously. He just shrugged. "They have the best strawberry milk shakes in town." Yeah, probably made with the original shake machine.

The inside wasn't as bad as I'd feared. It was old and needed a serious makeover, but it was clean and surprisingly busy for 8:30 on a Tuesday night. Beau led me past a counter with red and chrome swivel stools, over to booth towards the back. I slid on to the cracked, faded, vinyl bench expecting him to sit across from me. Instead he slid onto the same side, draping his arm across the back of the bench behind me. I peeked over at him to find him studying me. I just grinned back. "So I guess I should order a milk shake, huh?"

"It'll be the best one you've ever had." His eyes told me he wasn't just talking about the milk shake.

I swallowed, wondering if I really was ready for this. "So what else is good here?" I grabbed the menus from behind the napkin holder and handed one to him. He laid it down on the table, not even looking at it.

I barely got a chance to look it over before a bored voice asked, "What can I get for ya?" Two red plastic glasses of water were set in front of us. I looked up, half expecting to see the waitress in a candy pink uniform with a bouffant hairdo, chewing gum. Instead, there was a tired-looking twenty-something wearing jeans and a t-shirt with "Mick's" on the front. I assumed that was the name of the diner.

Beau ordered a burger and fries with a strawberry milk shake for each of us while I ordered the chicken fingers. The hand he was resting behind me began to play with my hair, combing through it, twisting it around his fingers. I started out with the basic getting to know you questions. "So are you from here?"

"No, I moved here a couple years ago. You?"

"No, I'm here for school. I grew up in a small town a few hours from here. I bet you never heard of it. Quarry Springs?" He shook his head slightly. "So where are you from then?" He had such sleepy eyes; the lids were only half open, barely showing the dark blue eyes behind them.

"Nowhere and everywhere. My mom and I moved around a lot when I was a kid. I came here to work for a friend." He was looking around the restaurant now. I wanted his attention back on me.

"What do you do?" I figured he wasn't a student. He looked older and a little rougher than most college students.

"I'm a tracker." He was looking at me, trying to gauge my response. I wasn't sure what a tracker was. "My friend Curtis owns a bail bond office and I find the ones who skip out on him."

"Wow, I bet you have some great stories. How did you get into that?"

"I was living in Tulsa and Curtis came to town looking for a guy. We had known each other for awhile, so he stayed with me. I ended up helping him find the guy, so he offered me a job. It seems I have a natural ability to just know where someone will try to hide. So what about you? What are you planning to do after college?"

"I want to teach classical literature at a college level. I'm starting the masters program this fall."

There was a pause in the conversation as the waitress brought over our milk shakes, placing a large glass in front of each of us. She also set down two silver mixing tumblers with the excess shake in them. Ordering milk shakes on a first date felt so innocent, when nothing about Beau seemed innocent. I took a long sip of mine. It was good.

Beau must have known that was what I was thinking because he chuckled, "Told you they have the best shakes."

We talked more about his job. He told me that was why he was at the bar last night. The bartender was a friend of the guy he was looking for. When I asked if he'd found the guy yet, he said no. But it was just a matter of time. His eyes bored into me, causing me to shiver. It was like he was sending me a message. I played it off as being cold from the shake. He just had this aura about him, drawing me in, wanting to see how close I could get, and waiting to see what would happen next.

Our meal came, and we ate while I told him about college life. We talked about motorcycles, which I really didn't know anything about. He suggested that I borrow my friend's so we could take them out together sometime. He laughed when I told him that I would much rather ride holding on to him.

I was just taking the last sip of my milk shake when he asked if I was ready to go. He stood up and held his hand out to me, pulling me out of the booth. He wrapped his arm across my shoulder and we walked up to the counter where he paid for supper.

"So where to next?" I asked, hoping he had more plans.

"I thought we could go have a drink. Maybe play some pool." We were already back at his bike and he handed me the helmet.

The bar we stopped at was in much the same condition as the diner. It was old and in need of repairs, one of the windows was even boarded up. I stood, looking it over, and Beau asked in a low voice, "You think you're up for this place?"

"Yeah I think I can handle it."

He sent me a lazy smirk "Hmm...we'll see."

I took a step towards the building and felt Beau place his hand at the lowest part of the small of my back and lead me to the door. His hand felt nice there. He opened the door and motioned me in first. It was about what I'd expected. It was dimly lit, with a scattering of tables around a few pool tables. There were a few booths along the far wall and an old bar taking up most of the near wall. There weren't many people there. A couple of old guys on bar stools watched the TV above the bar. Another couple were already playing pool and a handful more were dispersed around the room in small groupings. There was an old jukebox against the back wall between a couple of the pool tables that was cranking out what I thought to be Hank Jr., but I wasn't sure.

I stood there and looked around awkwardly, not quite knowing what to do. I was thankful when Beau handed me a $20 and said "I'll go grab us a table. Why don't you grab us a drink."

"Sure, what do you want?"

"Whatever you're having. I'm not picky when it comes to alcohol." He flashed a little grin at my look of confusion. "Just grab us a beer. I'll be over here." He motioned toward the closest table.

I headed up to the bar, not really sure what to order. I was used to girly drinks, and I never really paid attention to what Reed and Sloane ordered. The two guys sitting up at the bar were staring at me, and the bartender seemed amused at my discomfort.

"Um, two Coronas with lime wedges?"

"Don't have the lime wedge." He answered in a gruff voice.

"Okay then..." Quick, what was a normal American beer? "Two Buds?" I said the first name that popped into my head. They had to have that, didn't they?

He nodded his head and handed me two open bottles. I handed him the $20 and waited for the change, throwing a couple bucks back on the bar for a tip.

I headed back to Beau with what I hoped was a seductive sway to my hips. But since it was me, I ended up tripping, spilling half the beer on the floor and on him as he reached out to steady me. "Are you okay, doll?"

I felt my face flame up. "Um, yeah. Thanks. I kind of do that a lot," I mumbled.

I followed Beau's eyes as he looked around the room. "You play pool?" He asked, taking the beers from me.

"I've knocked around a few balls before."

He quirked an eyebrow at me. "So, a buck a ball then?"

I laughed. "Like I'm gonna fall for that. I may not have much experience, but I've seen movies. I know how pool hustlers work. I'm sure you're a very skilled player." I added, raising my eyebrows up at him, giving him a very pointed look.

"I've knocked around a few balls before." He threw my earlier statement back at me with a small smile. "Let me grab a couple more beers. I'll be right back."

"I'll rack 'em."

"I bet you will," he said in a low voice as he brushed against me on his way to the bar.

I watched him walk away, giving a little sigh at the sight of such a perfect ass. I turned back to the table to get the balls in the plastic triangle. I knew there was a correct way to place them in there, but I wasn't sure what it was. So I just alternated stripes and solids with the eight ball at the top. Beau came back over with a bucket of ice and four beers.

"Thirsty?"

He just shrugged. "It'll save time later. Why keep interrupting this shark game with extra trips to the bar? Besides, I don't like wasting time." He set it all down on the table and walked over to the balls, switching the eight ball so that it was in the middle. "You break."

I leaned over the table getting into position to shoot, but he was standing just to the right behind me, watching me. He was so close it made me so nervous I didn't hit the cue ball with near enough force to do more than bump a few out of the triangle. I blushed again at the pathetic attempt.

Beau just replaced the rack, gathered the few stray balls, and put them back in. He looked up at me with a grin. "Here, let's try that again, only let me help you a little."

"Sure." I repositioned for my shot.

He came up behind me, placing his right hand on my hip, and moved me closer to him. His body was so hard and he smelled good. Not a cologne smell, more of a natural musky scent. He grabbed my hand, repositioning it so I was bridging the cue differently. He covered my hand on the rear of the cue and started moving the stick back and forth smoothly as he softly spoke into my ear, "You need to focus on one spot on the cue ball. Then with a hard firm stroke, strike the ball and follow through." Then he backed away to let me shoot.

That try was much better. I got a clean break, pocketing two solids. "Looks like you're stripes." I took my second turn and this time hit the ball I was aiming at but knocked it wide of the pocket. "I guess I need another lesson."

"I'm not so sure you do. I believe that you are baiting me." He lined up what looked to be a fairly easy shot. "Eleven ball, side pocket." He bent over and, in one smooth stroke, put the eleven ball in. He stood up, looking me over. "That was a very nice break and I don't think you would have missed that second shot there if you were playing with your girlfriends."

"Are you saying I'm distracted?"

He lined up the nine ball for the corner and put that one in. "No, I'm saying you're better than you're letting on. I'm on to you. You think I'm just going to let you run me over?"

I smirked back at him. "I think you are more than capable of handling yourself."

Beau lined up and sunk a difficult shot on the twelve ball with the cue ball in a bad spot.

Finally, it was my turn again. I put my beer down and looked the table over. "I'm not calling a pocket. I'm not that experienced of a player." I lined up a shot on the four ball.

Beau finished off that game in his next turn. We played a couple more, flirting more and more outrageously with each other. He helped me line up a few shots and would trail his tongue along the shell of my ear or along my neck. I really liked the roughness from the stubble along his jaw when he nuzzled into my neck a couple times. I was definitely feeling it between my legs when he teased like that.

"Okay, final game," Beau announced. "How about some stakes? Every time I sink a ball I get to ask you one question and you have to answer it no matter what."

"Only if I get to do the same for every one I sink."

"Sure. Why not? My break right?" I nodded. "Rack 'em, baby."

I leaned in low over the table while I racked them, knowing that the front of my shirt was giving him a good view.

"You trying to use some kind of special warfare there?"

I looked up at him blankly. I knew exactly what I was doing, but I wasn't about to own up to it.

Beau lined up the cue ball and bent over low to get a better look as he lined up his break. He struck the cue ball firmly. It smacked into the other balls, spreading them apart wildly. But none went in. "I guess you'll get first crack at me, doll."

The balls were spread evenly over the table with several near the pockets. I lined up and sank an easy shot. "Hmmmm, what do I want to know?" I looked over at him, taking him all in with my eyes, biting my lip. "What did you plan on doing after this game?" While not an entirely safe or original question, it was the one top most in my mind.

"I have this vision of taking a beautiful woman home with me," He purred.

I looked around the room to relieve some of the sexual tension. "Really? Which one?" As if there were any question to who he was referring to. I looked back at him giving him an evil smile.

He dropped his chin a little, staring back at me. "It's still your shot."

I pouted, taking my shot and missing. "Your turn." I gave in and brushed my hand across his ass as he leaned over to shoot. My distraction didn't work, as he easily sunk one.

Looking over his shoulder at me I gave him an innocent smile. He asked me, "Do you like what you see?"

I let my gaze linger over his lips before drifting lower. I took a deep breath, letting it out with a quiet, "Yeah, I do."

He hummed low in his throat, turning back to the table. He sank the next one as well. "Are you enjoying yourself with your little innocent teasing?" He growled.

"I would be enjoying it a whole lot more if it were working."

Beau dropped the cue on the table and moved dangerously close to me, pushing me back against the next table over. He leaned very close to my face. "Who said it wasn't?" He pulled my hips up against him and I could feel just how hard I had made him. He was still looking into my eyes as he ground against me. I licked my lips in anticipation of the kiss I hoped was coming. "Let's go," he said, grabbing my hand roughly and pulling me towards the door.

I followed along the best I could, stumbling my way out the door.

Once outside, he spun into me, pushing me back up against the wall. Without a warning he crushed his lips to mine, kissing me hungrily. It was a rough kiss, he dominated my mouth. His tongue probed in me, hard and demanding. I kissed back willingly, giving him all I had. Just as I brought my arms around to grab that ass that had tempted me all night, he lightened the kiss and pulled away. "I think I should take you home."

"I think you should." I could not wait to get home.

On the ride back, I let my hands roam all over his body. I traced patterns over his hard chest, running my fingers from his pecs to his waist. I rubbed hard up the inside of his thighs from his knees to his waist. I loved having him stuck there in front of me, not being able to control my movements. A few blocks from my place, I started rubbing over his crotch, feeling the hardened length beneath his tight jeans. He sped up when I started to rub harder and I wiggled my hips against him and the seat of the bike, wanting to feel the friction.

We pulled into the lot and quickly hopped off the bike. I ripped the helmet off my head and he lunged down to me, capturing my mouth with his. His hands were on my back, pushing me into him. He pulled back. "You are such a little tease."

"Come up with me and see if you still think that." I knew I wanted him in my bed that night. It would be hard and rough, and I was looking forward to it. I pulled him with me into the building and practically ran up the stairs.

When we got to my door he had me pressed up against it before I could get my keys out. He began to kiss me with even more heat and passion. I gave just as much back, rubbing against him. His cock was so hard, pressed right against me. His hands slowly moved across my breasts and up to my cheek, then dropped down to my ass to pull me closer, as if that were even possible. He moaned into my mouth and broke away to move to my neck. I turned my head to the side, closing my eyes as he softly bit and nibbled along my neck and collar bone.

I looked back at him sharply when he suddenly stopped. He was looking over his shoulder, so I pushed up to my tip toes to look over his shoulder. I got a fleeting glimpse of a tall back topped by dark brown hair walking into the apartment across from me before the door shut.

I felt like I had been doused with a glass of ice water. I knew it couldn't be Quinn, but seeing hair that color was enough to make me lose all feeling, turning me numb. I had flashes of the previous panic attack I'd had after I'd talked to Kai on the phone. Beau started to kiss me again, but I pulled away.

"Are you okay?" He asked. His hands were still on my hips.

"I have to stop. I'm sorry, I just can't. Thanks for tonight. I just have to go. I have to get up early." I was rattled, and I just needed him to leave so I could calm down.

"What's wrong?" He looked around the hall to see if he could see what was bothering me. His eyes stopped on the new neighbor's door and he glared. That glare was very unsettling.

"Nothing, really. I had a great time but I do have to get up early. Maybe we can do this again?" I'd had an exciting night and I definitely wanted to do it again. I hoped this little display hadn't turned him off.

He started backing away from me. "Okay, sure. Some other time."

"Good night, then." I pulled out my keys and opened my door.

I leaned up against the other side of the door after shutting it, and slowly sank to the ground. I had so much racing through my mind. Beau had been totally hot, and my night with him had been good. I really wanted to see him again. I thought my bad boy may be just the thing for me to get over this. I resolved that tomorrow I was going to go with Kai and meet the new guy, just to put my mind to rest.

Chapter 2 - Quinn

IT WAS TOO FUCKING HOT. When the hell did Minnesota get so hot? Why didn't I listen to mom and hire movers? "Well Dad, this is the last of the boxes now it's time for the heavy stuff. Do you want a beer before we start in on that?" I sure as hell needed that beer and a shower. The sweat was dripping off me. I long since abandoned my shirt hoping that would help cool me down. It didn't and it would be awhile longer before I could get one.

"Sure. Good thing you brought those in first so they'd be cold. I'll wait here while you go get them." Dad had taken the day off to help me move. I moved back in with them for the summer. It had been a hard decision to leave Princeton to attend med school at U of M but dad seemed to really want me to come back home and eventually intern at his hospital. Mom was thrilled having me home this long for the first time in four years. At first she even wanted me to stay living with them but I wanted to be closer to campus and avoid a daily commute. Mom eventually gave in and found this apartment for me last spring. She said it would be perfect, close to campus, small with good security, seemed to be quiet with nice neighbors. From what I could tell she was right on all counts except I hadn't met any neighbors yet. I grabbed the beers and headed back down.

My dad was standing by the door shaking hands with a really big guy with a buzz cut. He had to be a football player, he was big enough to be one. Standing by them was another guy with blond hair pulled back in a band. He was almost as tall but not near as brawny as the first. Both were dressed similar to me, in basketball shorts and shirtless. As I came out the door my dad turned to me "Here he is now. Quinn, I just met a couple of your neighbors." I handed the open bottle over to my dad and turned to shake their hands.

The big one reached out his hand first "Hey man, I'm Reed Walker and this loser here is Sloane Evans." His grip was hard on my hand like he was testing my strength.

The long haired guy switched a basketball over to his other hand and reached out for mine. We shook as he said, "Hi" Then he jabbed the other guy in the ribs with his elbow. "You only won because you cheated. Just a warning if you ever play ball with this guy, he cheats." He had a southern twang to his voice.

"I'll keep that in mind." Both of them seemed pretty friendly.

"So your dad was saying that you're moving into 304 today. Do you need any help?" Reed offered. "We happen to have the rest of the day free and can help you out."

"That'd be great. We got all the boxes in already, it's just the furniture left. We were going to start on that when we finished these," I said motioning with the bottle.

"That will be perfect. I'll run this in and tell Kai. I'm sure she'll be out here right away to meet you." Sloane said as he headed into the building with the ball.

"That guy is so whipped." Reed laughed.

"I heard that. I'm going to tell Kerri." Sloane called back.

I looked at Reed as if to ask who Kai and Kerri were. Reed was already answering "Girlfriends. Kai has been wondering about you all summer. It kills her when she doesn't know everything. I'm sure she'll be out here and have your whole life story before you finish that beer."

Dad and I drank our beers while Reed told us more about the place. It seems that mom was right on all of it. Reed said the five of them had been living here for the last two years. I was getting ready to ask who the fifth one was when Sloane came back out.

"The girls went shopping so we really do have the afternoon free. When they go shopping they're gone for hours."

"That sounds like women." Dad added. "So what do you say we get this truck unloaded?"

Reed and Sloane were awesome. With their help we were done unloading in no time. Dad offered to take the truck back to the rental company and have mom pick him up there so I could unpack. It was too hot and I just didn't feel like it so I invited Reed and Sloane to stay for a beer. I found out Reed was the oldest of six boys. He was from Tennessee and did play football but blew his knee out in his third year and after that switched his major to sports medicine. Sloane was from a big ranching family in Oklahoma but decided the cowboy life wasn't for him. He was now in the graduate program for psychology. They met their first year and lived on the same dorm floor as their girlfriends who were roommates.

While they talked I kept thinking back to the girl I saw before I met them. She looked so much like Sylvia. But then I had been seeing Sylvia in every petite redhead I've had a glimpse of for the last four years. There was no way that she was still here at school. Last I knew she was planning on teaching and she was sure to be done with that in four years. And if she wasn't, well it's a big campus the odds of running into her couldn't be in my favor. Get over it and move on, she has. I had to keep reminding myself of the last time I saw her.

It was over winter break my first year away. I was back in Quarry Springs for the holidays and ran to town to pick stuff up for my mom. I parked out front of the grocery store and headed in only to remember I left the list in the car. I turned to go get it and saw a guy walking across the street with his arm around my Sylvia. My heart froze. It was that moment when I realized I could never go back like I had dreamed. I had lost my Sylvia forever. I got back into the car and didn't go back into town again. In fact that whole break I barely came out of my room and left early to go back to Princeton. Fortunately before summer break my dad took a job in Minneapolis and I never stepped foot in Quarry Springs again.

The three of us finished off our first beer and I was getting ready to offer them another when Reed's cell phone rang. "That would be Kerri. I bet the girls are back and wondering where we are." Sloane guessed.

Reed hung up and confirmed it. "So, Quinn, man thanks for the beer. You will have to stop in later and meet Kai and Kerri. That is if the pixie doesn't come up here to meet you first."

Sloane said his goodbyes too and I promised I would meet up with them sometime tomorrow. I turned and looked at the mess of boxes and decided to take that shower before I started to unpack. Unfortunately I had to find the box of bathroom stuff before I could do it. I had labeled all the boxes carefully when I packed them so it was just a matter of finding the right box. I plugged my iPod into the docking station and turned on the Stones and began the search. It didn't take long to find the right box and head to the shower, again thinking of the girl and of Sylvia.

The shower was just what I needed to get me motivated again. I came out of it refreshed and ready to unpack. I looked around, not really sure where I should start. The bedroom seemed to be a good choice. That way when I was done for the night that would at least be ready for me. I headed

in there, thankful that Reed and Sloane helped me set up the bed. I could
have done it by myself, but it would have sucked. At least now I only had
to make it. I found the box with the bedding and pulled it all out. Mom
insisted on buying me all new stuff, not only for this room but for every
room.

This was my first apartment. I lived in the dorms at Princeton not
wanting to have to find a place and furnish it when I wasn't sure how long
I was going to stay there. I was excited to actually have a place to call my
own. After I had the bed made I continued putting my clothes away and
set up my alarm clock. There were more boxes of books and other things
but I figured those could wait until tomorrow. It was after seven and I
really needed to get something to eat. I didn't have anything in the house
so I decided to run to the nearest fast food place I found.

A good thing about living close to a college campus is that there is any
number of food places close by. I opted for the first one I saw with a drive
through so I could get back to work. As I pulled away from paying at the
first window my phone began to play mom's ringtone.

"Hi Mom."

"Quinn, how is the unpacking going?" I had been surprised when
she didn't offer to come help me put my apartment together. Mom is
an interior designer. I offered her free reign with my place. She said she
would limit herself to helping me pick out what I would need but as for
arranging it and putting it away I would be on my own. She told me that
it would feel more like my own if I did it all myself.

"Well I have most of the bedroom done. Oh, hold on a minute." The
guy at the second window handed me my food and I thanked him quickly,
turning back to the phone. "Sorry, I'm in the drive-through picking up
supper."

"I knew I should have sent some things with you. You can always come
home and eat with your father and me too, you know."

"I know Mom. This was just close and easy. I still have a lot left to do
tonight. I thought I would unpack the kitchen stuff and then go to the
grocery store so I would have breakfast tomorrow."

"Well, it sounds as if you are off to a good start. Your dad said that you
met some of your neighbors. Anyone interesting?" I got the suspicious
feeling that she was fishing for information but I didn't know why.

"Just Reed and Sloane, the two guys that helped carry the furniture in.
I told them I would see them again tomorrow and meet their girlfriends."

"Your father mentioned that they live on the floor below you. You didn't happen to meet anyone on your floor yet?"

"Um, no but I'm sure I will soon. Why do you ask?"

"It never hurts to know your neighbors, just in case you ever need anything."

"Mom, this isn't the dorms. It doesn't matter who I live by. I could probably go the whole year without really needing to know my neighbors."

"Hopefully you won't. I need to go now. I will check in with you later. Oh, and bring your laundry home when you need it done."

"Mom, I can do my own laundry. I have been doing it myself for the last four years."

"I know that, I just didn't want you to have to pay for it."

"Thank you, Mom. Goodnight."

"I love you Quinn."

"I love you too." I closed my phone and waited for a motorcycle to pull out of the parking space I had vacated earlier. Going past the second floor I could hear Reed laughing from one of the apartments, that guy was so loud. I thought about stopping and saying hi but opted to eat and get the unpacking over with. There would be plenty of time for socializing after I was settled in.

I ate quickly and began putting things in the cupboards. It was going much faster than I had thought it would. I probably would already have it done, but I had to open or take tags off everything before I could put it away. I was about half way through when I found an unmarked box. That in itself was odd, since I had made sure to label all of the boxes, but it also didn't look like any of the other boxes I had used. All of the other boxes were either the original boxes from the store or brown ones from a packing company. This box was all white without anything written on it. It looked familiar but I couldn't place it. Mom must have slipped in something extra. She probably called to see if I had opened it yet. I'd have to call and thank her after I opened it so she didn't feel bad.

I ripped the packing tape off wondering what she would have gotten me that we didn't think to buy when we were out shopping. I pulled back the sides and looked in. Smiling happily up at me was Sylvia. My smile faltered and my heart stopped. Fuck! This box wasn't from mom. It was my Sylvia box. Four summers ago I filled this box, taped it shut, and put it in my closet never to look at again. How the hell did this get mixed in with all my other boxes?

Some strange compulsion had me emptying the box. It had been years since I had seen this stuff. I thought of Sylvia often, but always tried putting her out of my mind as quickly as I could before the pain could set in. Seeing all this stuff brought it all back. Yet at the same time it also gave me a perplexing sense of comfort. I spread the pile of miscellaneous treasures out, picking up one of the CDs she had made for me. I looked at the cover. She had worked hard Photo-shopping a collage of photos of the two of us together. I looked through the song list. Suddenly needing to hear them, I shut off my iPod and opened my laptop to play it. The first song was "our song." I closed my eyes and let the sweet sounds wash over me. I went back to the collection and the memories.

I pulled out an old biology paper first. This was where it had all started.

It was second semester of my freshman year of high school. Being ahead of rest of my class academically, I was used to working on my own in most of my classes. The first day back after winter break I was en route to Biology after lunch, only to be stopped at the door by Mr. Rasmussen. "Quinn, we have a new student in this class. She was in advanced placement classes in her old school so I would like her to work with you." I nodded and headed to my table. I had heard there was a new girl at school, but I had yet to see her. I started getting my stuff out when I felt eyes on me. I looked up to see the most beautiful face ever. Her green eyes peered into mine and I was lost. I couldn't even speak to ask her name. She sat down next to me and through the whole class all I could do was look at her. I knew I was being incredibly rude but I was just too shy and self-conscious to talk to her. I was just a skinny, geeky boy. She couldn't possibly have anything to say to me.

The next day I vowed that I would talk to her. She was just a girl after all; no different than anyone else, at least that's what I kept telling myself. That day we had to work in partners for a lab. Once we got started I found it was very easy to talk to her. She told me the reason she and her father, Kelly, moved to Quarry Springs and I began to see that she was just as beautiful on the inside as she was outside. After that, I began to look forward to Biology every day, to have 'Sylvia time'. Soon we had a project to work on outside of class. That project drew us together. We began to spend more and more time outside of school with each other and countless hours on the phone. Our relationship progressed so naturally that I can't even pinpoint when exactly we became a couple. People say that it takes chemistry for a good match. For us it was biology.

I put the paper in the box and picked up a small photo album full of pictures of our years together. Flipping through the pages sent a flood of contrasting emotions through me. The pictures bought me back to when they were taken and I could remember the feelings of happiness, contentment and love. But overshadowing those emotions were the fresh ones of hurt, loss, sadness and the ever-present regret.

It had been an exhausting week of end of the year tests added on top of that Sylvia had the flu. On Saturday, I convinced her to spend the day doing nothing but recovering. That was the day I learned Sylvia talks in her sleep. We snuggled up on the couch and watched movies together. At some point she fell asleep. When she first started talking I thought she was awake and couldn't understand why she was telling me to stay, I was behind her on the couch obviously not going anywhere until she moved. Then she said the words I would never get tired of hearing. "Quinn, I love you." My heart burst at that moment. I pulled her tighter to me and just reveled in the fact that this wonderful, amazing person loved me. Eventually I fell asleep too, and mom couldn't pass up such a sweet photo opportunity.

There were more pictures like this. Ones of the two of us in the midst of various activities: at the beach, prom, standing next to school projects, holidays, and many ordinary everyday candids. The difference between the two of us was remarkable. At fifteen Sylvia was just as beautiful as she was at eighteen. I, on the other hand, had been a gangly teenager with my hair longer than it was now, hanging over my glasses and covering my eyes. I wasn't what one would term handsome and could never understand what Sylvia saw in me. She always said I was "adorkable." Honestly, as long as she wanted me I wasn't going to question why.

The small splatter of a tear on the last page brought me back to the present. I hadn't even realized I had been crying. It had been years since I cried over the memory of Sylvia, the memory of us. I put the album in the box and blindly picked up the next item. It was the graduation card she had given me. The pictures of the two of us in our caps and gowns had fallen out. I picked them up and placed them back inside the card. My chest constricted and my breathing became labored. I didn't want to see the jubilant expression on Sylvia's face. I didn't want to think of how the next day I wiped that look off her face leaving one of anguish in its place. I put them in the box without even looking at them. I couldn't deal with this. It was too hard, the pain too much. What was done was done, and there was no turning back now. I quickly gathered the rest of the mementos, stuffing them back into the box haphazardly.

I brought the box into my bedroom where I shelved it in the back of my closet -- where, unlike my memories, it would stay undisturbed. I walked back to the kitchen to grab a beer when I realized the CD was still playing. I shut my laptop; cutting off the song that Sylvia always said reminded her of me, in mid verse. I went back to finishing off the kitchen and then out for groceries.

I had to drive around awhile before I found a grocery store. I should have looked up directions on the net first. At least the drive gave me time to clear my mind. I stocked up on everything I could possibly need, most of it consisting of prepackaged, microwavable meals. I may know my way around a laundry room but the kitchen was still mostly uncharted territory.

The damn motorcycle was back in my parking space when I returned home. Wow, home. That was going to take some getting used to. I have my own home -- well, apartment, but it's still all mine. I got my key out and ready then fumbled around trying to get all my bags on one trip. I managed, just barely, to make it up the stairs without dropping anything. Once I reached the third floor I was greeted with the sight of my neighbors making out against their door. Mom obviously forgot to add exhibitionist neighbors to the list of qualifications of this place. I tried to slip by unnoticed, but the guy turned to glare at me. If he didn't want to be interrupted then he should move it behind closed doors. Like I wanted to see that every time I come home.

I put all the groceries away and headed for bed. I felt good about how much I had done. Tomorrow I would set up my electronics and finish unpacking, but for now I was exhausted. I stripped down to my boxers as I made my way down the hall, tossing my dirty clothes on the floor just inside my bedroom door. I fell into bed without setting my alarm. Man, it was nice to have freedom.

God, she tasted good. I couldn't get enough. I felt her moan into my mouth as I moved to suck on her lower lip. I traced it with my tongue and kept going with little nibbles and licks all along her jaw to her ear. My hands were cupping the sides of her breasts, my thumbs rubbing slow circles over her nipples. I brought my hands up over the top, pinching her nipples between my thumb and forefinger eliciting a deeper moan from her. "You like that?" I growled in her ear.

"Yes, more." She pleaded arching her back and pushing her chest up to me. I ran my hands down her sides to the hem of her shirt. I pushed it up roughly and dipped my head to take her nipple between my teeth. I flicked at her nipple

with my tongue over the top of the soft lace of her bra. As I moved over to tease the other one the same way I slipped my hand into the cup of her bra lifting her breast out to have complete uncovered access. I slipped the other out and traced circles over her nipple with my tongue. Her little whimpers urged me on, faster and faster, until I sucked the whole bud in and pulled back, releasing it with a pop.

One of her hands was gripping my ass, pulling me in closer to her while the other was running over my cock on the outside of my now-too-tight jeans. I moaned around her nipple as she began undoing my pants. Soon I felt her hand rubbing me over my boxers until her hand slipped through the open fly, pulling me out. She used strong, slow strokes up, stopping to swirl her palm around my head before going back down. She slid down against the door to her knees. I couldn't believe she was doing this out in the hall where anyone could walk up and catch us.

She held the base of my cock tight in her little fist as she stuck out her tongue, tasting the tip. I looked down to one of the most beautiful sights ever. Bright green eyes looking back up at me so innocently as she teased her tongue over the tip before closing them and diving down, taking me all the way in. I slammed my hand against the closed door as she sucked me in. "Damn, Sylvia, that feels so good!" I moaned out. I pounded my hand against the door even louder every time she pulled back, only to come down faster on me.

"Quinn! Dude, get the hell up and answer your door." The gruff voice broke through the haze. I swear to God I'm going to kill the person responsible for interrupting us.

"Fuck," I yelled out in frustration. I opened my eyes realizing that my mind put that little fantasy together for me, punishing me for opening the Sylvia box and witnessing the make-out session out in the hall.

The pounding didn't stop. I threw my shorts from the night before on and padded down the hall to the door. "Damn it Reed, I'm coming."

I threw open the door to a laughing Reed. "That's what she said." I rolled my eyes at him.

"So what brings you up here pounding on my door this early?" I moved away from the door letting him enter.

"Early? Hell, man its 11:30. I thought maybe you would like to come play some ball with Sloane and me. You know, get a little break from..." He stopped and bent over to pick something up. He looked at it quizzically and then looked back up at me. "What the fuck?" He looked back down at it again and I walked over to him pulling it from his fingers.

It was my favorite picture of Sylvia. I must have missed it when I put everything back into the box last night. I stared at it momentarily, going back to that day.

We spent a perfect lazy summer day making love out at an abandoned farm house on the edge of town. It wasn't our first time together, just our first time there. I couldn't resist taking the picture of my Sylvia. She was beyond beautiful laid out on the grass. Her soft red hair was spread out behind her, with her arms thrown up over her head. She was playing with a lock of hair, twisting it around and around her small delicate fingers. Her green eyes were heavy lidded with a look of absolute contentment in them. Her cheeks were flushed and her lips were still swollen and slightly parted as if she were waiting for one more kiss. My shirt was over her chest barely covering her breasts. My only regret was that the picture wasn't taken with a better camera than the one in my phone. Right after I snapped the picture she pulled me down for that kiss and soon we were once again lost in each other.

I was still semi-hard from the dream and that little flash back had my dick twitching.

"Well?" I looked over at Reed realizing he must have asked me something and was waiting for an answer.

"I'm sorry, what?"

He looked rather pissed and I wondered if I should be worried. "Why the fuck do you have a picture of Sylvia?"

I looked back down at the picture. "How do you know Sylvia?" I was instantly cold. I hadn't talked about Sylvia with another person in ages. Now I have someone who obviously knew her standing in front of me.

"Sylvia is a friend. A good friend." His voice was menacing and he was looking at me with complete distrust. "How do you know Sylvia?"

"We were... friends once." He looked at me questioningly and back down at the picture.

"From the looks of that you were more than friends."

It felt wrong, someone else seeing Sylvia like that. That picture was for me alone. I pulled it away from his view and turned to go to my room. "Yeah, well, it was a long time ago. She's gone now."

Reed called after me, "Gone? Hell, she lives right across the hall."

Fuck! I stopped and took a deep breath. I let it out and continued to my room to get ready.

As I dug through my drawers I debated on what to tell Reed. My heart leapt at the thought of her that close. I could see her again. Talk to her, be a part of her life. She could be my Sylvia again. My mind was racing, overjoyed at the possibilities. Then, like a punch to the gut I remembered the couple outside what was probably her door. Fuck! I felt sick. I sat down on the edge of my bed. I put my head in my hands and leaned forward. She's not my Sylvia anymore. I made that choice. I had to live with it. I would just have to keep my distance. Just move on, like she clearly had.

"Q? What's the deal?" Reed questioned quietly from the doorway.

I knew I had to give him an answer. But what one do I give him?

I looked over at Reed. He had his hands raised above him, holding on to the top of the door frame. His face was a mix of irritation and confusion. My gut told me that Reed was a good guy, that I could tell him about the mistake I made and beg for his help getting her back. While my mind screamed at me that she had moved on, and not to make a big deal of this. In this case, the one that yelled the loudest won out.

I shrugged, "Sylvia and I dated in high school, but we went our separate ways when we left for school." Meanwhile my heart whispered that I still loved her.

He looked at me a moment longer before his face went livid. "You're the asshole!" He stalked towards me and now I was worried. I threw up my hands, not sure why he was so upset with me. "Don't pretend to be innocent. You broke her heart. What are you doing here? Did you come here thinking to pick up where you left off?" He was standing in front of me at the foot of the bed. He looked as if he were ready to pound the crap out of me. I briefly thought I was going to have to use my hard-earned Tae Kwon Do skills.

"We're not gonna let you fuck with her again! You had your chance and blew it. Sylvia is the happiest I've ever seen her and you are not gonna do anything to change that." I didn't understand why he was so upset.

"While I am happy that Sylvia has people who care about her, I don't understand what you mean that she is the happiest you've ever seen her."

"You should know exactly what I mean. You're the one who did it to her."

"I know I took her by surprise, and that she was hurt. But it didn't take her long to move on," I came back defensively. Who the hell was he to tell me what happened between us?

Reed scoffed at me. "Didn't take long? It only took her the better part of two years, and that was to just go out on a group date with us. It wasn't until last spring that she even dated a guy one on one, and that barely lasted a month. So yes, she did move on, finally."

I stared at him blankly. "But I saw her over winter break our first year with another guy and she was pretty cozy with him. Maybe she didn't date because she already had a guy back home."

Reed rolled his eyes. "Tall guy with blond curly hair? Total farm boy look?" I nodded. So he did know. "That was Jason."

"See, I told you. She moved on." I thought I should feel better that I was right but hearing about Sylvia hurting just made me feel hollow.

"Jason is her best friend."

No, I was her best friend. But I guess I fucked that up too.

"I guess it got so bad that her dad called a friend of his for help and Jason came with and finally got Sylvia to start talking again. But then you were the one who left, so why should you care?"

"I didn't know." I mumbled more to myself then Reed. I hurt her badly enough that she didn't talk? I looked at him for answers. "What else? What don't I know?" I had lived with the assumption that she was fine and better off all these years now. And here this guy was telling me that it had taken her years -- years -- to even go out with a guy. *Oh, Sylvia what did I do?*

"Man, it's not my place to tell you. I just want you to stay away from her." He didn't look as threatening anymore.

"Please I need to know," I pleaded with him. I had to know the damage I'd caused. From the sound of it, the damage wasn't just to myself.

He must have seen the desperation in my eyes, because he let out a frustrated sigh. "We all met Sylvia our first year here. She lived next door to Kerri and Kai in the dorms. Kai made friends with her first, and gradually we all got to know her. At first we only ever saw her walking to and from class. She was like a ghost. Sometimes she joined us for supper. She was a mess of a girl. She was always sad, never really talked; she spent most of the first year alone in her room. After that first summer, she came back a little livelier. She was still sad but she didn't seem like she was barely holding on anymore. Sloane thought maybe over the summer she'd started on antidepressants. Even if that was the case, they didn't completely work. She still holed up in her room more often than not. But she also went home more on weekends and would come back a little better each time. Finally that spring, Jason came up to tour the campus and we all got to meet him and see how normal Sylvia was around him, almost happy even."

My head snapped up. "You said Jason wasn't her boyfriend." I was confused. If he made her happy, why wasn't he?

"Oh it wasn't for lack of trying on Jase's part. Poor kid had it bad for her. No, Sylvia only ever looked at him as a friend. I think the first few dates she did agree to were just to discourage him. After he started school here that fall Sylvia wasn't a zombie anymore. Now she laughs and goes out and has a good time. She's alive." He tilted his chin appraising me but still warned me, "You are not going to ruin that."

"You're right. I'm not." I wanted him to know that I wasn't here to cause trouble, that really it was all just a coincidence. "I didn't know she was here. I mean I knew she was going to go to U of M, but I thought she would be done by now. Hell, when my parents moved I thought I would never see her again."

He still looked at me with distrust. "Then why was that picture of her out?"

I ran my hand through my hair pulling at it, not wanting to admit that I'd spent a chunk of last night reminiscing about her. "It must have fallen out of a box or something. Before you picked it up I hadn't seen it in years." At least that was true. I didn't see that one last night. "I'm not going to do anything. Really. I'm just here for med school. That is my top priority. In fact after last night, I see that she has priorities of her own." The last bit came out harsher than I would have liked.

"What the fuck does that mean?" He bristled up at me again.

Great, what the fuck did I say wrong now? "Just that when I came home from the grocery store, I saw a guy outside her door being very... *friendly* with someone. I didn't see who the girl was." *Please tell me she has a roommate*, my heart pleaded, not ready to give up.

Reed just laughed loudly and slapped me on the back. "Yeah, that sounds about like our girl now. It may have taken her awhile to date again, but she's more than made up for that now." I didn't think I even wanted to know what that was supposed to mean. Reed was still laughing as he headed back out the door. "Come on. Let's go play ball." Looks like he's going to let me off the hook.

I shook my head. It was a lot to digest. Sylvia was here across the hall. She hadn't moved on like I thought, but now she had a new life, apparently one that had no place for me. "I'll be there in a minute. I just need to get ready." I called out after him.

Reed must have been looking through the box labeled "games and movies" as I got ready, because every once in awhile he'd shout out something like, "Sweet, I wanted to play this one" and "I will so kick your ass at Halo" and "I haven't seen this one forever."

"Do you always open other people's unopened boxes?" I joked with him as I came into the living room.

"Yeah, if I think I might find porn in it. I mean it's labeled 'games and movies.' How could I not look through it?" He was grinning at me again.

I still had something I wanted to say to him about Sylvia, but I wasn't sure how he was going to react to it. I finished tying my shoes and let out the breath I was holding. "Reed? Can we keep this about Sylvia between us?" I motioned back and forth between us with my hands and then pulled my hair back off my forehead, combing my fingers through it. "I don't want everyone making a big deal of it. It was a long time ago and both of us are done with it. So can we just let it drop?"

"They're gonna find out. I mean Sylvia's gonna eventually see you, and I'm not sure how she's going to react." He had a point there.

"Well, let's just let them figure it out. I'll deal with it when they do. For now, I'll just keep a low profile until we figure out how to let her know I'm here."

"I don't know man. Kai is going to figure it out and if you think I was hard on you, it's nothing compared to the wrath of Kai-ying and Kerri. Alone, they are scary. Together..." he just shook his head. "I think maybe we should tell Sloane. He'll know what to do. He's better with this shit than I am. If nothing else, he'll at least help keep Kai in check." We were moving towards the door when he added with an ominous grin, "Still, if you do anything to make her sad again, I won't hesitate to let Kai rip your head off."

I gulped, and wondered just what kind of girl this Kai was.

This couldn't possibly be the terror both Reed and Sloane threatened me with. Kai was mesmerizing. How one so little could be so big in...everything...was fascinating to see. She was very pleasant, overly curious, and very hyper, but still charming. I could see that she was a fireball. She, for lack of better description, danced around the room as she talked to us. She reminded me of a humming bird, bright and colorful and constantly moving. Sometimes I wasn't sure which moved faster: her mouth, her feet, or her hands. She asked question after question. I looked to Sloane and Reed, and they just flashed knowing smirks back at me. Finally, Reed saved me.

"Kai, I think Quinn was still planning on unpacking in this century."

"Oh. So you need any help? We can all come and help you get settled into your place. Sylvia worked this..." I didn't hear anything else. I had to find a way out of meeting Sylvia for now.

I quickly jumped in. "I have to go home later this afternoon. I promised my mom I would come for supper." Thank God, they live in the same city. "I was just going to go up to shower and change and then take off." I glanced quickly at Sloane and he nodded.

"Okay. Well, then I guess we'll see you later," she said with a slight pout.

"It was nice meeting you, Kai. Reed, Sloane. Thanks for the game." I added with a wave, "I'll see you around sometime this week." I left, going back up to my place. I didn't really want to go home, but I was going to now. I couldn't stay here on the off chance that Kai found out and showed up with Sylvia. Sloane agreed that we should avoid it for now. He'd feel her out on how she would react to seeing me again, and how best to approach her.

Sloane was an interesting guy. He was fairly quiet, and even though he was defensive about Sylvia he was still insightful when we explained the situation to him. This was amazing, considering Reed's tact. While we were walking to the basketball courts, Reed had said, "So I met the asshole who broke Sylvia's heart."

Sloane gave him a dirty look and motioned over to me. "Oh, don't worry. Quinn here knows all about it."

Sloane glanced up at me curiously. "Do you know him?" Reed just laughed, and it dawned on Sloane that it was me. First he gave me a heated look, but he looked over at Reed in confusion as to why he was laughing. "What the hell is so funny about this, Reed? Nothing was funny about Sylvia when we first met her," Sloane chastised him while still flashing angry glances at me.

"It's alright Sloane. I gave him the riot act this morning when I found out. But he has a side, too. I think you should hear it."

Sloane looked expectantly at me, his green eyes drilling into me, waiting for me to speak. I wasn't sure what to say. I was the asshole who broke it off and left. I'm the one who didn't answer her calls and left for a month after I did it, choosing to hide with my grandparents rather than crawl to Sylvia on my knees, begging her to take me back. Sloane looked as if he could feel the guilt rolling off me, so I figured I would tell it as honestly as I could.

"Since you know about the break up then I assume you know about her and I dating since our freshman year in high school. When it came time for college I broke it off. I was heading to Princeton and she needed to go here. I didn't want to deal with a long distance relationship and the inevitable breakup that would ensue. We would have enough pressure with classes and being away from home. We didn't need the added pressure of a crumbling relationship. I ended it when we could both have the summer to get over it." That was the excuse I had been using, since I could never tell anyone the real truth.

"So what?" he was just as pissed as Reed but in a quiet, menacing tone. "Now that you're in the same city, you want to start it up again?" As if it was that simple.

"No. She seems to be doing fine on her own now." I thought bitterly of the image in the hallway. "I didn't even know she was still here. I just came for med school." I wondered how many times I was going to have to say this. "Honestly, my mom picked out my apartment. My parents left Quarry Springs over three years ago and I doubt my mom even thought about Sylvia when she looked for my place."

Sloane was still looking incredulously at me, so I continued. "Until this morning when Reed told me about her, I didn't know how badly it had affected her. I don't know how I would have reacted if I did. I do know that I never intended for it to be like that." Sloane was starting to relax, so I kept up the reassurance. "Really. I don't want to hurt her. I will do whatever it takes to make this easier for her. Reed said you could help with that." He looked over at Reed, so I did too.

"Sloane, I believe him. Plus, we're here now if he does try anything with Sylvia. We can deal with that if it happens. Right now, we need to figure out how Sylvia is going to take this." Reed said this seriously, and I was beginning to see that he didn't take much seriously. Sloane responded to that with a snort, but then took a deep breath.

"Well, just know that if you screw this up and hurt her, you will not only have to face Reed and me, but Kai will...well, I'm not certain what she will do. But it won't be good."

Reed laughed again and I was a little worried.

We played ball then as we discussed possible ways for Sylvia to find out. I sucked at basketball and only agreed to play because I wanted to get to know them. It looked as if I was going to need their help. It wasn't an overly sunny day, but it was very muggy. Between the humidity and discussion of Sylvia I was ready to be done way before either of them. Finally, we called it quits and headed back to the apartment. We still didn't have a definite plan, but Sloane said not to worry about it. If I kept a low profile he'd figure something out.

So, in keeping with the low profile, I was walking into my parents' house the day after I moved out. "Mom," I called out. Her car was in the open garage, so I knew she was home.

"Quinn, dear." She was surprised as I popped my head into the kitchen. "What are you doing home so soon? I was under the impression from our conversation last night that you were going to be busy today. Are you done unpacking so soon?"

I leaned down to kiss the top of her head. "What, I can't come home because I miss you?"

She arched her eyebrow up at me. "It's barely been 24 hours. What is the real reason?"

"Really Mom, can't I just come home for supper? You know I can't cook for myself." She looked like she didn't believe me but let it drop anyway.

I stood over the garbage can and started helping mom husk corn on the cob for supper. She told me about Grandma and Grandpa Lobato calling last night. She filled me in on all the family news. My cousin was engaged, Grandma wanted to come visit soon, and I heard how Grandpa's golf game was going. I listened half-heartedly while I wondered about Sylvia and what would have happened if I had known how sad she was. Mom cleared her throat and I came back, still holding a partially cleaned corn cob.

"So you just missed my cooking, huh?" She smirked at me but didn't push.

"Have you met anymore neighbors yet?" She asked in almost a giddy voice.

"Well I met Kai-ying, Sloane's girlfriend, after I played basketball with him and Reed this morning."

"You played basketball?" my dad questioned as he came into the room. "I didn't think you knew what one was."

"Ha ha. Just because I'm not a jock doesn't mean that I don't know how to play. I just don't know how to play well." I grinned back at him and gave him a hug. "I learned to do a lot of new things while I was away. Sometimes I played with some guys from my floor at Princeton." I shrugged. "After Michael got me interested in Tae Kwon Do, I started trying other normal guy activities." My roommate at Princeton had been a third degree black belt, and helped out as an instructor at a local place.

He got me interested with the promise that it would be a good place to relieve my displaced anger, which had started to flare up frequently within the first few months of moving into the dorms.

Mom broke in. "Well it's great that you are making friends already. So, anyone else interesting?" And right there it hit me. Mom knew. My eyes were wide with disbelief when I turned to confront her.

"You knew?"

She blushed and at least looked a little guilty.

"Why? Why would you do that?"

Dad looked between the two of us not sure what was going on. "Marie, what did you or did you not know?" His voice revealing his confusion. At least he hadn't known too and kept it from me.

"She knew that Sylvia was there." My eyes were still locked on Mom's. She fidgeted uncomfortably from my gaze.

"Sylvia? As in Sylvia O'Mara? Wow! I didn't even know she was still there." Dad sounded surprised.

"Yes, well, she is. And apparently she lives across the hall from me. Tell me, Mom: is it a coincidence or did you know?" I could only think of a few times in my past that I was ever upset with my mom. This surpassed them all.

"Quinn, I think we need to talk." Mom led me to the table to sit down and dad excused himself, with the lame excuse of wanting to change out of his work clothes.

I sat, but I just watched her, waiting for her to begin. Even with her creased brow and frown mom still looked much younger than most women her age. Looking at her so closely now I began to see the signs of age. There were more creases around her eyes and her dark hair had a few gray hairs. Her pale blue eyes were sad as she looked at me.

"I am sorry you are so upset by all this. Yes, I did know. When I went to tour the apartment building yours was still unavailable and the landlord knew that he was likely to have some available. So he showed me Sylvia's place. She wasn't home, but there was a letter addressed to her on a table by the door and pictures of her with others around the apartment. I asked the landlord about the girl who lived there. He told me about Sylvia. It wasn't until later that he called to tell me that the apartment across the hall from the one he had shown me was open. By that time I'd decided I didn't care what one it was as long as you would be in the same building."

I caught myself pulling my fingers through my hair again as I debated on leaving now instead of hearing her out.

"Look Quinn, you have not been the same since high school. I know you said it was better that you broke it off when you left, but it changed you. You became so distant and so focused on school. You didn't want to come home anymore, and even your phone calls were few and far between. After you talked about taking summer courses, I urged your father to take the job here in Minneapolis. I thought that if we left Quarry Springs you would come back again. I had hoped that you would even bring a girl home with you eventually. It didn't work. You were still just as distant as ever. I knew that it had to be because of her. When the two of you were together you were so happy. Oh, you were still focused on your goals, but you had fun, you even laughed. That's something you rarely do anymore."

I knew what she was talking about. I had been a real shit to everyone since then. Every call I wanted to ask how she was or if they had heard anything about her. I always stopped myself, but eventually I had stopped calling. I just didn't want the temptation. I didn't want to come home that summer because I knew I would go see her and I didn't want to see her with another guy. "But mom, did you think about what it would do to her?" I knew from the look that passed through her eyes that she did indeed think about that.

"Quinn, I know your leaving was very hard on her. I told you before about all the calls and the visits to the house while you were at your grandparents. I never approved of you running and hiding from her. You know that. And yes, I heard gossip about how depressed she was. Kelly was beside himself with worry over her. He even called us a few times. At first I thought it would be best if you did just stay away, that with time you both would move on. Most high school romances don't last anyway. But over time I heard more stories about Sylvia, and you were so unhappy, too." Mom reached out to rub my hand. I was still upset with her but I didn't pull away from her. "I started to hope that one day you two would meet up again. Then there she was, right where you were going to be. It was perfect. I was afraid that it was going to be her apartment but the landlord said that she signed a lease for another year when I asked if you would be getting that apartment. Now we just wait and see what fate has in store." She shrugged. Her eyes were hopeful, though.

I shook my head. Even my mom was plotting against us. "She has a boyfriend. I saw him."

Mom got up to check on supper. She smiled and added cryptically,

"Not everything is what it seems. Now go tell your father to come down here and get the grill started."

The rest of the evening was spent amicably. I told them about Reed and Sloane and they laughed at the description of Kai-ying. We talked about my schedule and other random things. By the time I texted Sloane to see if I could safely come back, my anger at mom was mostly gone. When her plan didn't work out it would be just one more blame to lay on me. I would just accept that.

Sloane texted back that the girls were all at Kerrington and Reed's having a girls' night while he and Reed were at their place playing the Playstation. He didn't offer for me to come over and I wouldn't have if he did. I just needed to be home and think over the day and all its revelations, theirs and mine.

Chapter 3 - Sylvia

O NE MORE HECTIC SHIFT OVER with. Only four more days until classes actually started. That meant a couple more weeks of insane shifts at work until next semester. Not being the lowest on the totem pole anymore, I thankfully got the weekend off. Friday was move in day for all returning students. I lucked out on the morning shift Friday so I would be off by the time most actually arrived. Then it was Kai's annual pre-year picnic on Saturday, which for the first time I was excited about. This year for the very first time I was going to take a date.

Of course I hadn't asked him yet, but I would when he called back. At least I hoped he was going to call. I really did have a good time with Beau. It certainly was the most unique first date I had been on. Not the activities, necessarily. I'd been on dates where we'd gone out for dinner and then to a bar. My experience of first dates was that they were more about impressing me with what the guy could do or what he had rather than who he was. I guess that right there was a clue to who they were, if they thought I would be impressed with outward appearances. Beau, on the other hand, had taken me to a place that couldn't possibly have been to impress. In fact, it seemed that he was doing the exact opposite. He took me so completely out of my own element that I'd had no choice but to trust him. We were in an area of the city that I was unfamiliar with and, as much as I hate to admit it, I was uncomfortable with. It made me focus that much more attention on him as I tried to not think about where we were.

Everything about the night with him was a contradiction. At times it seemed as if he didn't care whether I was there with him or not. That this was just his normal Tuesday night and I just happened to be a part of it. Then he would look at me like I was the only person in the room. I liked that look. The way his eyes would take me all in -- like they were seeing right into me -- was absolutely hypnotic. It was intoxicating. And then there was the challenge. Not the pool game, the one alluded to all evening.

Could I handle it? Or, more to the point, could I handle him? By the end of the night I was damn sure going to try.

And I would have, too, if we hadn't been interrupted. I was still kicking myself for that reaction. After a night to sleep on it, I had come to the realization that it was not Quinn. I was being ridiculous to even entertain the idea that it was him. What was between us was over and I was going to accept that. I resolved right then that if thoughts of Quinn Lobato should come creeping into my mind I would just push them right back out. This was another new school year. It wasn't exactly a new start. I was still a student, living basically the same life I'd lived last year. But I was still going to treat it like one. Kai predicted that I was going to find my guy soon. That certainly would be a new beginning.

Once my little pep talk was over I was ready to deal with Kai. I'd texted her this morning before going in to work. I'd apologized for not calling last night, stating that it ended up being a late night. I'd said I would see her after I got off work at two. I'd had several texts from her over the course of the morning. Every thought she had that was relevant to me she messaged, as well as a few that weren't. I should have gone to see her, but I really wanted a quick nap. I figured if I called her she would just talk me into coming, so I opted to text her instead.

```
Need a nap. Will call after & we can talk, bring
Kerri. - S
```

She immediately replied.

```
New plans. Pizza @ 5 @ Kerri's & girl talk after.
- K
```

I tried to nap. I felt tired enough that I should have been able to, but I just couldn't. Frustrated, I poured myself a glass of sun-tea. I took it out on my balcony and lost myself in a book. Reading can be as relaxing and re-energizing as a nap for me and this time was no different. Honestly, I wished I could have read all night. It was much better than whatever girl's night activities Kai had planned.

At five-thirty, I realized how lost in my book I had become, threw my book down and raced down the steps in my sweats. If I had to spend the night girl-talking, I was at least going to be comfortable while I did it. Reed called out to me to just come in when I knocked. I entered to find them eating already. From the looks of it, they were all about done.

"About time you got here. The boys were just about to leave. We saved you some but you better hurry up. Reed wants to take the rest of it with them," Kai said, in way of greeting from Sloane's lap. Kai had changed the formerly pink stripe in her hair to a bright green and had it in small pigtails jutting up from the top of her head. She wore a short lime green dress with rainbow striped socks and basically looked like a four year old who dressed herself. At least she didn't have any colored contacts in. I'd known her going on five years but her love for bright colored eyes still weirded me out.

"Hi to you too." I grabbed a piece and headed to the kitchen to grab a pop.

Kerri stopped me when I passed her on the couch and held out a glass with a slight pink tint to it. "Here, we made berry mojitos tonight."

I took it from her and went to go sit on the last available chair. Before I sat down I caught Reed staring at me. "Can I help you?" I asked him sarcastically.

"No. I just realized I can now picture you naked."

"Excuse me?" I wasn't all that shocked that he said something like that. I just couldn't figure out what would trigger him saying that. I looked around the room. Both Kai and Kerri looked clueless and Sloane was scowling at him.

"Reed, I think it's time to go get your ass handed to you in MGS4." Sloane leaned down and kissed Kai on the top of head as he stood. Kai slipped into his chair and gave him her usually overly sappy goodbye calling him *lianren* - sweetheart. Even though Kai never learned to speak Chinese before being adopted she liked to use little endearments she looked up on the internet.

"Bring it, tough guy. You are so going down." Reed continued to taunt him, grabbing the pizza box as they walked out the door.

"What was that all about?" I asked Kerri as I took a bite of my already cold pizza.

"I'm not sure. Those two have been acting weird all afternoon." Kerri rolled her eyes. "So, tell us about Beau." I was surprised that she asked before Kai did. I glanced over at Kai and she was bouncing in the chair with giddiness, waiting to hear about it.

"I don't know. It was alright." I didn't want to really say too much because he hadn't called me back yet or anything. Not that I expected him to call this soon, but I thought maybe a text or something.

"Come on Sylvia," Kai trilled impatiently. "We want the details. The good details. You promised."

I laughed at her ardent interest. "Well, he picked me up on his motor-cycle. And yes, he looked just as hot as he did that first night."

"I didn't think he was hot." Kerri added dryly as she flipped her dark hair back behind her shoulder.

Kai gave her a "shut the hell up it's Sylvia's turn" look.

"We drove for a long time before we stopped to eat." I took a sip of my mojito. I didn't really want to tell them about the place he took me. Sometimes the two of them can be judgmental, and I didn't want them killing my buzz about the night.

"Where did you eat?" Of course Kai would ask that.

I hesitated "Um, I'm not sure the name of it."

"Was it around here?" I could see Kai mentally flipping through all the restaurants around here.

"No, I'm not actually sure where we were. I didn't recognize anything around there." At least that was truthful.

"Oh. Then what? I know you didn't get home until after eleven." Kai was so matter of fact.

"Were you watching out your window for me?"

She pursed her lips and looked at the ceiling. She glanced to Kerri, but Kerri just shook her head. "Of course she was. She saw you leave and come home. That's why your phone rang as soon as Beau left. Do you really think we would have let her interrupt you?"

"So tell us about him." Kai couldn't hold back.

"He's a good pool player. We went to a bar and played pool after we ate. He spent some time teaching me how." I said as I blushed. Both Kai and Kerri smirked. Kai "needed Sloane" to help her play our first year too even though she was probably better at it than he was to begin with.

"Did it work?" Kerri asked. I felt myself redden even more. "I guess from that blush we can assume it did."

"Let's just say if we hadn't have been interrupted, Kai wouldn't have seen him leaving." I scrunched eyes up and covered my face with my hands. Kai and Kerri both freely shared their exploits but I was still bashful gossiping about mine.

There was a lot of squealing and Kai was clapping. Then she stopped dead and looked at me. "Wait, did Quinn interrupt you?"

"No, I haven't thought about him when I kissed a guy in a long time." Okay I lied but she didn't need to know that. "It wasn't the thought of

Quinn that stopped me anyway it was the neighb...oh." I looked up at her sharply. "You meant my new neighbor, Quinn right?" I took a deep breath. There are lots of people named with names that could be shortened to Quinn; Quinton, Quincy, Joaquin, it wasn't him. It couldn't be him.

Both Kai and Kerri were staring at me now wide-eyed. They both knew that Quinn was the name of my ex. "Was it him?" Kerri whispered.

"I don't think so, but I only saw his back."

Kerri turned to Kai. "You met him today. Is it him?"

"Wait, what? Kai, you met him? I thought you were waiting for me to go with." I wasn't really upset, I just kind of thought we were going to do that together.

"I was. He stopped in with Reed and Sloane after playing basketball with them."

Basketball? I let out a big breath in relief and laughed. "What? The guys play all the time." Kerri asked.

"Yes, they do but my..." wait, I about referred to him as my Quinn. "But the Quinn I knew wouldn't. I don't think he knew what one was unless maybe he was hit with one in gym." That was one thing I had in common with Quinn in high school...a mutual hatred of anything related to participating in sports.

I'm pretty sure both of them picked up on my slip but they let it go. "Well, Kai what did you learn about him? I'm sure you grilled him thoroughly." Kerri and I both smirked.

Kai looked indignant. "I was just getting to know him."

"You need to write a book on the 'Kai-ying Adams meet and greet method.' I'm sure it would come in handy during Government Interrogation training."

"Do you want to hear about him or not?" Kai pouted. Like she wasn't dying to tell us all about him.

I ignored her and hoped Kerri would catch on. "So Kerri, I don't think Jason is coming to the picnic."

Kerri shifted in a way that Kai couldn't see her face and winked at me. "Why? I thought he was going to bring that one kid from home. That other friend of yours that we haven't met yet. He is starting here this year, right?"

"Colby is starting here. In fact he moved in this week. Jase said since he's off-campus this year. A couple of the guys from back home are coming up Saturday. They have plans to initiate Colby to life without parents. I was surprised Reed didn't say anything. I would have thought Jason would have invited him and Sloane." At first Jason didn't like Reed and Sloane. I think he was jealous of the time I spent with them. But after he hung around us and saw just how devoted they both were to Kerri and Kai, he began to loosen up around them. Soon he was doing stuff with them all the time. It was only Kerri he seemed to not get along with. I never have been able to figure that one out. Sure, Kerri could be a bitch. But it was mutual. I didn't know how anyone could not like Jase. He was just so warm and fun loving.

"Good, then he won't be screwing up the picnic," Kerri said with a huff. If Kerri and Reed weren't so perfect together I would swear there was sexual tension between her and Jason.

"About Quinn..." Kai cut in. I knew she wouldn't last.

I turned to her with a grin. "Did you want to tell us something, Kai?" I said, as innocently as I could.

She didn't buy it and stuck her tongue out at me before she started. "I shouldn't tell you anything and just let you wait. Then, after you run into him wearing something like that," she said pointing at my baggy t-shirt and sweats. "And you'll come complaining to me because I didn't warn you that you had someone that hot living across the hall from you and I will just laugh. Maybe then you would throw out all that old stuff anyway."

I looked down at my faded gray t-shirt. Yes, it was old. It was one from our senior class trip, but it was so comfortable. I loved wearing it. I just glowered back at her.

"Fine. Quinn was very charming. I didn't catch his last name and Sloane said he didn't remember what he'd said it was either. He's from here in Minneapolis and his dad wants him to finish med school here. He's happy to be back close to home. He opted not to live with his parents so he could be closer to campus. This is also the first time he's lived alone." Kai said all of that with barely taking a breath.

I just blinked at her. Kerri asked, "Okay, that's good. But what did he look like?" Of course she would think of looks first.

"He was tall and really toned. They hadn't put their shirts on after playing ball so I got a good look." She grinned suggestively at us. "I think you would approve, Kerri. He had really dark sexy hair, but that could be because they were still sweaty from playing ball."

Okay. Tall - check. Dark hair - check. Toned body? Nope not him. Not that my Quinn didn't have a nice body, it just wasn't what one would de-

43

scribe as toned. It was just the body you would expect a nonathletic teen-age boy to have. It was a body Kerri would definitely not have approved of. I was feeling good that it wasn't him. I had just one last question. "Did he have glasses?"

"No." Kai looked at me and I could see the relief from her eyes too as she figured out what I was getting at. "He's not yours, is he?" She stated that more than asked it. So she did remember him from his picture. I had only shown it to her once, when she went home with me for a long weekend.

They were both looking at me expectantly. "No. I admit, I was worried that it was him. Just because that would be my luck. The one guy I never want to see again would move into my building." So why did my heart just twinge a little when Kai said it wasn't him? "Besides I'm done with it. I'm not going to let thoughts of him in anymore." I stated it matter-of-factly. I changed the topic, giving them the hint to let it drop. "I'm going to ask Beau to the picnic Saturday." This would definitely get their attention.

"Really? So why haven't you yet?" Kai, of course, took the bait.

"Um, he hasn't called back yet," I mumbled.

"Don't worry, Syl. He will. Guy rules say he can't call you right away." Kerri rolled her eyes.

"Guys and their stupid games," Kai giggled. "Like we don't know what they're doing."

We spent more time laughing about stupid things guys do, and talked about our upcoming classes. Kai and Kerri had another shopping trip planned for the next day. Kai promised to buy me something perfect for the picnic. I warned her that Beau wasn't much of a dress-up kind of guy. She just hushed me and told me to leave it all to her. She mentioned that she was going to ask Quinn to join us too since he was new and that the guys seemed to get along with him.

At the end of the night I came home much less stressed than when I left. Kai and Kerri reassured me that Beau would call and neither really questioned about where he took me. I did have to explain why we were not in my apartment and still in the hallway when Quinn interrupted us, which caused a round of teasing. Both said they wanted to get to know him better at the picnic. The most relief came from the knowledge that it wasn't Quinn Lobato across the hall. And even though I slept well that night, I still dreamt of dark chocolate eyes behind a pair of heavy glasses.

The next two days went by much like Wednesday had. Stupid customers in the morning, followed by an afternoon of reading. Jason and Colby came over for a little while Friday evening. It was great to see the kid again. He was always so happy, but Friday he practically rivaled Kai in energy with the excitement of being away from home for the first time. They invited me over to Jason's place Saturday night. I told them I wasn't sure what the plans for then were. I would have enjoyed their visit a lot more if I hadn't been worrying about the fact that I still had not heard from Beau.

I was really starting to doubt that he was going to call back. I wouldn't be taking a date to the picnic after all. I wasn't even going to get to meet the hot new neighbor. Kai said she had Sloane ask, but he wasn't able to go. I had yet to meet him. I asked Sloane and Reed about him. Reed just leered at me and Sloane just shrugged and said Quinn was busy. Kai insisted that those two were up to something. When she went home Wednesday night, they were talking on the couch. But when she walked in, they had quickly unpaused the game and acted like they were playing. Of course both she and Kerri were hoping whatever they were up to involved engagement rings, even if neither of them would admit it.

I had a weird encounter with Sloane on Thursday. He came up with Kai when she brought over the new clothes she bought for me. When Kai left to get the shoes she forgot, he asked me if I was really doing okay. I have always felt that Sloane, above all the others, knew just how heartbroken I had been before. I'd had some very insightful conversations with him over the years. Those were generally conversations I initiated. He always just seemed to get me better than anyone else, even Jason. Jase made me happy and I'd had good times with him, but I could never really talk to him like I could to Sloane. Sloane let me talk if I needed to without asking questions like Kai tended to do. He was more sympathetic and understanding than Kerri, who told me to suck it up and move on. And he was way more mature than Reed. I don't think I've ever had a serious conversation with Reed. In fact I don't think Reed knew what serious was.

It just took me off guard when Sloane asked. I didn't think I had let on to anything he would have cause to worry about. I reassured him that I was fine and was over the past. I even let him know that I was more than hopeful that things would work out with Beau. Of course that was before three days had passed and he still hadn't contacted me.

I didn't know if I should be pissed or relieved when he finally did call me around 1:30 AM Saturday morning. He told me he had been out on a job and couldn't call me until then. He was back in Minneapolis and wanted to see me again over the weekend.

I invited him to the picnic. He hesitated but finally agreed to go. I smiled and did a little victory dance even though I was in bed.

We talked some more about our week. If I hadn't been so tired I could have listened to his voice all night. I don't know if he was trying not to wake others at his place or if it was just the fact that it was night, but he kept his voice low for the whole call. The low, rough baritone of his voice left me wet and needy when he told me that he was looking forward to picking up where we left off last time. He ended the call not long after that, promising to meet me at my house around one the next afternoon. I rolled back over after he hung up and smiled into the dark. Tomorrow was going to be a good day.

I woke up to a phone call at nine. Normally I would have had Kai to blame for a call that early, but it wasn't her ring tone. I answered groggily.

"Sylvia?" Who the hell else would it be?

"Yeah."

"Hi. This is Bobbie. I'm so sorry to have to call you but Corrina can't come in and we need someone to fill in for her." Damn it! Damn it! Damn it! Something like this always has to happen. I couldn't turn it down either. Everyone had been so good to me when I took off a couple weeks to go visit my dad in June.

"What time was she supposed to work?" Maybe I would be lucky and be done at two then I would only miss like the first half hour of the picnic.

"She's on 10 to 6 today." Crap, there went that.

"Oh." I looked over at my clock. Damn, not very much time. "Sure. I may be a little late. I haven't really gotten up yet. I still need to get ready."

"That's fine. We're just happy you can come in and do it." I could hear the relief in her voice. I knew firsthand how bad it sucked to have to be the one to call around to find replacements at work. "See you later. Thanks Sylvia."

"Sure," I grumbled lamely, and closed my phone.

I let out a frustrated growl and called Kai. I knew she'd probably been up since dawn making sure every detail of our day was planned. She was disappointed and told me to check with them as soon as I got off, to see where everyone was going to be for the evening. Jason finally called Reed and invited them all over to his place for the evening if everyone wanted to come after the picnic. I told her I would and then texted Beau. I knew he wouldn't be up yet.

Picnic off. Have to work. Done @ 6 if you still want
to go out. - S

I threw off the covers, found clothes, and headed to the bathroom to shower and get ready for work.

As predicted, we were fairly busy until two when things started slowing down. The nice weather had everyone outside enjoying it. Several of us employees were standing around talking when the assistant manager came over and told me that since I came in on my day off I could go ahead and take off early.

I flew out of there. I called Kai first and told her. She said they were all still at the park and hadn't even started eating yet. I quickly called Beau, who thankfully answered, and he agreed to pick me up in a half an hour and we would go meet everyone there.

I rushed home, very grateful now that Kai had bought me something to wear. It saved me having to stare in my closet, trying to decide what to wear. Kai had actually done a decent job with this outfit. I was afraid that she would come back with a dress, but she surprised me with a light beige pair of capri pants and a deep emerald gauze shirt. It was a nice smock-like top with a little ivy pattern embroidered along the open v-neck. It was very comfortable. She finished it off with a pair of beaded flip flops. Thank God she didn't go with heels. We often played games like Frisbee when we went to the park, and I sucked at it normally. I couldn't imagine how much worse it would have been wearing a dress or heels.

Beau had gotten there really fast. I didn't have time to do anything other than leave my hair up in the loose ponytail I wore to work. When I answered the door, he looked me up and down again like he did the first time. When he met my eyes he smiled wide. "You look sweet enough to eat." So did he. His jeans were a little looser today riding low on his hips. The black sleeveless shirt showed off his impressive biceps.

I laughed at him even though I was blushing. His look and the way he growled the words out hit me at some base level. I briefly remembered just how good he felt pushed up against me on the other side of the door he just happened to be standing in front of. I had to stop those thoughts. "Let's go. We're already late."

"As you wish." He motioned me to lead.

He brought his bike. I told him which park we were going to. I loved riding behind him again. I wished I wasn't wearing the stupid helmet, though. I would have loved to lay my check against his back as I held on to him.

The park was busy. People were taking advantage of the nice days we had left before fall set in. Even though this was the park closest to the campus, there were still lots of kids running around. The slides and swings were teeming with them. I loved hearing their laughter and watching them run from one piece of equipment to the other. One little boy ran headlong into me from behind, toppling both of us over. I laughed as I pushed back up to my knees. I stopped when I saw Beau yank the kid up roughly and tell him to watch where he was going. He looked over at me then and saw my frown and his faced morphed completely into nothing but concern.

"Sylvia, are you okay?" He helped pull me up. I wanted to tell the kid it was okay, but he was already off running in the opposite direction.

"I'm fine. He was just having a good time playing tag. He didn't mean to knock me over," I chastised as I brushed my hands off on my pants.

Beau rubbed his hand up and down my back like he was soothing me. "I know. I was just worried you were hurt. I guess I was a little harder on him than I should have been." He looked away from me then. "Is that girl waving at you?"

It was Kai. She was jumping up and down waving both arms. I waved back to let her know I saw them. "Yeah, that's Kai. So are you ready to meet everyone?" I could see Kai and Kerri over by a picnic table. It looked like Kai had just set all the food out. She'd had one of the local delis make everything. It looked like she had quite a spread set out. "Hope you're hungry. From the looks of it Kai plans on feeding the entire park."

He laughed and kept his hand on my back. He was still slightly rubbing along my spine as we walked over to them.

"Wow, Kai, this looks amazing," I said when we got to the table.

"Oh, Sylvia, I'm so glad you got off early and could make it. Kerri, go tell the boys we're ready to eat. Hi, Beau. I'm so happy you were able to come with Sylvia. The guys are off playing Frisbee. We'll make sure you get introduced to everyone." Kai was dancing happily around the table, making sure everything was ready. She had all the food on one table and another close by for us to sit at.

I heard the guys laughing as they approached and looked from Kai to them. "Good news, Sylvia," Kai started to say, just as my gaze locked onto a pair of hauntingly familiar brown eyes. "Quinn was able to come after all."

Chapter 4 - Quinn

I SPENT THURSDAY AND FRIDAY laying low. I stayed in my apartment, just settling in. On Thursday, Reed and Sloane came over while their girlfriends were shopping. They hadn't told Kai or Kerri who I was yet. Sloane promised to talk to Sylvia soon and feel her out. I was torn between asking for every detail of the last four years of her life and not wanting to know anything about her life without me. Reed made the decision for me when he pointed to my Xbox and challenged the two of us to a game.

I spent the afternoon playing with them and getting to know them. Reed was competitive, loud, and crude, but made us laugh most of the afternoon. Sloane was quiet in comparison, but just as competitive. I realized that afternoon that I would get along great with these two. I hoped that my history with Sylvia wouldn't keep a friendship from developing.

I was lonely after they left, but we all agreed it was best if Kai didn't know I was around. Sloane was going to tell her that I was at my parents' house for now. That limited my ability to come and go as I pleased, but I had plenty to do to keep me in the apartment. Unfortunately, it also meant that I had to cook for myself. Thank God for microwaves.

Being home alone gave me a lot of time to think about everything. At first, I was still pissed at mom for taking it upon herself to put me -- us -- in this situation. The more I thought about it, I decided it was a good thing. It seemed that both of us had unresolved issues and probably needed the contact to get them worked out. While I had no idea what Sylvia needed from me, I did know she needed something. People talk all the time about the necessity of closure to move on. I thought that must have been what both of us required. I knew I'd taken the cowardly way out and hidden after breaking it off, denying us both that. Maybe if I had talked to her again, things wouldn't have been so bad for her, although I knew there was no way I would have been able to hold to my plan if I had talked to her.

I had left for my grandparents a couple days after telling her goodbye.

I'd had to turn my phone off the day before. She kept calling and texting repeatedly and I just couldn't allow myself to answer. I erased the messages, not even bothering to listen or read them. Mom was surprised when I emerged from my room after being holed up for two days only to ask to go visit her parents. I had gone to visit them in the past, and they were always asking me to come and stay so I figured this was a good place to run to. Yes, that's what I was doing. I was running. Mom called them and they agreed and I was on a plane that night. I stayed a month with them. It was undoubtedly the hardest month of my life.

I cut myself off from almost all contact with the outside world. I barely talked to my grandparents, which I knew worried my Grandma Spencer endlessly. I had even less contact with my parents. When they first started calling, my mom would tell me all about Sylvia and try to convince me to just talk to her. Mom was disappointed in me and let me know all about it. I knew she loved Sylvia like a daughter and I felt like shit that I had taken Sylvia away from her too. Not only that, Sylvia had looked to her as a mother after losing her own to breast cancer. It was just another relationship lost in this fucked up decision.

During that month I convinced myself that I was indeed doing the right thing. I was miserable without Sylvia but I had a plan on how to fix it. I decided to give it a year. By then she would be settled into life at the University of Minnesota and when she came home for summer break I would see her again. I could hold out for a year. I was doing this for her and I would do anything for her. I spent countless hours daydreaming about our reunion that next summer. How I would apologize and beg her forgiveness and we would work it all out. By the end of the summer we would be back to normal. We would be able to part again in the fall for school but still hold onto our relationship. It would work. It had to.

It didn't work. Winter break had changed everything.

By Friday I was convinced that this was a good thing. I could handle seeing her again. In fact, I wanted to see her again. At one time we were friends. Even though she was my girlfriend, she was my best friend. The same was true for her as well. She'd never really had any close friendship with any girls in school. She talked with a few, but the two of us were inseparable. We were everything to each other. Neither of us felt the need for other friendships.

It was about noon on Friday when Sloane stopped over. I had just made myself a sandwich, one of my few accomplishments in the kitchen.

I called out for him to come in before I remembered that I still had the door locked. I unlocked it and let him in.

"Hi, Sloane. What's up?"

"Kai sent me up to ask you to come to her annual pre-year picnic tomorrow. I also came up to tell you about my talk with Sylvia."

So he had talked to her. "Did you tell her I was here? How did she take it?" I was extremely nervous even though I spent the last twenty-four hours convincing myself I was ready for this.

"I didn't tell her anything." He looked a little sheepish. "I asked her how she was doing. She says she's fine and I really felt that she was. She's such a bad liar I would have seen right through her if she was lying."

"So what do I do now?" He was right on being able to know when she was lying. Sylvia couldn't lie to save her life.

"Reed and I talked it over this morning. We think it's time to let Kai and Kerrington know. It would be best coming from them. That way she can be prepared before she runs into you here or on campus." That sounded reasonable. "That brings me to the picnic. I promised Kai I would ask you. I don't think you should accept. Kai is all about planning this now and it would be best to wait until after the picnic to tell Sylvia. We'll tell the girls Saturday night and they can talk to Sylvia Sunday. Come Monday she will know and you won't have to worry about surprising her."

Great -- that meant two more days stuck in here. "I won't go to the picnic. Tell Kai I'm at my parents' for the weekend. When will you be gone Saturday? There are a few things I need to go out and get." I could always go home for the weekend but I didn't really want to.

"We should be gone all Saturday afternoon. Kai is planning for us to leave around one and eat at two so that should give you plenty of time to go do whatever you need to."

I nodded not really knowing what else to say. Sloane looked like he wanted to say something more but stopped himself. He just shook his head and said, "Don't worry about it. Sylvia can handle this. Everything is going to be alright." I hoped he was right.

I slept in Saturday. I couldn't leave until afternoon, so there was no hurry to get up and get things done. It was after eleven when Reed came up. I knew it was him before I even opened the door. No one else pounded on a door like he did.

"Quinn, dude! Kai ordered me to come up here and drag your ass to the picnic. She said she knows you're here because your car is in the parking lot."

"She knows what car I drive?" I briefly wondered if I should be concerned that she had stalker tendencies, but then I remembered Reed and Sloane joking about how OCD she was.

Reed just laughed at me. "Dude, Kai knows everything."

"Everything? So you guys told her who I am. Did she tell Sylvia already?" She must have. Why else would they invite me to the picnic if there was any chance of Sylvia freaking out?

"No. No-one has told her anything yet."

"Then what about Sylvia? Sloane told me that they were going to tell her tomorrow." I was confused.

"Sylvia can't come. She got called in to work or some shit like that, and now she isn't gonna be there. When Kai told me to come and get you, Sloane thought it would be okay. You can come hang with us and the girls can get to know you. When we do tell them about you they will see that you're okay and not some psycho out to hurt Sylvia."

"I guess if you think it will work. Anything I need to do or bring?" I was hesitant. "How much time until we leave?" I still had to run to the store for a few things. I should probably get that done with before Sylvia gets home.

"I'm not sure, maybe 2 hours. We eat around two." Reed seemed to always know when food was involved.

"I'm going to run a couple errands. I'll be back by then." I said as I glanced at the clock.

"Oh, we go before that and toss around the Frisbee or shit like that. We used to grill out and shit, but Sylvia always did the cooking. Kai and Kerri can't cook worth shit so we're gettin' food from somewhere else. Be back by one. You can ride with us." I glanced at the clock again.

"Yeah, I think I can do that."

After Reed left, I thought I should wear something slightly better than a plain white t-shirt and shorts I had on. I threw a dark brown button-up shirt on over my t-shirt and called it good. I wanted to make a good impression on Sylvia's friends. I rushed around and got all the stuff I needed at the store and was back with time to spare.

I went down to Reed's place around one. The girl who opened the door was stunning. Reed hadn't exaggerated about her at all. "Hello. You must be Quinn. I'm Kerrington. Come in. Reed and Sloane are going in Reed's jeep. You're riding with them." Though polite enough, her greeting was rather cold. I got the feeling that she was reserving her judgment on me and I wondered if that was good or bad.

"Hi Kerrington. Thank you for inviting me along today." I gave her my most polite smile. It didn't help.

"Oh, I didn't invite you. Kai did." Okay, Kerrington may be a problem.

"Hey, Q, you ready to go?" I cringed at Reed's shortening of my name.

"Yes," I answered simply.

As we walked down the hall, Reed opened Sloane's door and called in "We're going down to the jeep now."

Reed led me over to a big red hard-top jeep. It fit him perfectly. I let out a chuckle and Reed turned to me.

"What? This here is my other baby. Kerri first, then Ruby." I quirked my eyebrow at him. "Ruby Baby." I really laughed at that.

After Sloane came down, we all climbed in and headed to the park. Sloane said the girls were taking Kai's car because they were stopping to pick up the food. We were supposed to go ahead and find a couple tables to put together.

After we got there, we scouted out a spot and waited at the tables until the girls came. The park was busy. It seemed like everyone was out enjoying the day. I was surprised to see so many kids at a park near the college. In addition to the playground there were basket ball courts, horseshoe pits and some volleyball courts. Kai called Sloane and asked where we were, he started waving. They saw us from the street and parked close by and helped them carry everything over.

Kai sent us off to play Frisbee while she and Kerri set everything up. We threw the Frisbee around for awhile before Kerri came to tell us it was all ready. I followed behind Reed, whose arm was draped over Kerri's shoulder. He was leaning over and whispering something in her ear and turned to look back at me. I glanced over at Sloane to see if he knew what was up. He was looking towards the tables where Kai was. I could see Kai and some guy with black hair that looked vaguely familiar. I came around Reed to get a better look as I heard Kai chirp, "Good news Sylvia!"

Oh fuck. Sylvia was here. My breath hitched and I completely missed the rest of what Kai said as my eyes fell on the wide emerald eyes I had missed more than I ever thought possible.

Sylvia's face froze. Her complexion paled, and I noticed a slight tremble to her bottom lip before she bit it. I was trapped, and couldn't look away. I'd known, sooner or later, I was going to see her. I had tried to prepare myself for that. There was no preparation for the feelings that hit me. My heart ached in a way it hadn't in years. Not even seeing her pictures that night made me feel like this. God, she was beautiful. My Sylvia. I wanted to run to her and sweep her up in my arms and smother my face in her hair and breathe her in. My knees even twitched as if they were telling me to go, to do it.

I held myself still. She was not My Sylvia anymore. It took everything I had, but I tore my gaze away from her. That was when I remembered the guy standing next to her with his arm around her. His eyes narrowed when mine caught them and he pulled her tighter to his hip. I recognized him as the guy who was outside her apartment door Tuesday night. My first thought was, 'I could take him'. Ridiculous, I know.

The sight of Sylvia after all these years left me completely speechless. I looked first at Sloane, who was standing next to me. He was looking at Kai, who was staring intently back and forth between Sylvia and me. Her brow was furrowed and her eyes were narrowed. Suddenly, they went wide with understanding. She looked right at me and said, "Oh my God. You're Quinn Lobato." Then her eyes flew back to Sylvia. "I swear Sylvia, I didn't know."

Chapter 5 - Sylvia

QUINN. QUINN LOBATO. I STOOD frozen, my mind fracturing into several conflicting voices. Each voice shouted out its own warnings and advice.

Run. Just turn and run. Get as far away as you can before you lose it. Don't let him see you cry.

Here's your chance. Go up and punch him in the balls. Let him hurt the way you did.

Scream. Let it all out. Let him hear it. Call him every name you have referred to him as in the last four years.

Ignore him. He's nothing to you. He cut you out of his life. Don't let him back in.

Run to him. Throw your arms around him and never let him go again.

Whatever you do, don't let him see your weakness. Hold it together. Take a deep breath.

The last one is the one that broke through my temporarily frozen state. Somewhere in the fringes of my mind I knew that Kai had said something to me. I just couldn't process it. I took that deep breath and looked around. Everyone was staring at me waiting expectantly. I felt Beau next to me, his grip tighten around my waist. I glanced sideways at him. He wasn't watching me. He was glaring at Quinn. The atmosphere was thick with the tension emitting from all of us. I was the only one who could do anything to relieve it.

I exhaled the big breath I had been holding. "Quinn," I said in a half whispered voice with a nod of acknowledgment. It was all I could get out.

The voices all stopped. I felt like I was on a swing with my eyes closed. I swallowed back the nausea that was building. I leaned into Beau, letting him support me. He brushed my hair off my neck and whispered in my ear, "Are you okay? Do you want to get out of here?" I could hear the confusion in his voice, and also a slight bit of hope.

I shook my head and turned to Kai, who was still looking at me with eyes full of guilt. "Are we..." my voice cracked a little, so I coughed and started over. "Are we ready to eat, then?"

Then in a flurry of activity everyone started talking and sitting at the table. I still stood frozen next to Beau, his grip on me never letting up. In that moment, I was so thankful that he was there with me. I wasn't sure my knees would hold me up and I feared that I would collapse if I tried to move on my own.

I chanced a glance at Quinn; he was still standing in the same spot trying to look anywhere but at me. When he spoke I closed my eyes and just basked in the sound that started my heart fluttering. "Thanks for inviting me, but I really think I should go now." He was speaking to Kai. I opened my eyes and looked at him.

"No." That simple statement had everyone staring at me again. Even Quinn. I gulped and continued in a rush. "I mean you're already here. You might as well stay and eat." I wasn't sure why I said that, but I knew I didn't really want him to leave yet.

He nodded at me and went to sit next to Reed. Beau gave me another squeeze and kissed my cheek. "Do you want to sit down?" I nodded. He led me over to the opposite end of the table from Quinn.

Bless Reed. He started regaling everyone with a story about something funny that happened at a family reunion. His family stories were always entertaining. He was the oldest of five boys and from the sound of it they were all as much trouble as he was, that wasn't even taking in to consideration his uncles. While he was talking, I took stock of my feelings. They were still a jumble of conflicting emotions.

I still had the urge to run, but I wanted to stay just as much. I let my body work on autopilot as I put food on my plate that I wouldn't eat. It was really him. After all these years, why now? Why here? I looked him over as he sat there, feigning interest in what Reed was saying. I knew him well enough to know that he wasn't really listening. I wondered what he was thinking about. He glanced over at me and I quickly looked down, blushing at having been caught.

He was still Quinn, but he looked different now. He was no longer the awkward, skinny boy that I'd loved. His hair didn't hang down over his eyes. It was shorter, sticking up, still untamed. He must have been wearing contacts because he didn't have glasses on. His face was even more angular, having lost any remaining round boyishness in the past few years. Yes, he was still Quinn. But this Quinn was a man and not a boy. I had the sneaking suspicion that Quinn the man was even more dangerous to my heart than Quinn the boy had been.

With that thought, I let myself go numb. I wasn't going to let any more feelings come in. I was just going to block it all out and deal with it later behind closed doors, alone, where no one could see.

Beau wasn't eating either. Unlike me, he wasn't pushing his food around his plate, he wasn't even paying attention to his. He was openly staring at Quinn with a heated look. I'm sure he was confused about the tension and suspected that Quinn was the cause of it. I wasn't sure why he would feel this possessive of me after just one date, but possessiveness was exactly what he was showing.

I didn't like it, and I wanted him to let it go. I touched his arm to get his attention. "I forgot to introduce you to everyone." I spoke up then. "Reed," I interrupted. He looked over at me questioningly. "This is Beau Dalton. Beau, the big guy is Reed Walker." They shared the obligatory 'hey mans'. "Sloane. Beau. Beau. Sloane Evans." I pointed them out to each other. "You met both Kai-ying and Kerrington." Both gave him a quick wave. And then I stopped at Quinn not sure what I should do. Beau solved that dilemma for me.

"I take it that is Quinn. Isn't he your neighbor?" He had his brow furrowed as if was recalling Tuesday night.

"Apparently he is." I couldn't bring myself to make the introduction so I just left it alone.

Sloane came to my rescue. "So, Beau, are you a student here?"

I didn't pay attention to Beau's answer or the following conversation. I just stared at my plate and concentrated on holding myself together and blocking out all thoughts and emotions. Sometimes I could feel Quinn looking at me. I had to fight the urge to look back at him. I willed time to speed up. I just wanted out of there.

After a time Kai came over to me. "I was going to pack everything up. Do you want to help me bring it to the car? Reed brought a football and the boys can go play catch or whatever it is guys do with a football."

I nodded with relief at the thought of being able to escape both Quinn and Beau for a few minutes. "Beau, I'm going to help Kai and Kerri pack up. You're welcome to go play football with Reed and Sloane."

"Yeah, man. Come play. Then we can play two on two," Reed boomed out loudly.

Beau looked over at Quinn with a pointed look and said "I'd be happy to." He turned to me then and brought his hands up, one cupping the back of my neck and one against my cheek. He brought his mouth down to me in a strong possessive kiss. I wasn't expecting it and my mouth was slightly parted to start with, allowing him to slip his tongue in right away. I held back but he continued coaxing me with his tongue, alternating it with licking my lips. Finally he gave up, ending it with a couple quick pecks to my now closed lips.

He looked into my eyes. His blue ones glittered with something I couldn't name. He then turned and looked towards Quinn again but Quinn had already turned and was walking away with Sloane. Beau took off after them, following close behind Reed.

"I'm surprised he didn't just whip it out and start pissing on your leg," Kerri spit out.

"Excuse me?"

"Well, he was clearly marking his territory."

"He was just reminding me that he was here for me," I said lamely. I knew Kerri was probably right, but there was no reason for Beau to be feeling territorial over me.

"Sure he was," Kerri replied, sarcasm dripping off her.

"Sylvia, I'm so sorry. Are you okay?" Kai's concern was a little overwhelming right now.

"Yes, I'm fine. I just don't want to think about it right now." My voice was flat. I tried to hold to that, but I just couldn't. I had to get it all out. "I don't know what to do really. I guess there really isn't much I can do. So he lives across the hall from me. I just have to accept that. I can't move. I can't ask him to move. It's not like I have to interact with him on a daily basis." I realize I was spilling all my thoughts out unfiltered, but I needed to get it out. Maybe putting a voice to them would help me work through the confusion. Thankfully, both Kai and Kerri just listened to me, not stopping my verbal diarrhea. "I can do this. He doesn't have to affect my life if I don't let him." I was trying desperately to reassure myself.

Kai piped up, "We won't have anything to do with him either. I can't believe that we didn't know it was him." It was good to have friends to back me up.

"It's okay, Kai. He's changed a lot from the picture you saw. Do you think he knew I lived here?" My eyes went wide with that thought. Had he known? I looked from Kai to Kerri. Kai had her lips pursed like she was thinking it over. Kerri was looking off at the boys suspiciously.

"I don't know, but I have a good idea of two people who do." Kerri said, pointedly glaring at Reed and Sloane.

Kai caught on quickly. "That's what's been up with those two all week, isn't it? They knew. When I get my hands on them..."

I should have felt bad for Sloane and Reed with Kai on the war path, but I just couldn't find it within myself to care right then. Not wanting to talk about it anymore, I changed the subject. "Are you going to Jason's tonight?"

"I think so. Reed wants to go." Kerri answered off-handedly. She was still distracted, probably contemplating ways of torturing Reed for withholding information from her.

I glanced over at Kai for her input since she was, for all intents and purposes, the group coordinator. "Yes, I think it would be good for all of us to go. Are you going to bring Beau?"

I looked over at the guys, seeking Beau out. He was laughing at something Reed said. "Yeah. He seems to be getting along with them pretty well. I want Jason to meet him. You weren't planning on inviting Quinn were you?" I gazed back worriedly towards Kai.

"No. At least I hadn't said anything to him. I would hope that those two idiots would have the sense not to invite him there, either. They knew that you would be going. Not only that, but Jase would rip him apart if he recognized him."

I hoped Kai was right. "Good, because I really need to drink tonight."

Beau and I left for Jason's as soon as I was done helping pack the rest of the food up. I just wanted to get out of the park, so I had Kai tell Beau to meet me by his bike. He looked at me questioningly as he walked up to me, flicking aside the cigarette he'd just finished. "I just want to get out of here. I have another friend who's having a party tonight and I planned on going. Would you like to come with? Reed and Sloane will be there." I was really hoping he would say yes. I truly believed without him there today I would have fallen apart. The others knew my history with Quinn and I didn't even want to think of what my reaction would have been with just them there. I wouldn't let myself break down in front of Beau. Quinn was the past, and while I didn't know what Beau was to me yet, I did know that for right now he was the present.

Beau was quiet for a second thinking it over. "Will Quinn be there?" He asked suspiciously.

"Definitely not," I answered quickly.

"What's the deal between you two? He was eye fucking you all afternoon." His voice had an accusatory edge to it.

He was? I hadn't noticed that. I paused before answering that loaded question. How much should I tell him? "Quinn and I dated in high school. We split up when we went to college. Today is the first time I've seen him since the day after high school graduation." I kept my tone flat and unemotional, hoping he would just let it drop.

Beau scrutinized my face trying to decide if I was telling the truth. His deep blue eyes drilled into mine, but I didn't squirm. He must have liked what he saw. He flashed me the biggest smile I had ever seen from him. He pulled me to him and leaned in close. "Well then we'll just have to make sure he knows you're no longer interested." His lips met mine and I could taste the cigarette. I didn't care. I was just relieved that he wasn't upset by the whole Quinn ordeal. I kissed him back, demanding more, showing him that he was the one I was interested in, not Quinn.

Once his name popped into my mind I paused momentarily to push it away. Beau picked up on the pause and pulled back peering into my eyes again.

I tried to cover my lapse by saying, "We should probably get going. I told Jason I'd be over as soon as the picnic was over, and I'd like to get there before the others."

Beau nodded, asked me for directions, and we took off. I wrapped my arms around him and forced myself to think of Beau and the fact that it was his body I was holding onto, not the one I'd held so long ago.

Jason's house was in a neighborhood full of college students. Its proximity to campus and the size of the houses -- which allowed for maximum tenants -- made it an ideal location for off-campus housing. Almost every house had a party going on. The whole block was a complete cacophony with music pouring in from several different places. People were out in yards, both front and back. For only being late afternoon, several were notably intoxicated. I had every intention of joining them.

We had to park over a block away from Jason's big blue two story house. During the walk to the house Beau asked me, "So who is it that's having this party?"

"Jason. He's a friend from back home." Kerri's pissing comment came to mind and I felt like I needed to add a disclaimer. "He's like my younger brother." I peeked over at him to find him studying me with one eyebrow quirked. "He's having the party as a welcome for another friend from back home. I actually think Colby will be my younger brother someday. My dad has been seeing his mom for a while now, even though he doesn't think I know it." I laughed at the thought of my dad thinking he was getting away with hiding his and Shelly's relationship.

Beau smiled again and draped his arm across my shoulders as I pointed out the house. We headed up the sidewalk and around the house to the backyard where I knew everyone would be. Once we rounded the corner I paused, taking in the sight in front of me. Jason's roommates were there, of course, along with a couple of their girlfriends. There were probably about a dozen more people I didn't recognize. Off to the side of the cement patio, standing next to a keg, was the group I was looking for.

The group stood out from the rest. In all there were four of them. Four of the biggest all-American farm boys you would ever see. All tall, muscular with varying shades of blond hair. All could be confused for Norse gods come to life. They were all laughing at something. I couldn't tell what. I moved a little closer and saw that Colby was already swaying heavily, the beer splashing out of the cup he was holding as he moved his arms around animatedly as he talked. I couldn't believe they'd let him get this drunk already. Wait, I could believe it. In fact they probably encouraged it. I laughed at that and Colby looked up at me.

"Sylllllviaaaa!" He slurred loudly, almost falling on his face as he ran up to me. He plucked me up off the ground in a big bear hug. I could barely breathe, he was squeezing me so hard. "I'm so happppy ta seeee youuu. Ya need ta get beeeer. It's goooood beeeer. I had lots oſit taday." He was almost incomprehensible, he was so drunk. He swung me around; swaying as he did so and Ben grabbed me out of his arms.

"Damn, Colby. Be careful, you'll drop her." Ben held me just as tight as Colby had. "Sylly. It's good to see you." He handed me over to Danny and I got my greeting hug from him too before he set me down in front of Jason.

"Hey Sylvia."

I slapped his chest. "What are you thinking? The afternoon is barely over and Colby is sloshed." I reprimanded him. He shrugged and gave me a slightly guilty grin. I chuckled at it. "Now it's my turn. Where's my beer? I'm not leaving here until I'm in the same condition as Colby." After the day I'd had, I needed this release. I fully planned to use the vast amounts of alcohol that would be available to my advantage. I reasoned that the drunker I was the less I would think about my new neighbor.

I introduced Beau to the guys and got us both a drink. He didn't look real thrilled at having watched me being passed around by all of them. I let it go, he just didn't know them yet. Once he did he would see that they were just like my siblings.

Beau stayed by my side all night, only leaving to get me more to drink. He didn't really talk to anyone other than me. He wasn't being impolite, just more reserved. I think he was sizing up my friends and getting a feel for us as a group. I hoped he was having a good time. He didn't act bored or like he was anxious to leave. He just followed my lead around from one group to another, while I made sure I talked with everyone. I didn't get to see Ben and Danny often, and I'd missed them.

Colby passed out early and they dragged him off to Jason's room to sleep it off. That didn't stop the rest of us from having a good time. True to my word, I did drink plenty. Usually Kerri or Kai cut me off before I could get as drunk as I was. Tonight they just stepped back and let me go.

Beau was actually the one to suggest I stop. We had taken his motorcycle here and if I continued at the pace I was on, I wouldn't be able to stay on it on the way home. I definitely wanted him to take me home. In fact, the more I drank the more I wanted him.

He was just fine with my overt public displays of affection. He encouraged them. At one point I went down the hall to use the restroom and he followed me. We were alone in the hall and he grabbed me around the waist from the back, pulling me to him. He rubbed his hard cock against me and growled into my ear. "Feel what you've done to me? Why don't we slip into the bathroom there and you can do something about it." It was more of a command than a suggestion. Somewhere in my alcohol hazed mind I knew I should have been offended, but at the time, the drunk girl was in charge and she was all for it.

I gave a little giggle and reached back up around to his neck and pulled him in for a kiss. It was a wet open mouth kiss with our tongues slithering around the other's, more outside of either of our mouths than in. His tongue trailed along my jaw to my ear and I let my head roll to the side, allowing him better access to my neck. He found that spot just under my ear that made me melt and began to suck there. I let out a low moan as he began nipping at it.

He ground into me, pushing his length harder against my ass. I trailed my free hand down his side working its way between our bodies to cup him in my hand.

The bathroom door opened and Reed let out a whistle "Damn, Sylvia if you're going to give a live sex show you should at least charge for it."

Normally, that would have me blushing and pulling away. But by this point I was equal parts drunk and turned on. I just glared at him and told him to go find Kerri.

"Seriously, Sylvia get a room or go home." He walked away shaking his head and chuckling at me.

"That's a good idea. Why don't we go back to your place and finish what we started the other night?" Beau whispered in my ear before taking one last nibble on my ear.

"Mmmm, let me just go say bye to Jason and we can go." By this time I had completely forgotten why I started down the hall in the first place.

"You don't need to say goodbye to anyone. They'll figure it out or I'm sure Reed will let them know. Come on, I don't want to wait anymore for you." He rocked against me once more, pleading his case to leave quickly.

It was colder now and starting to mist. Neither of us had a jacket and the night air should have been cutting on the ride home. I didn't feel it. I kept myself pressed tightly to his back, teasing him the whole ride home. I stroked my hands up and down the length of his thighs and up over his chest. I just ghosted my hands over the bulge in his jeans, just enough to keep him wanting my touch.

We pulled into the parking lot and a slight wave of nausea hit me as I slid off the bike and into Beau's arms. He unstrapped the helmet and pulled it off me. I took a deep breath and felt a little better. He strapped the helmet on the bike as I teetered from side to side. He snickered at me and wrapped his arm around my waist.

"Steady there, little one. We still have to make it up to your place." As we walked, I felt the hand on my waist slip into my pocket, withdrawing my keys. I looked up at him questioningly. "Just want to make sure we make it inside this time."

As I waited for him to unlock the door I glanced over at Quinn's. I briefly hoped his door would open. That he would see that someone wanted me, even if he didn't.

Once we were inside my door, Beau turned me to him and crashed his mouth to mine. His lips were hard against mine. When he opened his mouth he took my bottom lip between his teeth and pulled at it, scraping it with his teeth as he let it pop out. His hands were at the bottom of my shirt pushing it up over me. I raised my arms letting him pull it completely off me.

His hands came back down, cupping my breasts roughly, pushing them together. He pinched my nipples between his thumb and forefinger roughly. I let out a moan. "You like that, don't you?" I let my head loll back, pushing my chest up further into his hands.

He bent down, tracing his tongue over the skin just above the lace of the bra. He let go of my breasts just long enough to reach back and undo the clasp and pull the straps from my shoulders. I dangled my arms down letting it drop off me.

He grabbed my breasts again, rolling the nipples between his fingers. "I could feel you behind me on the way here. Your nipples were hard pressing into my back. All I could think about was getting you home and getting that shirt off and feeling them in my hands." I raised my head and looked at him. His eyes were heavy lidded and gazing down at me. "And in my mouth." His words sent a little shiver through me.

With that, he flicked out his tongue, swirling it around my peak, causing it to harden even more. Then he closed his mouth around it, sucking hard. His hands roamed down my sides, sliding under the waist of my pants. He brought a hand to my front, expertly working the button and zipper while the other hand rubbed my ass.

My head was fuzzy, both from the alcohol and Beau. I swayed and tried to keep my balance. I giggled and grabbed at his hand he stopped everything. "You think you can tease me all night and then stop now?" He peered up at me, his eyes clouded with lust.

"I'm not stopping anything, just moving it along." I giggled again and stepped back, pushing the Capri's and panties off my hips and shimmying out of them. I dropped a little less than gracefully to my knees. Beau groaned as I undid his jeans pulling them roughly off his hips and down his legs.

He stepped out of them and I wrapped my hand around him. I brought my head forward, running the tip of my tongue around his head. I looked up at him as I did it, to see him watching me. It was all the encouragement I needed. I parted my lips and slid my mouth down around him hard as I squeezed tighter around the base.

I pulled back up swirling my tongue as I went. I pulled all the way up, freeing him from my mouth with a pop. I looked back up at him and smiled. His fingers were in my hair pulling out the band I had it pulled back with. He threaded his fingers in and pulled at the same time, pushing my head back down. He growled, "No more teasing."

I took him in as far as I could, until I felt him hit the back of my throat. I brought my hand up higher on him trying to keep him from going in so far. He set the pace, thrusting his hips forward into my mouth and pulling back on my hair. I tried to concentrate on what I was doing, but I ended up fighting more for a breath and keeping myself from gagging as he shoved in too far.

Finally he stopped and pulled me up. He kissed me hard, running his hands down from my hair all the way down my sides and around to my center. He rested his hand against me, making me writhe into his hand, wanting to feel more. "Mmmm. You're so hot and wet already. Just waiting for me." With that, he pressed one finger between my folds, dragging it back and forth. Finally he circled around my clit, causing me to groan and buck my hips into his hand.

He slid the finger back to my opening thrusting it up in me. I rocked into his hand and he added another finger and started to flick my clit with his thumb. God, it felt good. But I wanted more. I needed more. "Please," I whimpered into his shoulder.

"Please what Sylvia?"

"Please, I need more. Please." I begged.

"Oh, I'll give you more." His voice was low and gruff, sending tingles all through me.

He pulled his fingers away and quickly spun me around until I was facing the back of the couch. I wobbled and grabbed on to the back of the couch to keep myself from falling. I felt him reach down to the floor and heard the rip of a condom wrapper as he pushed me forward over the couch.

I spread my legs further apart as I bent over. I felt him behind me and was ready for him when he thrust in. Beau set the pace hard and fast. He had a tight grip on my upper thighs, thrusting in harder each time. He was talking to me telling me how he wanted me and how he thought about fucking me like this while he was gone. It was driving me crazy; the quick hard thrusts punctuating his words. He slid his hand off my hip and around me to rub my clit again. He gently slapped at me telling me to come for him. I could hear him groaning and I wanted to be pushed me over the edge with him. I felt his fingers tangle up in my hair again as he pulled causing me to arch my back. I was so close. He thrust in hard twice more and he gripped my hair and hip tighter, pulling me roughly to him as he came; leaving me frustrated and unfulfilled.

We were both panting and trying to catch our breath as we came back down. I was still leaning over the back of the couch when the nausea hit again. This time I couldn't choke it back down. I ran for the bathroom. Throwing the door open as I hit the light on at the same time. The harsh bright light had me flinching. I made it to the toilet in time, saving myself from getting sick all over the floor.

Oh, God. This is why I should never drink this much. I was too preoccupied with the heaving and gagging to be mortified at the fact that I just threw up after having sex.

"Are you okay?" I looked up to see Beau peaking around the door at me, already dressed.

I knew I must be a sight, naked and puking, sitting on the bathroom floor. "Yeah, just too much to drink." I groaned. I felt another wave coming up.

"You should drink some water or something." He sounded concerned yet disgusted.

"I'm fine. Just go. I don't want you to see me like this." The realization of what was happening was kicking in. I could even feel myself start to blush.

"Are you sure..."

I cut him off. "Yes, just leave. Please."

"Fine. Um, later then." I heard him turn and walk away. The door opened and closed and I rested my head on the edge of the toilet. I just wanted to die.

I woke the next morning on my bed naked and cold. I laid there for a few minutes trying to ease the pounding in my head. At least my shades were shut and it was still semi-dark in the room. I rolled over and threw my hands over my head. That's when the night before came rushing back to me.

I cringed at the memory. Why? Why did I drink that much? I couldn't believe I'd puked after sex. He was never going to call back. I could hear the low beep of my phone coming from the other room. I figured it was Kai. I would call her later. Right now I needed the bathroom and more sleep.

Looking in the bathroom mirror had been a mistake. My hair was tangled up, sticking up all over. My eyes were bloodshot and ringed with smudged make up. My lips were swollen. My hips and thighs hurt and I looked down to see finger print bruises on each side starting to turn purple. The rest of my body was sore, too. I checked it out, relieved to not find any more bruises.

I shuffled naked to the kitchen to get some water, aching just about everywhere. The knock on my door about killed my poor head. "Damn it Kai," I yelled. "Don't you know better by now than to come wake me up?"

The knocking paused, but then started up again. "I'm coming. Just a minute." Really, why does she always have to do this? It wasn't like I wouldn't go to see her when I got up. I grumbled to myself as I went back to my bedroom to grab clothes.

I pulled the big t-shirt on that was lying on top of the dirty clothes pile. I thought it was the one I'd worn Wednesday night, not that that mattered. At least I had something on now. I grabbed a pair of underwear out of the drawer and pulled them on as I stumbled down the hall.

My clothes from last night were still scattered around the living room floor. I wasn't even going to bother picking them up. Kai could see it and think what she wanted. I was just going to end up telling her about it anyway.

I got to the door and it wasn't even locked. I'm surprised she didn't just come barging in. "God, Kai. Could you not wait until I got up?" I huffed. "What do you want?" as I flung the door open.

There stood Quinn. Looking good, all showered and dressed and ready to start a new day. Whereas I, on the other hand, was so not ready for this.

"Sylvia, I think we need to talk."

Chapter 6 - Quinn

I COULDN'T SLEEP. I PACED the length of my apartment over and over. I just kept replaying the scene of Beau kissing Sylvia, over and over. I wanted to go pull him off her and knock him the fuck down. I knew I couldn't. Instead, I had turned away and left with Sloane.

The shock of seeing me was clearly evident on Sylvia's face all through the picnic. I kept looking at her, only once catching her looking at me. For the most part she just kept her head down, staring at her plate. I would have loved to have known what she was thinking. I knew exactly what Beau was thinking. He'd glared at me throughout the meal. Even when he was talking to Sloane he still threw looks of contempt my way. Then there was the way he'd held on to Sylvia, like she was his property. It sickened me.

We played that joke of a football game. At first, I thought it was just going to be a friendly game, more like playing catch than football. I didn't really know how to play. Sloane was on my team, and he just told me to catch the ball and run, or -- if the other team had the ball -- just tag them. He explained that they didn't get real physical when they played because of Reed's knee. I was fine with that.

Everything was going fine. Reed and Sloane taunted each other as they always did whenever they played any game. Beau was just quiet, watching everything I did. I would have asked him what his problem was, but I already knew the answer to that. I couldn't believe it when I got past both him and Reed on one play. I knew I was a fairly fast runner, but I didn't really think I would do very well playing football. Something in Beau's eyes changed after that. They became cold and calculating.

I tried to hang back and not put much effort into the game after that, but Sloane wasn't letting me get away with it. On the next play where I went to run the ball, I felt someone collide with me. I went down hard and felt my ankle give on me. I looked up to see who hit me. Beau's smug face was hovering over me. I knew the warning he was sending. 'Stay away from Sylvia.'

The game ended after that. Beau took off to find Sylvia, and Reed and Sloane were ready to go. On the way back to the jeep, Reed was the first to bring up the incident. "What the fuck was that all about? I told him it was just touch football."

"Don't worry about it. He was just letting me know where I stood with Sylvia." I just wanted to let it go. I didn't want any trouble with him. For whatever reason, Sylvia was with him and I wasn't going to do anything to cause trouble with her.

"I don't like him." Sloane said quietly. "This is only the second time he's been out with Sylvia. I don't get why he's being so possessive towards her."

Only the second time she was out with him? I wanted to ask more about that but didn't want them to think I was interested in her. I held on to that, though. If she hadn't been seeing him long, maybe it wasn't serious. I mulled this thought over again.

I remembered how she looked in the park. She was even more beautiful than she had been four years ago. I knew it was a completely girly thought, but she looked really good in that color. I always liked her best in green, green like her eyes. Her eyes. I missed her eyes. Today I saw them for the first time in years. First, they were filled with surprise, and then pain, and I wasn't sure, but I briefly thought I saw love. The look was gone so fast that I wasn't sure if it had actually been there, or if I was seeing what I wanted to see. It had given me a little hope that maybe we could work things out.

I had to stop thinking about it, and stop pacing. I went for a drive hoping that would help. I drove around Minneapolis aimlessly. I tried to pay attention to what was around, trying to familiarize myself with the area. I don't know how long I drove before I realized it wasn't doing any good. I went back to the apartment, intending to try to get some sleep. I saw the motorcycle in the parking lot and cringed. I knew it was Beau's. That bastard was probably upstairs right now with Sylvia. The jealousy was eating away at me.

I was almost to the door when he walked out. It took all the control I had not to just fucking hit him. How could Sylvia be with such a prick? He passed by me with a self-satisfied smirk. My jaw tightened and my fists clenched. I kept walking, though, hoping he wouldn't see how pissed I was. I really needed to get over this. Sylvia was free to date who she wanted. I could not stand in the way.

I went to bed, still thinking about Sylvia and Beau. I worried about how territorial he was with Sylvia. I didn't like seeing him act that way towards her. I'd seen relationships like that in the past, and I knew they never ended well. I wondered if Reed and Sloane would step in if he started getting even more controlling. I sure hoped so. From the little I saw of Kerrington, I couldn't imagine she would let that slip by.

Over the course of that sleepless night, I realized that I needed to just stay away from Sylvia. If we both happened to be in the same place, I would act friendly and nothing more. I could handle that. If Beau was there, I would just make sure to stay as far away from him as possible so there wouldn't be any trouble.

I knew she must have been worried about me being here. I decided I'd go talk to her and let her know that I wasn't there to cause any trouble. I waited until mid-morning since I figured if Beau was leaving that late, she probably would be sleeping in. I checked the clock every ten minutes, hoping it would be time to go. I needed to get this conversation behind me.

Admittedly, I took my time getting ready. I chastised myself when I debated on what to wear. I finally gave up, and just pulled a random shirt out of my closet and grabbed a pair of jeans. Everything went with jeans. It didn't matter what I was wearing anyway. I wasn't going over there to impress her. Sure I wasn't. That was why I'd spent so much time trying to get my hair to do anything other than stick up all over. No really, I was just going over there to tell her I wouldn't be any trouble for her.

Finally, I couldn't wait any longer. I made my way across the hall. The space couldn't have been more than five or six feet from door to door, yet it felt like I was crossing the Grand Canyon. By the time I got to the door, I started second-guessing myself. My throat was dry and my heart was racing. I raised my hand, but held off on knocking. If I knocked, there would be no turning back. I took a deep breath, closed my eyes, and knocked.

I heard her call out, thinking I was Kai. I debated on just turning around, but I'd come this far. I needed to finish it. I heard her yell from further away this time and couldn't make out exactly what she'd said. At last I heard her at the door.

"What do you want?" She practically spit the words out at me as the door was thrown wide open. There she stood glaring at me and it was too late to turn back.

"Sylvia, I think we need to talk."

There I'd said it. Now I had to finish it. I took a deep breath and waited for her to reply. She was just scowling at me. As I waited for her to say something, I took the time to really look her over. She looked like hell. I had seen Sylvia in many different situations; first thing in the morning, sick, after swimming, with windblown hair, and other times as well. At no point did she ever look this awful.

It went further than just messy hair and smudged make-up ringing her eyes. Her eyes were blood-shot and puffy, and even though they were currently shooting daggers at me, there was still an undeniable sense of tiredness. I moved from her eyes to her lips. They were swollen and cracked. As I looked at them, her tongue darted out, licking them. My gaze traveled lower, taking in the faded blue t-shirt. Damn, it was the one from our senior class trip. I momentarily remembered her asleep on the bus in my arms while wearing that shirt. I couldn't believe she still wore it. I glanced down at her feet, trailing my gaze up her bare legs to the bottom of her shirt. I caught a brief glimpse of her black panties. I quickly shifted my eyes back up to hers, before my thoughts could get away from my reason for being there.

"I don't have anything to say to you." She attempted to shut the door, but I stopped it.

"Then just listen to what I have to say." I kept my tone even as my eyes pleaded with her to just listen to me.

"Why? Why should I listen to you? You didn't listen to me when I wanted to talk to you. You never returned a call or even a text. You just left." Her voice grew louder and louder with each word. "Now you expect me to listen to you? Fuck you, Quinn! You have nothing to say that I want to hear."

I had expected tears or silence while I talked. I didn't expect anger. I was completely taken aback when Sylvia swore. I didn't think I had ever heard her say that before. "I'm sorry, Sylvia." I looked into her eyes, hoping she would see the regret in mine.

"You should be," she sneered back at me. She tried to shut the door again, but I held it steady. I wasn't done yet, and I needed her to hear me out.

"I just wanted you to know that I'm not here to cause you any trouble," I said quietly. "I will stay out of your way. I'll stay away from Reed and Sloane too, if you want." I really hoped she wouldn't want that. I let go of the door and started backing away.

"You can do whatever the hell you want with Reed and Sloane. I don't care. I don't care about anything you do anymore." She was still yelling at me as she stalked closer, pointing at me until she was poking me in the chest. "You. Are. No. Longer. Part. Of. My. Life." She punctuated each word with a sharp poke. "I don't know why you are here now, and whatever the reason is I don't want to know it. Just stay the hell away from me."

The tiredness was now gone from her eyes. In its place was a flame of anger and an ember of hurt. I wanted to soothe her and assure her that I would never hurt her again. "Sylvia, I didn't know you were here. I swear. My mom picked out the place."

She covered her ears. "I told you I don't want to hear it." Now she was just acting childish. I pulled her hands away and she glared up at me.

"Look. We were friends once. There's no reason we can't be again, or at least be civil towards each other." *Except I'll always want to be more to you than just a friend.*

She looked at me then and the anger in her face crumbled into pain. "Why?" Her voice was so soft; I read her lips more than heard the actual words. Her lips trembled, and she stopped it by biting her bottom lip.

"Why?" I raised my voice a little, frustrated that I would have to explain this to her. "Because we live across the hall from each other. Because we are going to run into each other occasionally. We can't have this ever present tension and anger between the two of us." I motioned between us. "Because I like hanging out with Sloane and Reed, and they are your friends, too. We're bound to end up in the same room together at some point, and we need to not end up yelling like this." My voice had reached its full volume now, and I was yelling just as loudly as she had been.

Her eyes were wide and starting to pool with tears. She quietly sobbed. "I meant, why did you leave?"

Fuck! Not that question. This time I knew I needed to answer her. And I needed to answer her with the truth.

The door next to mine opened and a girl peeked around the corner of it. "Not out here Sylvia," I said between clenched teeth as I looked over my shoulder at the girl behind the door. Sylvia nodded and grabbed my hand and yanked me into her apartment. I shut the door behind me and turned to look anywhere but at her while I collected my thoughts.

Even though we had been standing in her doorway with the door wide open, I hadn't looked in her apartment. I had just looked at her. Now, for the first time, I was seeing it. Seeing her clothes from the day before lying around on the floor. It hit me then just why her clothes were all over the floor and why she was only in a t-shirt. My eyes flew open and I looked from the floor to her face and back to her bra on the floor and back to her face again.

I felt sick. Beau's smug grin the night before flashed before my eyes, and I knew why he'd been gloating. Sylvia was red, but she made no move to apologize or pick anything up. She left the evidence of her new life laying there between us. How was I supposed to tell her the truth -- that I loved her so much I'd had to let her go -- with the remains of her night with another man right there in front of my face? I ran my hands through my hair, trying to calm myself down. I closed my eyes and pinched the bridge of my nose, trying to push away the vision of her removing those same clothes. Taking them off for an asshat like Beau.

"So, are you going to tell me or stare at my clothes?" Sylvia asked, annoyed. "I deserve an answer." She was right. She did. I took a breath in while deciding how to tell her. Should I tell her to sit down first? Should I just tell her quickly, and get it over with? Either way she wasn't going to understand. No one would understand. That's why I'd never told anyone.

I straightened up and looked her in the eye. I answered quietly, yet matter-of-factly, "Because you needed to go to the University of Minnesota." She gave me a puzzled look. "You needed to take the scholarship."

We were in our last week of school. Our graduation ceremony was going to be held on Saturday afternoon. It was an easy week for the seniors. With our tests behind us, we spent the last few days of school reminiscing with the others in our class and talking about our future plans. On Thursday, Sylvia was called to the counselor's office. She was notified that she was one of the recipients of the Governor's Scholarship. She would have a full ride to any in-state college or university. Only five students in the state of Minnesota were chosen each year for this. Sylvia had worked very hard for it.

When she came back from the office and told me, I was excited for her. I didn't understand why she wasn't. Then she told me she wasn't going to accept it. We had both been accepted to Princeton and planned to go together in the fall. She had been working and saving, and even though Kelly offered to help, it still wouldn't be enough to cover her first year's tuition. That didn't even include housing fees, books and just everyday living expenses. Sylvia had already completed all the paperwork for the massive amount of loans she would need to pay for it.

I couldn't let her do it. I couldn't let her pass it up. I mulled it over for the next couple days, trying to decide how to make her see reason. She absolutely wouldn't hear it when I tried to talk about it with her that first day. After that, I decided I had to come up with a better plan. During the graduation ceremony it hit me. If I broke it off with her, she would take the scholarship and go to the U of M. It broke my heart to even contemplate moving away from Sylvia, but I knew it had to be done. It was best for her, and that was all that mattered.

Sylvia blinked at me a few times, while my answer soaked in. "You broke up with me so I would go here? You broke up with me so I would take the scholarship?" She asked me incredulously. Her voice began to rise. "You left me over college tuition? Seriously? You left me broken and crying over money?" *Well, when you put it that way...* "Get the fuck out."

"Sylvia, wait. You don't understand," I tried to reason with her.

"No, I think I understand perfectly well. You decided what was best for me without my input." She was absolutely livid now. Her eyes were flashing and her arms were flailing. She was amazing. "You asshole. You goddamn motherfucker. What gave you the right to decide what was best for me?"

"At the time..."

"At the time I was completely capable of making my own decisions." She was pacing around the room now, her eyes were wild, and I was a little frightened. "I knew what I wanted. The University of Minnesota was not what I wanted."

"I know, but it was what you needed." I attempted to calm her down.

"NO! It wasn't what I needed. You were what I needed. You were what I always needed." She stopped pacing long enough to shout that at me.

"Sylvia, please..." My pleas were falling on deaf ears. She was in the middle of her rant, and nothing was going to calm her down.

"Please what? Please let you decide what would be best for me? Please let you take away my free will? Please let the past few years of absolute heartbreak and emptiness go like they never happened? Is that what you want, Quinn? Is that what would please you?" She was stalking towards me again. I have never in my life seen a woman as angry as Sylvia was. Her red hair was wild with tangles and curls and her eyes flashed brightly. "Did you feel that you needed to make my decisions for me? Was I so incapable of managing my own life that I needed you to take care of that for me?"

I shook my head. I raised my hands in an innocent gesture, even though

I knew I was anything but innocent. "Please, Sylvia. I did what I thought was right. I was 18. I didn't know..."

"You're damn right you didn't know. You didn't know how I fell apart. You didn't know how I needed you. You didn't know how much I loved you." She let her hands drop to her sides, defeated. She looked up at me under her lashes. "You were everything to me, but I was not enough for you." My heart seized up. Not enough? How could she even think that? She was everything.

"Sylvia, you were..."

"Stop!" She yelled it at me, effectively cutting me off. "No more. I don't want to hear it. It's been too long. My life is mine now. Apparently you made that decision for me. Now I make my own decisions. I want you to leave." She said this in a cold, detached voice.

"Sylvia, please..." I tried one more time, but she turned away from me. As she turned, my eyes were drawn to her hip and the way the t-shirt rode up on it. There on her hip was the most horrendous bruise. I knew Sylvia bruised easily. She always had some bruise or another on her, from tripping or running into something. This bruise was definitely not from her normal clumsiness. This was in the definite shape of a hand.

I sucked in a breath and asked, "Sylvia, what the fuck is that?" Like I didn't already know what it was. My brain just wouldn't process it. She whipped around and looked at me blankly.

"What is what?" She asked, clearly pissed at what she must have thought was a new tactic to distract her.

I pointed to her hip. "What is that?" She looked down. I saw comprehension cross her face as she realized what I was pointing at. She tugged the bottom of her shirt lower.

"That is none of your business." She glared back at me with a hint of challenge in her eyes. Daring me to say any more about it. She still held the hem of her shirt as she pulled it low over her hips.

"Did he do that to you?" It was starting to dawn on me just how in the hell those marks came about. My eyes were still wide in shock that someone could do that to my Sylvia. I was so distracted I didn't even catch my mental slip. She continued to glare at me her eyes no more then paper-thin slits.

"What he does or doesn't do to me should not be your concern," she snapped at me.

"Sylvia, I am not going to stand aside and let some jackass manhandle you." No matter what had happened between us, I would not let someone abuse her.

She thrust her chin in the air and said with an air of finality, "Quinn, get the fuck out of my place. Right now. My life is mine to live, and you are not going to make any more decisions for me. If someone leaves a mark on me that's my problem, not yours. You gave up all right to care about me when you decided I was better off going to U of M than being with you." She stated it all very calmly as she walked to the door. She opened the door while staring straight into my eyes. "Leave. Now!"

I swept my gaze over her one last time, looking for any other markings. I didn't see any, but that didn't mean there weren't any. My anger was barely contained. I wanted to find Beau and mark him. I wanted to kick the living crap out of him for doing that to Sylvia. "This isn't over, Sylvia. I'll leave now, but I'm watching. I will not let that bastard hurt you." I said this just as I reached the door.

As she shut the door I heard a strangled whisper, "No, you're perfectly capable of doing that on your own."

Chapter 7 - Sylvia

I COULDN'T BELIEVE THE NERVE he had. First, to not leave when I'd clearly told him to. Then he'd had the balls to get all overprotective over a little bruise! It wasn't any of his business anyway. I continued to fume as I picked my clothes off the floor. I was glad he'd seen them there. I hoped he'd gotten a good eyeful. He needed to know that I was no longer his. I lived my own life, and it most definitely did not include Quinn Lobato.

I threw my clothes in the laundry basket. I went to my drawer and pulled out a pair of sweats. I wouldn't have wanted anyone else to accidentally see the marks and jump to conclusions. I continued cleaning around the apartment, grumbling the whole time. When I got angry I cleaned. At that moment, I was downright pissed. I was even beyond the tears that came to my eyes when I was mad.

Not long into my rage-induced cleaning spree, there was a gentle knock at my door. *Oh, he'd better not be back for round two. There's no way he's coming out of this one unscathed.* I flung the door open ready to tell him to go to hell. Standing there was Kai, aqua eyes wide with curiosity. I shut my eyes and groaned. I wasn't ready for this yet. I was still hung over. My head still pounded and my emotions were nowhere near under control.

Kai stepped forward with her arms outstretched. I fell into them and cried. She stepped forward, shutting the door behind her, without moving me from her arms. Kai just held onto me. She didn't say anything, just held me to her and let me cry it out.

I poured four years of hurt and anger out on her little shoulders, each sob harder than the one before. I felt worthless. Money. It was all about money. I'd never even thought of that. Sure, the Lobatos had money. Quinn didn't need to worry about loans or scholarships to pay for Princeton. I'd never thought money mattered to him. It was starting to sink in that obviously he did not want to have to pay for two Princeton educations. I had planned to get loans but once we were married we would have had to pay back the loans. He must have thought about that and decided I wasn't worth it.

My sobs eventually slowed. My throat was tight and my chest ached. My head still pounded but my mind felt numb. I was aware that Kai's shirt was soaked. I pulled away and looked at her. Her face held nothing but love and concern. She reached for my hand and led me over to the couch. Her voice was soft and quiet. "Sit here. I'll be right back." She disappeared into the kitchen and I heard the fridge open.

She came back with a can of pop and Tylenol. She grabbed the box of Kleenex off the bookshelf and sat down beside me. If she hadn't already had my unending love and friendship, I would have given it all freely then. I sniffed and attempted a smile as I reached for the meds and the pop.

"I love you." My voice cracked. She reached over and gave me another hug.

"Do you want to talk about it? I didn't mean to eavesdrop." She let out a wry laugh. "Actually, I think the whole building heard you."

I groaned again and hid my eyes with my hand. "I'm sorry. I probably woke everyone. That sucks to be woken on a Sunday morning by a domestic spat between the neighbors."

"We didn't actually hear what was being said. Sloane and I just knew it was you and Quinn. I waited until it was quiet for awhile before I came to check on you. So what was the deal?"

I took another drink of my pop and launched into an explanation of the morning's shouting match. Kai, being Kai, stopped me often with a question or comment to add. When I got to the part about him telling me why he left, her eyes went wide again. Amazingly, she didn't say anything about that.

"And then he saw the bruise and was all 'how did you get that?'" I was giving my best angry, overprotective Quinn impersonation. "And I..."

"What bruise?" Kai interrupted me.

"Oh, it was nothing. Beau just held on to me a little too tight last night and left a bruise. It's no big deal." She still looked at me skeptically. "See? It's nothing." I pulled the top on my sweats down a little, quickly flashing a bit of the bruise for her to see.

Kai looked at me curiously. "How did Quinn see that?"

"What?" I was confused.

"It's on your hip. You just had to move your pants to show me."

"Oh, I didn't have pants on."

Her smile widened. "You were in your apartment with Quinn this morning, and weren't wearing pants?"

"No, it wasn't like that. He came to the door and I thought it was you so I quickly threw on a shirt and underwear. It wasn't like I was naked and yelling at him. He just saw it when my shirt rose up a little." I was blushing furiously. I tried to tell myself that it wasn't a big deal that I'd just had my first real conversation -- okay, argument -- with Quinn in four years, and I'd done it half naked. When I'd opened the door and it had been him standing there, every thought I'd had went out that door. I didn't think, even once, that I was only wearing a t-shirt and underwear. Not until he'd pointed out the bruise, anyway. By then, I was so pissed at him I just wanted him out.

"That's not what's important anyway. What is important is him acting all perfect and holier than thou, accusing Beau of 'manhandling me' when he just got done telling me how he'd made a life-altering decision for my benefit. That he was going to be watching to make sure Beau doesn't hurt me. Why can that asshole not get it through his head that he is doing the very thing he is accusing Beau of?"

Kai wasn't smiling anymore. She looked far away, like she hadn't even heard me. "Kai. Earth to Kai-ying." I said, annoyed, as I waved my hand in front of her face.

"I'm sorry, Sylvia. I heard you. I just had a thought..." She trailed off and looked at me curiously.

"And that thought was..." She didn't answer me. She just shook her head.

"Well, what are you going to do about all this?"

That I wasn't sure of yet. I took a deep breath in and released it slowly. "First, I need to stay as far away from Quinn Lobato as I can. I can't imagine that I will do anything other than go off on him again if he even says one little thing to me. Second...I don't know if there is a second." I sighed.

I then told Kai about my night after we came back home.

Her damn little eyes glittered with mirth when I relayed running to the bathroom to puke. "It's not funny. It was embarrassing. He'll probably never call me again after that." Thinking of it again, I wanted the ground to open up and swallow me. If he did call, how was I going to face him? I would be mortified, knowing he'd seen me sprawled out on the bathroom floor like that.

Kai reassured me that it would all work out. She stayed a while longer with me. We talked about other things -- stuff from Jason's party, Kerri and the others. I was feeling better by the time she got up to leave. I hugged her again.

"Thank you," I simply told her once again.

"Sylvia, I'm always here for you. We are all here for you. We just want to see you happy." She squeezed my hand once before letting go, and went out the door.

The rest of the day passed in a blur. I avoided my phone. I would call Jason and Kerri back later. Beau never called and Quinn didn't attempt to talk to me when I passed him in the hall on the way to do my laundry. I spent the day reflecting on the past and making plans for the future. By eight that night, I was worn out. Classes didn't start until Tuesday, but I still went to bed early that night. I just wanted the escape from my reality that sleep would provide me with.

THREE WEEKS PASSED by quickly. The days got easier. Soon I was into a routine. I had classes and work. Unfortunately, it seemed that I had classes at the same time as Quinn. Every Monday, Wednesday, and Friday morning we ran into each other as we left our apartments. He would say hi, and look me over.

I knew what he was doing. He was looking to see if Beau had left any more marks. The first few times I didn't even give him the satisfaction of a response. I would just lock my door and walk away. He walked the same way onto campus as I did. If I hadn't known Quinn better, I would have thought he was following me. At least he never tried talking to me more than just the perfunctory hello.

Slowly, my anger dissipated. I began to greet him back. One day, we even talked about the weather as we walked to the outer door together. I was still upset with him. I felt as if some part of me always would be. At least for the near future, anyway. I was still hurt by it all. I just tried really hard not to let myself think about it.

I stayed busy. I still had work, which was starting to wind down with classes in full swing. My hours there were slowly being cut down. That was always helpful, this year in particular. The classes weren't necessarily harder. They just demanded more time for work outside of the classroom. I spent a great deal of time in the library, getting my ideas for my major projects together.

I didn't see much of Kai, Kerri and the guys. They were all busy too, getting into the swing of the new semester. I had called and checked on Colby a few times. He even came over for supper one night. I had yet to see Jason. We just couldn't seem to find a time when we were both free. I missed him. I hadn't told him about Quinn yet. He'd gotten me through so much in the past and listened to so much of my heartbreak that I just didn't know how to tell him that Quinn had reappeared. I would tell him at some point. I just wanted to do it face to face.

Then there was Beau. He did call back. He called Monday night after the weekend party. He said he'd figured I'd had a pretty nasty hangover that Sunday and didn't want to be disturbed. We spent a great deal of time together when he was in town. It seemed like he was always leaving. I didn't realize that many people skipped out on bail. When he was in town, we tended to spend our time alone together. That first weekend I took him along with me when I went out with the others. The guys had invited Quinn, not knowing that I was coming. It wasn't quite a repeat of the park. I tried to ignore him as he glared at Beau all night. His eyes were hard, dark and full of animosity. Beau found it all very amusing.

At one point during the evening, Beau was telling Reed and Sloane about how on our first date I didn't know how to order beer. I knew I was blushing. I hadn't realized he had picked up on that. When he was done he made a comment about having broken me in then and asked me to go get us all another round. Kerri and Kai were in the bathroom and Quinn's glowering at us was getting on my nerves. I needed the break away, so I got up to go get the drinks. As I stood, Beau patted me on the ass. I glanced down at him to see him smirking at Quinn. I followed his gaze to find Quinn clenching his jaw and gripping the table. I rolled my eyes and leaned down and whispered in Beau's ear, just loud enough for Quinn to hear. "You can do that again harder tonight, when we get back to my place." Then I let my tongue slowly trace along his ear. I looked over at Quinn as I did it. He had his eyes shut and looked as if he were mentally counting to ten.

I ranted to myself the whole way to the bar and back. He had no right to care what I did with Beau. Did he really think that I would never date again? He left me. Was I supposed to just sit on my thumbs and grow old alone because he didn't want me? Who did he think he was that I would put my life on hold for him? He was just waiting for me to fall back into his arms. Well, that wasn't going to happen. Ever! I'd learned my lesson.

How long before he would have had another reason to leave me? Well, it wouldn't work. I did move on. Quinn was just going to have to get used to seeing me with Beau. If he couldn't handle it, he could leave. These were my friends first. He didn't have to hang out with us.

By the time I got back to the table, I had worked myself into a rage. I planned to tell Quinn just what I thought about his behavior. Then I stopped myself. That was exactly what he would want. If I let him know it bothered me, he would keep doing it. Instead, I just ignored him and turned my entire attention to Beau. I would show Quinn that his presence didn't bother me in the slightest. I would show him that I had someone else in my life, and he never would be again. I made sure I was touching at least some part of Beau the entire night. I even laughed at his lame jokes and acted like he was the only person in the room. I barely paid attention to Kerri and Kai, even. I didn't go dance with them like I normally would have. I only went out to dance when Beau went with me, which thankfully was only once.

When we all left for the night, I saw Quinn leave with Reed and Kerri. They were still standing outside our apartment building as Beau and I came up the walk. I said a quick goodnight to all of them and pulled Beau up the steps behind me. I didn't look back to see if Quinn was following us but I heard his door slam seconds after I closed mine.

The next day, Kerri told me that the tension between Beau and Quinn was too much and I needed to find a way to fix it. After that, I just tried to avoid doing group activities with Beau along. He asked why we didn't go out with them again, so I just invited Kai and Sloane over on a night I knew Kerri would be busy. I actually asked her, too, but I knew the answer I would get. That night didn't go as well as I'd hoped it would. Beau and Sloane were both pretty quiet. Who could get a word in with Kai around most of the time anyway? She quizzed Beau the whole time they were there. I could tell Beau was getting annoyed with her, so I faked a headache and told them I should just go to bed. I hadn't attempted to join any of them again with Beau.

Beau seemed to be fine with that. He was only in town for about eleven days during those first three weeks. I spent all of those with him at my place. We went out alone a couple times, but he was fine with just staying in with me. I cooked and we watched movies or found other ways of entertaining ourselves. He only stayed the night once, that second Friday. He left Saturday night saying he had to be gone again by Monday morning. He called or texted when he was on the road. Not every day, but often enough that I wasn't concerned that he'd forgotten me.

Kai was making plans to go to Chicago on our next three-day weekend. After hearing that Quinn was going I declined, using work as an excuse. I wasn't about to go for three nights and the better part of three days with his constant presence. I didn't think I could handle it and I knew Beau would have gone ballistic if I'd told him I was doing that. Beau detested Quinn and he made no attempt to hide it. Quinn let it be known that the feeling was mutual. I knew Quinn's dislike was due to the bruises he'd jumped to conclusions about. I just couldn't completely figure out Beau's anger. He knew about our past, but I tried very hard to show him that was all Quinn was to me -- the past.

Of course neither Kai nor Kerri believed me. Kerri called me out on Beau not letting me go. I tried to explain his position on Quinn but Kerri wasn't hearing it. She said he was just a territorial pig and I shouldn't let him make my decisions for me. I couldn't get her to see that he just really cared for me and was worried about me being upset by Quinn. Kerri rolled her eyes with a "whatever". Kai begged me to change my mind. I held firm to my answer, though. Also, I had hoped I would get the whole weekend alone with Beau.

Things had been going well between the two of us. I'd learned more about him. He had had a rough life. It had only been him and his mom. He said he had never known his dad. They moved around a lot. He figured he had been to over twenty schools in his life. He said he envied the stability I had.

I told him how hard it had been to watch my mom suffer from breast cancer, about the emotional roller coaster we lived on every time a new treatment was presented. I talked about having to care for both my mom and dad through it all. He pointed out that that was why I was so good at taking care of everyone. I asked him if he wanted to meet my dad, but he said he wasn't good with parents and we should wait. I was hoping that by Thanksgiving he would change his mind.

I still hadn't seen his place. He said my place was so much nicer and he wasn't ever really there anyway. I couldn't help but wonder, if my place was so much nicer, why he always left at night. I would have loved to spend the night in his arms, maybe wake up and have some morning fun. Beau was still rough when we had sex. I didn't really mind that. What I did mind was how fast it always seemed to be over. I was almost always left wanting more as he would get up and go out on my balcony for a cigarette. I held firm on him not smoking in my apartment. I wanted to talk to Kerri for advice on how to get him to slow down but I knew she didn't like him. So I just bit my lip and kept hoping that eventually it would get better.

On two separate nights I joined the group for a games night. We used to have them all the time. I was sure once we all got into the groove with our schedules we would start having them frequently again. In the past, Jason had often joined us, so I would partner up with him. If he couldn't come, we would just play games that didn't require partners. Without Jason available I figured that was what we would do again. Of course, Quinn ended up being there. Kai started to suggest that we be partners but Sloane quickly spoke up and claimed me for a partner. I could have kissed him. He and Kai shared a quick private conversation with just their eyes, and then Kai announced that it was time to start.

I expected the games nights to be worse than they were. Quinn and I interacted very little. We only spoke to each other if need be. If it continued like that, everything would be fine. I could handle seeing him as long as he kept his thoughts to himself. I heard more about his family. I had been dying of curiosity about them. I had always loved Marie and Alex. I missed them deeply. Losing Marie was like losing my mom all over again. It was a relief to hear that they were doing fine. When he shared tales from Princeton, I excused myself to the bathroom. I just couldn't stand to hear about what should have been my life, too. I knew that if I had gone there, I never would have met my friends. Yet it still stung to hear about it.

Kai and Reed showed up at my place one night wearing matching lime green bowling shirts. And just to make my life better, Kai bought one for me too. I had no idea why I let them talk me into going bowling with them that night. I hated bowling. I was horrible at it, and more often than not someone ended up injured when I bowled. I only went along out of sheer boredom. Beau had been gone for three days and I was caught up on my class work. I'd figured Quinn would be along, but that didn't bother me. We had gotten along well enough at the games nights. So I let Kai dress me in lime green that went so well with my red hair. I slapped on a smile that was just as comfortable as the rented shoes.

Quinn did indeed go along, as I had expected. It seemed that he had solidified a place within our little group. I tried not to feel as if I had been stabbed in the back. They were my friends first, and they knew my history with Quinn. I really didn't want to let it bother me that they were so easy to forgive his previous treatment of me. Sometimes, though, when they all laughed at a joke Quinn made or asked for his input on something, I just wanted to scream. That night was particularly bad. It may have been due to the fact that I was already on edge having to participate in something I knew would only end embarrassment. Or maybe it was because Quinn was in such a good mood.

He showed up at the bowling alley after the rest of us. He, too, wore a lime green shirt. Of course it looked just as silly on him. I couldn't keep my eyes from his. They appeared to be lighter and had more sparkle to them. What pissed me off the most, though, was that damned crooked smile he wore most of the night. It didn't matter to him that he was bowling like shit. In fact, his score was only slightly higher than mine, which wasn't saying much at all. He joked about it and smiled. Every time I looked over at him he had that smile on his face. It did things to me that I didn't ever want to admit. It made my stomach tighten and tingles run through me. My breath would hitch and I would have to remind myself to breathe. I just wanted to go over to him and wipe it off his face. *Yeah, with a kiss.*

It would figure that my irrational inner voice would choose that night to pick a fight with my reasonable inner voice. I barely spoke to anyone the whole night. I was afraid of which voice would come out at any given moment. The mental battle going on inside had my head aching. At times I wanted to go sit next to Quinn just to feel the electricity that he emitted to me. Once I 'accidentally' brushed against him when I had to retrieve the ball I dropped that had rolled over to him. More than one time, I caught myself staring at his ass when it was his turn. At one point, he turned around as I was lost in a memory of what it looked like naked. He caught my eye and that wicked grin appeared. I blushed furiously and tripped as I excused myself to the bathroom to get my mind under control.

The whole night went like that. One side of me wanted nothing more than to slap him silly for being so carefree and happy and turning my insides to mush. The other side of me wanted to join with him and let myself be dazzled by that smile. I started naming the battles in my head. We had the battle of 'Asswatchington' - which irrational won. Of course reasonable came back with 'Beaustlak'. That was when I told Kai how I was anticipating spending the next weekend with Beau while they all went to Chicago. Irrational won another with 'Suck Quinnsville.'

'Suck Quinnsville' had been a particular eye opener for me. I had just bowled my fourth gutter ball in a row when Reed suggested, "Syl, you and

Quinn suck so bad that even if we combined you two together you would still be in last place." All I heard was Quinn and suck, and my mind went off to some long-forgotten happy place. I couldn't believe that I would go there. I realized I had a goofy grin on my face when Reed started laughing and crossed off our names on the board and wrote Quilvia with our combined score. Kerri smacked him on the back of the head but he refused to change it. Irrational took another victory with 'Quilvia.' I momentarily liked the sound of it.

By the end of the second game, I'd had had enough. I was ready to go. Unfortunately, no one else was. I sat down with my head in my hands. Sloane came over and sat down next to me. "Not feeling well, Sylvia?"

"Not really. I hate bowling." I muttered between my fingers.

"Uh-huh. And you're sure it isn't anything more?" His tone suggested he knew more about the internal struggle raging through me than I wanted him to know.

I peeked at him and squeaked, "No."

"Suuurree it's not." He was smiled at me before he spoke up. "Sylvia's not feeling well. Maybe we should call it a night so she can get home."

"No way, man. We're tied one apiece. We need to at least have a tie breaker." Ever competitive, Reed had to open his big mouth.

Sloane jumped on the challenge. "Why? You'd just lose. You should quit now before I finish you off."

"Finish me off. Ha. That's what...." Kerri hit him again. He rubbed his head. "Damn Kerri. Stop it."

"I can take her." Everyone stopped and gaped at Quinn. He looked around at each of us. "I mean, I'm terrible at this and I really do have some studying to do, so I could just take her home." His voice got quieter and quieter as he finished, realizing that we were all still gawking at him. I just blinked and wondered what riding in such close proximity to him would do to reasonable voice.

Kai was the first to speak up. "That's an excellent idea. You don't mind, do you Sylvia? I know the guys want to finish the game, and we all rode together. So you should just let him take you home." She was giving me her puppy eyes that she knew I could never turn down even if they were the unnatural green to match her shirt.

I huffed and agreed. I said good night and headed to the parking lot. Quinn was still inside, but I knew his black Camry. I waited beside it. Always the gentleman, he came over and opened my door for me before he got in. I didn't say anything the whole ride home. I couldn't trust myself to. I sat there, surrounded in his scent. I closed my eyes and took a deep breath of it. I missed him. I knew I missed him, but I couldn't give in to past feelings. I knew on some level that it would be easy to, but easy didn't make it right. Thankfully, it was a short ride. Quinn still drove like a maniac, and we were back in record time.

He didn't turn the car off right away. I turned toward him. He was looking out the window straight ahead. I quickly looked for what he was looking at. Part of me feared that it was Beau. Fortunately, there was nobody there.

I sighed and said, "Thank you for the ride." I got out of the car quickly and Quinn was still sitting there. I gave the Camry one more glance when I reached the door. He was still sitting there; his head was down against the steering wheel. My heart gave a little tug and I briefly wondered if he had the same battles being fought in his mind as well. I was tempted to go back and talk to him, but my phone rang.

"Hi beautiful. What are you up to tonight?" I walked into my apartment as I relayed most of my day to Beau, leaving out bowling completely.

Chapter 8 - Quinn

I HAD MY BOOKS SPREAD out in front of me. I had a pharmacology test coming up on Thursday and I couldn't concentrate on anything. It had been four nights since I had gone bowling with everyone. I didn't really want to go. I hated bowling. I never could get the hang of it. I even had trouble Wii bowling. When Kai brought up the shirt the night before we went, I tried to get out of it. I told her I may be late getting out of the library and to just start without me. Kai insisted that no one goes to the library on a Friday night. I contended that I did. She said, "That may be but Sylvia doesn't." When she left I vowed that I absolutely would not go after that. I tried to discourage them from thinking that I wanted to get back together with Sylvia. I didn't, I just wanted to be friends again. I figured I would let Kai think I was coming and then text Sloane once they were all there and tell him that I wouldn't be able to make it. But it's funny how just a smile can change your whole day.

I was locking my door that Friday morning as Sylvia came out of her apartment. We had been doing this little morning routine since the first Wednesday after classes started. I had left early that first morning. I wanted to stop for some coffee before my first class.

I attempted a "hello" that first morning, not knowing what reaction I would get. I had never seen the side of Sylvia that came out that Sunday morning. We had never really argued in high school. There was never a need to. Of course we had disagreements, every couple does, but they were always small ones. Most of them were about her absolute stubborn-ness when it came to me spending money on her. She didn't like gifts or going out to expensive places. She just didn't get that I wanted to do those things, not because I could, but because I wanted to. I wanted to share those experiences with her or give her things to make her smile or make her life easier. I would have done anything for her. It didn't matter if it cost my whole savings account or nothing at all. I just wanted her smile and her love.

She was so independent when it came to such things. I respected and admired that about her, yet I still wanted to take care of her, too. She took care of me in so many ways that I never felt as if I showed her just how much I appreciated all she did for me. I just wanted to be able to give something back in return. Whenever I tried she would tell me that if she couldn't afford it she didn't need it. She would tell me in no uncertain terms when I was doing something that bugged her, but she never went off on me like she had that morning. Even though I was upset with myself for causing her to be so angry, I couldn't help but think about how beautiful she had been. All the clichéd phrases about tempests and wild animals came to mind, but she was more than that. Just thinking of it again had me hard. I knew it was wrong, but God she something else.

Once I'd seen the bruises, I just wanted to go out and pound him. I tried to make her realize that he was an ass for leaving those marks but she wouldn't hear it. She shoved me out the door and that was that. I debated on telling Reed and Sloane about it. I'm sure they wouldn't have approved of Beau hurting her. In the end, I decided not to say anything to them. Sylvia made it very clear that she wanted to make her own decisions. Telling them would just be meddling in her affairs, which she was absolutely correct about. I'd given up the right to do that. It didn't mean that I would stand aside and let her get hurt though. I planned to keep a close eye on Beau, and didn't ever want to see marks on her like that again.

So that first day when we met in the hall on our way out I looked her over. I didn't think he had been by in the past couple days after that, but I still wanted to be sure. Sylvia didn't respond to my hello and she didn't appear to be hurt anywhere. She just locked her door and walked away like I wasn't even there. I followed her down the steps and halfway across campus before she turned into a building. I realized that she must have class then, and decided that if I left at that time every morning I would be able to catch her coming out of her apartment. It would let me check on her without her realizing that I was doing it.

It turned out she only left at that time three days a week. At least I had those three days. I greeted her every morning. Eventually, she started coming around. At first it was just a greeting back. After the last time we had been at Reed's for games night we even talked about the weather. I had sincerely hoped that she would talk to me again that morning. She came out of her apartment all smiles. I didn't know what had her in such a good mood but I had hoped to work it to my advantage. I told her hello and she responded with a good morning. This time I went down the steps first, but I waited outside until she caught up with me. I walked alongside her all the way to her turnoff point. We never said a word to each other, but she smiled at me once more when she turned to go up to the steps of the building.

I walked away whistling. I decided then that bowling might not be so bad if she was going to be there. I had been encouraged by her smile and cheerful good morning. I hoped the friendliness would carry over through the evening.

Of course it didn't. I tried very hard to keep smiling, even though it was obvious that Sylvia wanted to be anywhere but there. I caught her several times looking at me. I would have given anything to know what she was thinking. After one particularly good round I turned around and found her staring at me. I gave her the grin she always accused me of using to 'get into her pants'. She blushed a deep scarlet before taking off for the bathroom.

I knew Sylvia hated bowling, probably even more then I did. When she wanted to leave and no one wanted to take her, I volunteered. I wanted to talk to her. I didn't really have anything to say. I just wanted to have a nice, easy conversation with her. One like we use to have. She waited out by my car while I said my goodbyes. I opened the door for her, purely out of habit. Once in the car I glanced over at her and all my thoughts of conversing with her left me. She was so tense. I hated that I was the one who had caused her to be like this. She should be able to go out and enjoy her time with her friends. I realized for that to happen I wouldn't be able to join them, but I liked spending time with them. Kai radiated so much energy and life that I was just drawn to her. Sloane's quiet, introspective demeanor always made me feel comfortable. Reed's humor made me smile, even on the worst of days. Kerrington was still cold to me but she was coming around. I kind of liked that she was loyal to Sylvia and wasn't as trusting of me as the others were. Not that I had any intention of causing Sylvia any trouble. There had to be a way for Sylvia and me to coexist without all the tension. I was determined to make that happen, no matter what it took.

It was a quiet ride home. Neither of us said a word. When we pulled into the lot outside our apartment building, I really wanted again to tell her that I was sorry. I was so sorry for it all. I stared straight ahead of me.

I was trying to find the words. I was too late. She thanked me for the ride before she got out of the car. After the door shut, I let my head fall against the steering wheel. One more chance at fixing this, once again lost. I sat there like that for awhile. Her scent still lingered behind, and I just couldn't bring myself to leave it.

I stayed in the rest of that weekend. Mom and Dad came for a visit on Sunday. Mom hadn't been to see the apartment since I'd moved in and she wanted to make sure I had everything I needed. I think she really wanted to go see Sylvia, but it was too soon for that. She settled for meeting Kai and Sloane. Kai and Mom really hit it off. At one point, Kai pulled her down to her apartment to show her something she had designed. They were down there over an hour. Mom and Dad left after that, but I over-heard Mom and Kai making plans to meet up for lunch.

With my concentration totally shot, I had no choice but to go along with Reed when he came up to tell me that it was Tequila Tuesday at their place. Kerrington had had a bad day, and Reed had decided that she needed a good drunk night. So he got everyone together for a completely inebriated games night. Even though we all had classes the next day, we still joined in.

Everyone was there when I got there. From the looks of it they had already started on the tequila. Even Sylvia seemed more relaxed and cheer-ful. Kai handed me a margarita and asked me what game I wanted to play. I really didn't care, so I told her whatever was fine with me. Kai wanted to play *Yahtzee* for shots. She explained the rules. "It's simple. Whoever has the lowest score after each round does a shot." I was up for that.

It was funny how Kai always had the highest scores after each round. I don't think she ever took a shot. Which is probably just as well, because I couldn't imagine her little body could handle much. The rest of us evened out fairly well. We were all pretty close with our final scores, and we were all pretty buzzed. We were all laughing and enjoying the night. Sylvia even talked to me a little. She asked about Mom and Dad and told me to tell them hi, and that she missed them. I smiled and told her they missed her too and that Mom would like to see her sometime. She looked wistful and said maybe someday.

Kerrington picked the next game. It was some card game I had never played before. It required partners and Kai was adamant about having Sloane as her partner and there was no way Kerrington was going to give up Reed. I looked over at Sylvia, ready to offer to sit it out and wait for them to be done, but Sylvia surprised me with, "So partner, are you feeling lucky tonight?"

Hell, yes! After that I felt as if everything was going to go my way. I gave her my best smile, which this time she returned. We all rearranged around the table so that partners weren't sitting next to each other. Sylvia and Sloane explained the rules to me as Kai and Kerrington made more margaritas and Reed found the cards.

We all chose our cards and passed them off according to the rules. I was given three red threes off the bat. It seemed like a sign. I knew I could close them, and Sylvia and I would be able to win. When I laid them out, she glared at me. It must not have bothered her too badly, though, because she still laughed and joked with the group. When we didn't close the book that first hand, Sylvia pretended to be mad about it. I knew she was only kidding, though. So the next round I did it again. I knew it was just a matter of time before we closed one.

We all kept drinking steadily. The conversations got more and more ridiculous. Reed regaled us all with nasty sex stories and jokes, each cruder than the last. He told us about a 'friend' who'd had anal sex only to wake up in the morning to find a 'present' in the bed. Kerrington choked on her drink, and I had a feeling that Reed was a dead man. After that, he toned them down but didn't stop completely. Sloane joined him with a couple, but I had none to share so I just laughed along with everyone else. Sylvia shocked the hell out of me when she shared the story about one time when we had sex outside in her backyard. It was dark and we didn't exactly check out the ground before we did it. After, we realized that we had rolled into cat shit, and it was all over our shirts. I was more surprised at the fact that she had acknowledged us as once having been together than that she shared that story.

Sylvia and I were way behind on our last round. I had attempted a book of red threes every round. If I hadn't we would have been far out in front of everyone else. Reed was giving me shit about it. I shut him up when I winked at Sylvia and said "I'll get lucky one of these times." She blushed a deep, dark red, but didn't say anything. When we lost that round, too, she threw her cards at me playfully and said next time she wanted Sloane for a partner. I knew she wasn't really mad. Her face gave her away. She was so much more at ease that night. She laughed along with everyone else. She only shared the one story, but she did make witty comments after some of the others.

After cards, we moved on to *Pictionary*. Sylvia and I ruled at it. It was amazing how we just clicked. It was like old times. We knew exactly what the other was trying to convey. Sylvia was not the best at drawing, but it didn't matter. I felt so in tune with her that I was able to get every one of them right. It was the same way when we moved on to charades. Drunken charades was an entirely new experience for me. The rest had played it several times. Kerrington insisted that it was the only way to play it.

We were all fairly wasted by the time we started playing. Sylvia could barely stand when it was her turn. It was yet another side of Sylvia I hadn't seen before. We didn't really ever drink in high school, and the few times we did had been nothing close to this much. She was adorable in her drunken clumsiness. Several times I had to catch her or steady her. I loved being able to touch her, even if it as just briefly. Kai seemed to be having the most trouble. Sloane had drawn the word minivan. Kai quickly got the van part but just couldn't think of the word for mini. She said small, tiny, little, even compact but not mini.

Sylvia was sitting on the couch in front of me, rocking back and forth with laughter over it. She kept brushing against my leg. I wanted to pull her onto my lap and hold her, but I knew that I couldn't do that. I had to be happy with the fact that at least we were getting along. It started to feel like old times between us. We were slowly slipping back into a friendship role, and that was more than I had hoped for this soon. I didn't want the night to end. Of course, it had to. We all had classes the next day.

We called it a night when Kai passed out against Sloane on the couch. Sloane carried her back to their place, and Sylvia and I left at the same time. I walked her up to her door, making sure she didn't fall and hurt herself. I stood outside her door for a few minutes, talking. I really wished that she would be going to Chicago with us. The night had been so promising. I knew with some more time she would come around and everything would be okay. I told myself that my previous idea of staying away so she could be happy with her friends was not the thing to do. The night proved I could be one of her friends, too.

Eventually, we both knew it was time to say good night. The silence grew between us. She was so beautiful standing in front of me. Her heavy-lidded eyes watched me and her hair was coming out of the messy bun she had it in. It was falling down over her face, so I reached over and brushed it back behind her ear. I felt the heat of her skin against me, and I wanted to keep my hand there, cupping her cheek. I pulled it away, knowing that she was drunk and her reaction to me tonight was alcohol-induced. Tomorrow we would probably be back to normal. I whispered "sweet dreams" to her, and opened her door. She held my eyes to hers for a few beats of my heart, and I would have given anything to know what she was thinking. She didn't say anything. She turned, went in, and closed her door.

I couldn't help but smile to myself while I got ready for bed. I cleaned all my books up off the table. I doubted I would do very well on the pharmacology test. I didn't care. I could retake pharmacology again if I had to, whereas I may never get another night like that with Sylvia. I went to bed thinking about it. Someday, Sylvia would see that we were just better together, even if it was just as friends.

Chapter 9 - Sylvia

IT WAS SUPPOSED TO BE my quiet weekend all to myself. Everyone was going to be gone. Kai and the others were all going to Chicago to enjoy the rare three-day weekend we had. I was okay with them all being gone, though. I was still mildly upset with Kai. I wasn't sure I could even call it being upset. I was more like jealous. Kai had met Quinn's mom. Not only that, she'd gotten along with her and even had plans to go to lunch with her. I missed Marie. She had been almost a mother to me after I lost my own. I loved her, but I just couldn't go see her after Quinn left. I thought about her frequently that first year of college. I would come home over breaks and often get to the end of her driveway before I'd talk myself out of it. Then they moved, and I never got the chance to renew my friendship with her.

I tried to not let it bother me when I agreed to go to Kerri's for a games night. I even resigned myself to partnering with Quinn. The others were starting to complain about not being partners with their loves. The funny thing was that together as partners we dominated about any game they threw at us. Any game except Hand and Foot. We had yet to win even a round at that one. During every round dumbass Quinn would attempt to keep a book of red threes. We never, never, closed them. We never even came close to closing them. The last time Reed was giving him crap about it, Quinn just winked at me and stated that one of these times his luck would change. I'm not sure if that was directed at me or not, but the wink made me sigh inside. Everything after that was just a blur. It all just seemed like a dream. I remembered the idea of what happened, but I couldn't quite recall the details. The plus side of not remembering the details was that I didn't feel like I was completely lying to Beau about what I had done that night. I just told him I had been to Kerri's for games night.

Beau was out of town again, possibly in Texas. I wasn't sure. He was gone all week and didn't expect to be back anytime soon. I missed him but I was so happy to have the time to myself without anyone around. I needed to get some homework done. I also planned to give my apartment a thorough cleaning. I hoped to see Jason at some point during the weekend, too. I missed him and I still needed to tell him about Quinn.

Friday night I came across a weekend-long marathon of my favorite TV show. It had been a few years since I had seen it, and decided to sit up and reacquaint myself with it. It was one I had watched all the time with Quinn. In fact I hadn't ever seen the last season of it or any of the reruns when it went into syndication because it was just too painful. Friday night, though, I decided enough was enough. I watched it until I fell asleep on the couch.

Saturday morning, I was startled awake by a particularly loud crack of thunder. We were under a severe storm watch for most of the weekend, another reason I think Kai wanted out of town. She hated storms, and always wanted out of town when we were in for a big one. As my heart calmed back down I looked around the living room, trying to determine what time it was. The sky was dark from the storm, so I couldn't tell. The TV was on, still playing the same show. I recognized this episode as one that was really good. I waited for the commercial to go to the bathroom and check the time. It was just after nine. I figured I probably wouldn't get back to sleep for the day.

I grabbed a pop and headed back to finish the episode. I curled up on the couch under my favorite soft pink blanket. It was old. It had been on my bed in since I was little. It was my security blanket. Many days I'd spent cocooned in its cozy warmth. It had seen me through both the loss of my mom and Quinn. It was one of the few reminders of Quinn that I kept around. We snuggled under this very blanket several times while we watched TV or movies. I tried to not let myself dwell on that thought again.

I was drawn into the story on TV. It was one of the more complex mysteries. While I could remember who'd done it, I couldn't remember how it was solved. I figured there were about ten minutes left of it when someone knocked on my door. I smiled widely with the thought that Beau got into town earlier than he'd planned and had come to surprise me. I imagined us curled up on the couch together, watching the rest of the marathon. I wondered if he ever watched it. I ran my fingers though my hair, I regretted not having brushed it while I was in the bathroom. I looked down at my clothes. I still had on my black yoga pants and an old sweatshirt of Kelly's that I'd cut the neck and sleeves off of. It wasn't what I normally wore when Beau was over here with me. I shrugged and figured it wouldn't be on long anyway.

I briefly entertained the thought of answering the door naked. Kerri would be proud of me doing something so daring. Of course I couldn't do that. If I tried that, it would be the landlord or something. I heard some serious coughing coming from the other side of the door. I opened the door to find a hacking mess under a red plaid blanket. I furrowed my brow trying to make out who was under it. The coughing stopped and Quinn turned around. He was pale, and his eyes were kind of glassy. I could hear his every snuffled breath. He looked and sounded miserable.

"Quinn? Are you okay?" Obviously he wasn't. *Wait, what is he doing here? He's supposed to be in Chicago.* I answered my own question with, "Are you sick?" *No, he's coughing up a hairball.* I mentally kicked myself for that stupid question.

"Sylvia," his voice was so raspy that even I cringed at it. "I'm very sorry to bother you, but with everyone gone I didn't know who else to ask." He coughed into the side of his arm again.

"What do you need?" I was surprised that he was actually at my door. I had a vague recollection of Quinn walking me to my door after games night, but I didn't know if that had really happened. I wasn't sure if I should ask him in, but he looked like he could collapse at any moment. "Come in here," I urged as I ushered him in.

He took a couple steps and stopped to cough again. "I just wanted to know if you had some cough medicine. I coughed all night and I just really need to sleep this cold away." His voice just sounded raw.

"Oh, that sucks. Yeah, I have some. Sit down while I get it." I went back to the bathroom to look in the medicine cabinet. I had a whole bottle of *Nyquil.* I quickly brushed my hair while I had the chance. I could hear him coughing the whole time I was in there. The poor guy. He sounded really bad. I knew from experience that Quinn rarely got sick, but when he did it was bad.

I brought the *Nyquil* out to him and paused on the way. He was sitting on my couch with his head thrown over the back of it. He looked so vulnerable like that. My heart ached. I wanted to go over and run my fingers through his uncharacteristically limp hair and just comfort him. He turned his head and saw me and gave me a weak lopsided grin.

"Ah, you're an angel." I smiled back and walked towards him. "Really,

Sylvia. I can't thank you enough for this."

As he stood he pulled the blanket tighter around him. I realized then that he was shivering. I kept it fairly warm in my place, so I knew it couldn't have been that. He had to have had the chills. I was really worried then. "Quinn, I don't think you should be alone. Have you called Marie?" Surely his mom would come if he was sick.

He chuckled a little but it turned into a cough. "I'm a big boy now. I don't need my mommy to come running for just a little cold. I just need some cough syrup and some sleep. Besides that, I wouldn't want her out in this storm." I had to agree with that. The thunder and lightning hadn't let up at all. I wouldn't have wanted that either.

That was when I made a snap decision that I knew I would regret later, but the words were out of my mouth before I could stop it. "Well, I'm here. I could stay with you awhile." His chocolate eyes went wide in complete shock.

"What?"

"I mean, you know, just sit with you to make sure you're okay and all." I stumbled over the words with embarrassment. I was looking down at my foot twisting against the carpet. He didn't say anything, so I looked up at him. He stared at me with a mix of consternation and what I thought could be relief. I don't know why, but I quickly added, "I mean I'm not doing anything and, well, you really shouldn't be alone." What I wanted to do was get him a hot cup of tea with honey and lemon for his poor throat.

"If you want to. But really, you don't have to. I would be boring company. I will probably just take this and sleep." He held up the *Nyquil* bottle I had given him.

"That's okay; I'll just bring my work with me. I planned to get caught up on it this weekend." I suddenly looked forward to staying with him. Really, it would be okay. He'd likely sleep, and I could get my work done. It would be a win-win situation for both of us.

"Um, okay. Thanks." He turned and headed to the door.

"Give me a couple minutes," I called out to him. I wanted to get a few things together. He stopped to wait for me, leaning against the door. He looked so awful. I had just seen him the previous morning and he didn't look that bad. His normally uncontrollable hair was lying limply across his forehead. He was scruffy like he hadn't shaved in a couple days. He was even paler than I was, yet he had bright red cheeks, signaling a fever. What bothered me most, though, were his lifeless eyes behind his glasses.

I hadn't seen him with glasses on since he'd come back. He always had his contacts in.

I hurried back to my kitchen and grabbed the ingredients for the tea. My books and laptop were all still in my bag, so I didn't have to get anything else together. I added the stuff from the kitchen and threw the strap over my shoulder. "Okay, I'm ready," I said as I turned my TV off and picked up my keys. I followed him out the door, and locked it behind me.

I had never seen the inside of his apartment. I knew it was a mirror opposite of mine: L-shaped living room, with a small dining area in the hook of the L. I knew the kitchen was to the right of the dining nook, and further down the hall that ran between the two would be a bathroom on the right and his bedroom at the end. I just didn't expect it to be decorated so simply. I had seen Marie's work before and figured she would have it a veritable showplace.

I took my time looking all around. I was astonished at the lack of items in the room. The walls were painted a coffee color but were completely bare. He had a large black leather sofa in the middle of the room. It was facing a metal and glass entertainment center. There was a large TV and speaker system on it. I rolled my eyes. Of course Quinn would have a sweet set up. He'd always liked his electronics. The TV was on what looked to be CNN. There was a laptop sitting on top of a coffee table that matched the entertainment center. The table was covered with used Kleenex. I wrinkled my noise and glanced at Quinn, who was watching me intently. I pointed at the mess on the table.

"You need to clean up your own messes, though. I'm not a nursemaid."

Quinn smiled, "Right away. Anything else?" I shook my head.

He headed to the kitchen; I followed him, telling him that I was going to make him some tea. I put my bag on the dining table and got out what I needed. He reached into the cupboard under the sink and came up with a plastic bag. I watched as he set it on the counter and read the directions on the *Nyquil* bottle. He pulled out a shot glass and poured himself a shot's worth of the nasty green liquid. I wanted to gag for him. I knew how bad that stuff tasted. He slammed it back quickly, as if it were a shot. He winced and shook his head.

"I hate that stuff. It tastes like black licorice. I can't stand that, either." He filled a glass of water from the fridge. The apartments came with appliances but none of them had fancy fridges like his. Kai and Kerri both replaced theirs for bigger ones like this that had built in water and ice dispensers. I still had the plain old white one with a burned out light bulb.

I stood in the doorway of the kitchen, waiting for him to leave. These kitchens were small, and I didn't want to accidentally bump into him while I made the tea. "Why don't you go lay down? I'll bring you the tea when it's ready."

Quinn nodded and thanked me again. I was relieved when he went to the couch instead of his room. I didn't want bring him anything in his bed. I went about getting the tea ready. I chose the right cupboard on the first pick. I smiled at the fact that he had his dishes in the same location I did. I filled a cup for him and decided to make one for myself, too. I put them both in the microwave and went back to the dining table to wait for the water to heat up.

Quinn had cleaned up the Kleenex mess. He lay on the couch, still wrapped up in the blanket, and flipped through the channels. I unpacked my bag, setting all the books on the table. I had to write an in depth analysis comparing and contrasting the works of the Bronte sisters. I knew all the works well, so I didn't expect it to be hard -- just time consuming.

The timer on the microwave went off, so I went back in and added the honey and lemon to Quinn's cup. I set mine on the table and brought his over to him. He was coughing again and I really hoped it would help. He truly did look exhausted. He was still flipping through channels. What is it with guys and remotes? Why can't they just find a channel and leave it there? He paused long enough to take the cup from me and give me an appreciative grin.

"Drink that. It should help your throat. Then try to get some sleep. I'll just be right over there doing some work." I pointed to the table. "Do you mind if I plug my laptop in? I should be able to connect to my network from here."

"I don't care. You do what you need to. If you can't get a connection let me know and you can log into mine." His eyes were so heavy. I momentarily wanted him to lay his head on my lap and let me run my fingers through his hair until he fell asleep. I shook that thought away and headed to the table to get started on my work.

About ten minutes later Quinn finally quit flipping channels. "Hey, look what's on."

He had it turned to the show I was watching earlier. "It's on all weekend. I started watching it last night. I never did see the last season. Did you?"

He was lying on the couch, all stretched out with his feet hanging off the edge. He shifted up a bit to look over at me. "No, I gave up on it. Maybe we can catch it this weekend."

Wait, what? We can catch it this weekend? I wasn't going to be there the whole weekend. I glanced up at him, wondering what he was thinking. When I didn't answer he lay back down and I turned back to my laptop. I couldn't concentrate, though. My mind was at war with itself. *What am I doing here? I'm in my ex-boyfriend's apartment, alone with him. I have a boyfriend. I shouldn't be here. He's sleeping now. I should just go home. But he's sick. I can't leave him alone like this. I'll just wait here and when he's feeling better I'll leave.* I replayed that argument over and over in my mind for the next couple hours while Quinn slept. I finally gave up completely on getting any work done. I closed the laptop and put it all away. I went over and sat on the floor by the couch and watched TV.

I slipped out during a commercial to run home and take a shower and pick up a couple things. I wanted to make him some chicken soup, but he didn't have anything except TV dinners, frozen pizzas and cereal. No wonder the guy was sick. He wasn't eating healthy enough. I got everything I needed and brought it back over to his place.

He was sitting up on the couch, bent forward with his head in his hands. When he heard the door he jerked upright. "I thought you had left me. I mean, I woke up and you were gone and I didn't see your stuff here so I assumed you'd gone home." His throat sounded a little better, but it was still scratchy.

I couldn't help but smile at the hopeless-little-boy look on his face. "I just went home for a shower and to get real food for you. Seriously, hot pockets and cereal? You need to eat better."

"Yes, Mom." He smirked at me.

"If your mom knew you were eating that crap she would have a fit. I'm surprised she doesn't make you come home for dinner every night. She used to be so adamant that you be home to have dinner as a family." I fondly remembered dinners at Quinn's on the nights that I didn't make dinner for my dad. We would all sit around the table and talk about our day and what was going on in our lives. It was just what I remembered family dinners could be like, and I loved being part of it.

"She would love that. She always complains that she doesn't see me enough." He rolled his eyes and looked over the bag I was carrying with interest. "So what's in there?"

"Just some stuff to make chicken soup for you. Nothing helps get over a cold like chicken soup." I went into the kitchen and got started. I had thawed out the chicken breasts in the microwave at my house while I was in the shower. Now I just had to cook them while I chopped vegetables. I was working away and didn't notice Quinn standing in the doorway watching me until he started talking.

"So you still like cooking, huh?"

I glanced over at him. He looked so much like he used to. His hair was lying over his forehead as if it too were too tired to stick up. He was wearing his glasses. I thought they were the same ones he'd had in high school. There were definite changes, too. The way the plain white t-shirt he had on clung to him. I could see the faint definition of muscles in his arms and chest that had never been there before. I wondered what his chest felt like now. I bit my lip and turned away. I had to stop these thoughts.

"Yeah, I still like to cook. I used to cook for everyone more, but I've been pretty busy lately." I thought of Beau and how he didn't like getting together with my friends. He did like it when I cooked for him though, and told me so often.

Quinn let out a snort. I thought I heard him mumble, "Held prisoner, more like it." I should have said something to him about that comment, but I really didn't want to argue with him today so I let it go.

"What else do you like to do now?" He still watched me as I started to add everything to the big soup kettle I'd brought over. I had to really think about that. I really hadn't done anything for myself other than read in so long.

"I guess just reading. I like to hang out with Kai and Kerri. I could do without the shopping trips and the makeovers, but I always have a good time with them. You haven't met Jason, but I like to spend time with him.

I finished adding the water and spices to the pot and left it to simmer. I washed my hands and then turned to Quinn, who had moved further into the kitchen. He was now very close in the too-small kitchen, which shrank even more while we were in there. I searched his face, trying to read his mind. He appeared to be deep in thought. He was staring right at me but I didn't think he was actually seeing me.

I took that moment of his inattention and really looked him over. Even sick, he was impossibly handsome. To me, he had always been handsome. I knew others didn't see him like I did in high school, but it was always there. His current hair cut fit him much better. His jaw was much more defined now, too. Before I realized what I was doing, I reached out and ran my fingers along it.

His eyes flashed to mine and I quickly pulled my hand away as if it were burned. "I'm sorry, you were so lost in thought and I just..." I trailed off, not really having an answer to what I was doing.

His gaze lingered on mine a little longer. Both of us seemed to have trouble pulling away. I felt my heartbeat pick up, and my breath hitched. I lowered my eyes to his lips. They were slightly parted. I wondered if they still felt the same. Did he still taste the same? At that moment, I wanted nothing more than to find out.

Quinn let out a soft sigh. "So how long until the soup is done?" That effectively snapped me out of my fantasy world and back into this one.

"Um, a little while yet." Quinn's eyes held a hint of disappointment. Whether it was because the soup wasn't ready or something else, I couldn't say.

"What do you want to do while we wait? Did you finish your work?" Quinn asked as he walked out of the kitchen.

I let out a big breath, and wondered what had come over me. I followed Quinn out of the kitchen. "I gave up on my paper. I'll work on it later. We could just watch some TV. I think it's about the middle of season one. You were so off on your prediction of how it would end." I chuckled remembering his guess at the ending.

We sat on his big, black leather couch, one on each end, the gap in the middle mirroring the gap in our relationship. We spent the rest of the afternoon on that couch, watching TV and talking about trivial things. We even ate our soup sitting there. Over the course of the afternoon and evening, that gap closed a little more with each passing hour.

It was getting late and I should have gone home, but Quinn's fever was back and I couldn't leave him like that. He had been sleeping on and off for about three hours, but it was a restless sleep. He woke up shivering and I went to get him another blanket.

His room was similar to the living room. He had minimal furnishings and the walls were unadorned. It was done in the same black and tan color scheme as the rest of the apartment. I wondered again at his lack of trappings. He didn't even have pictures on any of the walls, or anywhere for that matter. Not even of his parents. The most he had on any wall was a clock in the dining area. I made note to ask him about it later.

There was a loud crack of thunder as I brought the blanket out to him.

The storm had let up in the early afternoon but was back in full force. The lights flickered and went out. Great, no power. Now what do we do? "Quinn?" I tried to feel my way to the couch without tripping over everything. I was clumsy enough with the lights on. With them off, my chances of injuring myself and others tripled.

"I'm still here on the couch. Just go slow. You'll find it."

I did take it slow, but still managed to stub my toe on the end of the couch when I reached it. Quinn laughed when I swore at it. I handed him the blanket and he wrapped it around himself. We sat on the couch in the dark, neither of us said anything. The silence wasn't uncomfortable. It was actually peaceful. The wind and the rain raged outside and the thunder was deafening. The worst of the storm must have been right over us. The lightning lit up the room and allowed us each occasional glimpses of the other.

At some point I became aware that Quinn was still shivering. Even the extra blanket hadn't helped his chills. I knew full well that I shouldn't do it, but I quietly said, "Quinn, come here. Let me help you warm up."

"I'm f-i-i-i-n-n-e," He whispered with his teeth chattering.

"No, you're not. Let me help." I moved closer to him and wrapped my arms around him. He was stiff in my arms at first. Slowly, he started to relax. "Are you getting tired again? Your cough has been a lot better. Maybe you'll be able to sleep tonight."

"Yes, I'm tired. How about you? You've been so helpful today. I can't thank you enough for being here, taking care of me like this. You really didn't have to do it."

"I know, but I couldn't leave you alone in this state, either. Now stretch out and get comfortable. You sleep while you can. I'll go home when you're doing better." We shifted around on the couch until I had my back pressed against the back of the couch and my arms around Quinn in front of me. It was a little awkward with him being so much taller than me. I didn't care though. I just wrapped my arms around him and pulled the blanket tighter around him.

I felt Quinn slowly relax into sleep. Occasionally his muscles would twitch and make me smile. I was torn apart as I laid there holding him. The guilt ate at me. What would Beau say if he knew where I was? It was all innocent. I was just helping a friend. I would do the same for Kai or Reed. Would I? Would I really hold Reed the same way I was holding Quinn right now? I told myself yes, but the voice in the back of my mind snorted in disagreement. I tried to push all the thoughts away. I didn't want to think of any of it right then. I had been here with him the whole day, and no matter what I thought or did that wasn't going to change. He still needed me there.

I drifted off to sleep with hazy thoughts of how good being there felt, how right everything felt at that moment. I dreamt of Quinn out at our old farm. He was holding me and telling me I was his world and about all the things we were going to do together. I smiled at my dream Quinn and sighed, "I love you, Quinn," as I lay my head on his chest. I snuggled closer to him on the couch as we both dreamed on.

God, my neck hurt. And my hips. Wait, what are my legs around? I opened my eyes and to see two brown pools peering into mine. I blinked. I must still be asleep. Nope, they're still here. Then I remembered where I was. I was still on Quinn's couch, with my body completely wrapped around him. His face was so close to mine that our noses were practically touching. I could feel his breath across my lips. His arms were around me, holding me close. I was pretty sure I knew exactly what was pushing against my hip. I sighed. It felt so good being there, but it was so wrong.

"Good morning." Damn, his voice was sexy. It was barely audible, and not because he whispered. Unfortunately, it sounded like he was losing his voice.

I gave him a lazy smile. "Good morning."

He pulled back slightly and traced my face with his eyes. He took a deep breath and let it out as he said, "I should let you go." I was sad when he moved to get off the couch. It had been so long since I'd felt like that. Been held like that. I knew the right thing to do -- the smart thing to do -- was to get up out of his embrace and out his apartment. Knowing this, I still offered, "I thought I should stay and make you breakfast." He gave me a speculative look. I looked down, avoiding his gaze. I didn't want him to read too much into the offer. "I mean, all you have is cereal, and that's not going to feel good on your sore throat. I could make you something else." I peeked up at him through my lashes. He had on his little half grin and a twinkle in his eye. Damn, he knew.

"I would love to have breakfast with you, Sylvia," he rasped out. I cringed, and went to make him some more honey and lemon tea. He stopped in the doorway of the kitchen. "I'm going to take a shower. Will you be here when I get back?" He actually looked worried.

"I should be. I want to run home and change and grab a couple of things to make." I didn't look at him while I answered. I kept myself focused on filling the cup and putting it in the microwave. "I'll leave your tea on the counter in case you're done before I get back." I gathered together what I needed for the tea. When I looked over, he was gone.

I heard the shower come on as I took the cup out and added the teabag. I let it soak as I folded the blanket left on the couch. My internal monologue started back up. *Sylvia, what are you doing? There is no reason you should even be here now. Now you're staying for breakfast? How much longer are you going to let this go on? He's Quinn Lobato. He broke your heart when he left. Yes, but he's back. Not for you, he isn't. It is nothing but a coincidence that he's even here. If you weren't in the same building he wouldn't even know you were still on campus. It's not like he searched you out. But he does know and he hasn't once acted like he wants anything other than friendship. We can be friends. Friends don't spend the night together. They do when one needs the other.* With a sarcastic snort, the voice went quiet. By the time I remembered Quinn's tea, it was fairly strong. I added extra honey, hoping that would cut down on the bitterness. I left it on the counter and went home.

I briefly debated on a shower. I decided I could skip one for now. I did need to change my clothes. I didn't think I would need to go anywhere later, so I threw on a different pair of old sweats. It was amazing Kai hadn't confiscated these yet. She hated the old blue ones. It wasn't because they were holey or even because they were sweats. She hated them because they had "QSHS" across the butt. She questioned the sanity of those in charge at my former high school when I explained to her that these were part of our gym uniform. I grabbed an old cream color tank top and one of my dad's old flannel shirts to go with it. I ran a brush through my hair and pulled it back up into a bun. I brushed my teeth and added some deodorant and body spray. I may have skipped a shower but I wasn't going to smell like it.

I wasn't sure what to make him for breakfast. I wanted to make sure it could be easily swallowed. I looked at the oatmeal but that seemed so boring. In the end, I took all my eggs and cheese. I had left the unused part the onion from the soup in Quinn's fridge yesterday. I wished I had fresh mushrooms, but settled for canned. I put everything in a cloth grocery bag and headed back to Quinn's.

I could hear the opening and closing of drawers from his bedroom and figured he was in there still getting dressed. I blushed, catching myself picturing him naked. I mentally kicked myself for going there and went to the kitchen to make the omelets.

While I cooked them, Quinn came out and drank his tea. He set the table. We didn't say anything until we sat down together to eat. Quinn took one bite and closed his eyes and moaned. "Sylvia, I don't think I can ever let you leave. I'm going to keep you here just so I can eat this well every day." Between the moan and the smile I felt myself clench and my breath catch. I cast my eyes down to my food and muttered thanks.

"So, tell me about how you met Kai and Kerrington." I noticed that he still referred to Kerri as Kerrington. She still hadn't loosened up around him enough to allow him to call her Kerri. I was sure she would come around and soon be just as friendly with Quinn as the others were.

I chuckled at my memory of meeting Kai for the first time. "It was our second day at the U. I still hadn't come out of my room to meet anybody, so I had no idea who I was living around. My roommate decided at the last minute not to come, so I had the room to myself. When Kai found out that I had an extra closet, she wasted no time in coming to claim it." I laughed again, remembering her. "I was sitting on my bed reading when my door flew open. She didn't even knock. Kai just walked right in and -- you know how she is. She said, 'I'm Kai. We're going to be such good friends. Now which closet is empty?' All I could do was stare at this spunky little thing in purple pigtails with matching eyes. She talked so fast I could barely understand her. I just pointed to the one by the window and looked at her. She then launched into a thousand questions and eventually Kerri walked by and heard her and came in to see who Kai was quizzing. She had been subjected to similar treatment the night before. They met the guys on their way to supper after they left my room."

Quinn snickered along with me. "I heard about how they all met. Kai truly believes in all that psychic "gift" shit, doesn't she?"

"Yeah. The spooky thing is she's so often right that I catch myself believing it, too."

We talked some more about the others: about how different we all are, yet how we just all work so well together. During that conversation I realized just how much time Quinn spent with Reed and Sloane. I wondered just how much of my past they'd told him about. He seemed to know quite a bit about Jason when I started to tell Quinn about him. It reminded me again that I still needed to talk to Jason. I planned to do that this weekend. I resolved to do it the next day. We sat there talking long after we finished eating. Finally, I got up and gathered the dishes. I watched Quinn load the dishwasher. I knew I was dawdling. I wasn't needed anymore, but I wasn't really ready to leave, either. Suddenly my weekend alone just felt lonely.

Quinn finished and closed the dishwasher. "So now what? Wanna finish watching season two?" Hmm, it seemed he wasn't ready for the weekend to end either. Quinn grabbed each of us a pop and joined me on the couch. It would be a lie to say Beau never crossed my mind. I just chose to ignore it when he did. Yes, I felt guilty but it didn't stop me from enjoying the time with Quinn. There were still times when the elephant between us made a pass through the room. Something one of us would say would call it out. For whatever reasons we had -- whether it was just to keep the friendly atmosphere up or just because we couldn't talk about it yet -- both of us let it go without comment.

The afternoon stretched out in front of us, and soon it was evening. I made us an early supper of reheated soup and turkey sandwiches. We started a game of Scrabble, but Quinn had a headache and his throat was hurting again, so we quit. I teased him it was because I was winning. After the game was cleaned up, I started to stand. "I should go so you can get some sleep."

Quinn caught my hand before I could step away from the table. "Please don't leave yet." His eyes pleaded with mine. He felt it, too. I knew as soon as I walked out of his apartment whatever momentary truce we had would end. I knew this weekend had changed how I felt towards him. My anger was mostly gone. Of course the hurt was still there. It was just buried deeper. It reminded me just how much I'd missed his friendship. I couldn't ever go back to the way things had been, but I could move forward to something new. We were both adults now and could handle a friendship without the past interfering with it. Quinn had been trying to show me that all along.

I nodded and sat back down. "I'll stay, but you really need to rest. I'll work on my paper while you go get some sleep."

My heart squeezed from the smile he gave me. He got up and moved towards the couch. I stopped him by touching his arm. "Go sleep in your room. You'll get a better sleep there. That way the lights and my constant tapping on the keyboard won't keep you awake." I let my hand slowly trail down his arm to his hand and gave it a gentle squeeze before I let go.

"Thank you," Quinn whispered. I found myself staring at his lips, and pulled my gaze away to his eyes. He was still wearing his glasses but I still felt that, even through the glass, we saw right into each other with that gaze. Quinn broke away first. "Just tell me goodbye when you leave. Even if you have to wake me, I want to know."

"Okay." I watched him walk down the hall and part of me went with him.

I worked on my paper. It was much easier to concentrate this time, perhaps because Quinn wasn't in the same room with me where I could hear his every breath. I lost track of time as I worked. Before I knew it, the paper was finished. I still needed to proofread it for any mistakes, but that could wait. I found it was always best to put something away for awhile before I edited it. It was easier to find the mistakes when I hadn't been staring at the same thing for hours. I looked at the time and saw that it was after eleven. Quinn had been sleeping for almost five hours. I figured it was time for me to go home.

True to my word, I walked down the hall to his room to tell him I was going home. I cracked his door open and spotted him on his bed. He had all the blankets thrown off and was laying there in just sleep pants. His radio was on, and I thought it may have kept him from hearing my light knock on the door. I called out to him. He didn't answer, so I crept closer to the bed. I reached out to shake his shoulder. He was burning up. I moved my fingers and palm around on his shoulder. My whole hand burned from touching his skin. His fever was back.

"Quinn. Wake up Quinn." I shook his shoulder lightly. He groaned and opened his eyes, but they fluttered closed just as quick.

"Quinn, I'm going to get you some Tylenol and a cool cloth. I'll be right back." I slipped into his bathroom and opened the cabinet. I was relieved to see that he did have some Tylenol. I found a wash cloth in the drawer and got it wet. I went to the kitchen for some ice water. I filled the cup with more ice than water, hoping it would help cool him down faster if he sucked on it.

He was awake when I brought it all back to him. He pulled himself upright and reached for the Tylenol and water. I watched his throat bob as he swallowed them. I took the cup from him and set it on the bedside table. He lay back down and I brought the cool cloth up to his forehead. I moved it gently over his face to cool him down. He let out a sound that could only be described as half moan, half sigh.

He reached over and grabbed my hand and put it on his chest over his heart. At first all I noticed was the feel of his heart beat. It wasn't slow but it wasn't racing, either. The rhythmic beat was slightly fast and irregular.

Then I noticed how hot his chest was, too. I ran the cloth along his jaw passed his neck down to his chest. As I rubbed his chest down I became aware of just how hard his chest had become. His abs weren't quite "chiseled," but they weren't too damn bad, either. I flicked my eyes back up to his. Thankfully, his were shut. His head was thrown back on the pillow, exposing his neck. I watched his Adam's apple bob again as he swallowed. I continued to move my hand with the cloth over his chest as I examined his face. His jaw was tight. It was much more sculpted than it used to be. He didn't shave that morning, either, so he had at least a couple days' growth going. It intrigued me. He never really let it grow like that in high school. I wondered how it would feel against me.

I snapped my mind back to what I was doing. He was sick and I was ogling him. I should have been ashamed of myself. The cloth was warm already, so I went back to the bathroom to re-cool it. I brought it back and sat down beside him on the bed as I started the cooling process all over again. The light from the bathroom was shining through the door, right in to Quinn's eyes. He covered them with his arm and I got my first real good look at how muscular his arms had become. His fist was clenched, causing his forearm to tighten up even more. I'd never asked what he did to bring about the changes. I didn't want him to think I had noticed.

As I stood to go cool the cloth once more, my eyes fell on the glass of ice water. The ice had barely melted. If I put that in the cloth it would take longer to warm up. It seemed like a good idea at the time. I realized quickly that once the ice did melt, I'd need to rinse the cloth out to avoid soaking everything. I thought maybe it would just be better to use the ice directly on his skin. That way it would dry off faster than it would with a wet cloth constantly leaking. I went back to the bathroom and squeezed it out and brought it back with me just in case I needed it.

I closed the door most of the way when I came back in so the light wouldn't bother him. I sat down next to him and ran the first of the ice cubes over his chest. He sucked a breath in and pulled his arm away and raised his head to look at me. His eyes were heavy lidded as he gazed at me. He opened his mouth but all that came out was, "Sylvia." His voice was so low. I realized the ice was gone, but I was still running my hands in soft, slow circles over his chest and stomach.

I stopped and started to pull away when Quinn's hand came over the top of mine. He held my hand and continued to use it to trail against his body. His eyes never left mine as he pulled my hand down lower. I hesitated when I felt the soft waistband of his pants. I looked into his eyes, questioning him. I wanted to make sure he was aware of what he was doing. I was damn sure of what was happening, yet I felt powerless to stop it. Quinn made a whimpered choking sound. "Sylvia, I don't have the strength to fight this anymore."

He tugged my hand lower, placing it right over his length. This, too, was burning, just like the rest of his body. I gasped. "Quinn, you have a fever. This is not something we should be doing right now." Or ever. He groaned, and dropped his head back. Then he moved, flipping me back on to the mattress, much quicker than someone with a fever should be able to.

"Sylvia, it's more than just the fever that has me burning." His face was over mine, just inches from my mouth. I could feel his hot breath over my lips. I knew it was wrong. I knew I should not be there. I should not even have been considering this. But at that moment, nothing was going to stop me from kissing Quinn Lobato.

I reached my free hand up to the scruff of his neck and pulled him to me. His lips were hot against mine, yet they were so soft. He barely touched mine. I parted mine slightly to encourage him. He deepened the kiss but still kept it soft. I felt his fire pour through that kiss onto my lips and into my mouth. Slowly it crept on, burning me as it went. His hands joined in, sliding up under my shirt. They seared me as they moved up my side. I was burning with him, for him.

His tongue sought out mine, twining around mine, not battling mine for control but dancing with it. I moaned against him and he pulled back a little, not taking his lips off me but just moving them to my jaw. He shifted slightly, allowing his hand room to slide from my side to gently cup my breast. His move freed my hand that had been trapped between us. I moved it up from his waist, over his hip and up his back. The feel of his muscles all hot and hard under my hand had me groaning and raising my hips to his.

He slipped a leg between mine and glided the hand that had been lightly massaging me back down my stomach and over my hip, stopping once he reached my thigh. He wrapped his long fingers around it and hitched my leg up, bringing his leg closer against me. He stroked my thigh and hip as I arched into him. I needed to feel the heat and the friction of him against me. I could feel him, so hard, pressed against my hip.

His mouth was at my ear. He took a small slow swipe around the outer edge, causing me to shudder. I felt his hot breath as he whispered, "I've wanted this, Sylvia. I've dreamt of this. I don't even know if I can trust that you're really here." He slid his teeth over my earlobe and pulled it gently.

"Quinn, this is real. I'm here." *Oh, I'm most definitely here*, I thought as his lips came back to mine. His hand came back up to my shirt this time, trying to push it off. He forgot about the flannel over the top. I moved my hands off his back to tear at the outer shirt. He realized what I was trying to do and brought his hands up over my collarbone and to my shoulders, pushing it off for me. One hand he tangled into my hair and the other he ran down my arm to my hand. He used my hand as his own again. Together we pulled the tank top up over my head. He disentangled his hand from my hair and cupped my face. I just wanted to nuzzle into his hand.

His thumb brushed over my lips, and I had to taste him. I opened my mouth and slowly ran my tongue over his thumb. I could feel the ridges of his fingertips under my tongue. I could taste the salt of him. I wanted to taste more of him. I sucked his thumb into my mouth, closing my lips around it, curling my tongue around it. Quinn let out a little hiss that had my insides tightening. I slid my mouth off his thumb and licked at the next finger. I started at the base and dragged my tongue up the entire length of his long, long fingers. I sucked that one in, just like the last.

"God, Sylvia," Quinn practically growled.

He brought his mouth down to my chest. He didn't even wait to take my bra off. Just settled his open mouth over the ice blue satin covering my tip. It wasn't long before he was pulling at it with little nips. He pulled his wonderful fingers from my mouth when I opened them to let out a sigh. He traced his finger along the exposed skin under my bra before pushing up under it. Those magic fingers went to work on me, pinching and kneading, twisting and flicking. He pulled the straps off my shoulders and bared me to him. I felt more than heard the rumble from his chest. "Sylvia, you are so beautiful." He brought his mouth down to me and rubbed his jaw against my skin. I loved the feel of his stubble as it brushed across me. It was rough and slightly scratchy, but it sent little tingles shooting through me.

I arched my back and reached back to unhook my bra. He hooked a finger around it and pulled it off and dropped it somewhere beside the bed. By then I was losing myself to him. I was writhing against him so hard; I could feel the heat of him. I wanted to wrap my hand around him. I pushed at his pants, getting them off his hips and as far down as I could.

Quinn raised his hips to assist me in the effort. I took the opportunity to wrap my hand around him. I tightened my grasp and slid it up. His pants were still around his thigh, but I managed to snag them with my foot and pull them the rest of the way off.

I continued to pump my hand around him. He was so impossibly hot. His skin was so smooth. I wanted to feel that heat against me, in me. As if he read my mind, he moved his hands down to my pants. I curved against him as he pushed them off my hips. He moved away from me as he pulled them off. He trailed his hands all the way back up, from the arch of my foot, around my calf, behind my knees, and up the insides of my thighs. I was yearning for him. I needed him. I burned for him.

Finally, he made his way to where I most wanted his touch. He lazily ran one finger over me. I arched into him, begging for more. He made a second pass, adding a second finger. Both just traced over me, barely touching me. I shivered at the feel of his fingers ghosting over the satin of my panties. His husky voice was pure sex as he groaned out, "Sylvia, you are so wet for me. I just want these off you and feel your skin against mine." With that, he tugged my panties down and I wiggled my legs, sliding them off.

Quinn leaned in for a kiss as he curved his fingers around me. His lips took mine deeper this time, yet just as sweet. The kiss was hot but the fire didn't need to travel through me this time. I was already a raging inferno. He used one finger to slide in between my lips and stroked up and down along my slit. After a few passes, he stopped right on my clit. He rubbed slow circles around it, and I was dying for more. I thrust my hips to him, but he continued to torture me with the slow circles and easy kisses. It may have been torture, but it was a sweet torture. He was building me up, and I knew that when I released it was going to be huge.

Everything started to tighten. My hand was back around him, my grip tight around him as I felt it approaching. Quinn knew my body so well. It was like he hadn't forgotten anything. He slid two fingers in, hooking them against me as he thrust them in and out. My breath matched the pace of his fingers. When his thumb came down pressing on my clit, I was lost. I called out his name as I tightened all around him. He slowed his strokes as he brought me back down.

I was still slightly panting as I looked him in the eye, telling him that I still needed more. I needed him inside me. Even though it was fairly dark in the room, there was still enough light for me to see his eyes. They were a mix of lust and something else. I wasn't sure what, but I was sure they were telling me how much he wanted me too.

I looked away and hated the fact that he had to reach over to get a condom out of his nightstand. I had always been on birth control so we never worried about them. I heard the rip of the package and felt the bed move. Quinn positioned himself between my legs. He cupped my face and turned me to look at him.

"Sylvia?" He breathed the question. I knew he would stop if I said so. But I was too far gone. I wanted him at that moment more than I'd wanted him at any point in my life.

"Yes." It was all the answer he needed. With one smooth thrust, he was in and it felt like home. All my senses were alive. I could smell our scent mixed together when I took a deep breath in. I tasted his mouth on mine, his tongue again calling mine out to play. I could see his eyes gazing into mine. They were black in the dark, but still as intense. I could feel the heat and hardness of his body against mine. My hands rubbed at his back and clutched at his arms. He was thrusting slowly, teasing me, feeling me. And somehow, with all that consuming me I still managed to catch the faint strains of a guitar and a soft melodic voice breaking through my consciousness, as Deep Blue Something sang the words, *"You say that we've got nothing in common. No common ground to start from and we're falling apart. You'll say the world has come between us. Our lives have come between us still I know you just don't care."*

In that moment, my heart began to cry again. I pulled Quinn tighter to me to drown out the song. To drown out the world. All I wanted to know and feel right then was Quinn. I kissed along his neck, loving the taste I'd remembered a hundred times over. Our lives may have come between us, but in that moment they were joined together, even if it was just briefly.

Quinn's voice pushed the song from my mind. "Oh, Sylvia. I just want to stay here forever with you, in you." He let out a small moan and he began to thrust faster. I was there with him. Between his hands, his mouth and the feel of him moving in me, I felt the fire building again. I met him thrust for thrust. I was so close and I needed him. He growled my name and I went over the edge. I bit down on his shoulder as I grasped him to me. I felt myself still spasming around him as he pulled back and thrust harder into me, once, twice, and yet again. He threw his head back. His brow furrowed, causing the veins to pop out. He let out a loud groan and I felt him jerk a little and knew that the fire had consumed him, too.

He was still breathing deeply as he bent down to kiss me. His lips were ever gentle against mine as his fingers stroked my cheek. "Sylvia," he sighed once, and then pulled away from me. It felt like he pulled the condom off and dropped it on the floor beside us. He turned on his side and reached for me. He pulled me to him and nuzzled his face into my hair. I felt him take a deep breath and I smiled at the thought of him breathing me in.

We didn't say anything as we lay there in the dark. Neither of us wanted to ruin the moment. I lay there, tangled up in his arms, and stroked his hair. I thought about how it felt to be there with him wrapped around me, holding me so close that I not only heard his heartbeat as it slowed, but felt it as well. I knew he was asleep from his even relaxed breaths. I realized he wasn't as hot anymore, that somewhere in the middle of all that his fever had broken. I squirmed out of his embrace just long enough to pull the covers up around us. I didn't want him to get chills in the night as the sweat from our bodies cooled against us. He pulled me back to him. Even in his sleep he wanted me near. I drifted off, too, with the line, *well that's one thing we got,"* echoing in my head.

Chapter 10 - Quinn

I HOVERED IN THAT STATE somewhere between waking and dreaming. My dream was so amazing that I didn't want it to end. I fought the consciousness that was threatening to overtake me. I tried to hold on and fall back to sleep, back to Sylvia in my dream. It was a losing battle. My eyes opened and I stared up into the darkness. As the dream slipped away, I became aware of my surroundings. I could hear quiet breathing and felt her small body pressed against me. I smiled into the dark, happy that it had been more than just a dream. Sylvia was here. I pulled her tight to me and buried my face in her hair.

I played back the last couple days in my head as I tried to fall back to sleep. When I'd gone over to her place on Saturday morning, I'd never expected her to actually offer to stay and take care of me. That was my Sylvia though. She would always put her own problems away if someone needed her. Having two full days and two full nights with her had been everything I could have wanted. I'd thought it would be awkward when she first came over. I'd figured she'd stay a couple hours and be gone. The longer she stayed, the more she seemed to want to stay.

We fell in to an easy rhythm, and it was just like it use to be. I started to think that we could be friends. There were a few uncomfortable moments, but nothing too serious. On Saturday night, she wrapped her arms around me while she was sleeping and a spark ignited in my mind. Maybe, just maybe, Sylvia felt more for me than she let on. She was beautiful in the morning, all sleepy and smiling. I really, really missed her smile. Knowing that I was the one who made her smile and laugh and that it was for me alone was one of the best things about the weekend. I wanted to make her smile and laugh all the time.

I was awake long before she was on Sunday morning. My body was stiff everywhere from the uncomfortable night on the couch but I wasn't about to get up when I had Sylvia there with me. I watched her sleep, wondering if she had talked in her sleep during the night. I had been exhausted and slept well despite the cramped quarters. I'd slept though any talking she might have done. I probably wouldn't have wanted to hear it anyway. I watched the way the light played over her face as the sun crept through the window. Her lashes were long and her hair was swept over her cheeks. I brushed the hair off her face and traced one finger over it. I skimmed lightly over her closed eyes and wished I could follow my finger with my lips. From her eyes, I stroked down her cheeks to her lips. I rubbed my finger over her slightly parted lips, back and forth. They were soft to the touch, and her warm breath tickled over my finger.

I remembered what it was like to kiss those lips. I could imagine what it would be like to do it again. There were only inches between us. I wanted to close the distance and press mine to hers. I wondered what she would do. Would she kiss back? Would she hit me? Maybe she would yell at me again. I couldn't do it. I couldn't risk this fragile friendliness between us. I sighed and closed my eyes and tried to forget about her lips. That only made me aware of other parts of her body, and how closely they were pressed into mine. Her arms and legs were around me. Her breasts were pushed against my chest causing another whole new fantasy. Of course I was hard. We only had a couple thin layers between us, and I could feel her heat pressed against me. I shifted slightly and she gave out a little moan. I loved that sound.

I glanced back up at her to see if she had woken up. Her eyes were still closed. I went back to memorizing her face, mentally connecting the freckles as I had done so many times before. I always told her I could make my initials by connecting them, that it was, a sign that she was meant for me. Soon her eyes opened. Staring into those twin emeralds was a better morning pick-me-up than any caffeinated beverage. I was sure that would be the last of my time with her. I was stunned when she said she wanted to make me breakfast.

I hoped I would be good for the day after taking care of things in the shower but when I came out and found her bent over looking in the fridge, I was afraid I was going to have to go back for a second one. Those old blue sweats with the QSHS across her ass shouldn't have affected me as badly as they did. Yet just seeing them stretched across her had me hard. I picked up my tea and tried to do anything but draw attention to myself. I didn't want her to see my reaction. I didn't think she had noticed when we were on the couch, or if she did she pretended not to. I didn't want to scare her away. Friends don't get hard just from seeing a friend dressed like that. I was pretty sure Sloane or Reed wouldn't react that way to seeing Sylvia in those old sweats.

The rest of the day I tried to keep my mind on the present. I had to push memories of her away and shut down any new fantasies that threatened my sanity. We talked and laughed and had a wonderful day. I learned more about the rest of the group. She even told me about Jason. I can't say that I was exactly interested in meeting him but I was thankful that she had friends in her life. I avoided anything related to Beau. I just didn't want to hear it and I was afraid that I would say the wrong thing and wreck the mood of the day. I also avoided any mention of our past. I wasn't sure how to talk about it. I knew that if we spent more time together we would need to talk about it. Things were going good but were far from perfect.

When I went to bed, I had asked her to say goodbye before she went home. I really didn't think she would, though. I was pretty sure, when I left her by the table, that that would be the last time I saw her that weekend. Never, not once, did I ever think that we would have a hot night like that. Sylvia was *amazing*. I just had no words for how good it was between us. This was beyond anything we had had before. If it could be that powerful between us, there must have been feelings there. I had heard that when you were with the one you loved, sex was so much more meaningful and incredible. I had no idea if that was true, since Sylvia was the only girl I had ever been with, but I couldn't imagine it could be any better than that.

As I laid there with her in my arms and thought about it, I worried that maybe it would have been better if she had left. What if she regretted it? I sure as hell didn't. I told myself that she wouldn't have done it if she hadn't wanted to. She must have felt something for me. What did I feel for her? I knew I loved her. I told everyone I was only interested in being friends. In fact, I tried to convince myself that was all I wanted. I was only lying to myself and everyone else. Mom knew. She knew all along that I needed Sylvia. I could see that now. I needed Sylvia like I needed air or water or food. She was essential to my life. There was no way I could just be friends with her. Not after that. No, even if we hadn't had sex I would still need her. It just took her sharing herself with me -- showing me that she could feel more about me -- for me to admit it.

No matter what the daylight would bring, I would not let Sylvia go again. I was going to tell her everything I felt. I had made a mistake, and now it was time to correct it. I would do everything it took to get her back.

There would be no running away this time. We also needed to talk about the past. We had to get that cleared up before we could move on. Once that was done, we could build something new. We couldn't just rebuild the past. We were different people now. We needed to build something different between us. Not saying we should forget the past entirely, just move on from it. I guess that was easy for me to say. I was the one who fucked up the past.

I sighed into the darkness. She had to forgive me. I couldn't let her out of my life again. I couldn't just be friends. I certainly would never be able to see her with another guy without wanting to rip him apart. I would do whatever it took to get her back.

Determined, I cuddled up closer to her. We were both still naked. I didn't even care if I was going to be hard the rest of the night from sleeping against her bare warmth. I stroked my hand over her stomach and breast. I could never get tired of touching Sylvia. Her skin was so soft. I nestled my face into her hair and fell back to sleep, lulled by her quiet breaths.

I woke up on my back again, having rolled away from Sylvia at some point. When I rolled over to pull her back into my arms, there was nothing there. My first thought was panic. *She left. I knew she would.* I told myself to calm down and check it out before I jumped to conclusions. I got up and pulled my boxers on. I started down the hall and came to a dark and empty bathroom. The kitchen was the same way. No sign of her in the living room either. She had to be back at her place.

I went back to my room and threw on a pair of jeans. I didn't even bother with a t-shirt or shoes. I needed to talk to her. I needed to do it before anything could get worse. I knew Sylvia. She was probably just as scared and worried about what happened between us as I was. I would bet anything that she was internalizing it and finding everything wrong with it.

I pounded on her door but she didn't answer. I tried the knob, but it was locked. Maybe she was in the shower. That had to be it. I waited outside her door, pacing for what felt like forever. I knocked on her door again. Still no answer. I tried the knob. I called out, too, hoping that she would come. Finally the same neighbor that looked out her door that first morning came up the stairs with a bag of laundry. She stopped and stared at me. I ran my fingers threw my hair and wondered what her problem was.

"Are you looking for Sylvia?" She finally asked warily. She kept eyeing me like she wasn't sure I was all there.

I wanted to snark at her for asking such an asinine question. I stopped myself. I wasn't her fault that Sylvia was gone and I was standing in the hallway half naked looking like a crazed psycho. I didn't respond with a verbal reply, though. I just nodded my head, as I pinched the bridge of my nose.

"I saw Sylvia about an hour ago. She was walking towards campus with her backpack." Neighbor Girl still looked as if she was worried about having told me that.

"Thank you," I responded. I was relieved. She'd probably gone to the library or to a computer lab to print out the paper she'd been working on. I went back to my place and finished getting dressed. I would track her down and talk to her.

I was back at my door three hours later, Sylvia-less. I'd gone to every possible place I could think of. I'd asked all the people on staff at the various locations if they had seen her. I knew I must have looked like a crazy-ass stalker, but I didn't care. I had to find her. The bookstore she worked at was the last place I checked for her before heading back to our apartment building. The girl I talked to said she hadn't worked all weekend, that she had asked for it off.

I tried her door once more - no answer. The others weren't back yet. I texted Sloane for her cell phone number. He sent it but asked if everything was fine. I told him yes, I just had a question for her. I tried her phone and it went straight to voicemail. Great, where ever she was, she didn't even have her phone with her. There was nothing to do now but sit back and wait. She had to come home eventually. I was just afraid that by then, she wouldn't want to hear anything I had to say.

Chapter 11 - Sylvia

THE FIRST THING I WAS aware of when I woke was the feel of Quinn next to me. I could feel the strength of his arms around me, the heat coming off his chest, and how hard he was pressed against me. I sighed contentedly and replayed last night in my head. It was so good but oh so wrong. I needed to make a decision. I could no longer deny any feelings I had for Quinn. The attraction was definitely still there. The weekend proved I could get along with him, too. Could I love him again? Did I ever stop loving him? Those were harder questions to answer. Well, the answer was easy -- yes, yes I could. The million dollar question was: Did I want to?

What about Beau? I was dating Beau, sleeping with him. Yet there I was in another guy's bed. I never, ever thought I would cheat on a guy. What should I do about that? Should I tell him? I couldn't lie worth shit; he was going to find out. I started to panic. I needed to clear my head and figure out what I was going to do.

I took one more minute to enjoy being in Quinn's arms and then carefully slipped out of them. I didn't want to wake him. I knew we would need to talk but I wasn't ready for that yet. I had some more thinking to do.

Once I was off the bed I stood there looking around trying to find my clothes. My sweats were on the floor at the foot of the bed. My tank top and flannel shirt were still on the bed by the pillows. My bra was hanging from the open bedside drawer. My underwear was nowhere to be found. It was probably tangled up in the blankets. I would have to get them later. I pulled the sweats on and went to get the bra. The drawer it was hanging off of must have been where he had the condoms. Something caught my eye when I picked my bra up. I picked up the picture in the drawer. It was the one of me in the grass out at the farm. Why did he have that here? He didn't have any other pictures around. It was actually in the drawer, not out. But still it made me wonder why. I put it back in the drawer. I didn't have time to think about that right now.

I finished getting dressed and stopped to look at Quinn one more time. He was sleeping so peacefully. He looked so young while he slept. The crease in his brow was smooth. He had the hint of a smile. Just looking at his lips made me long to kiss him again. I didn't want to wake him, but the urge to touch him was too strong. I stroked one finger along his cheek and jaw. I loved the feel of his stubble. I took a big breath in as I remembered how it had felt against my breast that night. He let out a soft sigh and moved towards my hand. I couldn't resist giving him one last kiss, so I bent over and put my lips to his forehead. *Goodbye Quinn. I don't know when or if I'll be back, but last night was magical.* With that thought, I left his room.

I grabbed my bag and headed home. Once I was out in the hallway I didn't think going home was the best idea. That would be the first place Quinn would look for me, if he even looked for me. Beau could show up if he was back in town. Kai would come find me when she got home, and I wasn't ready for her either. I decided a walk would be a good start. I could clear my head some and then think about going home to face everyone. I didn't even stop to drop my bag off, maybe I would go to the library and print my paper off.

I started walking and thinking. The more I thought, the more confused I became. This was way more than I could deal with. I walked farther and farther. Soon I found myself on Jason's street, walking to his door. I suppose some part of me had known all along that I would end up there. I knew it was early and no one would be up yet. I dug in my bag for my cell phone to call him to come open the door for me. Great! No phone. I realized I hadn't used it all weekend. I must have left it at my place when I went over to Quinn's. Beau was going to be so pissed if he tried to call me. Just one more thing to deal with. It seemed to just keep piling up. I sat on Jason's steps to wait for someone to wake up.

As I sat on the steps, I replayed the weekend in my mind. Our friendship just fell right back in place. It was as if those four years had never happened. Was it because of our past or in spite of it? Was it all out of past feelings or was it something new between us? I couldn't tell. We could never go back, even if we wanted to. We both knew that. Was the weekend our attempt at reliving the past, or was it more? So many questions went through my mind, yet the answers didn't come. I wondered if it would have been like that if we weren't in our own little bubble for the weekend.

If the others had been around, I doubted we would have been like that.

It wasn't long before the door opened and a girl I didn't recognize came out. We exchanged quick hellos and she headed off down the street towards campus, doing the typical morning-after walk of shame. I wondered which of the boys she had stayed with, and why they didn't take her home. I started to judge, then remembered I was in the exact same predicament. I was sure her reasons for leaving like that in the morning were different from mine, yet we still had something in common.

I walked into a quiet house. Everyone was still asleep. I headed to Jason's room, hoping it would be empty. We talked so infrequently lately. I didn't think he was seeing anyone, but I wasn't sure. For all I knew, the girl that left had been with him. I opened his door to peek in. He was stretched out on his bed. At least he was alone and had boxers on. He must have heard me because he sat up rubbing his eyes.

"Syl?" He questioned sleepily.

"Jase?" my voice quivered and I started crying. My emotions had gotten the best of me and everything was just so mixed up and confusing.

"Oh, Sylvia, come here." He reached out for me and I fell into his arms. Jason was my comfort, my warmth. "What's wrong Sylvia? Did Beau break up with you?" He still sounded groggy.

I shook my head and sniffed. "I, I, I, slept with Quinn," I stuttered out between gasping breaths.

Jason rocked me back and forth and stroked my hair. "That was a long time ago Sylvia. I thought you were beyond all that now."

I remembered that I still hadn't told Jason about him being back. I swallowed and tried to get a hold of myself. I had a lot of explaining to do. I sat back up and wiped at my eyes. "Jason, I have a lot to tell you about, but I really, really need some caffeine right now. Do have any pop or coffee?"

He looked at me with confusion and concern. "Yeah, I think we have some Coke or something. Let me go check. Do you need anything else? Kleenex or something?"

"Probably," I nodded.

Jason left the room. While he was gone, I took the time to look over his room. Everything looked normal. I didn't think the girl had been in his bed last night at least. Not that I cared if Jase was getting some. I just didn't want him to be bothering him if he was sleeping off a late night.

He came back with a couple Cokes and a roll of toilet paper. He tossed it to me and shrugged. "It was the only thing I could find. Seriously, in a house full of guys you're lucky we even have that around."

I couldn't help but give a weak chuckle at that. Jason and his roommates didn't strike me as being responsible enough to remember stuff like that to put on a shopping list. They probably didn't even make shopping lists.

Jason plopped down on the bed next to me and slid up so his back was against the wall. He didn't have a head-board on his bed. He patted the bed next to him and I moved up to sit alongside of him. We both took a couple drinks of our Cokes as we sat in silence. Jase was waiting for me to talk, and I was trying to collect my thoughts.

Finally I decided I just needed to start at the beginning and get it all over with. "Well, you know I got a new neighbor right?" Jason nodded so I continued, "It's Quinn."

His light blue eyes went wide and then narrowed into a glare. "Wait. Your new neighbor is Quinn and you're just telling me this now? Like what..." he counted off on his fingers, "...six weeks later?"

I blushed. I knew I looked guilty. "I know. I just wanted to tell you face to face, and we never seemed to find the time to do that." I said it quietly and looked down at the bed, playing with a loose string on the quilt.

"Jesus, Sylvia. I would have been there for you. Do Reed and Sloane know? Did they kick his ass? Wait, why didn't they tell me?" Jason was pissed. I didn't blame him. He picked up all the pieces of the shattered Sylvia I had been and patiently glued them back together. I knew the guys kept their promise and didn't tell him because he would have been over to my place before they'd finished the sentence if they had.

"I was okay, after the initial shock. The others met him before I knew he was there. I guess Reed and Sloane found out who he was. They didn't tell me how. They all got to know him first, before I found out. They all get along with him."

Jason reached over and grabbed my hand and held on to it tight. His jaw was clenched and his eyes were furious. "What the hell, Sylvia? How could they do that to you?" He muttered something under his breath. I couldn't tell what it was, but it sounded like beating Reed's ass.

I needed to reassure him that the rest weren't trying to hurt me. "Jason, it's okay. In fact after the picnic..."

"He was at the picnic? The one before you came over here? And you still didn't tell me?"

"Yes, but I was fine. I had Beau with me, and having him along kept me from losing my shit." He loosened his grip a little after that, which was good because his grip could break my hand. "After that we've basically gotten along whenever he's around the rest of them."

"Has he tried to talk to you? And what was that crap about sleeping with him?" He looked at me suspiciously and I blushed. "God, Sylvia, you didn't. Why the fuck would you do that?" He yelled the last part at me, and I cringed back a little. I didn't answer right away. "Sylvia?"

I took a deep breath and looked up at him. I knew this was not going to go well. Why did I ever think I could talk about this with Jason? "I will tell you all of it, but you have to be quiet until I'm done. Got it?" Jason nodded, so I started in. I told him about the argument the morning after the party. I didn't mention the bruises. Jason so didn't need to know about that or that Quinn had seen them. I talked about running into him in the mornings. I explained about getting together with the others and Quinn being included. How it got easier and easier the more I was around him.

I finally got to the weekend. Jase tensed up when I told him about Quinn coming to the door and me going over to his place.

Jason interrupted me. "Sylvia, how could you even want to be around him?"

"It's not like that. He was really sick and needed someone with him. I just went to help him out. I would do the same for any of you."

Jason snorted, "Sure you would." His sarcasm was palpable.

"Not do…that, but that was…" I didn't really know how to explain it. "We were getting along so well and things just happened. Feelings were there and…God, Jason I can't talk about this with you. You aren't going to understand no matter what I say." I was frustrated.

He let go of my hand and turned to face me. "You're right, Sylvia. I don't understand. I don't get how you could just let all those years go. Man, Sylvia, you were so fucked up after he left, it was like you weren't even human. You were a ghost. I just can't see you like that again." He was clearly agitated, talking fast and loud. "So what are you going to do now? He shows up, so you're just going to run right back into his arms? What are you going to do when he leaves you again? What if all he wanted from you was sex? He is a guy after all. Maybe he just wanted to see how easy it would be to get in your pants again."

The tears started up again. I was so confused about all of it. I thought back to Quinn having a condom in his drawer. Maybe I was just a fuck to him. Maybe I didn't mean anything. I hadn't thought of that. It just seemed like there was more there between us, but what if I'd read him wrong? What if Jason was right, and now that he'd had me again he wouldn't want any more to do with me? What if it was all a game to him? I couldn't believe that. Quinn was never the kind to treat a person like an object.

Jason wrapped his arms around me and pulled me to his chest. "Syl, I'm sorry. I didn't mean to make you cry. I just want you to really think about this. You have no guarantee that he won't hurt you again."

I pulled away from Jason and reached for the toilet paper. I blew my nose and swiped at my eyes. I knew Jason was just looking out for me, but the truth hurt. I couldn't give into my feelings for Quinn. I couldn't leave myself vulnerable to him again, no matter how much I wanted to.

"What about Beau? You are still seeing him right? What are you going to tell him?" Jason looked in my eyes and I felt like he was judging me. I couldn't sit next to Jason right then. I got off the bed and started pacing. I felt so guilty about Beau. He really didn't deserve to be cheated on.

"Yes, I guess I'm still seeing Beau." Jason raised an eyebrow at that. "I mean he's gone a lot, but when he's in town we spend time together."

"Have you slept with him too?" Jason's tone was so damning. I blushed and felt the tears stinging my eyes again. My throat constricted and I couldn't answer so I just nodded. Jason let out a big breath. "You've made a mess of this, Syl."

"I know," I choked out quietly.

"So what are you going to tell Beau, then?"

"I can't tell him. It was a mistake. It won't happen again. He just doesn't need to know about it. Besides, I don't know if it's really cheating. We haven't exactly discussed what we are together."

"Sylvia, you are just justifying now." His voice was hard. He was right, I was. "Well, you need to figure that out, too. You can't have them both. As far as I'm concerned, you shouldn't even be considering Quinn." He said it with such resentment that I wished I hadn't said anything to him about it at all.

"You're right, Jason. For now I'm just going to figure things out with Beau and forget about anything with Quinn." My heart tightened at the thought, but I ignored it. Doing that had to be for the best.

Jason stood up and hugged me one more time. "I think that would be good, Sylvia. So now what do you want to do? Can you stay around longer? I've missed you."

I hung out at Jason's the rest of the afternoon. I wasn't in a hurry to get back to my place. I didn't want to face anyone else yet. I ended up showering at Jason's. I could smell Quinn on me. As much as I liked it, I had to get rid of it. It kept reminding me of the night before and how good it felt to wake up in Quinn's arms. I caught myself a few times wondering how different my day would have been if I hadn't left his bed. I couldn't go there, though. I'd done what I'd done and now there was no changing it.

I went over my paper one more time and used Jason's roommate's printer to print it out. After that, Jason and I just spent the day watching stupid movies on cable. After our morning talk, neither of us said anything more about it. I enjoyed the rest of the day with him, yet I still felt all mixed up inside. Finally, it was getting late and Jason wanted to get some course work done. He drove me home and I promised to call him soon and let him know how things were going.

It was almost six, but Reed's jeep still wasn't in the lot. I assumed that meant they weren't back from Chicago yet. I quickly scanned for Quinn's Camry. That, too, was gone. I felt a twinge of disappointment at that, but it was probably for the best. Even after my talk with Jason, I still wasn't sure what I was going to do.

Jason was right about so much, but I cared about Quinn. I was torn. I wanted Quinn -- I had always wanted him. If I were being honest with myself, I never stopped loving him. I wasn't ready to be honest with myself. I had to face the facts -- Quinn could really hurt me again. I had to make sure that I wouldn't let him get to my heart. Still, I didn't know what Quinn wanted. I decided the best thing to do was to let Quinn approach me. It was just as likely that Quinn regretted it and wouldn't want anything to do with me as it was that he would want to see me again. I would leave the next move up to him and proceed from there.

I trudged up the stairs. Everything was still weighing on me. When I got to the top, I nearly jumped out of my skin when I heard Beau.

"So how was Chicago?" His voice was so quiet I almost didn't hear him. He was standing in the shadow against my door, wearing his old ripped jeans with his black leather motorcycle jacket. I wondered how long he had been there.

"I didn't go to Chicago. What are you doing here?" I was quite shocked to see him standing there.

"I've been waiting for you. Where the hell have you been, then?" He was locked onto me with a very menacing glare.

"I was at Jason's." I knew he meant for the weekend, but I hoped playing dumb would help.

"For the whole weekend? Why didn't you answer or text back when I called?" He was still so very quiet.

I pulled my keys out of my bag and moved to open my door. Beau put his arm across the door, blocking me from unlocking it. I looked into his sapphire eyes. Those normally heavy-lidded eyes were now just little slits, barely open as they stared back at me so intently. I was instantly alarmed. My glance flickered briefly from his gaze to Quinn's door. I knew that Beau and I were probably going to be having a heated discussion. I didn't want that to be out in the hall where Quinn could witness it at any point.

Beau followed my gaze to Quinn's door. His grip tightened. "Were you with him?" He nodded his head towards Quinn's door.

"No," I answered quickly, and prayed it wasn't too quickly to raise his suspicion. "He went to Chicago with the rest of them."

Beau still glared at me. He clenched his teeth and said very slowly, "No. He. Did. Not."

My eyes flew open. How did he know that? Had he been here this weekend? I knew I needed to play dumb on this for sure. "What do you mean he didn't go? Kai assured me he was going."

Beau didn't release me, but his grip relaxed some as he let out a harsh laugh. "Sylvia, honey, I saw Mr. Rich Boy get in that wussy old man car of his and take off about two hours ago."

"Then Kai and the rest must be back."

"Wrong again, sweetheart. When you didn't answer your door, I went and knocked on theirs to see if you were there. No one answered. Your big guy's jeep isn't here either, so I'm guessing they took that to Chicago." He tilted his head, reading my expression, trying to determine if I was lying or not.

"I don't know why Quinn was here, then. It's not like I go knock on his door asking for his every move." I didn't lie, I just evaded. "I didn't leave my apartment until this morning." I hoped he hadn't been here before that. I suspected that if he had been here he would have knocked on Quinn's door. Surely if he checked at Kai's and Kerri's then he would have checked at Quinn's, too. "Now, let's go in and talk about this. I don't want to stand in the hall where anyone can hear us." He let my wrist go, and I opened the door.

As we walked in I turned my lights on. I scanned the room and it looked exactly like I'd left it. I let out a little breath. I didn't know why I was worried that it would look different.

I turned back to Beau. "Okay, now why exactly are you standing outside my apartment waiting for me?"

He pushed past me and stood in the middle of the living room. I moved to stand closer to him. "Well, Sylvia, I tried calling Saturday night to tell you I was on my way back. When you didn't answer, I sent you a text. I thought you were just out with friends and I'd hear from you when you checked your phone. When I didn't hear from you by Sunday, I tried calling you again. Your phone went straight to voice mail. I got worried and drove straight through the night to get here."

"I can't find my phone." I glanced quickly around the room hoping it wasn't out in the open. I didn't see it so I hoped I was safe. I had to dig it out of the couch cushions often, so I hoped that I would get lucky and find it there. "I've been looking for it all weekend. I didn't have anyone around to call me so I could find it. The battery is probably dead."

"Oh, and it doesn't beep when the battery is dying?" He was still eerily quiet.

"Yes, but if I lost it I wouldn't always be able to hear it, would I? How else do you think I missed your call?" My voice was beginning to raise. What exactly was he accusing me of?

He stood there eyeing me like he was debating on whether to believe me or not. "When was the last time you had it?" I felt like I was on trial. What did I have to be guilty about? Oh, yeah, that. When I blushed I sincerely hoped that he thought it was out of anger instead of guilt. My body always betrayed me. I was never going to get away with lying to him.

"When I talked to Kai, Friday after class, before they all left." I looked him in the eyes as I answered him definitively.

"And she was the last person you talked too?" His question really angered me.

"What does it matter who I talked to last?" I didn't care if he was quiet. I yelled. "What gives you the right to come in here and start quizzing me like this?" I wanted to add that we had never discussed what the other expected out of our relationship, but I was too chicken to say it.

"I'm doing it because I care about you. I don't want to lose you." He reached out to me and stepped forward so that he could wrap his arms around me. I stood unresponsive in his arms. "Sylvia, it makes me a little crazy when I'm gone from you for so long." He was whispering into my hair. "I get worried when I can't find you. I'm sorry I'm acting this way. I just need you. But I guess I don't mean that much to you." His voice sounded so sad and contrite. I had to hug him back.

What had I done? How could I have been so upset? Obviously he was just reacting to not being able to get a hold of me. Here I'd made him feel bad. What did I expect him to think? I would have thought the same thing if I was in his place. I stepped back a little and reached up to cup his face. I hoped my eyes could convey the sincerity of my feelings. "I'm sorry I worried you. I didn't mean to. Honest." It was true. I didn't mean to worry him. "You do mean something to me." *I'm just not sure what that is, or even if it's enough.*

He leaned down and captured my mouth with his. It was a deep and demanding kiss but I gave in to it. I wanted to make up for hurting him and show that I was sorry. I reached up and twined my fingers into his thick black hair which he had left down that day. Often times he pulled it back into a loose ponytail. I liked to pull it out and run my fingers through the back of his hair when he kissed me like this. Then I thought of someone else's hair and how that had felt around my fingers the night before.

Breaking the kiss, I stepped away from Beau. He smirked at me. "I bet pretty boy never kissed you like that." I didn't get why he always made comments like that. Like he expected me to compare him to Quinn or something. Like I would tell him if I did. Not that he could ever compare. No one could, and last night had just reminded me of that. I rolled my eyes at Beau.

Before I knew what happened, he had me shoved against the far wall and ground his lips into mine. I pushed at him to get him to stop. "What? Pretty boy ever kiss you like this?" His eyes were hard blue steel, and I was once again frightened.

"This has nothing to do with Quinn," I hissed at him.

"Oh, Sylvia, dear, this has everything to do with Quinn." With that, he crashed his lips to mine again. He stuck his tongue into my mouth. When I didn't respond, he stopped.

He looked me in the eye and said, "If pretty boy ever tries to kiss you like that... fuck that, if he even looks at you like he wants to kiss you, I will end him." His voice was ice cold. I had a shiver crawl up my spine. I knew that he wasn't kidding. My decision about Quinn was just made easier. If I cared about him at all, which I knew, deep down, I did -- no matter what happened -- I would need to stay away from him. *That much is clear,* I thought, as Beau brought his mouth back down to mine.

Chapter 12 - Quinn

OWN THE HALL, INTO MY bedroom, turn around, back down the hall, pause look at the clock on the wall in the kitchen, around the couch, and back down the hall again. I paced like a caged animal. The time crept slowly. I didn't turn TV or music on in fear that I wouldn't hear Sylvia come back home. I thought about propping my door open so I could watch for her. I didn't want to scare her.

By the time my dad called, it was after three. He said my mom was worried because they hadn't heard from me all weekend. Not thinking I told him that I had been sick. He started to ask questions and I tried to insist that I was better and I thought I was about to get away with it until I heard my mom in the background. After that, there was no getting out of seeing them. I was given two choices: go there or they were coming to my place. As much as I needed to talk to Sylvia I couldn't risk my mom seeing the two of us right now. She would immediately know something happened between the two of us, and I wasn't ready for her intrusion.

After I hung up I paced around some more. I texted Sloane again to see if they'd heard from her. I knew I would raise suspicions about why I was so concerned about Sylvia, but I didn't care at this point. I would tell anyone anything just to know she was alright.

She's probably at Jason's. What's going on? -S

Jason's, right. I forgot about him. I decided that I couldn't ask Sloane for directions to Jason's without alerting them to something being afoot. I thought maybe if I played it casual and avoided answering the question it would throw them off.

Ok. Let me know if you see her when you get back. -Q

If she was at Jason's she was at least somewhere safe, I hoped. At least she wasn't at Beau's. I prayed she wasn't with Beau. I started to worry more about the possibility of her being with him. I clenched my fists and felt my jaw tighten. I started pacing again. My second pass through, I realized that this wasn't doing any good. I grabbed my keys and headed to see Dad.

I checked Sylvia's door one more time. Still no answer. I took the steps two at a time. I wanted to hurry and get this over with. I got into my car, but before I turned the key I felt someone watching me. I looked around, hoping desperately that it was Sylvia. No such luck. Beau stood on the sidewalk right in front of the car. Our glares met through the windshield. I broke my gaze away first to look around to see if Sylvia was with him. She wasn't. I started the car and pulled out. At least I could cross that worry off my list.

I only stayed at Mom and Dad's long enough to for Dad to look in my throat and call me in a prescription for strep throat. I may have played the sore throat up a bit, but being sick kept Mom from questioning me. She wanted me to stay with them so she could look after me. I quickly used an upcoming test I had to study for as an excuse to hurry back to my place. Her raised eyebrow led me to believe that she didn't buy that for one minute. At least she let it go. I was out of there in less than fifteen minutes.

Dad called the scrip into a pharmacy by their house. I was able to pick it up without a problem. I figured while I was out I would drive around campus and just see if I would be lucky enough to run into Sylvia. I was slowly starting to realize that if she wanted to talk to me she would have been back by then. I reached for my phone, hoping that she would answer. It again went directly to voicemail. So she wasn't home yet, or hadn't turned on her phone yet.

If it was already that long since she'd left, it probably meant that she didn't want to talk. What if she did go to Jason's and he told her to stay away from me? From the way everyone talked about him, you'd think he was Sylvia's personal sun after I left. I worried that she would take whatever advice he would give. No, I wouldn't let that stop me. Even if she didn't want to talk, I would make her listen. I screwed up before. I was not going to screw this up again. I was going to make her see that I was right for her.

It was after six and I'd still had no sign of her. I stopped to pick up sandwiches on my way back to the apartment. I got one for Sylvia, too, in the hope that she would be back and be willing to eat with me. I knew it was a long-shot but it couldn't hurt anything, right? I remembered the kind she always liked. I hoped it was still her favorite.

There was still no sign that the others were back from Chicago. I didn't bother stopping at either couples' place. Instead I went straight to Sylvia's. I should have tried calling her first, I thought as I knocked on the door. I heard a voice and then the knob turned. I was ready for Sylvia. I knew exactly what I wanted to say to her. I wasn't ready for Beau. My eyes widened when they came into contact with his instead of Sylvia's. He smiled widely at me.

"Quinn," he said brightly and way too smugly for my taste, "What can I help you with?" He opened the door wider and a saw a very panicked Sylvia peeking around the kitchen door. As soon as Beau looked over at her, she dropped her gaze to the floor. He looked back at me and motioned me in. "Sylvia, I think Quinn is here to see you." His tone was over-friendly but I didn't look at him. I focused on Sylvia.

Her eyes were wide and slightly pleading. She gave her head the slightest shake. I knew she was trying to tell me something. When Beau looked back at her she looked down again. That couldn't be good. She looked back up at me and this time her face was blank.

"Quinn?" She wrinkled her nose and questioned as if she were trying to recall who I was. I saw how intently Beau was watching her, and I gathered that we were about to play pretend for his sake. "What are you doing here?" Her eyes flashed to Beau quickly and back to me. I still wasn't sure what was going on between them but I had a real bad feeling about it all.

"Um, yeah, Sloane texted and said Kai wanted me to check on you since she can't get a hold of you." *Please let her phone still be off.* She let out a breath of relief and then rolled her eyes.

"Oh, my phone is lost. Will you just let Sloane know everything is okay?" She stressed the last a little harder. She walked up to Beau and put her arm around his waist. *Was this how she was going to play it? My insecurities kicked in. Did she plan to sleep with me and then go back to her boyfriend? Was she trying to hurt me? No, Sylvia wouldn't do something like that. Maybe she regretted last night and was choosing him over me. Wait, I haven't even told her how I feel. How would she know that I even wanted more if I hadn't told her? I needed to tell her.*

I was about to ask her if I could talk to her in the hall for a minute, but Beau spoke up first.

"So, Quinn, I thought you were going to Chicago, too." He tilted his head to the left as he waited to assess my answer. "Have you enjoyed having Sylvia here alone all weekend?" Having Sylvia alone? That right there sent a big red flare up in my brain. Normally he was all about reminding me that Sylvia was no longer with me. If he was willingly informing me that he hadn't been with Sylvia all weekend, it could only mean that he was questioning where she had been. I glanced at Sylvia to see what was going on. Her face wore a painful mask. Her eyes pleaded with me. "Don't look at her!" Beau snapped at me, pulling my full attention back to him.

"Sylvia, are you sure everything is okay here?" I was very concerned about the way Beau was acting. I pictured Sylvia's milky-white skin with those hideous deep purple bruises and became immediately alarmed. I pulled up to my full height and stepped back, shifting my weight to my back foot. I had never had to actually use my Tae Kwon Do training outside of class, but my body just took over. I turned slightly so that I was facing him more from the side then straight on. This would allow for a slimmer target for him and give me the advantage of stepping into my punch or block if needed. I hoped I wouldn't need it.

"Well, it was until you showed up. What is your deal anyway?" She squeezed Beau tighter, wrapping her body more in front of him than to the side. Her head was now against his chest. From that angle he couldn't see her face. Her beautiful green eyes were silently begging me to be quiet. I wasn't sure if it was to cover her own ass so her boyfriend wouldn't know that she had slept with me, or if there was another reason. "Why are you here? Kai said you were going with them." So she wanted me to play it that way.

"Strep throat," I said it a little harsher than I'd meant to. I didn't know if she was worried about what Beau would do if he found out. I wouldn't be the one to tell him. Sylvia needed to make her choice. It clearly wasn't the time to talk to her about it, but I still had to leave her a clue and hopefully throw off whatever suspicions Beau had. "I was sick in bed all weekend, but I had the sweetest little nurse taking care of me." I made my voice go wistful, like I was thinking about something good and wanted to rub it in her face. Her eyes fell open like she couldn't believe I would tattle on her. "Now if you'd turn your damn phone on so Kai can get a hold of you, I can get back to her. I've been gone long enough and I'm sure she's starving." I held up the bags with the sandwiches. I guess getting two was worth it.

"Fine! I'll turn it on when I find it." She ushered me to the door. "You better get back to your little...whatever," she said with a flick of her wrist and annoyed huff.

I walked out and turned to her. I couldn't see Beau and I hoped he couldn't see me. I looked hard at her and mouthed, "We're not done here." She shut the door in my face.

I was no longer hungry when I got back to my place. I threw the sandwiches in the fridge and paced again. Beau was going to be a problem. I really needed to find out how Sylvia felt about me. Obviously she didn't want Beau to know where she'd been all weekend. What I didn't know was why. Was she scared of him? Was she letting me know she'd made her choice and I wasn't it?

I lost track of time as my mind played out different scenarios of what could happen regarding Sylvia. I was so far in my own thoughts that I jumped at the sharp rap on my door. I wanted it to be Sylvia but worried that it was Beau. I opened the door ready for either. It was Sloane. Over his shoulder, I saw Kai standing at Sylvia's door.

"Are you gonna let me in, or are you gonna keep staring at my girl's ass?" He drawled at me. I shook my head and looked back at him. I hadn't been staring at Kai's ass. I was watching to see who opened Sylvia's door.

"Sorry, man, my mind blanked. Too much cold meds." I stood back and let him in.

He walked over and plopped down on my couch. "So what happened with you and Sylvia while we were gone?" *What the fuck? Him too? Why would anyone even suspect us? We hadn't given any reason for anyone to. Maybe Sylvia called Kai and told her. No, she wouldn't do that in front of Beau, unless he'd left.*

I played dumb. "What do you mean 'what happened with Sylvia?'" I imitated him. "Why the fuck would anything happen with her?" I tried to sound offended.

"Let's see, you contacted me to get her number and you were looking for her."

"I had a question for her." I didn't join him on the couch. I ran my fingers through my hair and resumed my pacing.

"Uh huh. What exactly did you have to ask her? It's not like the two of you have any common classes or anything." He was looking at me with one eyebrow arched.

Several questions flashed before me, none of them sounded plausible. Then, "I needed to ask her about a former classmate," came to mind.

Sloane gave a little snort. "Sure you did."

"What? We graduated together. Remember?" I stopped right in front of the couch and looked at him.

"Well, Kai seems to think that something happened this weekend. She's over at Sylvia's right now and you know she won't let it go until she has the truth. That, and you look guiltier 'n a fox with hen breath and feathers between its teeth," he drawled out.

I sat down hard on the other end of the couch and pinched the bridge of my nose. "I don't know what happened." I said it more to myself than Sloane, but he still heard it.

"So something did happen then. Kai always knows," He said with a fucking smirk as he shook his head.

"Look, I don't really want to talk about it. I doubt Kai will get any answers from Sylvia, either. Not with Beau there. Fucking prick." I added under my breath.

"What did that asswad do now?" I was slightly surprised to hear Sloane use that tone. No one but Kerrington ever said anything about Beau in front of me. It was like an unspoken rule they had between all of them. I really didn't know how any of them other than Kerrington felt about him. She couldn't stand him, that much was obvious. But she limited her thoughts to snide comments when Sylvia didn't join the group because she was otherwise occupied with Beau. From his pissed tone of voice, I gathered that Sloane must not be Beau's biggest fan, either. Maybe I could confide some of my fears about him without coming across as the jealous ex-boyfriend.

"It's not really anything he's done, more of just a feeling I get around him."

"I know what you mean."

"I didn't ever tell you, but that morning after the picnic I went to talk to Sylvia." I figured he probably knew this. He nodded so I continued. "She had bruises on her."

His eyes went wide. "Where? Why didn't Kai tell me? She was up there after you left." He shot me an apologetic glance. "Sorry, we all heard you two. Kai went up there to check on her when it quieted down. Surely she wouldn't have let that go."

"Well, Kai might not have seen them." I said fast. I probably said too much, but I wanted to get it all out there. "They weren't exactly in a visible location." I rubbed my hands over my face and peeked at him through my fingers. His eyebrows were raised and he had the 'this is going to be good' grin. "Well, um," I swallowed. "She was only wearing a t-shirt when she opened the door. She thought I was Kai," I added quickly, hoping that he wouldn't think I'd intentionally wanted to see her in just a shirt. "I couldn't help but see them when she moved. I wasn't looking there on purpose or anything." I felt myself blushing.

"Just tell me where they were."

I blew out a breath and sat back. "On her hips and upper thighs. They looked like finger prints."

"Sylvia gets hurt easily. She always has bruises or cuts." I knew he was just playing devil's advocate.

I shook my head. "Not that easy. I know how accident prone she is, and I know with her fair skin evidence of that shows more than it would on most. But these were left from force. They were too dark."

"She could like it that way?" He winced as he questioned it, like it was his sister's sex life he was discussing and he wasn't comfortable with that.

I wondered the same thing myself. Sylvia was always...open to new things, but I couldn't see her liking pain. It just wasn't like her. *Of course, people can change.* I shrugged my shoulders. I had no answer for that.

"I got a real bad feeling when I was over there earlier. I stopped because I needed to talk to her. I didn't know he was there. At first he was just too friendly with me. Then he accused me of spending the weekend with Sylvia."

"Did you?" he interrupted.

I just shot him a quick look, letting him know I wasn't going to answer that. "She was all over him but her eyes were telling me something was wrong and to be careful with what I said. You know Sylvia can't lie. Something was wrong. I just don't know what it was. She didn't appear to be hurt or anything, so I guess..." I just let myself trail off. I couldn't prove anything. I probably sound like the crazy stalker ex-boyfriend trying to sabotage the new relationship.

Sloane was all serious-looking. "Quinn, where was Sylvia all weekend? Was she here? I need to know so I can help figure out if she's in trouble and what we need to do about it." He waited for me to answer.

I manned up and confessed to it. "She was here. But it wasn't what you're thinking. I was sick and she came over to..." Babysit me? Take care of me? Help me out? It all sounded bad. I might as well just say sleep with me... "To make sure I was okay." He gave me a very knowing look. I wasn't going to divulge any more info than that.

"So Beau knew that?"

"I don't think so. I don't recall her ever using her phone all weekend.

She said she lost it. I don't know if he ever showed up and she wasn't there until today."

"How long was she here to 'make sure you were okay'?" He mocked my words.

"Saturday morning until this morning." I didn't look at him as I answered.

Sloane let out a low whistle. "Wow, I guess Kai's spidey senses were spot on again."

I threw a scowl his way. "I didn't say anything happened. I just said she was here," I snarled at him.

He raised his hands in innocence. "I'm not judging, man. Whatever did or did not happen isn't my business. I'm just trying to figure out where she was." He still shot another fucking presumptuous smile my way.

"So anyway, I don't know if he came earlier. I saw him this afternoon for the first time. Sylvia wasn't back yet." He looked confused at that. "She took off sometime early this morning and I have no idea where she went. She didn't exactly leave her agenda for the day, let alone say goodbye." I muttered the last.

"That's why you were looking for her," he said as if suddenly it made sense. I nodded. "She was probably at Jason's."

I just let out a big breath. "So I don't know what's going on with Beau, if he's pissed 'cause she wasn't home or if he really knows she was here or what. I just don't like it."

A light tap at my door alerted us to Kai's presence and I called out to her to come in. Sloane and I didn't say anymore about Sylvia.

"Well, Sylvia is fine." She rolled her eyes. "She lost her phone. I don't know, she was all cuddly with Beau. I bet she was just all cozied up with him all weekend and turned her phone off." Sloane and I exchanged knowing looks over her head. I hoped he wouldn't share the secret. I wanted to wait and see what Sylvia would do. I shook my head and hoped he understood what I wanted. Kai was still talking and I caught the end of, "what did you do?"

"What?" I asked a little alarmed.

"I asked what you did for the weekend." She looked up at me expectantly.

"Oh, nothing. I had strep throat and just stayed in."

"Sorry. Chicago was great. It's too bad you couldn't come."

She looked like she was going to say more but Sloane suggested they go home so I could rest.

We said our goodbyes and I sat on the couch, wondering just what to do.

I tried every day for the next two weeks to get Sylvia alone to talk to her. I was blocked at every turn. If she wasn't with Beau she was with Kai, Kerrington, and even Jason, but mostly with Beau. He seemed to be over all the time.

I tried to call, but I only got her voicemail. She never returned my calls. I tried to text her. She just replied back that she wasn't interested in anything I had to say. I tried again a few days later.

```
I need to talk to you -Q

I can't - not right now -S

I'm here when you can. Anytime about anything -Q
```

A reply never came.

She didn't even leave at the same time anymore. I thought she was leaving earlier, but I couldn't seem to pin down the time and catch her. I didn't want to make it look like I had been stalking her for the past few weeks. I lived for any information I could glean from the others. Sloane didn't know what was going on either. He said that Kai was pissed because Sylvia was always with Beau. She still hadn't said anything to Kai about that weekend. I debated on leaving her a note but I was afraid Beau might see it. I didn't know what that asshole would do if he knew. I was fairly certain that he didn't have a clue about Sylvia and me. I was also sure that was why Sylvia was avoiding me.

I didn't want to have Kai or Sloane slip her a note like we were in junior high, either. I wanted to talk to her face to face. I wanted to see her face when I told her how I felt. I wanted to read for myself just what was going through her mind. I wanted her honest reaction.

My time would come. I was sure of it. I would wait patiently. One of these days I would get my chance to tell her. Until then, I would wait and watch, and if she needed me I would be there in a heartbeat.

Chapter 13 - Sylvia

"WHY WON'T YOU LET ME see what I'm wearing?" I whined at Kai.

She and Kerri were at my place, having a traditional girls getting ready together pre-party. Kai insisted on the pre-party, since I wasn't actually going with them to Jason's party. Instead, I was going out with Beau again. We had spent almost the entire past couple weeks together. He had even stayed over for the first time, and then stayed again the next night. For the most part, it had been good. He didn't ever once bring Quinn up. I started to think he was just trying to intimidate me the night he made the threat against Quinn. I doubted he would really make a scene if the three of us were ever in a room together. At least I hoped that would be the case.

Not that there was a chance Quinn was going to look at me ever again anyway. I had just left him like he left me. I walked away due to a bad decision without a real explanation. I doubted I would even be able to talk to him if I got the chance. I didn't think I could look him in the eyes. I didn't want to see how he would be looking back at me. He had called and texted. The calls were harder than the texts to avoid. I wanted to hear his voice and know how he sounded. If he was pissed, it would be easier to avoid him. But if he was hurt, how could I keep myself from running to him? I deleted them unheard. The texts I answered because I wanted him to know he needed to stop. I wasn't ready for whatever he had to say to me. After the last couple weeks, I had started to have a good idea of what I would need to say to him.

"I don't have it yet. Sloane had to go pick it up. You'll love it. I promise." Kai had the *'you'll wear it because I say you will, bitch'* glint in her eye even though she had the smile of an angel on her face. And most of the time she would be absolutely right. I would wear it if she told me to, especially if she and Kerri were going to be with me. I always felt that when I was with the two of them, they both way outshone me. No one would look twice at me in the tight or barely there clothes Kai would convince me to wear as long as she and Kerri were dressed similarly. To be fair to Kai, the clothes she picked out for me were in decent taste. They didn't scream "skank."

But I wasn't going to be with them. I didn't know what the exact plan was with Beau yet. When he'd left that morning, he wasn't sure what time he would be back. He said we'd figure it out when he got here. He said he just wanted to be with me. He really had been sweet lately. He was starting to open up to me, too. He said he felt like I was the first person he could really talk to. He told me about how hard it had been to start over at so many different schools. One night, he got all quiet and talked about how he had always missed his dad even though he really didn't know him.

My heart wrenched that night. We had been kissing on the couch when my phone rang. It was my dad, just checking in on me. We talked a bit, just sharing some of the events of the past few days. We talked briefly about my upcoming trip home for Thanksgiving. We said our 'love yous' and hung up. I looked over at Beau often during the call. He just watched me with a curious look, tilting his head from one side to the other as he visibly thought through things. I set the phone down on the table in front of me. I pulled my legs up under me as I sat in the corner of my worn couch. He moved closer to me and started asking questions about my dad.

He asked what growing up with a cop as a father was like. I told him that I guessed it was like any other father-daughter relationship would be like. Don't ask, don't tell, and don't ever get caught. Dad and I got along well, as long as I didn't cause any trouble, which I never would have dreamed of doing in the first place. He asked about the type of hours my father worked and how much longer he planned to work. I asked him why he was suddenly so interested in my dad. He replied that he was always fascinated with what it would have been like to have a dad around. He laid his head in my lap and closed his eyes as he told me about how he would pretend that his mom's various boyfriends were his dad. How he hated it when they would leave.

I brushed his hair off his head as he bemoaned a childhood bereft of a father. I waited for his blue eyes to open. I wanted him to see that he could trust me with his feelings. When he finally did open them, he looked so empty for a couple heartbeats that my heart just broke for him. He blinked, and then asked me a few more questions about my dad. I asked him again about coming home for Thanksgiving with me. He said he thought it might be a good idea.

That night I felt so close to him. I knew what it was like to only have one parent. Just like him I had pretended that Marie was my mom too. It made me feel sick to long for her and ultimately Quinn as I held and comforted Beau.

I looked back at Kerri and said, "Why does she have hers?" Kerri was the perfect Alice in Wonderland. Her dark hair was covered with a golden wig held back by a blue band and fell softly down her back. She was wearing a short pale blue silk dress with a white apron on the front. I had expected something straight out of an adult costume shop, but hers wasn't bad. It was on the short side of course but covered way more than I had thought it would. Hopefully that was a good sign for me. She was wearing striped blue and white thigh high stockings and heels that made my feet hurt just looking at them.

"Kerri picked hers up yesterday. Yours wasn't ready yet," she said nonchalantly with a shrug, as she walked past me to the bathroom.

I looked over at Kerri, but she was just looking at Kai walk away from us. When she didn't look back at me I followed Kai down the hall.

Kerri stopped in the kitchen. She had brought a bottle of pre-mixed lemon drop martinis. She met up with us with three cups in hand. In the bathroom, Kai rummaged through my stuff.

"You must have a clear hair band here somewhere. Aha! I knew you would. Now let's go out to the table and we can get started on your hair." I groaned. If we were going to the chairs, it meant it was going to take a long time. I took a big drink for my patience and my sanity and sat down to let the Jack Bauer of makeovers get to work.

"So Sylvia, how are things going?" Kai prodded as she brushed through my hair while spraying it with water. "We've barely seen you lately. And did Beau stay here the last couple nights?"

Of course she would know that. "Yes, so..." I dreaded her asking about sleeping with him. I didn't want to talk about the fact that I hadn't wanted to sleep with him since... well, since Quinn. And that I had been lying to him to hold him off. At first I told him I was afraid I was getting a urinary tract infection, and the next day said that I went to the doctor and he confirmed it. Then I told him I got a yeast infection from the antibiotic. Thankfully, I got my period then and it gave me some more time to figure things out.

"Just wondered how that was," she answered vaguely.

"About like you'd expect it would be with a penis-wrinkle," Kerri added dryly.

I just glared at her. I know she didn't get on with him at first, but she could have given it a second chance. Kai, of course, giggled and asked what that was.

"A man is a penis-wrinkle when calling him a dickhead would be a compliment." Kai giggled harder, and even I let out a bit of a smile. It was a pretty good term, even if I didn't agree with her.

"Kerri, really he's not that bad." I knew it would be useless to defend him to her. She had her mind made up and Kerri was nothing if not stubborn.

"Sure, he keeps you locked up in here when he's here. But do you really know what he's doing when he says he's 'on a job'?" she even used air quotes. "Maybe he's married or has another girlfriend."

"Kerri, you said you wouldn't do this," Kai hissed at her.

I glared over at Kerri. She just looked back at me, her violet eyes issuing a challenge. I wasn't going to let her provoke me. I wanted to enjoy this time with them and not argue about stuff she didn't understand. "I know because I've gone out with him a few times and met some of his friends. I even met his boss."

"Oh, what were they like?" Thankfully Kai jumped on that to change the conversation. I was sure Kerri would find a way to bring it up again. Her expression told me this wasn't over.

I described Beau's friends to her and how I met them.

After the last time Quinn showed up unannounced, I had been worried about him coming over to talk and Beau being there. So every time Beau was over I suggested we go out. At first Beau was against it. He said he was tired or he just wanted to spend some time with me. I wouldn't admit it to Kerri but after a few days I had started wondering the same thing. When I asked him straight out if he had someone else he was hiding from me, he laughed louder than I had ever heard him.

"Sylvia, why would I want to deal with two of you when you give me enough trouble?" I was relieved and hurt at the same time. Was I trouble? I was going to ask him, but he surprised me by offering to take me to his boss's upcoming birthday party. He had planned to just skip it, because he didn't think I would want to go. I assured him I did. So when Tuesday night rolled around, I reminded him and we took off for the same little dive bar he had taken me to on our first date. Now that it was colder, he took his truck instead of his motorcycle. He had a nice extended-cab pickup. He said he needed the extra room when he came back with his cargo, and then he laughed again.

I told Kai about how he'd stayed with me all night, even when some drop-dead gorgeous woman slinked up to him and attempted to flirt with him. It was pretty clear from the start that they knew each other well. I wondered how long it would take him to look over at me and realize that I couldn't compare to her. I was amazed when he pushed her hands off his chest and reached over to me. He pulled me in front of him and introduced me to the woman. It was clear that he was telling her I was with him and he wasn't interested.

I didn't tell Kai how later she stopped me in the bathroom and told me to watch out. She said she knew Beau well, and he wasn't someone who stuck around long or got involved with anyone he wasn't getting something from in return. She sneered at me as she examined me head to toe, and then turned to the mirror as if I wasn't worth her scrutiny. Looking at me through the mirror she said she wondered what that could be since I wasn't his normal type. I walked out and chalked it up to a jealous ex and tried to not let her words hurt me.

That wasn't the only thing I left out about that night. I didn't tell her about the fight he got into. He and his buddies had played pool most of the night. I was getting tired and had class in the morning, so I asked Beau if we could leave soon. He told me after the game we would go. I went to stand over by the wall and chat with his boss Curtis. He was a cross between the character of a bounty hunter and a pimp. Curtis was a huge African American with a penchant for heavy gold chains. I liked him though. He spoke quietly and was fairly easy going. As I walked over to stand by him a guy playing on the neighboring table called out, "I'll take ya home, baby." I ignored him but Beau sent him a frightening look.

The guy continued to make crude comments to those around him. Beau finally threw his stick down and stalked over to him. He got right in the guy's face. "What are you saying about my girl?"

The guy raised his hands in a peace gesture. "Whoa, man calm down. I'm just fuckin' with ya."

Beau held his gaze a little longer, and then stepped back. I'd thought for sure there was going to be trouble, and let out a breath of relief as Beau turned to come back to me. He took one step towards me as the guy said, "I'd rather be fuckin' her." Beau spun so fast I didn't see him do it. My eyes flashed to the guy now leaning back over the pool table with blood dripping out of his nose. Beau had a fist full of the guy's shirt, and his other hand raised as he held him against the pool table. I couldn't hear what he said to the guy, but I did hear the guy spit back a "fuck you".

That set Beau off. He pulled the guy up and took another swing at him. I stepped forward, not knowing what to do. Curtis put his arm out to stop me. I glanced up at him and he whispered down to me that Beau would be fine and he could take care of it. I wasn't worried about that. I just didn't want anyone hurt. I would have just ignored the guy. I kept my eyes on Curtis. I couldn't stomach seeing what Beau was doing to the guy. I never liked violence, and blood made me nauseous.

I looked back over when Curtis moved his arm. Beau was being pulled back by a couple of his buddies. The other guy was a bloody mess on the floor. I had to turn away. I couldn't handle the sight of the blood dripping from his nose and mouth. My stomach was rolling. I was afraid I was going to be sick all over. Curtis lead me towards the back door, suggesting that I get some air. Beau and his friends followed. They made comments to him congratulating him on the beat down. I shuddered inside, and just wanted to get out of there. He leered at me and until that moment, I had never felt true fear.

His face held an expression of confused concern. "Sylvia? Are you okay?" I just stared at him. I didn't know what to say. I had just watched him beat a guy in front of me. I was scared of that temper and strength. I must have shaken my head a little because he slowly came up to me.

"Sylvia, it's okay. I wasn't going to let him get away with talking like that about you." Was he serious? He thought I was upset about being talked to like that. I still trembled a little as he bought his arms around me. "It's okay, Sylvia." He cooed it again and patted my hair. I stood still, paralyzed with the realization and Beau could be very dangerous. I let him believe that I was just upset about that guy, and he took me home.

A sharp tug on my hair brought me out of the memory. "Oops. Sorry," Kai apologized as she pulled another chunk of my hair back into some intricate braid.

"I'm not complaining, but why are you braiding my hair instead of torturing me with the curling iron like you usually do?" I wanted to forget about that night and hoped that getting Kai to talk about our costumes would take my mind off it.

"That way the little ears I got to go with your costume will stay on easier and not get lost on all this hair you have."

Kai had decided we were all going with an Alice In Wonderland theme. Kerri was Alice, Sloane and Reed were Twiddle-Dee and Twiddle-Dumb, I was to be the Cheshire Cat. Kai declared that she was the white rabbit and was leading us all down the hole. I pointed out that actually, Alice was the only one to be lead down the hole, and the rest were already there.

I thought about asking to see if Quinn was going, but I figured since it was at Jason's he probably wasn't. Jason and Quinn had yet to meet, and even if they had there was no way Jason would invite him over. Jason had called and checked on me a few times over the past couple weeks. We met with Colby on campus a couple times for lunch. Jason promised me that he would try harder to be there for me. I thought about telling him how Beau threatened to end Quinn, but then figured that Jason would just offer to help him with that.

Kerri came over and topped us off. "When are the guys coming up?" I looked at Kai, but Kerri answered.

"Anytime now, so you better hurry and finish, Kai."

Kai fixed a headband with little black and pink ears to my head and dragged me off the bathroom to finish with makeup. "Kerri when they get here just bring our costumes to Sylvia's room." Kai called out to Kerri. I was beginning to suspect that I wasn't going to like my costume. If it was really bad I could just put it on until they left and then change before Beau and I went anywhere.

I looked in the mirror to check the damage and was pleased that Kai kept a light hand with the make up. She made a light, shimmery, pink mask around my eyes and a light gloss on my lips. I was worried about the eyes when she took so much time working on them but they looked great. My hair had been pulled in to a braid with the bottom of it tucked under. I was a bit uncomfortable with all my hair up like that. I felt like my neck was too exposed.

I heard the door, and Sloane talking to Kerri. It wasn't long before she brought in our costumes. Kai grabbed hers and put it on the bed before showing me mine. "Now Sylvia, I know you're going to think it's too short. But it's really not that bad compared to some I saw." She held up a cute little black and pink horizontal striped dress. It looked like a long tank top with a short flared skirt attached below the waist. It really wasn't too bad at all. Then again, that could be the two lemon drinks talking.

I couldn't let her think I liked it, though. I pursed my lips. "I don't know Kai. I think maybe I should wear something under it. I think I have a black turtleneck somewhere."

Kai acted like I just insulted her grandma. "You can't wear a turtleneck with this. It's perfect as it is, Sylvia." I flashed a smirk at Kerri. She knew what I was doing but didn't call me on it.

"I suppose, Kai, but I'm taking a shirt in case I get cold." I would too, once I knew where we were going. "I heard Sloane out there. Where's Reed?"

"Oh, he had to get something. He'll be here soon," Kerri answered as she handed me a pair of pink and black stripped leg warmers. I raised my eyebrow at her and she shrugged. "Kai said they were better than the furry Uggs." I cringed, at least Kai knew me well enough to know I wouldn't have worn Uggs.

We finished getting dressed. Kai had white knee-length tight shorts on with a little pink satin top with a white cropped tux jacket with tails and pink trim. She finished off the look with a little cotton tail, a pair of bunny ears, pink eyes and a pocket watch. It was perfect. Sexy without looking like a playboy bunny.

"I bought you ballet flats too. I didn't think you could handle heels if you were drunk." Sometimes I really loved Kai.

As I was putting the shoes on and scrunching the leg warmers over my calves and shoes the way Kai showed me to, I heard Reed come in. I thought I heard a third voice and wondered if it was Beau already. I had been hoping for some more time with the rest of them before they headed out. If Beau was already here, that wouldn't happen.

Kerri was already out of the room, and Kai was right behind her. I trailed after them turning the lights off. As I walked down the hall I ran smack dab in to Quinn coming out of my kitchen. I was so taken aback with him being there that I didn't say anything. I just looked him over. He was clearly the Mad Hatter. He was wearing a black tux with tails and emerald green lapels. His unbuttoned vest matched the lapels. He wore a black shirt with the top three buttons undone and an emerald tie hung loosely around his neck. The black top hat with green band completed the look.

He was sexily disheveled looking the part of an absolute rake. I couldn't pull my eyes away. My breath hitched and I was torn. I wanted to run back to my room just as much as I wanted to stare into his eyes the rest of the night.

He examined me as intently as I had examined him. My body tingled with the nearness of his. I was already warm from the alcohol but I still felt the blush creep up on me from his intense stare. "Sylvia." As soon as he said it, I snapped back to my senses and backed away from him.

"Hello Quinn," I greeted him as I joined the others in the living room. Reed and Sloane were wearing matching blue and red plaid shorts with short-sleeved white button up shirts and thick black-framed glasses. The best part was the suspenders. Sloane was wearing blue and Reed, red. I immediately thought of the fun that could be had snapping those later. It was too bad I wouldn't be out with them.

Kerri had turned on some music. Reed pulled out a flask and handed it first to Kerri, who then passed it around to all of us. I tried to relax and joke around with them, but I was always conscious of Quinn nearby. I hoped Beau would call or text me before he showed up. Maybe I could get them all to leave before that. As the alcohol did its job and I started losing my inhibitions, I started to include Quinn in when talking to the others. He started to respond to me too. Soon we were talking to each other.

I knew it was just small talk. There was so much more both of us needed to say, but we knew that this wasn't the time or place for that talk. He asked about classes and I asked about his parents and how he was feeling. We danced around what we both wanted to say. His eyes questioned me though. I knew he was looking for answers in my own eyes. I had the answers I knew I should tell him. I needed to tell him that I'd made a mistake. That I never should have gone to his place. I needed to let him know that I was staying with Beau. Yet the more I looked at him, the less I wanted to say those things.

There was a lull in the conversation and we exchanged awkward glances. I bit my lip as Quinn started, "Sylvia, we need to talk about it. I know that something is wrong." I prayed my eyes weren't giving anything away. "Sylvia, I know this isn't the time but you keep avoiding me and I need you to hear this." I was somewhat stunned when he reached over and took my hand. When I didn't pull it away from him he continued. "I need to tell you that it killed me to find you gone that morning. Why did you leave?"

I pulled my hand away with a resigned sigh. I glanced around at the others. They were wrapped up in whatever story Sloane was telling. None of them even bothered a glance over at us. I had to tell him. I could do this. I could be strong and get this over with. "Quinn, I just wasn't ready to deal with it yet. It was too much all at once and I had things to think through."

"Have you thought it through now?" His voice was so quiet that I barely heard him.

I felt my eyes pool and a lump rise up in my throat. I opened my mouth to tell him but the pain in his eyes stopped me. I couldn't do this. I couldn't hurt him. No hurting him would be to let this continue. "Quinn, I think..." I paused as I tried to find the right words. I never had to find them. A knock at the door interrupted me. There was only one person it could be. I blinked my eyes a couple times to clear them. Everyone stopped talking and looked over at me standing with Quinn.

"Are you going to get the door, darlin'," Sloane drawled.

"Yeah, you better go let dick-face in," Kerri added.

I nodded and went to the door trying to conjure up a smile. As expected, it was Beau. He was still in the same jeans and faded blue shirt that he left in that morning. So at least I knew then that he whatever he had planned didn't involve dressing up. I felt a little silly standing in front of him in my little striped dress and leg warmers. I suddenly felt like twelve year old caught playing with Barbies by her older friends. I fidgeted around him as I asked if he remembered everyone. He nodded and said hey to them. Reed went and grabbed him a beer from the fridge and asked him about his truck. While it was enough to break the ice, the carefree mood from earlier never quite returned.

It appeared that no one was particularly interested in leaving. I asked Beau if we should get going, if we had to be somewhere. He said that he had a long day and really just wanted to stay in. I shrugged; I had been looking forward to going out. I understood that he probably was tired. I resigned myself to staying and decided that since I was, I was going to enjoy my friends while they were still here.

I spent the next hour chatting and joking with the others. The drinks flowed freely and I hoped that Kerri was up to the task of taking care of all of them. She was the DD for the night. Although I suspect that if anyone passed out at Jason's she would just leave them there. Beau was reserved. He talked with the others but he mostly watched me. I would feel the hair on the back of my neck prickle and I would turn to see him staring. Whenever I was anywhere near Quinn he had the same curious look on his face that he had this morning when I opened my eyes. It looked innocent enough but something about it just bothered me.

Quinn too, was quiet. I could feel the tension between him and Beau. It was constricting, I felt the need for fresh air. I opened the balcony and took a step out. Beau followed me and lit a cigarette. "So how long are they sticking around?" He motioned his head towards the living room. I heard Kai giggle but the room had grown silent for the most part. I hoped they weren't trying to hear us.

"I'm not sure. I can ask them to leave if you'd like." He was leaning over the railing and looked over at his shoulder at me. His eyes were flat and unreadable.

"You do whatever you want, Sylvia." He turned to look away as he mumbled, "You care about them more than me anyway." I felt bad. I wanted to spend time with them but I knew Beau was tired out and just wanted some peace and quiet.

I turned and went back in the apartment to tell everyone goodnight. I walked into the living room. In the rocking chair, Kai was sitting on Sloane's lap per usual. Kerri and Reed were cozied up on the couch and Quinn was pacing behind the couch. He had his top hat in one hand and was dragging his fingers through his hair with his other.

As I stepped over to the couch, Quinn came around. Before he could say anything, Beau sneered, "She dreams about you, you know." All eyes flashed to him. He stepped from the balcony and walked over to us. "When she's sleeping she talks about you or to you I guess." His eyes were hard.

"Beau," I tried to sound menacing. This did not to be brought up now.

"What? Don't you think he should know that you call his name when you're in bed with someone else?" His voice was cold and he didn't take his eyes off me. I braved a glance at Quinn. His jaw was clenched tight and I could see his hands were clenched into fists as well.

I turned and put my hand against Beau's chest. "Beau, please don't do this. Not here, not now." I begged him. This could turn real bad. Not only was he pissing Quinn off, Reed and Sloane were shooting daggers at him as well.

"But then that's okay 'cause I'm the one in her bed." He sent a smug grin Quinn's way in an attempt to provoke him. I stepped between them remembering the bloody mess of a man Beau left laying on a dirty bar floor. I couldn't let him do that to Quinn. I knew that Reed and Sloane were there and there was no way Beau could take on Reed. Still I saw first-hand how fast Beau moved and knew that Quinn wouldn't have a chance. As far as I was aware, Quinn had never had to defend himself before.

"Beau, stop!" Everyone else was still watching us but I could see that Kerri was about to let loose. I tried to pull him back towards my room.

"Let's talk about this without all of them around. Please, just come with me." It was too late, Kerri stepped forward. The contrast between her sweet little girl costume and her ice-cold bitch face would have been comical had I not been the one caught in the cross fire.

"How dare you! What makes you think that you can just say things like that? I don't know what Sylvia sees in you or why she would even allow you in her bed but I hope to hell she sees what a fucking prick you are after this. I've been trying to tell her to drop your piece of white trash ass but whatever bullshit you feed her has her coming back. Keep it up, now she can see just what an ass you are." Kerri stood right in front of him. I prayed he wouldn't hurt a girl. I tried to step between them but I felt Kai's hand on my arm.

Beau scoffed at Kerri. "Bitch, please. I make her scream my name. That's what has her coming back." He looked at Quinn then, "she likes it when I slap her ass. She ever let you do that? The harder I..." Kerri stepped forward and shoved at him. He just laughed as Sloane got between them. He had been closer to her than Reed.

"Reed why don't you take Kerri out to cool down. I think we can handle this." Sloane said in an even tone. I knew that if anyone was able to diffuse a tense situation it would be Sloane.

"Kerri honey?" I didn't take my eyes off Beau but I caught a glimpse of Reed wrapping an arm over Kerri's shoulder. She stood still and glared at Beau.

I tugged at him again. "Please, let's just talk about this." He finally looked back at me and smirked. I continued to pull at his hand as I turned to go down the hall.

Once in my room I flipped the light on and closed the door. "What the hell are you doing?" I hissed at him.

"What am I doing? I would say the question should be what the hell are you doing? You're all whored up and flirting with every guy in the room." His face was livid. I trembled a little more from anger than fear.

"I was not flirting. Those are my friends out there. I was having a good time with them." I said it low hoping the others weren't outside the door listening to us.

Beau let out a short gruff laugh. "Princess you lead every guy on. Look at what you're doing to Quinn." Then his face changed and I did feel a tremor of fear shoot through me. Beau tilted his head to the side like he always did when he was thinking something through. "You slept with him, didn't you?" He said it as more of a question than an answer.

Never had I hated my god damn blush more than I did in that minute. I couldn't stop it. I felt it creep up and mix with the heat I was already feeling from the anger and the buzz I had going. I didn't answer. There was nothing I could say that he could read on my face already.

"I thought so. You sure had me fooled. I thought you were so sweet and innocent. You're just a fucking slut like all the rest." He stared me down. His eyes judging and disapproving. I looked down, not being able to stand what I saw in them. He was right. I was far from sweet and innocent and now I had made a mess of everything and someone was going to get hurt.

"I'm sorry." I didn't know what else to say. I didn't need to say anymore. The door flew open and Quinn stormed in. He got right in Beau's face.

"Get the fuck out! Now! You will not talk to her like that!" Quinn was livid. His face was bright red and his dark eyes were flashing. I could see his chest raise and fall quickly with his heavy breathing.

Everything felt in slow motion to me. I was still reeling from the fact that Beau was right. Then to have Quinn in my room defending me. It was too much. By then everyone else was in the room too.

Beau was looking them all over. His eyes stopped at Reed. He raised his hands up and looked over at me. "Sylvia, were not done talking about this. Why don't you ask your friends to leave and we can continue this?" His voice was flat once again but I could detect the edge of anger he was holding back.

"No, I don't think that's going to happen. You're the one who is going to leave." Quinn's voice was ice.

Beau looked at him and laughed. "What are you going to do about it pretty boy? Let the ice queen step in and save your ass again?"

Bringing Kerri into it was definitely the wrong thing to do. Reed stepped forward and grabbed Beau by the arm. "You need to leave. Now!" The others followed him down the hall. I stood still, stunned and hurt. I could still hear Reed threatening Beau as he led him to the door. I looked back at Quinn; he was watching me with cautious eyes.

"Sylvia, are you okay?" He asked so quietly and sincerely that I just couldn't face him right then. I didn't know what to say. He just heard that I dreamed about him even when I was in bed with another man. What must he be thinking about me. God, maybe he thought the same thing as Beau. I was just a mass of confusion and I knew it was wrong but I lashed out at him.

"How do you think I am? I'm embarrassed and pissed and...fuck!" I just didn't know what to say. I didn't want him looking at me like that. He looked so concerned. It ripped at my heart to see that. How could he be worried about me after all he heard? "Just go. I'm fine. Really. Thank you but I will be fine." He stepped close closing the distance between us.

"I'm not going anywhere." He reached his arms around me but I pushed him away.

"No, Quinn. You heard him. You know what he said about me. It's true." I couldn't stop the tears by then.

Kai stuck her head in the room. She looked from me to Quinn and back again. "It's okay Kai. I can handle this." Quinn whispered. "Why don't the rest of you go on to Jason's. I'll make sure she's fine."

"We're not going to Jason's." She hesitated looking back at me. "Sylvia, we will be right down stairs if you need us." She looked once again at Quinn and motioned him over. I couldn't hear what she said to him but he nodded. Kai turned away and closed the door behind her leaving Quinn and I locked in a stare-down.

Chapter 14 - Quinn

A s I turned away from Kai and back to Sylvia, I heard the door click. It left me aware of just how alone I was with her. It was what I had been waiting for. No Kai or Kerri, no Reed and Sloane, but most of all no Beau. The opportunity was there. All I had to do was open my mouth and let it all out. Just tell her how she was everything to me, how I had been so empty without her. Now that I'd seen her -- held her -- loved her. Confess how scared I was that she wouldn't return it. Beg her to forgive me. Declare my love for her. All I *had to do* was *speak*.

All I *could do* was *listen*. I heard my heart beat rapidly with equal parts adrenaline, hope, and fear. I heard Sylvia inhale and exhale a little fast and a little hard, yet starting to slow. It was perfectly in tune with me. The two of us in post sex come-down bliss flashed in my mind, with our breaths coming so similarly. The problem wasn't that my words weren't there. Hell, they had been there for two weeks. They may have been there even longer than that, had I just listened to my heart before. No, the problem wasn't a lack of words. The problem was Sylvia.

Sylvia reminded me of a guitar string pulled so taut that one little pluck would snap it. She glowered back at me. Tears filled her eyes, leaving them a distorted pool of anger, fear, and shame. It was the last that troubled me. I heard what that bastard had said to her. I knew I was being an overprotective asshole, but as soon as I heard the door shut I followed them down the hall. I was so afraid that if I didn't I would be too far away to protect her when he hurt her. I was absolutely sure he would hurt her physically, as he had just done emotionally.

As soon as I heard him call her a slut I was in there. I could not stand back and let him speak that way to her. I went in with my hands ready, either to defend or attack, I didn't care which. Either way he wasn't going to touch Sylvia. The others must have followed me, because after I told him to get out he looked around me. I glanced at Sylvia, her face unmasked with fear and guilt. Sylvia had nothing to feel guilty about. That fuck-head was the one who should feel guilty.

I looked back at Beau and got the distinct impression that he was sizing up the room, which was obviously in our favor. Not that I couldn't have handled him alone. I wanted to -- damn, did I ever want to -- but I knew Sylvia wouldn't want that. I knew how she felt about violence and blood, although I wasn't about to let him hurt her anymore either. Then he had the balls to order her to tell us to leave so "they could finish this." I felt my jaw tighten and my muscles tense. I tried desperately to calm myself as I ordered him to leave. When he challenged me, I was ready to show him exactly what I would do about it. I wondered if he picked up on that, and knew if I started Sloane and Reed would be in on it too. That was maybe why he threw the bit about Kerrington in there.

When I was sure Reed had him, I focused on Sylvia. I was worried about her. I knew that she would always be affected by guilt trips. That was just Sylvia. She never wanted to disappoint anyone. She wouldn't even look at me. I needed to know that she was okay, but her reaction wasn't entirely what I was expecting. I couldn't believe that she would want to be left alone right then. What if that motherfucker came back? How could she even think that I would leave her alone?

I tried to take her into my arms to comfort her, but she wasn't having that. She stepped back and confirmed my suspicions that she had believed that shit he'd told her. Kai popped in and distracted me. She looked at me and for just a second there was the tiniest hint of her annoying know-it-all smirk. This was just as much about me and Sylvia as it was about Sylvia and Beau. We needed to get this shit clear. Sylvia could not take this all upon herself. I let Kai know that they could leave, that I would be okay with Sylvia.

Before she left, she told me to "think of everything you would like to do to Beau right now. That's going to look like a trip to a day spa compared to what I'll do to you if you hurt her again." I was pretty frackin' sure she would do exactly that, too. She gave me one of her mystical angel smiles and a wink before she pulled her head back.

I was left standing there, face to face with a Sylvia that looked so broken that my heart was breaking along with her. I did this to her. My leaving her with that lie did this. I caused her to doubt herself. She knew what she wanted all along and my questioning that and making her decisions for her led to this. To this brilliant, beautiful girl standing here before me feeling as if she deserved what an asshat like that would say to her.

"Quinn," her voice hitched a bit as she spoke. "Go. Please."

"Sylvia, I won't let anything hurt you -- not even yourself. You can't believe what he said."

She scoffed at me. "You don't know me anymore." She pushed past me towards the door. When she reached the knob she tossed back, "You know nothing about my life these past few years." Then she walked out.

I went right behind her. "Sylvia, you're right. I don't know your life, but I do know you."

I watched as she picked up the stupid flask Reed had left out on the table. She unscrewed it and threw it back like it was water. How she was able to swallow that much without choking was beyond me. Reed's "Tennessee Tiger Sweat" was some powerful shit. She slammed it back down on the table. "You know me so well that you knew I would climb right into your bed the first chance I got."

"Sylvia, it wasn't like that and you know it. I never, never, expected that." She continued to glare at me as she picked the flask back up. "If you don't sit down, you're going to get a nasty headache from that shit when your head hits the floor." She looked straight at me and took another big drink. "Seriously Sylvia, slow down." I knew that stuff was going to hit her hard.

When Reed showed up at my door before we went to Sylvia's he handed the flask to me with a smirk. I took a big drink of it and sputtered. "What the fuck is that?" It tasted like kerosene. He just laughed and explained to me that it was Hillbilly Pop, aka moonshine. His uncle makes it and he brings some back with him every time he visits home. It had to be over 150 proof. It was some serious shit.

Sylvia made her way over to the couch ungracefully taking the flask with her. I hoped to hell there wasn't much left in there. I went over and sat on the couch next to her.

She just looked at me, her eyes were so forlorn. "You don't know the things I've done." She covered her face with her hands as if she was trying to hide from me.

I pulled her hands away. "Sylvia, look at me." I gently tilted her chin up with my knuckles, so she could look in my eyes. "I'm sure you have done nothing wrong. Don't listen to what an asshole like Beau says."

"It hasn't just been Beau. There were others." I didn't understand. Others? Had she dated other pricks like Beau?

"Other what Sylvia?"

"Others. As in I slept with guys other than Beau and you." She choked out the words and I was afraid she was going to start sobbing.

"Sylvia, it doesn't matter. Whatever you've done in the past just doesn't matter. It is not who you are." I brought my fingers up and brushed away the tears. I wanted to lean forward and brush my lips across the same path my fingers just took. This wasn't the time. Sylvia's eyes were swimming with remorse and I needed to make that go away, not add to it.

I pulled back and looked her in the eye and tried to firmly tell her, "Sylvia, stop. You don't have to be telling me any of this." I wasn't going to let it bother me, but I didn't want the thought of Sylvia with anyone else in my head either.

She sat up a little straighter, and then listed to her side so that she was propped against the back of the couch facing me. She choked back a sob then gave a little giggle. Her eyes flashed the hint of sparkle and then went dim again. "It was all before I knew you were coming back. You were gone." She was really slurring her words. I'd known this was going to happen. I took the flask from her and shook it a little. Not much left in there. I took the lid off and threw the rest of it back. It burned like a motherfucker. I put the lid on and let it drop to the floor. All the while Sylvia was still mumbling about me being gone.

She looked so forlorn, looking up at me, asking my forgiveness. I was the one that needed the forgiveness, not her. Whatever had happened in the last few years was my fault. I reached out for her and she practically fell into my arms. Her warm cheek was pressed against my heart and her arm was around my waist. Those damn cat ears were tickling me so I gently pulled them off and dropped them.

Sylvia was still sniffling a little bit, but was starting to calm down. She snuggled tighter in to me and I wrapped my arms around her. I wanted nothing more than to run my fingers through her hair as I told her it was alright and that I was sorry too, but that damn braid had it all bound up. I felt around looking for the end of it. Once I slipped it off I began systematically unwinding it with one hand, just letting my fingers twine through it. I realized I was zoning out and once I focused on what Sylvia was saying.

"I just couldn't let him hurt you."

What? Who hurt me? I stopped undoing her hair. "Sylvia, who was going to hurt me?" I had a good idea who she was talking about.

"Beau." She wasn't crying at all anymore and her breathing was slowing down. I was worried she was going to pass out on me.

I straightened her up so I could get a good look at her and her at me. I wanted to be sure she understood this. I held her gently by her shoulders facing me. Her eyes were a little unfocused, but she seemed to understand that I wanted her to pay attention to me. "Sylvia, no one is going to hurt me. Not Beau or anyone else."

"But he said if he ever caught you looking at me, he would end you." That sounded like it had to have been a direct quote from the prick. "And then I thought about that night, and how the blood made me sick and..." The blood made her sick... what? Did that bastard hurt her?

"Sylvia. Did he hurt you?" I looked around her arms to see if there were any marks. There didn't appear to be any, and that striped dress was covering everything else up. I felt the anger rising up again. Why didn't I hit him when I had the chance? I should have just taught that asshole a lesson.

She shook her head. "Not me. The guy at the bar. He didn't even do anything and the blood was everywhere and Beau just kept hitting him." Her shoulders shook a little as she shivered. She must have been seeing it all again. From the look of horror on her face, I knew it must have been bad.

I pulled her to my chest and held her tight. I felt her take a deep breath and knew she was smelling me. I smiled, thinking about how she used to do that all the time and thought I didn't know about it. I went back to unbraiding her hair. It was so soft, falling through my fingers. I felt her warm breath against my neck and I knew I wanted this girl again. I had to have her back. I ached with the knowledge that tonight wasn't the night.

"Sylvia, I promise I can take care of myself. No one will hurt me. I'm more worried about you. I don't want him coming back and hurting you." I bristled at the thought of him coming back. I was sure that Reed and Sloane would have made sure he was gone tonight, but we couldn't watch her 24/7.

Sylvia pulled back from me with panicked eyes. "I don't feel well." Her eyes were darting around the room.

I knew she would get sick. God damn Reed. I helped her up from the couch and guided her down to the bathroom. I flipped the light on and helped her over to the toilet, lowering her so she wouldn't slip and crack her head open. "Sylvia, I'm going to go get you some water. Are you going to be okay?" She nodded and I backed out.

I took off the stupid tux jacket and vest. The tie was already loose so I pulled that off, too. I left them all on her dining table and went into the kitchen for a glass of water. She didn't have a fridge dispenser so I started the water in the sink. Not even thinking about it I opened the same one that had my glasses at home and sure enough that is where she kept them. I took some ice out of the freezer and added it to the glass and filled it. Once the water was off I could hear her in the background.

I went back to the bathroom and knelt down by her. She looked over at me and was blushing brighter than the pink of her dress.

"I'm sorry. You don't have to help me. I'll be alright." She turned her head back and put it down on her arm which was across the toilet. I smoothed her hair back and leaned over and kissed the top of her head.

"I'm not going anywhere. I'm not leaving you again." We sat there like that for a few minutes. Sylvia didn't throw up any more and I finished taking the braid out. I kept it brushed away from her face with one hand as I rubbed soft circles on her back with the other. I was thinking about what Sylvia had told me. Obviously, Beau had threatened her. I wondered if there was more to it. I couldn't honestly see what Sylvia saw in him. Every encounter I'd ever had with the prick, he'd acted like he'd owned her. That was so different than the independent Sylvia I knew. I wondered what he was holding over her.

"I think I'm going to be okay now." Sylvia's voice was so hoarse. She sat up straight and I gave her the water glass. She smiled weakly at me.

"Do you have any Tylenol or anything?"

She nodded. "In the kitchen. I can get it." She moved to stand up. I took her arm and helped her up.

"Sylvia, why don't you go change and I will get it for you." I led her into her room and turned to the kitchen. I checked her door and locked that, too. I was staying the night. I didn't care what she said. I wasn't leaving her alone. I texted Sloane before getting the Tylenol.

```
Sylvia will be ok - very hung over but ok. Is he
gone? - Q
```

I found the bottle and filled two more glasses of water, one for me and one for her. I took a drink of mine and my phone buzzed.

```
Reed led him right to his truck and he took off. Kai
said to stay with Sylvia just in case. - S
```

I planned to. We need to talk tomorrow. - Q

I went back to Sylvia's room and found her laying face down on the middle of her bed, still in her costume. I knew it was wrong to be looking at her like that, but that dress was one of the sexiest things I had ever seen on her. With the way she was laying on the bed it was hitched up in the back, barely covering her ass. I briefly thought about what it would be like to run my hands up under it and feel her smooth, soft skin. I couldn't let myself think about that.

I rolled my eyes. Of course she would pass out before changing. I set the water glasses and Tylenol down on the table beside her bed. I stood there a few seconds, debating if I should just leave her there like that and go sleep on the couch or change her into something more comfortable. It wasn't like I hadn't seen her naked before. Hell, it had only been two weeks since the last time I had. I couldn't leave her there like that.

I went over to the dresser and opened a couple drawers before I found one with t-shirts. I noticed she had many from high school in there. I smiled even bigger when I saw a faded blue one with *Lobato* on the back. It was from our junior year softball game against the seniors. It was a requirement that everyone in the class be on the team. Sylvia and I hated every minute of it. She said the only good thing to come out of that was the shirt in my hands. I knew this was the one to put on her.

I moved back to the bed and laid the shirt down beside her. I slipped the little slipper shoes off her. I knew Kai picked out her costume and I was pleased to see that she didn't try to force her into heels. Sylvia, heels, and alcohol would not be a good combination. I suspected Kai had learned that lesson at some point. Once the slippers were off, I rolled down the sock-like things on her legs. I wasn't sure what in the hell they were for. They just covered her legs and not her feet. Once those were on the floor I moved up to the zipper on the back of her dress. I hesitated, took a deep breath and undid the zipper. I hoped Sylvia wouldn't be pissed at me. I raised her shoulders up a bit and inched the dress down her body and over her legs. I dropped it on the floor with the shoes and leg things.

She was now laying there in nothing but a small shiny strapless black bra and panty set. I groaned. I should have left her. I would never get this image out of my head. The pale skin against the black reminded me of pearls in a black velvet case. She was so beautiful, even like this. I knew this was a good time to check to make sure she didn't have any bruises elsewhere. I swept my gaze over her and didn't see any. I exhaled in relief

161

and crawled up on the bed next to her. I pulled the shirt over her head and then put each arm through. I pulled it down over the rest of her body and then reached back under and unhooked her bra. I lifted her and turned her to me. I pulled the bra off and laid her back on her pillow.

I moved to get off the bed and pull the covers over her. She moaned a little and whispered "Quinn," so softly I wasn't sure I heard her at first. Her eyes were open though. "Stay."

I smiled down at her. "I'm not going anywhere but to turn the light off." I stood and kicked my shoes off and pulled my socks off after. I walked down the hall and turned the other lights off and then the one in her room.

She was still awake when I came back to the bed. She rose up letting me pull the covers back. I laid down next her and gathered her into my arms. She snuggled in, nestling her nose into the crook of my neck. Her leg bent over mine. *How did I ever let this go?*

I raised my head back up and rested it against the pillow. I kept my arms around her, tracing patterns up and down her arm and across her back. I still hadn't told her how I felt. I hoped at least my actions tonight would show her that I wanted her back in my life. Of course she needed to hear that, too. But this was a start.

My mind turned to Beau. He would come back. I was sure of it. I needed to talk to Reed and Sloane in the morning and see what they thought about it. I didn't think threatening him would do any good. I was sure now that Sylvia had to see what an ass he was. I would be sure to tell her again not to worry about me. It made sense that he would use something like that against her. Sylvia always thought of others first. She always took care of those around her. Now it was our turn to take of her.

I wrapped my fingers in her hair and pulled her into me tighter. I knew she was asleep, yet I still needed to tell her. "I love you more than the world, Sylvia." I whispered against her head as I kissed her again. "If you let me in, I will never let you go again. I will be yours forever." I let myself drift off, relishing the feel of her warmth against me. I desperately hoped that, come morning, she would still want me there.

Chapter 15 - Sylvia

T HE FOUR OF US -- Kai, Sloane, Quinn, and I -- were sitting outside a small ice cream shop close to campus. The others were chatting away about something. I wasn't sure what it was. I was too entranced with the amazing things the bright sunlight was doing to Quinn's hair. In the shadow it was its normal deep brown and even black. Then the sun would peek out from behind a cloud and it would shine a deep shade of bronze with hints of copper. It reminded me of watching autumn leaves change through time-lapse photography.

Kai gave me a little nudge. I knew I was busted when she smirked at me and pointed at my caramel sundae. "Are you going to eat that, or drink it?"

I wrinkled my nose at her and took a bite of my sundae. It was starting to melt, but it was right where I liked it. Frozen enough that it didn't drip off the spoon, yet soft and creamy and melting as soon as it hit the tongue. I took a second bite and leaned back against my chair. They had all resumed whatever it was they were discussing before. I glanced from Kai to Sloane to see if I could catch up with them. On my second pass through, I realized I didn't understand anything they said. I looked towards Quinn to see if he would be any help.

He must have just been listening to Kai and Sloane and not joining in with them. He was leaning back in his chair, his long legs kicked out in front of him. His feet were all gimpy as one pushed against the pavement, causing his chair to rock back. The other was almost laying sideways, crossed over the first. I tilted my head, trying to figure out how he could get his foot in that position. I started at the foot and moved up to see if his ankle had the answer. Of course I couldn't just stop at the ankle; I proceeded on up his legs. What was supposed to be a deep blue was now faded and washed out to slate in some spots. There were hints of tears along the sides and visible holes along the pocket. The left knee had a rip from one seam to the other, leaving a hint of skin showing through the frayed bands still intact.

I studied the jeans, trying to figure out how they got so dirty. I counted eight separate spots, the largest of which was on his thigh, which may have been made by wiping his hands off against his pants. There were four evenly spaced ones under a horseshoe on his right leg. Those were definitely made from resting his left shoe across his knee. I followed one up near the inseam that I was pretty certain was a spill of some sort. The spill stain ended by where what was probably the original indigo of the jeans began. I was intrigued by the yellow of the stitching along the fly against the dark blue.

I liked the way the fly pulled over on the left, revealing the top two buttons. I worried that I may have been blushing a little when I thought about unbuttoning those two buttons. I bit my lip remembering what it was like. I may or may not have been a little tingly in the right places, too. I quickly looked up at Quinn to see if I was caught. I forgot that he had sunglasses on. I couldn't really see his eyes to see if he was watching me. I sighed when I realized I was safe.

He seemed to be absent-mindedly licking his ice cream cone and nodding to whatever Sloane had just said. Two places of my body involuntarily clinched when I saw his tongue flick out in a pink flash and a little swirl along the cold white cream and retract it back into his mouth. After it unclenched, my heart beat a bit faster. As his lips briefly closed, I thought about how cool they would feel against my lips. His tongue peeked out, removing the trace amount of cream left on his lips. It would be sweet and cold and oh so hot all at the same time.

The tingles struck again as he stuck his tongue back out more slowly. This time it wasn't a quick, curled tongue. This was a slow, flat against it, smoothing it out lick. My breath came a little quicker as I imagined the feel of that drawn out lick. I sucked in a breath and sighed as he turned the cone, sweeping his tongue along it as it turned. He drew it back in his mouth once more. When it shot out again it took quick little laps. It seemed to just flick against the ice cream, when it touched it, rather than actually take any away.

I definitely felt a flush creeping up my chest, past my throat and onto my cheeks. I blinked, hoping to clear the image but when I opened my eyes, he had his mouth closer to the cone. His lips were parted just a touch as he leaned forward slightly and kissed the ice cream as he took a bite. I may have moaned a little at that. All my girly parts were absolutely alive, and I couldn't tear my eyes away from Quinn's mouth. He had a tiny drop of sweet vanilla right on the top edge of his upper lip. The pink of his tongue was slightly diluted with white as he skimmed his lips with it before flipping up to remove the sticky sweetness.

I think my mind may have exploded.

Kai gave my shoulder a tiny shove and I turned to glare at her, embarrassed that she caught me staring again. She just pointed at my now melted ice cream. Kai shook her head and laughed at it.

I knew I was bright red by that point. "Stop laughing Kai. I wanted it to melt."

Her laughter didn't stop, and soon I felt the vibrations of that chuckle along the side of my head. I slowly woke up only to comprehend that I was dreaming. Kai's high pitched giggle changed into Quinn's low rumble. As I became more alert I gradually became annoyed with the tickling of his chest hair against my nose. I wiggled my head to try to relieve the itch.

"Sylvia?" He asked quietly checking to see if I was awake.

I made some sort of noise that could have been a snort or a moan. *A snoan? A moart?*

He must have taken that as confirmation that I was. "What did you want to melt?"

"What?" I was confused. I vaguely remembered Kai laughing in my dream as I woke up but I didn't remember anything melting. I sat up. The pain slammed into my head and my stomach flipped. I dropped back down with my hand pressed against my forehead. *Why? Why? Why did I drink that crap last night?* I knew perfectly well what it would do to me. Everyone else had tried it that first year but I hadn't until the second. I slept on the floor of the communal bathroom on our floor and then was sick for two days after I tried it the first time. After that, I never had more than one drink when Reed would pass it around.

I felt Quinn shift from below me and sensed that he was looking at me. I lifted my hand so that I was peeking up at him. He was still in the same black shirt from the night before. It was unbuttoned and very wrinkled. It had obviously been slept in. I realized that he had slept in the bed with me. I knew I should care about that, but my head hurt so bad I just couldn't bring myself to.

"Sylvia, are you okay?" He whispered. "You never did take that Tylenol. I'll grab it for you." My eyes followed him as he got off the bed, picked up a water glass, and walked to the door. Once he was out of sight I flung my arm over my head, covering my eyes. If I held real still, my head didn't hurt as bad.

I tried to recall just why Quinn was in my bed. I thought back over the night and remembered what happened with Beau. I wanted to die. I couldn't imagine what the others were thinking about me right now. I didn't know what I'd done to cause him to behave like that. I had talked to Quinn in front of him, but not more than I did with anyone else in the room. I was torn. If I talked to him, Beau would be pissed. If I didn't, the others would suspect something.

I guess the little that I did was enough to piss Beau off. On the plus side, hopefully after that he wouldn't be coming back. I was hurt and embarrassed that he'd said that in front of my friends but I was angry, too. How dare he? That was no one else's business. I planned to tell him that, too, if he called. I wasn't about to call him. As far as I was concerned it was over between us.

That still didn't explain why I'd woken up with Quinn. The fact that he was still wearing his clothes gave me hope that nothing had happened. My memory was fuzzy about everything after everyone left. I remembered arguing with Quinn and drinking Reed's flask. I wanted him to leave then, so I was confused about why he was still there.

I risked the pain and dizziness and raised my head to see what I was wearing. It wasn't the dress so I must have changed at some point. The shirt I had on was blue and I tried to recall which one it was. Then I realized it was Quinn's shirt from high school. How the hell did I end up in that? It was at the bottom of my drawer. I hadn't worn it in forever. I somehow doubted that I was the one that had put that on.

Those thoughts were stopped when Quinn came back in.

"Sylvia?" He whispered.

I sat up, and instantly regretted it. I winced as the pain and dizziness washed over me. Quinn sat down beside me. In one hand he held two Tylenol and in the other a bottle of *Powerade*. I wondered where that had come from. I didn't have that in my fridge.

When he saw me staring at the *Powerade* he said, "I had some at home. I thought this would be better for you than just water. You know, rehydrate you and all." I took the Tylenol out of his hand and he opened the bottle for me. He rubbed soft circles on my back while I drank. "Is there anything else I can do for you?"

"No, I just need to take a shower and get some caffeine." Quinn chuckled softly when he steadied me after I stood up and swayed towards him. I tried to glare at him but it hurt my head when I did. He walked with me all the way to the bathroom. I was wondering if he planned on staying or if he would be gone when I got out. I had a nagging memory in the back of my head of him telling me he was never going to let me go again, but I couldn't bring it into focus. I wasn't sure if it was a real memory or just one from a dream.

We stood awkwardly outside the bathroom door, neither knowing what to say. "Um... so... yeah, I'm just gonna go..." I motioned behind me towards the shower.

"Oh. Sure. Sorry." Quinn fumbled as he backed away from the door. We kept eye contact as we both moved away. Finally, I turned and shut the door.

I don't want to even describe the mess I saw in the mirror. I took care of all my pre-shower needs and then climbed in under the hot spray. I stood there gratefully and let the hot water beat against me, relaxing me yet waking me at the same time. I stretched my neck from one side to the other, just trying to work out the headache that refused to leave. I tried to recall what Quinn and I had talked about after we came out of the bedroom. I wasn't sure, but I thought I may have told him about Beau's threat. I was thankful and relieved that he told Beau to leave, but I was also worried that he might try to hurt Quinn because of it. If I didn't tell him last night about the threat, I needed to today. Beau left because Reed and Sloane were there, too. But Reed and Sloane wouldn't always be around Quinn. I was trying to puzzle out what would be the best thing to do about Beau and Quinn when my water started to get cold. I quickly washed my hair and body and got out.

I looked around and realized the only clothes I had in there with me were my underwear and the Lobato shirt. I could either put those on or wrap the towel around me. I opted for the shirt and underwear, figuring he'd already seen me in that. I smiled down at the shirt in my hand. I knew Quinn had to have been the one who put it on me. For some reason, it felt good that he wanted to put his name on me. Which was silly. He probably just reached in the drawer and pulled out the first thing he touched. *Yeah, 'cause the one on the bottom is always the first thing you touch.*

I opened the door. I could hear him doing something in the kitchen. I quickly slipped into my bedroom to get dressed. My head still hurt like a bitch, but the dizziness was gone. I pulled on my faded QSHS sweats and thought about leaving the shirt on. I ended up changing into the one that said, "I do all my own stunts." Reed thought it was hilarious when he gave it to me last year. Fall down the stairs a couple times and you never live it down. I could smell toast as I stopped in the bathroom on my way to the kitchen to grab my comb and a hair band. I snickered, remembering the contents of his cupboards, that was probably about all he could make.

Quinn was sitting on my couch with a couple bottles of Coke, two glasses of juice and plates with toast. He didn't hear me come out. He was sitting on the edge of the cushions. His forearms were resting on his knees and he was looking down between them at the floor. I studied him, sitting there like that. He looked so stressed. He must have gone home and changed. He was in a pair of jeans now and a plain white t-shirt. His hair was still everywhere. If I didn't know him better, I would have doubted that he'd even combed it when he'd gone home. I knew he had, but his habit of playing with his hair when he was upset made it appear as if he hadn't touched it. I estimated the scruff he had along his jaw was now four days old. I liked how it felt against my ear and neck this morning when he leaned down to whisper to me. I sighed and dropped my gaze to the plates. He had made toast, and on mine he'd put my favorite, cream cheese with raspberry jam. His had peanut-butter.

"Still won't eat jam, huh? Some people just don't know what they're missin'." He looked up at me as I clicked my tongue and shook my head.

"Why would I want to put smashed berries all over my perfectly good peanut-butter?" He grinned up at me, remembering our long-running argument about the best thing to put on toast.

I sat down next to him and reached for the pop. There is nothing better than the tingly burn of a carbonated beverage in the morning. Others could have their espressos and lattes. Give me a twenty ounce Coke and I'm a happy person. Or at least a content one. After my initial caffeine fix I gingerly picked up the toast and took a bite. It looked so good, but my stomach just didn't want it. I set it back down, grabbed the pop, and sat back against the corner of the couch. I pulled my knees up and wrapped my arms around them. I watched Quinn as he ate his toast.

"Can't eat yet?" He asked with his mouth full. I shook my head. He swallowed. "If you ate normal stuff on your toast you probably could."

I kicked my leg out at him, making contact with his thigh. He grabbed my foot and started tickling it. "Stop it," I pleaded through the giggles. I kicked both feet at him and he finally let go. He sat back against the couch. The smile was gone and a serious look was in its place.

"Sylvia, we need to talk." I cringed. I knew this was coming. I wasn't exactly sure what he wanted to talk about, so I waited for him to continue.

He shifted on the couch so he was facing me. His brow was slightly creased and his lips pursed like he was debating on what to say. Finally, he took a deep breath and looked me in the eye.

"I've been wanting to tell you this for the past couple weeks. I hated that you were gone the next morning. I had so much I needed to tell you."

"I'm sorry. I just had to work some things out," I mumbled.

"I know. I figured you were out over-analyzing it." He flashed me a little grin. "You just didn't wait until you had all the information." I really didn't have anything to say, so I just waited for him to continue. The silence stretched as he searched my face. I didn't know what he was looking for, but he must have found it because he continued.

"Sylvia, I know I screwed up when I let you go. I have never gotten over you. Now that I have found you again I want nothing more than to be in your life forever." He reached over and took my hand and gently squeezed it. "I love you. I never stopped loving you. These past years have been empty without you. The weekend you spent with me made me realize just how much you mean to me."

This was not what I was expecting. I was a little stunned and not sure how to respond.

"I don't expect for you to feel this way. I know you need some time right now with everything going on. But I promise you I'm not leaving. I'm not giving up on this. What we had was special and it could be again. Sylvia, I will wait for you. Just don't shut me out."

His brown eyes were so sincere. I could see the love in them. They looked at me just as they had years before. I wanted to tell him that I felt that way, too, but I didn't and I couldn't lie to him. My eyes pooled and I felt a tear slip down. He brushed it away and leaned in for a hug. I rested my head on his shoulder and just enjoyed the feel of his arms tight around me, the warmth of his hard chest against me. I hoped that maybe someday I would be ready for this again. I felt him kiss the top of my head, and I smiled.

He pulled away as my cell phone rang. I debated on answering it, but it was Jason. I figured it was important. I gave a Quinn a reluctant smile and answered.

"Hi, Jason."

"Syl, are you okay? Reed just called and told me about last night. I'm on my way over." He sounded like he was actually running. Damn Reed. I didn't need Jason brought into this right now. I had enough going on.

"Jason, stop. I'm fine. You don't need to come over." I glanced over at Quinn. Jason had yet to meet him, and that was just something I didn't need that day. Quinn was watching me intently.

"Reed and Sloane are meeting me there. We're going to come up with a plan to keep you safe." I had a sneaking suspicion that the man on my couch was behind this meeting.

"Really Jason, I'm fine. You don't need to come over. I'll send Reed and Sloane away, too." Quinn coughed behind me, confirming my suspicion.

"Too late, Sylvia. I'm on my way. See you soon." Jason hung up on me. I knew it wouldn't do any good anyway.

"So, were you going to tell me I was expecting company?" I was fairly upset about him just deciding that I needed their help.

"Sylvia, he's going to come back. You know that. We all know that." Quinn said it in a calm voice, almost as if he were talking to a child.

"Look, I can deal with him if he does. He isn't going to do anything to me. If anyone should be worried, it's you. You're the one he said he would hurt." The whole conversation felt like déjà vu. We must have talked about this last night.

"Like I told you last night, he can't hurt me." He held up his hand. "Before you start, let me tell you why. When I got to Princeton I was angry and moody all the time. I was mad at myself after breaking it off with you. I had never had reason to be so mad before and I didn't know how to deal with it. It got to the point where every little thing set me off. My roommate, Michael, was a Tae Kwon Do third degree black belt. He got me to come with him to class. At first, it was to just be able to channel my aggression. But I also learned a few things there, too. So really, don't worry about me."

Well, that explained the hard chest and firm arms. I still wondered, though. I'd seen what Beau had done to that guy at the bar. I shuddered and closed my eyes.

"I will be okay. Right now we need to worry about you. Sloane and the others are supposed to be here about noon to talk about it."

I looked at the clock on my phone. That was just a few minutes from now. God, could this get any worse? No one needed to worry about me. I'm sure he would just leave me alone. I didn't want anyone else to get involved in this. I noticed I had nine missed text messages. I assumed they were from Kai and possibly Beau so I didn't want to open them in front of Quinn. Especially not after he had everyone circling their wagons around me.

As if on cue, there was a knock at the door. I went over to answer it, but Quinn stopped me.

"Aren't you going to ask who it is?" He asked quietly. Like he didn't know who it was. I rolled my eyes at him and flung open the door. As expected, it was Kai and Sloane.

"Good morning, Sylvia." Kai was her normal peppy self. Why did she never get hung over? She leaned around me and waved at Quinn. "Hi." She flashed me a quick knowing smile and slipped past me.

I gave Sloane a tentative look. I wasn't sure what the others were thinking after Beau's comments. Sloane gave me a reassuring grin back. It wasn't a full smile, just a hint of dimple showed, but it was still a smile. "Hey, Sloane," I said quietly as I let him in. I heard Reed and Kerri on the stairs, so I just left the door standing open and went back to sit with Quinn.

Kai was still standing talking to Quinn about his mom. Sloane pulled out my dining chairs so everyone would have a place to sit. I sat still and sulked. I resented everyone there like that. I looked at Quinn, who was talking calmly with Kai.

His eyes were tired. The creases in the corners of his eyes matched the one on his brow, telling me he was stressed. I could make out traces of purple shadows just above his slightly flushed cheeks. I wasn't sure what he was blushing at. Kai must have said something to him. The blush was cute, though. It made me think of our early days together and how nervous he would get around me. Of course I'd felt the same way, so the pair of us often looked like a set of Raggedy Ann and Andy dolls with our constant red cheeks.

Reed came in, loudly greeting everyone. Quinn reached back and slapped something against Reed's stomach. It must have been rather hard because Reed let out a little huff.

"What the hell, Q?" He lifted it up and I could see that it was his flask. I gagged a little thinking about how much of that I had drunk and how I was still slightly sick from it.

"You forgot something here last night." Quinn had an edge to his voice. I didn't know why he was pissed. It wasn't like he was the one who'd been sick after drinking it.

Reed scanned the room for Kai. "I thought you said you'd grab that for me?"

"Oh, I must have forgotten it." Kai seemed just a little too innocent as she brushed his question off and moved to sit on the floor in front of Sloane.

Kerri came in and shut the door behind her. She was beautiful, as always. Like Kai, she never seemed to be affected by late nights and too much alcohol. Her black hair flowed behind her, shiny and soft. The only flaw with Kerri was the bitch face she had on. She already didn't like Beau, and I was sure after that, it was only worse. I have to admit, though: after saying the shit he had, he was a penis-wrinkle.

"Jase's on his way over too. I talked to him this morning," Reed told the room.

Quinn nodded. "He just called Sylvia."

"You didn't have to call him. There is not a problem and I don't need you all here," I snapped at them, crossing my arms. I knew I was acting like a child. But I felt like they were treating me like one. It was completely stupid, but I felt like it was an intervention. I looked around, wondering if there was a camera crew coming to tape it. *Do they send someone to rehab for picking bad boyfriends?*

"Since when do you keep secrets from Jason?" Kai piped up. I glanced over at Quinn and turned red, thinking about just how much of my life Jason knew. I bet Jason knew me even better than Quinn did.

"It's not a secret, and there is nothing to have him to know about."

The door opened as I was talking. Of course Jason would just walk in without knocking. "What's a secret Syl?"

He stopped short when he saw Quinn. The two of them just stared at each other. Nobody said anything for several seconds. Then Jason shot a glare over to Reed. "What's *he* doing here?" He jerked his thumb at Quinn.

I spoke up before anyone else, "Jason, this is Quinn Lobato. Quinn, this is Jason Bratt." I knew they both were fully aware of whom the other was, but I hoped this would break the ice, so to speak.

"Dude, chill." Reed patted the chair by him. "Quinn was here last night when it happened. I told you that."

Jason threw a cautious look at Quinn. Instead of sitting next to Reed, he sat on the couch next to me. *Great. Just where I always wanted to be, between Jason and Quinn. Like this wasn't already awkward enough.*

Kerri started. "You guys should have just kicked his ass last night. I told you he was a prick, Sylvia."

"Yes, Kerri, you did. And you were right, but I don't think this is necessary. He's not going to do anything. If you want, I will text him later and tell not to call me anymore. You are all making a big deal of nothing. He never hurt me." I glared at Quinn because I knew he was behind the worries of Beau hurting me. Damn bruises. Everyone just looked at me like I'd lost it.

I knew I was fighting a losing battle, so I just sat back and let them discuss it. I only half listened to what they were saying. I was thinking about what I was going to text to Beau.

I still couldn't believe he'd acted like that. I was so embarrassed. Who tells other people that stuff? The more I thought about it, the more upset I became. Even though Jason had his arm around me, pulling me to his side, Quinn must have sensed my mood shift. Every once in awhile I caught him watching us out of the corner of his eye.

I looked over at Quinn. He was listening to Sloane. I watched his hand twitch towards mine a couple times, and I smiled. I knew he must have sensed my mood shift and wanted to comfort me, but didn't know what to do with Jason there. I felt someone watching me and looked up to see Kai staring at me blankly with a mysterious smile. She was up to something. I was sure of it. I just didn't know what it was.

I saw movement to my right and realized Kerri had stood up. Reed was following her. I heard him say something to Jason about spending the night.

"Wait. What?" I looked at Jason, confused. "You're not staying here."

"Sylvia, it's just until we know that he won't come back." Jason rubbed my shoulder as he explained it to me. "One of us will walk you to class and back again. It's only for a few days."

"NO!" I was putting my foot down. This had gotten ridiculous. "I am just fine. No one needs to walk me to and from class or stay with me. You all live in the same building. If I need you, all I have to do is yell or pound on the floor. Not that I'm going to need anyone."

Jason started to argue with me but Quinn stopped him. "Jason," he held up one hand and Jason stopped talking but didn't let up on his hold of me. "If Sylvia doesn't want us to stay or help, I'm sure that her dad, Kelly, would come up if we called him."

Goddamned overprotective asshole. He knew just how I would respond to that. If Dad even thought that I was in danger, he would drop everything to come up here. He would probably drag me back home to Quarry Springs and lock me up; just to make sure I was safe.

Jason -- the traitor -- responded to Quinn with a conspiratorial grin. "Kelly may be better to deal with this. We should call him." I knew from the calculated tone of voice they were using, that they were just trying to get me to agree with what they wanted. Although I had a feeling that if I didn't, they just might call him.

"Fine! Don't call my dad. There is nothing he needs to worry about. You can sleep on my old cramped couch instead of your big comfy bed for a couple nights for no reason. It's your body." I shrugged, still upset, but I tried to pass it off as if I didn't care.

"What, Sylvia? You're not going to let me sleep in your bed?" I knew Jason was finally past the little crush he had on me, but he still made comments like this every chance he got. I felt Quinn bristle beside me. I worried that he was going to believe Beau, and think that I'd slept with every guy I knew.

I rolled my eyes at Jason. "The only way you'll be sleeping in my bed is if I fall asleep on the couch first."

"Sweet. Then I can carry you to bed." He winked at me. I stuck my tongue out at him and stood up.

Quinn sat there tensely, looking from Jason to me, trying to decipher if we were joking. Jason stood up, too, and said he was just going to run home to get stuff and he would be back. He left with Sloane. Kai pulled me over to her by the door.

"Call me later. I want to know what's up with the details." She whispered to me.

"Whatever," I answered her. Like she didn't already know that he stayed and obviously nothing happened. "Goodbye, Kai." I opened the door for her.

"Talk to ya later, Sylvia. Goodbye, Quinn." She gave a wave and went out the door.

I came back around the front of the couch. "You guys don't need to be doing this. Nothing will happen." I glared down at Quinn.

He pushed back against the couch, reaching up to rake his hands through his hair. He ran through it twice and stopped midway through the second pass and just pulled on it a little bit. That was a common sign of sheer frustration on his part. He turned those penetrating eyes on me and huffed. "Sylvia, you're right. We don't *need* to be doing this. We *want* to be doing this. Did you hear nothing we said?" I looked at the floor guiltily. "We all hope that nothing will happen. That would be great if last night was the last any of us see of him. We just want to make sure of that. We're your friends, Sylvia. We don't want to see you hurt. If that means taking unnecessary precautions, then so be it. We will do that. You would do the same for any of us. Now stop pouting about it and deal with it."

Wow. My eyes flashed to his face as the last of the words came out. Even though the words sounded harsh Quinn had the tiniest bit of a smirk on his face. God, he was handsome when he did that. Tired eyes and all, he still made me melt.

"Alright, but only for a couple days," I agreed hesitantly.

"Only if he leaves you alone," Quinn said sternly.

"Whatever," I grumbled as I sat back down and picked up the glass of juice and the remote. I turned the TV on so I wouldn't have to have and more serious conversations with Quinn. I had enough flipping through my head. I didn't need any more added to it.

My phone buzzed, alerting me to a text. I reached for my phone. It was from Beau. Quinn was watching me. I briefly debated on whether or not to read it. If I didn't, he would know who it was from. If I did, he would ask me about it. Either way he'd figure it out. I opted to check it.

```
Sylvia plse plse call back - B
```

"What does he want?" Quinn asked in a cold voice.

"He just wants me to call him." I met Quinn's eyes with mine. "I'm not going to, so calm down."

I looked at the text list. Six of the nine unchecked were from Beau. I opened them all; starting at the earliest one which was sent in what I assumed was less than an hour after he left.

```
Sylvia we r not done yet call me - B

Sylvia stop being a bitch call me - B

Im srry call me - B

I just need 2 tlk 2 u - B

he doesnt care 4 u like I do - B

I need 2 c u plse - B
```

"Are there more?" I nodded and deleted them as I read them.

"He just wants to talk to me. If I just ignore them, he'll stop." Quinn just looked at me.

I ignored him, too, and watched TV. He sat there quietly next to me for a few minutes. "Sylvia, I'll just be across the hall if you need me. If you ever want to talk, I will be there for you. Anytime." He reached for my hand and just held on to it.

I squeezed his hand. "I know you are. Thank you." I leaned over and hugged him and Jason came walking back in.

I pulled away and Quinn glared at him. "Don't you ever knock?"

"Not at Sylvia's. Don't you ever just stay away?" Jason glared back.

I jumped up and immediately felt my head start pounding again. Stupid fucking moonshine. "Just stop it, you two. I don't need your bullshit right now. Jason, go put your stuff over there and Quinn, I will talk to you later. Thank you for helping me last night and this morning." I heard Jason huff.

"Bye, Sylvia. Remember what I told you. I meant it. All of it." His eyes were serious and his voice was soft. He left and I just watched the door, half hoping he would come back for something.

"What did he tell you?" Jason sounded suspicious.

"Seriously, Jason it was nothing. He just told me he would be here to help if Beau came back." I'd never kept things from Jason before, but this just wasn't something I wanted to share. I needed to figure myself out first.

"I need a nap. Just...do whatever. I'm going to sleep." I knew Jason was watching me. I picked up my phone and headed down the hall. I didn't need Beau to text or call and have Jason answer it. And he would answer it. The kid had no boundaries. I turned my phone off once I was in my room. I didn't want to hear from anyone right now.

I laid there with my head pounding, wishing I could sleep. My head was all sorts of messed up. I didn't want everyone else to know it, but I did have a tiny fear that Beau wasn't done. I figured at some point I would need to talk to him. I planned to tell him it was over, to not call, not text, and just forget about me. I just hoped he would, and would leave my friends alone, too. It wasn't like we'd dated long enough for him to get psycho over me. It was just me anyway. There is no way he would even feel that way about me. I wasn't the kind of girl guys went crazy over.

Crazy. What was crazy was what Quinn had told me. How could he still have feelings for me? I guess truthfully I still did for him, too. I just was so confused about it all. At one point in my life, he was all I ever wanted or needed. Was he still? Could he be again? What if it ended badly again? Could I do this? Did I want to? I just didn't know how to answer.

I thought about how it felt waking up with him. I felt safe and happy in his arms. The way he felt against me. He was warm and hard. He was definitely hard. I smiled at the memory of the morning. I knew I wanted him in my bed, but was I ready for him in my life? What if he was confusing lust with love, too? What if I fell for him again and it wasn't real for him? I didn't know if I could survive that again. I knew I needed to forget about it and just let whatever would happen, happen. I just didn't know if I was ready for it.

Chapter 16 - Quinn

I HATED LEAVING HER THERE with him. Jason Bratt: the guy who made Sylvia smile again. His opinion of me was so blatantly obvious. He didn't like me, didn't want me there, and wanted me nowhere near Sylvia. He kept his arm around her the whole time. She could barely move. Every so often I could see him glowering at me. He was so juvenile, with his ridiculous display of over-protectiveness. I was surprised he even left her there alone with me while he ran home. At least he played along with me threatening to tell Kelly.

I wanted to go downstairs and talk to Sloane, but I needed a shower before I went to see what he thought about Beau. I knew everyone in the room was holding back on their true thoughts about the situation with him. Sylvia wanted to play it down, and if we tried to push her and take too much control from her she would push back and probably end up hurt. I needed to make sure she was safe, but do it from a distance. I couldn't do it alone. I wanted to see if those guys were on the same page as I was. We would need to figure out a plan that would keep Sylvia from being suspicious. Fortunately, she was such a bad liar that she would believe anyone who was even passably good.

I turned the water on hot and waited. Once the room was steamy I got in. I tilted my head back and let the water run down over my face. I thought about Sylvia and how she looked in my shirt as she stood in her bathroom door. I would have liked nothing more than to have followed her into the shower. I raised my head straight and shook the water off my face. I grabbed the soap and rubbed it between my hands. I pictured her pulling me into the room with her, biting her bottom lip with her eyes all half-lidded.

I thought of her standing under the spray. The water would be dripping down her. I pictured a drop running down her cheek, dripping onto her collar bone and down the center of her chest. I wanted to bend down and start right between her breasts and lick the same path as the drop. Once I got to her jaw I would work my way over to her lips. I thought about how warm she would be pulled against me. I'd hitch her leg over my hip and push us back until her back was against the shower wall. She would already be wet but I'd still use my fingers just to feel her warmth and wetness on them. Then I would slide in as I pulled her down onto me. I imagined Sylvia moaning against my lips as we kissed. I loved watching her come. I pictured her face, head tilted back, eyes closed, her lips slightly parted. It was so good to have Sylvia back in my life. I let out a harsh chuckle. *At least now I had new images of Sylvia and not ones of her from high school.*

I quickly finished with my shower, threw my clothes back on, and headed down to Sloane's. I could hear Reed talking from the hallway, so I knew he was already there. I knocked and they told me to just come in. I looked around the room when I walked in and noticed they were all there, including Jason. I didn't see Sylvia. I was concerned that she'd changed her mind and didn't want our help.

"Where's Sylvia?" Everyone in the room turned to look at Jason.

"What? I told you all already -- she's napping. I locked the door when I left..."

"You left her alone? What the fuck were you thinking?" I stepped closer to Jason. I couldn't believe that he would leave her alone.

"It's not like we aren't all right here if she needs us." Jason was defensive.

"That's it. We're here, she's up there." I motioned to the ceiling. "We can't exactly tell if he is up there or not."

Jason bristled at me. "Sylvia will call us if he shows up. Then we just go up and make him leave." He stepped closer to me.

"And if she doesn't?" Knowing Sylvia's stubborn streak, I wasn't entirely sure Sylvia would let us know.

Jason scoffed and rolled his eyes. "Why wouldn't she? She's not dumb enough to let him into her place alone."

"Sylvia is definitely not dumb. Trusting -- yes. It wouldn't surprise me if she's already talked to him." My hands clenched and released as I stepped further into the room. I should have turned around and gone back up-stairs to Sylvia, not argued about it with Jason. Obviously he didn't know her as well as he wanted me to believe if he thought that Sylvia wouldn't think she could handle this.

"She hasn't even heard from him yet," Jason threw me an over confi-dent smirk.

"Except for the texts he sent last night and today." I couldn't help myself and smirked back.

His eyes narrowed and his voice lowered. "What texts?"

I was pleased that Sylvia shared that with me and not him. "When you went home, Sylvia got a text from him. After that she checked her phone. She had several texts from him. She just said he wanted to talk to her, but from the look on her face I think she was leaving something out."

"Did she answer him?"

"Not that I am aware of. She told me she wasn't going to call him."

He took a couple more steps closer until he was right in my face. "So what do you want me to do, take her phone? Treat her like she's a child? That's what you would do, isn't it?" I wondered when our past was going to come up.

"This has nothing to do with that," I tried to keep my voice calm. The tension in the room increased and everyone was looking at us.

"Then why are you even here? Why are you involved in this?" Jason's glare turned colder. "Why did you spend the night with her?"

That's what his problem was? I'd spent the night with Sylvia. "I stayed to keep her safe. I was there as her friend."

"Is that what it was when everyone was gone a couple weeks ago? Were you just being her friend then?" So Sylvia told him about staying with me that weekend. I wasn't completely sure if she had. I wondered how much she had told him.

I needed him to stop talking. As far as I knew only Sloane was aware that she had stayed with me the whole weekend. I didn't want Jason giving out more than Sylvia wanted people to know about. We certainly didn't need a repeat of the previous night's confessions.

We were toe to toe, glaring at each other. I was so focused on Jason that I missed Kerrington walk past him. I tore my eyes from Jason's to see what had just swished down between us. It appeared to be a short, wooden ruler. I flicked an annoyed glance over to a smirking Kerri.

"Whip 'em out boys. We'll measure them right here and now." I assumed from the amused look in Kerri's eye that Jason was wearing a similar look of astonishment. She arched one brow as she waited a beat to add, "That's what I thought. So quit verbally measuring and let's get Sylvia taken care of."

Reed laughed loudly. "Kerri would be disappointed in you both, anyway. Let's get this done with so I can watch the rest of the game." With that, the tension in the air relaxed.

I spotted Kai mouthing, "I told you so," to Sloane as she grinned like the Cheshire cat. She had that damn all-knowing look in her eyes. I was really beginning to hate that look.

Barely under an hour later, I was on my way back to my place. Kai knew Sylvia's class schedule, so it was fairly easy for us to coordinate our schedules to hers. I was happy that Jason had classes at different times and would only be able to meet with her a couple days for lunch. It was something they did often anyway. Jason even called someone named Colby who was able to meet with her after a few classes and walk with her to her next one. He was a freshman and had the easiest schedule. Kerri had most of the other times. I didn't know this Colby kid, but the fact that Reed and Sloane were okay with him reassured me that it would be all right. If he was as big as Jason I knew Sylvia would be all right. Jason was big guy. He was damn near as big as Reed.

I was going to go back to walking with her three mornings a week. I was looking forward to that. Unfortunately, my first class was too far from her next one to be able to walk her there and then make it back to mine. I was able to meet with her two days for lunch, though, and a couple other times after classes.

The only problem we could think of was what to do while she was at work. The bookstore was a pretty big place and had a few different exits. We wouldn't be able to cover all of them all of the time. I didn't like it, but knew Jason was right when he said we would just have to trust Sylvia to take care of herself. Sylvia wouldn't allow a scene to be made at work, but then there would be plenty of people around to keep Beau from trying anything. Kai was going to call a couple of the girls that she was mutual friends with through Sylvia and give them a heads up.

I was outside my door when I heard Jason come up the stairs behind me. "Quinn." I turned to see what he wanted. He stopped right in front of me. "She's tougher than you think. And she's been through worse." I knew he was referring to my leaving. The glint in his eye and the tilt of his chin challenged me. "I won't let you hurt her again. I can see that the others are okay with you being around, but I'm not."

"Get used to it, 'cause I'm not going anywhere." I lowered my voice to match his. "I made the biggest mistake of my life leaving her. I'm not going to do it again. As long as she wants me, I'm here. And I intend to do everything I can to make her want me here."

I didn't wait to see if he had more to say. I reach back for the knob and opened my door. I stepped backwards inside and abruptly turned, leaving Jason standing there as I shut the door in his face. I wasn't going to let Jason Bratt get under my skin. I had enough to deal with about Sylvia. I didn't need to start anything with him. For whatever reason, he was Sylvia's best friend. If there were any more to her feelings for him, she would have acted on them before now. Even with my reasoning, I was still jealous that he was staying with her and I wasn't.

I didn't bother calling or texting Sylvia the rest of the night. I attempted to study. I let her have her time with Jason and gave her space on whether or not she called Beau back. I thought I caught sight of his truck parked along the street that our balconies faced. It was far enough away that I wasn't sure if it was his.

I walked Sylvia to class the next morning. We met out in the hall like we used to, before she started leaving early. She looked tired. Her eyes were puffy and looked a little unfocused. She didn't appear to be upset with me walking her to class, though.

"Good morning, Sylvia." Her smile greeted me.

"Hi, Quinn." I followed her down the steps to the door. I caught my-self thinking of walking her to class in high school. We'd had our first hour together senior year and I'd walked with her from my car to class every morning. There had been a few too many mornings where we'd rushed in right after the bell, earning us trips to the office for tardy slips. And one time...well let's just say the detention was worth it.

"What are you smirking at this morning?" Sylvia's voice was quiet yet amused.

"I was just thinking how this feels like senior year all over again."

Sylvia shook her head and masked her face in perfect parody of Senora Martinez. "*Senor Lobato y Senorita O'Mara llega tarde de nuevo. Informe a la oficina.*" We both fell into easy laughter about the phrase we were all too familiar with.

"How many times do you think we were sent to the office by her that year?" I mused once the laughter died down.

"Thirty-seven, not counting the detention," Sylvia said, still giggling a little. My eyes widened. Did she really know the number? She blushed. She did know.

"Thirty-seven, huh?" I quirked an eyebrow at her.

"What? I know, okay? I had thirty-seven tardies my senior year and six point five missed days. It said so on my final report card and I had to explain the tardies and half day to my dad." Her voice was still full of amusement. "It was a good thing you were already gone 'cause he was about..." Sylvia trailed off and looked away.

I sucked in a big breath and put my finger tips to her cheek and gently turned her face to look at me. I looked into those beautiful jade eyes and my heart constricted. "Sylvia," I let all the air rush out ending her name in a sigh. "I would spend the rest of my life making it up to you if you would let me." I whispered it to her and brushed her cheek with the back of my knuckles.

She minutely shook her head. I knew it was still too soon for her. I didn't regret saying it though. She needed to know that I meant it when I told her I loved her. She sighed and turned to look up the path and started back up it. I followed along with her. Neither of us said anything all the way to her class. One minute she was walking alongside me and the next she was headed towards the door of her building. I wasn't worried though. She would come around. I hoped.

Late that afternoon, I got a text from Sloane that said when Sylvia and Kerri walked up to Sylvia's place there was a rose outside her door with a note that said "Sorry." I called Sloane after my class and he said no one had seen Beau anywhere around. Kai confirmed that he had tried to call Sylvia again, but Sylvia was still refusing to talk him. Jason was due back at the apartment any time, so I just told Sloane to keep me updated.

The rest of the week went about the same. Sylvia received a few calls and texts from Beau, but she never called him back. A few of us thought we saw him near the parking lot or along the back street. None of us could confirm for certain that it was him. Sylvia and I walked between classes a few more times. Each time there was tension between us. Gone was the easy air we had that first morning. We talked of upcoming projects for our classes and about some of our professors. Of course, the antics of our mutual friends was always a good topic. Both of us avoided what was really right there between us. It was tangible by the last time. It was as if it were a third person walking with us that spoke to us, but we were making a conscious effort to ignore him and continue to speak over him.

On Friday, I opened my door to find Beau standing on the stairs. I stiffened immediately. Our eyes locked and I wondered if it was finally going to be the day I had been waiting for.

Beau smirked at me. "What, are you walking her to class again, pretty boy? Are you going to carry her books, too?"

"You're not welcome here," I answered him with ice in my voice. "Just go now and there won't be any trouble."

As he chuckled, his face twisted and the bright splotches of light coming through the big window over the stairs made his face appear to melt. He stepped forward and walked up to Sylvia's door and knocked. He was daring me to make the first move. I dropped my bag down and loosened my arms. Before I did anything else Jason called out, "Sylvia said to go without her today." He opened the door still talking. "Her class isn't meeting..." His face went hard when he saw Beau. "What are you doing here?"

He glanced up over Beau's shoulder and looked at me. I felt the adrenaline pumping. The rush of it made my stomach tighten. I was ready for this. I just wanted him to give me the reason.

"I want to talk to Sylvia," Beau said it more politely than I thought him capable of. "I know she's home. I just have a couple things to say to her."

"Look, Beau, Sylvia doesn't want to see you right now." Jason met my eyes. I suspected that he was being quiet because Sylvia was awake and he didn't want to alert her. "I'm sure Sylvia will call you when or if she is ready to talk to you. Until then, just give her space."

"Look, kid," I could hear the sneer in Beau's voice. "Why don't you just step aside and let me talk to her."

I was ready to speak up when Sylvia walked in to view. "Beau?" I couldn't make out her face but I could hear the surprise in her voice.

Beau stepped to the side of Jason so he could see Sylvia, effectively cutting off my view of her. "Sylvia, I need to talk to you."

Jason stepped back into the apartment. I wasn't sure if he planned to just shut the door or what. Sylvia put her hand on Jason's arm stopping him from doing anything. "What do you want to say, Beau?"

He looked from Jason and back to me. "I would prefer to do it alone." His smirk in my direction spoke volumes of his confidence that Sylvia would tell us to leave.

"Why, Beau? You seemed just fine talking in front of my friends last weekend. Anything you have to say can be said in front of them now." *That's right, Sylvia, call him out on it.* I stepped closer as Beau moved past her doorway.

His voice was low and I had trouble hearing him. It sounded as if he told her he was sorry. I was to the door and Jason had stepped away from it and put his arm around Sylvia. *That's right, Jason, pull her out of the way.* I slowly crept forward, aware of my surroundings yet still focusing on Beau.

Sylvia spoke in a flat voice. "Beau, just leave. I don't have anything to say to you right now. I don't care if you are sorry. This is over."

"Sylvia, please." His voice wavered and I thought for the briefest second that he was sorry. Sylvia kept her face stony. Beau threw his shoulders back and looked from Jason to me and back to Sylvia. "Sylvia, when you get away from your keepers, give me a call."

Surprisingly, he turned to leave. His eyes met mine as he walked past. They held a calculating look that made the hair on the back of my neck stand up. I wasn't sure what game he was now playing, but I knew there was no way he was giving up this easily. Jason and I both watched him retreat down the steps before we turned back to Sylvia.

I walked over and picked up my bag before I stepped in and shut her door.

"Quinn, I don't have class, so just go without me," she said.

I looked over at Jason, who said, "I have to leave soon to meet up in the library for my group project."

"It's okay. I can stay." I was rather pleased with these turn of events.

Sylvia furrowed her brow and looked concerned. "I'm just fine. You don't need to skip classes for me."

"I'm not missing anything. I don't have class for another hour."

Sylvia's face changed from concern to confusion. "Where do you go then when we leave together in the morning?" Oh, yeah. That. "Wait. If you don't have class, then why do you leave that early?"

I tried to keep my face from showing how guilty I felt. I didn't want to tell her that I left that early as an excuse to see her every day. I absolutely didn't want to confess that to her in front of Jason. I figured the best answer was at least mostly truthful. "I go get coffee or go to the library."

She glared at me briefly before she sighed. I wasn't sure what she was thinking but at least she didn't seem pissed about it.

Jason spoke up before she could say anything. "I need to get going. Syl, you gonna be okay? I can see if Kai or Kerri are home."

"Jason, just go. I'm fine. Kai and Kerri don't need to come babysit me. You saw for yourself that he isn't going to do anything. Besides that, Quinn's here, so I'm not alone." Sylvia and Jason stared at each other for a few minutes, communicating some silent message that neither seemed too interested in sharing with me.

Jason strode across the room and picked his stuff up off the table. He went over to Sylvia and gave her a hug. It was clearly for my benefit. Sylvia half-heartedly hugged back, looking a little surprised. "Just call me if you need me to come back. I can make some excuse to the group and be back."

Sylvia rolled her eyes and pushed him towards the door. "Go. You need all the help you can get with your grades. You can't afford to screw up with this project."

Jason didn't say anything. He just glared at me as he passed by. When he was gone, I walked over and helped Sylvia fold up the blankets Jason left lying on her couch. I knew she told him that he would be sleeping on the couch, but the evidence that he actually did made my day. Sylvia and I made small talk as we finished clearing the couch.

"Did you eat yet this morning?" Sylvia asked as she took the blankets down the hall.

I found myself following behind her. I just wanted to be near her. She was wearing the old Quarry Springs High sweats again with a white t-shirt, and I was fairly certain she wasn't wearing a bra. She still had wet hair, so I figured she must have just finished her shower when Beau came to the door.

"Kind of," I answered her with a shrug.

"What kind of answer is that? Yes or no. Did you eat?"

She placed the blankets on a chair in her room and I stood in the door-way, looking around. Even though I had been in it before, had even spent the night in it, I hadn't really looked at it. Of course it was the same layout as mine. Her walls were the original white. Sylvia's room was simple. It wasn't near as small as hers room back home had been. She had the basic bed and dressers with bed-side tables. All were mismatched. None of it had been hers from before. The walls had several pictures hanging up. Some I could tell were her parents. The others I couldn't quite make out from where I was standing. I moved closer to get a better look, and real-ized that most were of her friends here. A couple I assumed were friends she knew through Jason. There were four boys in them, one of which was Jason. Most looked to be about the same age, but one was much younger.

Sylvia came up behind me. I watched as her tiny hand came up to the frame and she began to point and name people. She was close enough that I could smell her, all sweet and clean the scent of shampoo and soap and her. She started with Jason, so I nodded my head. She went around to each face, stopping at the youngest. "That's Colby. You'll probably get to meet him soon. He's the pup of the group. In fact, there's a good chance that he's going to end up being my step-brother." I heard what sounded like a bit of hope in her voice. I turned to look at her. She had a soft smile on her lips and a happy glint in her eye. "Dad has been dating his mom, Shelly, for a while now. He doesn't think I know. I'm planning on getting it out of him at Thanksgiving."

"Kelly's dating someone?" I shouldn't have been as surprised as I was. "Has he ever dated anyone before?" I tried to think back, but I only remembered Kelly doing things with a friend named Brad or going fishing.

"No, I think Shelly is the first since my mom died. He met her through Jason's dad. Not sure how they got together, but Colby told me all about it one weekend when I went home with Jason."

"And how do you feel about having a step mom?" She seemed to be okay, but I wanted to hear what she had to say about it.

"Shelly's great. And honestly, if Dad's happy, then I'm happy." It was a typical Sylvia answer. "So what about breakfast? Did you have any?"

I looked back at the picture, and briefly wondered if the kid in the picture would someday be my family, too. Without even having met him, I hoped he would be.

"Yes. Breakfast sounds great. I had pop tarts around six when I got up to work on pharmacology stuff. Like I would ever pass up a chance to eat whatever you make." I gave her the smile that I knew always used made her weak in the knees. I did an internal fist pump when her eyes focused on my mouth, and she bit her bottom lip and blushed a light pink. *Good to know that still has an effect on her.*

Sylvia made us stuffed French toast. She even made mine with peanut butter instead of cream cheese and jelly. We talked about our plans for Thanksgiving break. It was only a couple weeks away. I was happy to hear that Sylvia was going home with Kelly. I knew that everyone else had plans to be gone for the week. I didn't want her here alone and I knew that she would be safe going to Kelly's. I helped her clean up, and suggested she go get ready for class. I planned on walking her to her class and then going to mine. I would be late but I didn't care today.

While she was changing her clothes I looked out her balcony door. The pick-up was there again. I was sure it was Beau, watching her. It made me nervous to think of him out there. I tried to anticipate his next move, but there were just too many options. The only thing I could do was keep Sylvia close.

I stepped away from the window and went to get my bag that I'd left next to the couch. Sylvia came out and was all ready to go. She had changed into a pair of jeans and a tight-fitting long sleeved t-shirt. I had simultaneous urges to cover her up and stare at her chest. Afraid of doing either I turned away and headed to the door. She grabbed a hoodie and we left for class.

Chapter 17 - Sylvia

STUPID JASON. HE WAS SUPPOSED to wait for me and give me a ride home for Thanksgiving break. Did he wait? No, he had to go back early with Colby. Stupid boys skipped class just so they could be home early and party. Who parties on a Wednesday night anyway? I only left four hours later. Really, they could have waited for me. I'd been on the road for awhile, in fact I was over half way to Quarry Springs, but I was still all mumbly and grumbly, and I knew it.

I only skipped one class, and that was to take Kai and Sloane to the airport. At least Kai let me borrow her car for the break. I suppose Jason would have waited for me if I didn't have Kai's car. There would have been no other way for me to get home otherwise. I really needed to get myself a car. I had some savings after working all summer. Maybe I could find a car with that.

For now, I was driving home to Quarry Springs in a very posh car. Kai had all the add-ons. I loved driving her car. I hated the bright blue "look at me" color, but I loved the heated seats. At least I didn't have to listen to Jason all the way back. I was getting seriously sick of that boy. I get it. He didn't like Quinn. His non-stop complaints about him were really starting to grate on me. You would think he was more concerned about me getting back together with Quinn than he was about Beau.

I would love for Jason to just go home but it wasn't likely since Beau had still been calling and texting and Quinn pointed out that he was watching me from the street. I sent him a text on Monday telling him to stop trying to contact me. I hadn't heard from him since. I hoped he'd finally gotten the hint, but Quinn doubted it. He was sure that something was going to happen. I just wanted my life back. I wanted Jason to leave. I needed some time to myself.

I had been looking forward to the drive back. Three solid hours, all alone. It gave me plenty of time to think about things. I knew the time with my dad would be good, too. I missed him. I hadn't seen him since this summer. I planned to tell him that Quinn was back in my life. I didn't know exactly how he was in my life, but he was there. I wasn't about to tell him anything about Beau, other than I broke it off with him. I didn't need him getting all overprotective, too. He would probably send me back with pepper spray or something.

I smiled, thinking of Dad. Dad was a big gruff man. Often intimidating to most, he didn't ever say much but when he did he was loud and commanding. He had the typical Irish look that I inherited -- the red hair and green eyes. He took it very hard when mom died. He did all he could for her. I was so young when she was first diagnosed. She went through all the treatments and we thought it was gone only to be told two years later it was back and it was at a stage four and spreading. There was nothing we could do but enjoy the time we had left with her. It was so hard. Dad tried to keep up the smiles and act like everything was okay. I played his game too. I hoped that it helped mom. I never wanted her to see just how much we were hurting too, she already had too much of her own pain to deal with.

As hard as it was for both of us once she was gone it was almost a relief. Still, it was hard for us to stay there in that house, in that town. Too many expressed their condolences on a daily basis and all it did was remind us of what we had lost. Then one of dad's old friends from his hometown called and said they had openings on the police force there. We decided together that the change would be good for us. Dad still owned Grandma O'Mara's home. It was the one he had grown up in. We moved there and attempted to start over. All in all it had been a good move for us.

I liked taking care of my dad. I had been doing it for as long as I could remember. It always made me feel that it was the least I could do for him since he tried so hard to give me a normal life. This year I was planning to make us a big Thanksgiving meal. I hoped he would invite Shelly and her kids. Even if he didn't, I was still going to get him to confess to dating her. I had three whole days with him. I was sure I could get him to break at some point. Maybe I should just invite them over myself. I giggled a bit at the idea. Yeah, I could do that. If they couldn't come on Thursday I could ask them all over on Friday. Maybe then Brad and Jason could come. They were going to Jason's grandmas on Thursday but I didn't think they had plans for Friday. That's what I would do. There would be plenty of leftovers, and I could make us all a big meal on Friday night.

Now I just needed to keep Jason's big mouth shut about Beau. Dad didn't know that Jason had been staying with me. I could just see Jason making some bone-head comment about it and dad picking up on it. Even worse he could say something about Quinn. I knew how Dad felt about him. He had always gotten along fairly well with him while we were dating. As far as he knew or cared to know it was all innocent between Quinn and I. To his credit Dad never once said anything bad about Quinn leaving. I knew he was worried about me and was very unhappy with Quinn but at the same time I always wondered if he wasn't slightly pleased that I was no longer involved with a boy.

I thought about Quinn and how wonderful he had been lately. Oh, I was still annoyed with his constant worrying about Beau, but I knew he was doing it because he cared about me. We had been getting along extremely well these past couple weeks. Ever since the day Beau showed up. There was some turning point there. I couldn't put my finger on just what it was, but something was different with us. I spent a great deal of time with him after that.

Whenever Jason was gone I opted to hang out with Quinn more than Kai or Kerri. Sure I still saw them, too. I just preferred to be with Quinn. We would quietly study or watch TV together. I had started to teach him how to cook. It was nothing fancy -- just some basic things -- but it was so much fun working in the kitchen with him. We had even gone grocery shopping together. There was just something comfortable being with him. I didn't know how I ever thought I could live without him.

I thought I was getting over him, but now that he was back I could see that I wasn't ever really over him. I thought about him every day. There was always some little reminder that would bring his face to my mind. I would feel a little blast of pain in my heart every time I thought of him. It felt as if it were an egg being cracked against a bowl, just a quick crack and it was over. I knew my heart had never healed properly. But now, with him back in my life, it was starting to feel as if it were becoming whole once again.

I rounded another curve and realized the turnoff for our abandoned farm was up ahead. I made the snap decision to turn off. I hadn't been on this road in years. I went once that first summer. I just needed something to hold on to. It was so painful I could never do it again. I pulled in and parked on the dirt path. It was too dark to actually see much. So I sat there and looked at the trees surrounding the path. I couldn't see our normal parking spot from where I was, but I could close my eyes and see it. I remembered perfectly what it was like.

The images fluttered behind my closed lids. The soft green grass splattered with little wildflowers in the late spring and summer. The trees and rundown buildings circling it, casting shadows across the ground. The sun shining in the middle like a spotlight. And Quinn. Always Quinn. His smile dazzling me and his eyes, the deep brown pools, shining with love and clouding with lust. I remembered his touch. The way he made me feel so alive, so beautiful, and so loved.

My eyes flew open when I realized I wanted that back. I had seen that look on his face a few times in the past several weeks. At the time I'd ignored it. I didn't want to see it. It hurt to see it because it made me remember what once was. I hadn't thought about what could be. Quinn still looked at me like maybe he really had never gotten over me. I thought back to his confession the morning after Halloween. He told me he loved me. That he had never stopped loving me. He said he was empty all those years apart, too.

I felt the warm wet trail of tears as they slid down my cheeks. The past couple weeks had been so good. I wanted to be with him as much as possible. I craved his company. When we were apart, I missed him. He was the first person I thought of when I wanted to share how my day was. Quinn was the one I wanted to whine to when things weren't going right. It was his laugh I wanted to hear when I thought of something funny. It was his arms I wanted to hold me. It was him, and I knew it had always been him.

Quinn had told me he knew now wasn't the right time but he would wait for me. I didn't want to wait anymore. There had been way too much time lost already. I smiled and wiped the tears away. I was done thinking about it. My decision was made. For better or worse I belonged to Quinn and I would risk my heart for him.

My phone buzzed alerting me to a new text. I was still leery when it came to checking my messages. I sighed and checked it. Thankfully, it was just Kai.

We just landed. Take care of my car. Be safe. -K

I rolled my eyes.

Don't worry about me just have a good time with
Sloane and his family. - S

Almost immediately after sending it another came in from her.

```
"The bad things in life open your eyes to the good
things you weren't paying attention to before." - K
```

I let Kai's message float through my mind. I wasn't sure why she was quoting *Good Will Hunting* to me. I had no idea what she was referring to. Was it regarding Beau and our breakup, or was it Quinn coming back? Maybe it wasn't either of those, but something entirely different. I was still puzzling it out when my phone sang out in Dad's ring tone.

"Hi, Dad."

"Hey Syly-girl. How far out are you? I'm just getting done with work and I thought I would pick us up a pizza so you wouldn't have to cook tonight."

I smiled at my Dad's thoughtfulness. "Thanks, Dad. That's a good idea. I'm about ten minutes away."

"Well, drive safe, and I'll see you at home."

We said our goodbyes and hung up. I looked out at the darkness once more. Maybe someday Quinn and I would visit here again.

That night passed quickly. It was good to be home with Dad again, even though it always left me with a longing for my mom. He arrived just ahead of me. While we ate our pizza, I asked him about the plans for tomorrow. I decided it was time to put my plans into action.

"So I was thinking maybe you had someone you wanted to invite to dinner tomorrow." I watched him carefully. He just continued chewing while he shook his head.

After he swallowed, he answered, "No there really isn't anyone. Just you and me, Syl." He picked up his beer and I couldn't resist asking him.

"Really? So I shouldn't call and invite the Williams? I thought maybe this year Shelly would like to join us." I looked Dad in the eye with one brow cocked.

He sputtered on his beer and coughed.

I just laughed. "Yes, Dad, I know. Did you think you could keep it hidden?"

"I wasn't hiding anything." He looked down at the half-eaten piece of pizza on his plate, talking more to it than to me.

"Sure you weren't. That's why Colby had to tell me about it, and not my own father," I teased him playfully. It was fun to watch him squirm.

"Damn kids. Yes, I've been seeing Shelly. There, are you happy now that I told you?" He even had a hint of a blush.

I decided to let him off the hook. "Yes, Dad. I am very happy. I'm happy that you have someone on your life. Now about tomorrow, would you like to ask them?"

"Sorry to disappoint you, kid, but they already have plans. Some of their family is coming to town and Shelly is making a meal for them. I didn't know how you would feel about going so I turned down her offer to have us over."

"Well, Dad, if you want to go, we can."

"Then what do we do with the turkey I bought at your suggestion?"

"I could cook it and we could take it with," I suggested hopefully.

"No, Syl. I think we should just stay here. It's nice having you all to myself for awhile."

I was disappointed, but I didn't let him see it. "Well, maybe sometime while I'm home we could invite them over. If we did it Friday, Brad and Jason could come too."

"That's a fine idea. Now tell me, how are your classes going?"

We talked more about my classes and I filled him in on how the others were doing. Dad had been taken with Kai-ying since the first time he'd met her. He always asked after her. I finally caved and told him about Quinn moving in across the hall. As I suspected, he wasn't thrilled to hear about it. I spent a great deal of time reassuring him that I was fine with it and that we were getting along. I explained how Quinn got along with the others and that everything was truly all right.

I opted to go to bed when the news came on. I knew he would want to watch that in peace. I was tired anyway. There was always something comforting about being in my old room, in my old bed. When we first moved I had trouble sleeping. Everything was unfamiliar and the unfamiliar night sounds kept me up. Now it just made me drowsy as I laid there and relaxed. My phone buzzed and I reached over to check it.

I was just thinking of you. Hope all is well. Good night - Q

My heartbeat picked up, and I smiled. He had been thinking of me, too.

Everything's great. I was thinking of you too. Sweet dreams - S

I thought about telling him I stopped at the farm, but in the end I decided to keep it short and sweet. I waited a few minutes but he didn't reply back. I put my phone on the table and drifted off to sleep, thinking about the weekend I stayed with him.

I got up early the next morning to make a pie and get the turkey ready. Dad and I watched the Macy's parade together. When it was over, I went and took stock of the kitchen. I had sent Dad a list of things to get at the store, but he'd forgotten butter, of all things. Thankfully, the store was open until two.

I got in Kai's car, and picked up the butter and a couple other things that I thought we could use over the weekend. On the way back to the car, I had the oddest feeling. I just couldn't shake it. There weren't many people out, so I was surprised to see someone driving behind me. My heart dropped to my stomach and I became instantly nauseous when I recognized the face in my rear view mirror.

I momentarily panicked as my heart raced. I tried to calm myself by reminding myself that I was going home to Dad's and it would all be okay. I sped up and debated about trying to lose him. In the end, I knew it wouldn't do any good. Quarry Springs was so small all he had to do was drive around a bit and he would eventually see Kai's damn blue car out front and know exactly where to find me.

I regretted not telling Dad last night about breaking it off with Beau. I hadn't brought the subject up, and dad tended to stay away from the subject of boys. Beau knew my dad was a cop so I can't imagine he would start anything. I pulled up in front of the house and grabbed the bags and got out. I hoped to get to the house before he could talk to me.

Of course I wasn't fast enough.

"Sylvia," I heard him call out to me before he even shut his pickup off. I pretended I didn't hear him and he called it out louder as he ran to catch up to me. I stopped and turned to him.

"What are you doing here?" I hissed at him quietly. I didn't want to alert Dad if there was a chance I could just get him to leave.

"I needed to see you, but your goons are always around." His heavy lidded eyes were pleading with me.

"Beau, I have nothing to say to you." I turned to go towards the house but he grabbed my arm. I froze. "Let go before I scream," I said between clenched teeth. He immediately released me but he didn't step back.

"Please Sylvia just hear me out. I'm sorry. I was just jealous. Please, I need you in my life. I miss you. Sylvia, I…"

"Hey, kid, you need any help?" Dad was standing in the doorway. I breathed a sigh of relief. "Who's your friend?" He was eyeing Beau suspiciously.

"Dad, this is Beau, Beau Dalton. Beau, this is my dad, Deputy O'Mara." I wanted to remind Beau that my dad was in law enforcement.

Beau walked up the steps and held out his hand. "Hello, Deputy O'Mara. It's nice to finally meet you."

Dad shook his hand and looked over at me. I didn't know what to say.

"Thanks for letting Sylvia invite me to dinner today. I've been looking forward to it all week."

My eyes flew open. What the hell was that? Did he not realize any invitation I made was rescinded when I'd told him I had nothing to say to him?

"Sylvia?" My dad looked at me questioningly. "You didn't tell me we were having a guest."

"I didn't..." Beau cut me off before I could finish.

"I wasn't sure I would be able to make it. The last time Sylvia and I talked about it, I wasn't sure." Beau smiled triumphantly at me. I had two choices. I could play along with this and hope it was over quickly, or I could make a scene and get Dad worried about me. I had enough people in my life worried and watching my every move. I didn't need Dad doing it, too. I chose the former, praying that it was indeed the lesser of the two evils. At least I would be here with Dad.

Dad was still looking at me. I gave him a weak grin and a shrug. "I guess I'm setting one more plate."

We headed into the house. Dad went to his chair to watch the game and Beau followed him. I brought the groceries into the kitchen and put them away. I stood next to the sink and looked out at the back yard. My nerves were on edge. What the hell was he doing? I could hear him in the living room, chatting with Dad about the game.

I hid in the kitchen. At least I could blame my absence in the living room on needing to cook. I really wanted to call Quinn. The only thing that stopped me was the thought that he would probably insist on coming here right away. I didn't want to ruin his Thanksgiving. That would also leave me even more explaining to do with Dad when he showed up and the unquestionable showdown that was sure to take place between him and Beau if he did. I just fumed to myself and willed time to speed up.

Eventually the food was ready. I set the table and called them in to eat. Dad sat at the head of the table and I sat on his right side with Beau on his left. There was an awkward silence around us as we started to eat. I'm sure Dad could sense the tension between Beau and me. I didn't have anything to say, so I kept my mouth shut. Beau and Dad talked more about the game they had been watching.

"Sylvia, Curtis was asking about you. He wanted me to ask you to come out with us again sometime soon." Beau was smiling at me pleasantly.

I didn't know what to say to that. "I'm heading into a busy time now with classes." I answered to my food.

"Oh, I'm sure you can find time. You know what they say about all work and no play." He continued on like everything was sunny between us, and I hadn't been avoiding him for three weeks. "Sylvia, is this the same cranberry dish you made for me one night?" He was referring to my cran-apple salad.

I nodded.

"Deputy O'Mara, your daughter is an amazing cook. I'm sure you miss her cooking. She keeps me well-fed." Beau looked over at me and winked.

I didn't understand how he could be acting like this. I wanted to scream at him to just leave. Instead, I quietly pushed the food around on my plate. I had long since lost any appetite I'd had.

"Sylvia, is something wrong with your food?" Dad asked as he scooped up another helping of potatoes.

"No, I think I just taste-tested too much while I was making it."

"Sylvia, when should we go Christmas shopping? I found that place you were looking for that has the gift you wanted to get Kerri." What the hell was that? I never even mentioned a gift for her.

I looked up to see him grinning playfully at me. My eyes narrowed and I whispered, "I changed my mind about it. Kai and I are looking at something else."

"Sylvia, what are you getting for her?" Dad was still watching me. I figured he knew that Beau was the reason for my rude behavior but he didn't say anything.

"Kai suggested jewelry." I left it at that and stood up to get the pie.

Dad asked Beau a few questions about himself. Beau gave him a very edited version of his life. I brought the pie to the table and cut them each a slice with a generous amount of whipped cream. They talked a little about how boring stakeouts could be. I just tuned them out and watched the clock. It was only a little after five. I wondered how long Beau was going to stay.

When we were done eating, Beau offered to help me with the dishes. I didn't want to be in the same room with him, so I shooed him out with my dad. I took my time putting everything away and cleaning up in the kitchen. By the time I was done it was close to seven. I finally couldn't put it off any longer and joined the guys in the living room. There was nowhere else to sit so I sat next to Beau on the couch.

I still didn't initiate conversation with him. I answered his questions but stayed quiet. I could tell Dad was clued into something being wrong.

"Syl, didn't you say you wanted to call Kai and Kerri before it gets too late?" I smiled at him in relief.

"Yes, I should. Beau, this could take awhile and I'm sure you would like to be getting on the road soon. So I will say goodnight now." I looked at him, daring him to challenge me on this in front of Dad.

Beau eyed me for a few moments before saying, "You're right. I should be getting back. When are you returning to Minneapolis?" It figures he would ask that in front of Dad. There was no way I could get out of answering it.

"Sometime Sunday." Quinn was picking Kai and Sloane up from the airport at three and then getting Kerri and Reed at eight. I hoped to be back in time to see him before he went to get them.

"Well then I will see you when you get back." He stood up then. "Goodbye, Deputy O'Mara. It was nice to finally meet you. Thank you for sharing your Thanksgiving and your daughter with me."

Dad gave him a measured look. "Goodbye, Beau. Drive back safely."

I led Beau to the door. I was not going to walk him to his truck. I stopped at the door and held it open. He leaned in and quietly whispered, "See, Sylvia, we can make this work. I liked spending the day with you. Thank you for dinner. When you get back to Minneapolis and get rid of your watchdogs, call me." Then he leaned in to kiss me. I turned my head at the last minute and his lips contacted my cheek instead of my lips. He pulled back and glared at me. I met his icy stare with one of my own. "I'm sure once you have some time to think things through you will come around. Good night, beautiful."

He left then, and I shut the door behind him a little harder than I'd meant to. I leaned against it and looked over to see Dad leaned back in his recliner watching me.

"Everything okay there, Syl?" His voice was laced with concern.

"Yes, it's just fine."

"Anything you want to talk about?" *Yes, but not with you.*

"No, I think I'm just going to go call the girls and go to bed." I walked over to him and gave him a hug and kissed the top of his head.

"Sylvia, you know I'm here if you change your mind." I smiled at him. He was trying.

I nodded. "There's nothing to talk about. I love you. Good night."

He looked my face over carefully. "I love you, too, kid."

With that, I headed upstairs to call Kai and Kerri.

DAD CAME IN early after a long sleepless night. "Sylvia?"

"It's okay, Dad I'm up." I sat up pulling the covers back. He hung back by the door.

"Hey, kid, there are reports of a severe storm moving in this afternoon. It's supposed to last through the weekend. First freezing rain, then snow. I hate to cut your visit short, but it might be best if you head back early. I talked to Shelly and Brad, and the boys are going to head back this morning, too." I could see the sadness in his eyes. He had been looking forward to having me home as much as I had been looking forward to being home.

I huffed, "Sure Dad. I guess I'll just get my stuff together and take a quick shower."

"I'll see you downstairs then."

Dad left my room and I reached over for my phone. Beau had me concerned with the way he'd acted the day before. I didn't want to be home alone when I got back. I called Jason. I didn't tell him about Beau. I just asked when he was leaving. He said he didn't know yet, Colby was still asleep. I told him to call me when he knew.

I gathered my stuff up and took my shower. I had everything ready to go, so I went down to make us some breakfast. I started to get stuff out, but Dad stopped me when he came into the kitchen.

"You don't have to make me anything. I ate earlier. You should just get going before the roads get bad." Typical Dad always worried about driving conditions.

"Oh, okay. I'm going to make something for the road and then I will get going. Jason didn't know what time he and Colby were leaving yet. I had hoped to follow them, but I guess I can just go." I was a little annoyed. Not at Dad, just the whole situation.

"I'll go take your stuff out to the car."

I decided to let Quinn know I was on my way back.

```
There's a storm coming in and dad wants me to go
back early. Leaving soon. Will you be there when I
get back? - S
```

He answered immediately.

```
I'll be waiting at my place for you. Drive safe. - Q
```

I finished making a couple sandwiches and grabbed some pop. I put my jacket on and met Dad out by the car.

"You drive safe, kid. Little cars like this weren't made for bad weather."

I put my stuff in the passenger side and came around to hug him.

"I will, Dad. I love you. I'll call you when I get home." I broke off the hug and got in. He stood by my open door.

"Sylvia, if there is something wrong you can tell me." His green eyes so much like my own were questioning me.

"Dad, I'm fine. Everything is going to be just fine. I'll be back at Christmas and you'll see. We'll make up for this missed weekend." I smiled at him and prayed he would let it go.

"Love you, Syly." With that, he shut my door and I headed back to Minneapolis.

I had a quiet ride back. I thought about the differences between Quinn and Beau. I was so worried about a broken heart that I had put myself in danger of having way more than that broken. I had to tell Quinn about Beau showing up in Quarry Springs. I wondered if I would have to file a restraining order. I wasn't sure if I could do that, since he never actually hurt me or threatened me. I knew Dad would be able to tell me, but I didn't want to alarm him. I figured I could just Google it when I got back.

I also planned to send Jason back to his place. I'd had enough of him being there. If I got a restraining order, then Beau would have to stay away and there would be no need for Jason to stay anymore. If I was met with resistance I would ask Quinn if he would stay. I really wanted the time with him anyway. We had a lot to talk about since my revelation. I was ready for it. I fully believed that what I told Dad was the truth. Everything was going to be just fine. I turned the volume up and enjoyed the rest of the drive back as I counted down the minutes until I would see Quinn again.

True to his word, Quinn was waiting for me at his place when I got back. He helped me carry my stuff in and then we sat down and talked about our Thanksgivings. He told me about his. It made me miss Marie even more.

"I really want to see your mom soon."

Quinn smiled at that. "She wants to see you, too. In fact she's been waiting for that since she found out you lived here." He told me about Marie's plotting and how she chose his apartment because she knew I lived here. Part of me wanted to be upset with her meddling, but I just couldn't be. Her meddling brought Quinn back into my life.

I told Quinn how I'd gotten Dad to fess up about seeing Shelly. We laughed together when I told him that Dad even blushed about it. I figured I couldn't put it off any longer.

"Beau showed up Thursday." His eyes went wide and the grin disappeared. "He followed me home from the grocery store."

"And Kelly didn't kill him?" I shook my head. "Did you even tell Kelly?"

I looked away guiltily as I bit my lip, trying to figure out how to tell him about Beau coming in and all.

"Sylvia, you didn't tell him, did you?" His tone was judgmental.

"I didn't want to alarm him," I whispered.

"What if he'd done something to you? How alarmed do you think Kelly would be then? You know he just wants to keep you safe, too. He wouldn't be mad." My eyes filled with tears and I just nodded. I couldn't get any words around the lump in my throat. Quinn pulled me close and just held me. He smoothed down my hair and whispered quiet calming words to me.

When I felt like I could talk again I pulled away and told him all about how Beau ended up staying for dinner. His eyes were angry, but he didn't say anything. He just let me finish. I didn't tell him about the awkward conversation we had while we ate. When I was done, we discussed the possibilities of getting a restraining order. Quinn assured me that Beau didn't actually have to hurt me or threaten me to be able to get one.

"Sylvia, you need to tell your dad. He will find out about this. How do you think he will feel if he hears his daughter filed for a restraining order without telling him?" He was right. I knew it.

"I will call him. Crap! I forgot to call and tell him I was home." I got up to look for my cell phone. "I can't believe he hasn't called to find out what's taking me so long." I looked through my pockets and my purse, but I couldn't find my phone. Quinn ran out to Kai's car to see if I had left it in there.

When he came back empty-handed, I sat down on the couch to think about the last time I'd seen it. I realized it had been after Quinn's text. I'd put it on the counter while I made the sandwiches.

"I think I left it at my dad's." Great. Now I would have to drive back for it or have him mail it to me. "Can I use yours to call him?"

Quinn handed me his phone and I called dad. It rang until voicemail picked it up. I left him a message telling him my phone was there, and this was a number he could reach me at. It was after two and I hadn't heard from Jason yet either. I called him next. Jason and Colby were still on the road. Jason said it was starting to get bad out. I told him Quinn was here with me and to just go home. He argued but I held my ground. Finally, he gave in.

I hung up with Jason and yawned. Quinn smiled softly and wrapped an arm around me. "You're exhausted. Why don't you take a nap? I'll wake you when Kelly calls." I didn't really want to sleep yet. There was still more I wanted to tell him. I yawned again and agreed. I rested my head against Quinn's shoulder. He turned the TV on and soon I was out.

I woke up when I heard Quinn's cell phone go off. I sat up and blinked as I rubbed the sleep from my eyes. It was already fairly dark. I must have been out for a couple hours. I was trying to gauge the time when I noticed how still Quinn was beside me. I turned to face him and he was sheet white.

"You're sure? No, I can tell her. Where is he?" The hair on the back of my neck stood up and chills coursed through my body. Something was very wrong. "Thank you. No. Just call me." Then he ended the call.

He took a deep breath and pinched the bridge of his nose. He turned towards me and took my hands. His eyes were wet and full of pain. I could tell that he was fighting to keep his face controlled. *This was bad, very bad.* My heart was pounding and my stomach was rolling.

"Sylvia, that was Jason." He swallowed and continued. "He's at the hospital here in Minneapolis."

"What..."

Quinn held a hand up to stop me before reaching back down to take mine again. "It's not Jason. He's fine. Kelly and Brad were on their way here. Nobody knows why yet. They were in an accident. Brad is in ICU. Jason is with him." He squeezed my hands tighter and my heart screamed *NO!*

"Sylvia, Kelly didn't make it."

Chapter 18 - Sylvia

"**H**AS SHE CRIED YET?" I could hear the hushed tones of Jason and Quinn as they talked about me. I didn't even bother to look up from my book. At some point in the past few weeks, my friends had all taken to talking about me as if I were absent. I knew I should be mad about it, but I just couldn't find it in me. Right now I was doing everything I could just to make it through each day.

I continued to stare at the open book in my hands. I couldn't even tell you which book it was. It didn't matter. They were all the same right now. They were an escape. Not that I actually read any of them. The words on the pages were nothing more than black ants crawling across the pages. The books were my shield. When I held an open book, no one asked me if I was okay, if I wanted to talk, or if I needed anything. I'd had enough of those questions.

"No, but my dad said to just be patient. Everyone reacts to grief in their own way. Sylvia always works things out in her own mind before she lets others in. She's doing that now. Just let her process this in her own way." Quinn was beginning to show his frustration with the questions too, or maybe it was his frustration with me. He had spent day and night at my side and it was really wearing on him.

"It's been almost a month, and she hasn't cried since the night it happened?" Jason asked. Had it really been that long? All my days just seemed to blur together. I didn't hear anymore, I didn't want to hear anymore. I looked at the book, but all I saw was Dad's ashen face, lifeless and gone just like my mom's.

That was when I had stopped crying and let the numb soak in. That wasn't Dad there. It wasn't him on that table, it couldn't be him. I didn't want it to be him. I wanted Dad to remain warm, and thoughtful and comforting. I wanted him to be trustful yet worried. I wanted him alive like I'd left him. The body laying there was not my dad. The sobs slowed to nothing but a hiccup as I turned and walked from the room. I didn't know what Quinn said to the man in that cold, stark room. I just wanted to leave. There were things to be done and calls to be made.

Try as I might, that was still the vision I saw. I had to go identify the body and now that would always be the last image I had of him. There was no coffin and no viewing of the body at the funeral. Dad hadn't wanted any of that. It had been too hard on both of us with mom's funeral. In its place, there was a picture of him in a big frame on an easel with a plain, black urn sitting on a table next to it. That was all I remembered of that day. The fucking plain black urn that held my father.

It was all so sudden. With my mom I had time to prepare. Not that it was easy or that I wasn't sad when she passed away. I was just ready for it. Relieved even. I had been able to show her my love and say my goodbyes. I knew that last time I hugged her that it was the last. I knew I never would feel my mom's arms around me or hear her heart beat as I held myself close to her. I didn't get that with my dad. We had plans to see each other again. Our hug and goodbye was cut short with the risk of the oncoming storm. It didn't bother me then. I knew we had Christmas coming and I would see him soon. I just wanted to hurry and go before he asked more about what was bothering me. The regret of it all settled in me causing me to internalize it all. I just didn't know how I should react. So I just sat in my silence.

"Is she at least talking?" I knew Jason's concern over this. He was worried that I had reverted back to the way I had been when Quinn left.

"Yes, Jason. I am talking." Silence fell across the room as both turned to look at me. "I am talking, and now I am tired and I am going to bed." With that, I got up and went to my room. I was tired, but I wouldn't sleep. I just wanted out of the room.

I was being incredibly rude and I knew it. I had used up my quota of quiet graciousness within the first few days. For being a terrible liar, I felt I had put on a good act for everyone. Between Shelly and Quinn's mom, Marie, everything had been taken care of. All I had to do was shake hands and receive hugs and listen to countless numbers of people tell me they were sorry.

I gave a short bitter laugh. They were sorry? They weren't the ones who caused him to be out on icy roads. No, I was the one who caused that. If I had told him about Beau, he wouldn't have been on his way to see me. He should have heard it from me and not as secondhand stories passed from

Jason to Brad. I lay on my bed and stared at the ceiling.

Quinn's voice was quiet and restrained as he talked to Shelly on the phone. I didn't process much of the conversation, one-sided as it was. I did get that Dad had his suspicions about Beau, and had gone to the station and run a background check on him. He went home and tried to call me, only to find my phone on the counter. He brought it out to Brad's, hoping Jason could take it back to me. Jason had already left, but before he had he told Brad all about Beau. The combination of the background check and Jason's stories spurred Dad into coming to Minneapolis. I don't think there was any more I needed to know from that conversation.

The background check had shown that Beau was wanted for drug trafficking. There was more there, too, but that was the current and biggest of the red flags. At least I hadn't heard from him since Thanksgiving. I don't know if he knew Dad was aware of him or what, but he didn't try to contact me again. Quinn had his own suspicions on that, too, until Brad had woken up.

"I still think Beau had something to do with it." Quinn's voice was bitter as he talked to Reed and Sloane. I don't think he was aware that I was awake. I had been on the couch fighting the odd floating sensation that kept trying to pull me into the void of nothingness. Quinn had talked me into taking the *Ambien* that his dad had prescribed for me. They both thought I needed to sleep. I didn't need to sleep. I needed to have my dad back.

I laid there and listened to the three of them talk about the possibilities of Beau having been responsible for the accident that took my father from me. I tried to hold on and understand what they were saying, but the words were jumbled in my altered mind. I wasn't even sure that had all happened or if that was just my brain flipping through random files and putting them together as I lay in some quasi-conscious state.

I thought about what Brad had told Jason once he was off the respirator. It had been ice and nothing more. Dad had been driving too fast, intent on getting to me as soon as he could. The freezing rain had turned to snow, and the road crews couldn't keep up with the clearing and sanding. Dad had taken a turn too fast and tried to slow down, but ended up skidding off the road and into the trees.

"There was nothing that could be done." Alex's voice was still calm, even though it was laced with sadness. He was explaining to Kai and Kerri what had happened. I suppose he had told me, too, but that was the first time I remembered understanding it. "Even with the seat belt and airbag, it sometimes happens. The force of the impact caused a significant rip to his aorta. He bled internally before help could even get there. Even if they had gotten to him quickly, I don't think it would have made any difference. The tear was too severe."

I rolled over and buried my head in the pillow. I constantly had flashes like this over the past couple weeks. Sometimes they were mixed in with the events surrounding my mother's death too. I couldn't seem to stop them. They came mostly at times when I tried to sleep. After the night I had been given the *Ambien*, I'd refused any type of sedative. I didn't like the void -- the sheer nothingness -- I couldn't pull myself out of. I would rather deal with whatever state my own mind put me in than that black hole. I actively tried to push any thoughts from my mind as I repeated a lullaby in my mind over and over. Finally, Quinn came in and laid down beside me. He pulled me to him and just held me with my ear resting against his chest. Soon the lullaby turned into numbers as I counted the beats of his heart.

I felt him drift off to sleep next to me. Quinn had been my constant these past few weeks. I was grateful for his presence. He let me be without asking questions. He didn't try to push me to deal with my grief. He just accepted whatever mood I was in and adjusted himself accordingly.

It was hard to watch all those around me go on with life as normal. I wanted badly to do that, too. I needed the escape it would bring me. Kai had made arrangements with all my professors to turn my work in and take my tests after break. I appreciated it, but I needed to be doing something. I turned most of it in. Quinn convinced me not to take any of my end of the semester tests until I came back.

Everyone was finished now. They had all left for their vacations. Kerri and Reed went to visit Reed's family. It would be the first time Kerri would meet his family. Kai brought Sloane home with her. They had all invited me to go with them. I knew they really meant it, and it wasn't just out of pity. But I didn't want to bring down anyone's holiday cheer.

That was the reason Jason had been over earlier. Brad had been home for awhile. He was recovering from a collapsed lung. Jason had wanted me to go to Lakeport with him. I couldn't do it, it was too close to Quarry Springs. That and there was just too much of Dad there, and I knew that I wasn't ready for that yet. I had to keep the bandage on however I could; because once it came off I knew I wouldn't be able to stop whatever poured out. I wanted to be alone when that happened. I went back to counting Quinn's heart beats until I dozed fitfully.

Quinn was already up and in the other room when I awoke with a start. I had dreamed that I was in Kai's car, telling Dad that everything was fine and I would see him at Christmas. Then the picture morphed into that black urn with a red bow on it. I laid there and let my heart rate slow down as I realized today was the day I would have been heading back to Quarry Springs to have Christmas with Dad.

I finally got up and gathered things for a shower. I could hear Quinn in the kitchen. I hoped he wasn't making anything for me. I didn't feel like eating. I slipped into the bathroom as quietly as I could. I didn't want Quinn to know I was awake yet. I was in a bad mood, and I just wanted to be alone.

This would be my first Christmas alone. Christmases had never been a huge affair for us since mom's death, but I had always had Dad. Now it was just me. I was an orphan. I would never go home again for my family Christmas or Thanksgiving or Easter or any holiday. I was truly alone. I was empty and hollow and just couldn't make myself feel anything.

I didn't know what to do with myself. The others had agreed to have our own little Christmas party after everyone came back from break. I hadn't been ready for anything before they left, and they were all giving me time. I would have to go shopping before they came back and buy some gifts. Maybe shopping would help me feel normal again. I hadn't even been to the grocery store. Quinn had been taking care of all of that for me.

I finished my shower, dressed, and went back to the bedroom. I just wanted to be alone. No one left me alone. I wasn't going to do anything and Beau wasn't in the picture, so I didn't understand why they couldn't just back off and give me my space. I opened the curtains to look out at the gray day. It was a lot like my mood.

I stood there and watched the cars drive by. Everyone was going on and I was here. I needed to move on. Dad wasn't coming back, and I had to get use to that. It wasn't fair. It shouldn't have been him. He should have just waited. Damn Jason for telling Brad. No, it wasn't Jason's fault. It was mine. I slapped the wall next to me in frustration. It was my fault that Dad was out in that weather. If I had just told him the truth.

There was a light tap on the door as it opened. "Sylvia?" Quinn whispered his voice full of concern.

"What Quinn? What do you want?" I had no excuse to snap at him like that, but I couldn't stop it.

"I just wanted to see if you wanted something to eat." He was standing in the doorway with his hands in the pockets of his jeans. His eyes were scanning my face, trying to figure out where the attitude was coming from.

"If I wanted to eat I would come out and make something for myself. You don't need to be doing everything for me. I'm a big girl. I can make my own food. You can barely cook anyway." The last I muttered under my breath.

"I'm sorry, Sylvia, I'll just let you rest." He started to back out of the door but I wasn't done with him yet.

"Just go home, Quinn. You don't need to be here." I had had enough of him.

"Sylvia, I just want to make sure you are okay." He stepped towards me with his arms outstretched. I stepped to the side to avoid his arms. He sighed and ran his hand through his hair before dropping them to his side.

"Don't you get it? My dad is gone and it's my fault. I am not okay. I will never be okay. But I can't stop life for everyone else." I yelled it as I stepped away from him.

"Sylvia..."

"No. I don't want to hear it. Just leave. I can't breathe with everyone hovering around me all the time. You all think I'm just going to get over it and get back to normal, but it doesn't work that way. It's not going to be normal ever again. He's gone. I need to cope, to get used to it, to adjust. But going back to the way things were is never going to happen."

"We all understand that. No one expects you to just go back. We just want to see you doing alright. We're worried about you. You never leave the apartment, you barely eat or sleep. You just sit and stare at books you aren't even reading. Please, Sylvia..."

"Do you know what today is?" Quinn shook his head. "Today was the day I was supposed to go home for Christmas. When I left, I told Dad everything was going to be fine and that I would see him for Christmas. I lied to my dad the last time I saw him. Everything wasn't fine and because of that he's not here for Christmas."

I had to turn away. Quinn's brown eyes were full of pity and my own were starting to sting.

"Go home, Quinn. Go see your parents. Enjoy them while you have them. You need to be with them for Christmas, not here with me." I said it quietly, trying to get the words around the lump that was forming in my throat.

"Sylvia, I'm not leaving you. I told you that. Mom and Dad know that I'm not going to leave you alone and they are fine with that. They understand." He moved closer to me again. This time I pushed him away.

"You don't get it. I. DON'T. WANT. YOU. HERE." I shouted it at him giving him a shove with each word. "Just get the hell out."

He wrapped his arms around me and pulled me to him tighter. I didn't want this. I struggled in his arms, fighting to get myself free. I kicked out at his shin and he let me go. I backed away feeling a little like a trapped animal.

"Sylvia, just calm down. Take a deep breath. It's going to be alright." I think he was trying to convince himself of that more than me. I could feel the tears coming. It was all just building, and I didn't want him to witness it when the dam broke.

"I never asked you for your help. I don't want it. I'm sick of you being here. If it weren't for you, I would never have stayed with Beau so long in the first place. It's your fault I stayed with him, and it's your fault I didn't tell Dad." The pressure was building with every lie I told. I couldn't take the look on his face. He was crushed. His whole face crumpled with pain and guilt. I forced myself to stay and watch as I completed this. "So just get the fuck out!"

I watched as his eyes welled up with tears and his lips trembled. I pointed at the door. I could see that he was warring within himself. I was afraid he wouldn't leave.

"If you don't go, I will."

He turned and left the room, his shoulders hunched in utter defeat. I watched him walk down the hall. I stepped to the door in the bedroom and kept my eyes on him as he grabbed his jacket and a few other things. When he reached the front door he turned back to look at me. I stared back, trying to keep my face hard and the tears hidden. It looked as if he wanted to say something but thought better of it. He opened the door and walked out. As soon as I heard the door slam, I threw myself on my bed letting it all come out.

I cried for hours. I let all the hurt and frustration out. I screamed and I kicked. I yelled at my father for being so damn overprotective and going out in a storm. I yelled at him for leaving me when I needed him. I paced around the apartment ranting about Jason telling Brad. I cursed at myself for being so stupid to have fallen for someone like Beau. I raged over everything in my life, things that were long past I let out. For my mom dying and my dad for him never moving on, for always having to be the one to take care of everything. It wasn't fair. Nothing had been fair. I cried for Quinn leaving me, for never being more for Jason, and for losing my dad. Finally I cried for myself.

I let all the hurt, anger and guilt pour from me. The tears came in torrents, flooding down my face, soaking my clothes and my pillows when I finally went back to my bed. Slowly they turned into a trickle. My head hurt and my throat ached and my body was too heavy to lift. I laid in my bed and let the darkness pull me under into a full, dreamless, healing sleep.

The first thing I was aware of was the complete stillness around me. There were no voices in the other room, no TV or music, no Quinn moving around, and no Quinn breathing beside me. For a moment I was just relieved. Then I remembered the day before, and all the things I had said to him. My heart ached for what I had done. I hadn't meant any of it. I'd lashed out and hurt the one person who honestly loved me and just wanted me to be okay.

I had to tell him. I had to let him know I didn't mean it. I went over and knocked on his door. When he didn't answer, I was worried. Maybe he didn't want to talk to me. I walked back into my apartment and searched all over for my phone. I'd thrown it down the hall last night when it had started ringing. There were missed calls from Kai. Nothing from Quinn. I didn't know if that was good or bad. I stared at the phone, working up my nerve to call him. Finally I hit his number. It went to voice-mail. I left a message telling him I was sorry and I hadn't meant it. I begged him to call me. I was still apologizing when it cut me off. I debated on calling him back, but sent him a text instead.

When I didn't hear back, I decided to clean myself up. I felt like hell and I was sure I looked like it, too. I went to my room to get clothes and saw some of Quinn's clothes in a pile on top of the dresser. I hadn't noticed them before. I looked around and saw more signs of Quinn. There were shoes and books and other little things of his. I walked back to the bathroom and saw his shampoo and soap in the shower. There was a razor and deodorant on the counter. When my eyes landed on his toothbrush in the holder next to mine, it hit me. I wanted him there. With him here I wouldn't be alone.

I went back to my room to get clothes. I grabbed a simple white t-shirt off his pile of clothes and some stuff from my drawers, then I went back and showered. Once I was in the shower I realized there was the faint scent of him still lingering behind. I picked up his soap and inhaled deeply before lathering it into my loofah. I smiled when I thought of him being in here.

I don't know when he moved more of his stuff over. It must have been a gradual process. I did know I didn't want him to take it all back. In fact, I wanted more of it here. I got out, ready to do whatever I needed to get him back. I hurried and dressed and checked my phone. There was a new text.

How are you today - Q

I smiled and realized that for the first time in weeks I didn't feel numb. There was still the lingering deep sadness over Dad and the guilt of what I had said to Quinn, but there was feeling.

I'm better than I have been. Did you get my messages? - S

He replied quickly.

Yes. It's good to hear that you are doing better. What are you doing now? - Q

Missing you. What are you doing? - S

My phone buzzed as there was a knock on my door. I walked over to answer it as I checked Quinn's text.

I'm about to knock on your door. - Q

Chapter 19 - Quinn

THE DOOR FLEW OPEN AND Sylvia stood there a few seconds -- with the biggest smile I have seen on her face in a long time -- before launching herself at me. I wrapped my arms around her as I stumbled back a couple steps to regain my balance. She let out a little giggle as we moved. It felt so good to have her in my arms like this. This was the Sylvia I knew. The Sylvia that I had been afraid was gone.

She pulled back just enough for me read her face. Her eyes were a bright green, shinier than they had been in days. The purplish smudges under her eyes were so faint they could barely be seen. She appeared to be well-rested at last. Her smile was what did it for me. It was huge, and it was all for me.

"Good morning. It looks like someone woke up on the right side of the bed today." I couldn't help but smile back at her.

"Oh, I did." She said it with a little smirk and an enticing raise to her brow. Sylvia dropped her arms from around my neck down to my hands, which she clasped tightly in hers. She stepped back through her doorway, pulling me along with her.

"I missed you." She surprised the hell out of me when she went up on her toes and kissed me. Her soft lips against mine were just what I needed this morning. I came over not knowing what today would be like with her. I wasn't sure if she would still be angry or back to the ghost that had been haunting the apartment for the past weeks. Never did I expect this from her.

It wasn't a quick kiss either. I felt her lips part against mine and the tip of her tongue sweep across my lower lip. I opened mine to her and let her take the lead. I didn't want to push her further than she was ready to go. I pulled her tighter to me as she teased me with her mouth. Her tongue darted into my mouth, coaxing mine to play. I grew harder with every pass her tongue made against mine. When I felt us growing breathless, I pulled back and she slid down, standing flat on her feet.

"I missed you, too," I said, still slightly breathless.

"I am so sorry for yesterday. I didn't mean it. Please understand I didn't mean it." She was talking fast while she pleaded with me. She looked scared like she was worried that I was upset.

"Sylvia, I know you didn't." I leaned down and just brushed my lips against hers briefly. "So...you look better. Looks like you got some sleep at last."

Her face lit up. "I did sleep. I don't even know how long I slept, but it felt like forever." She started to walk over to the couch and I followed, taking my coat off and dropping it on the chair as I passed.

"Sylvia, do you want to talk about yesterday?" I didn't want to push her, but I really wanted to know what had brought about this change. I joined her on the couch, sitting sideways so I could look at her. She was radiant today. Her hair was still drying, but it shined. The strawberry curls bounced against her as she sighed and shrugged. I noticed then what she was wearing. I was pretty sure the white shirt was mine. I smiled to myself at the thought of her choosing to wear my shirt.

"I don't really know what to say. I just had some things I needed to get out of my system and I couldn't do it with you watching me. You wouldn't have wanted to see me anyway. I was a complete mess."

"That wouldn't have bothered me. I would have been here for you, helping you through it." She shook her head.

"No, Quinn. This was something I needed to do alone." I hated leaving her yesterday but I was so afraid that she actually would leave when she threatened it. I was hurt at her words, and feeling guilty for being the source of her pain once again. I had intended to just go for a drive and clear my head and then go back and check on her. Those plans changed when I found myself in front of my parents' house.

Mom took one look at me and opened her arms. I felt like a child again as I let my mother envelop me in her arms. Her comforting embrace was something I could always count on. After that, she led me to the kitchen and made me hot chocolate as I unloaded everything to her. I told her about the ache of seeing Sylvia so unhappy and being powerless to do anything about it. I guiltily confessed the anger I was starting to feel towards her for just seeming to give up on everything. Mom listened and offered bits of advice or encouragement, until I relayed the events of the morning.

Mom chastised me for not giving Sylvia room to grieve. She pointed out how I should know by now that Sylvia would need her own space to think things through. Mom insisted I spend the night and leave Sylvia to work it out on her own. She assured me that Sylvia would call if or when she needed me. It was a long night of worrying about her. I woke up early and paced around the house wondering if I should just go to her. I wanted to call and check on her but realized my battery was dead. I plugged it back in and went downstairs to have breakfast with my parents.

I had joined Mom and Dad in the little breakfast nook off the kitchen. It was the usual place to find them in the morning. There were windows on three sides which allowed the sun to shine brightly through. Mom liked to sit here in the morning and look out over her garden. Of course now it was covered with snow with little tufts of yellow dead grass poking through. In a few months it would be filled with color and life. As I sat through breakfast I didn't hear anything Mom and Dad said. I just looked out the window and thought of Sylvia. Slowly, I began to realize that Sylvia was like the garden. Right now she was dormant, waiting for the sun and the warmth to come back. After a time it would. All I had to do was sit back and give her the time she needed. She too would renew, just like the garden did. With a little patience and love and caring she would come back to life, too. I sat back and smiled. Sylvia was going to be fine.

It was after breakfast that Mom suggested I go to Sylvia's and take her back to their place for Christmas and the rest of the weekend. My grandparents were flying in later that morning. I liked the idea of having Sylvia come and stay.

Sylvia shifted on the couch and reached out for my hand. I focused all my attention back to her.

"I know. Mom made me see it. I'm sorry it took me this long to let you have your space." She was visibly relieved at that. "Still, I sense there is more to your mood than just having been given some space."

She smiled sadly at me, and it didn't reach her eyes. "There is. I know my Dad isn't coming back any more than my mom is. I just have to try to go on." Her eyes started to water and I wrapped my arms around her comforting her the only way I could. She stayed tucked against my chest for a few minutes, not saying anything, just pulling herself together.

She sat back and took a deep breath. "I also came to another realization in my time alone." She took my hand again and turned her attention to it as she traced along my fingers. Her feather light touch was nice, but I was curious about what else she had to say. I could tell she was searching for the words.

When she finally did start speaking, I could barely hear her. "I haven't been very nice to you lately..."

I sighed. "Sylvia you had so much going on that..."

"Don't interrupt me." She looked up at me and there was something more in her eyes. Something I had caught brief glimpses of before the accident. "I don't mean since the..." she swallowed, "...the accident. I was so angry when I found out you were here. I still had feelings for you, and I was afraid that they would intensify being around you again. I was right. They did. What I wasn't expecting was you feeling the same way. I'm sorry for pushing you away all this time. I was just scared." I squeezed her hand so she would know I understood. "I'm not scared anymore. I woke up this morning and saw all your stuff around, and it just felt right. Like this was what was supposed to be."

"Sylvia it *is* supposed to be. And it may have been what *was* supposed to be, but we can't change that now." She nodded.

"Quinn, thank you. Thank you for giving me my time to grieve last night. I truly needed that time to get my mind straightened out." Her voice quivered but she continued. "Thank you for not giving up on me, for staying with me." Her eyes were watering up again. I brushed away the tear that had spilled over onto her cheek. I leaned over and kissed her softly to silence her. She didn't need to say anymore. I understood her perfectly.

"Sylvia, I love you. I know that everything isn't perfect, yet and we still have things to talk about. But for now, can we just enjoy the holiday?" Sylvia smiled at that and nodded.

"I would like that very much."

"Mom would like it if you would come for Christmas and stay the weekend at their place. It would mean so much to her, and me too." I could see the hesitance in her eyes as she bit her lip, thinking it over. "Please Sylvia."

"When would we go?"

"Well, since its Christmas Eve, I thought we could leave as soon as you are ready." I knew I must look like an eager puppy. I sure as hell felt like one. I really wanted her to come with me. I wanted to spend the holidays with her. I could see that she was thinking it over, and that gave me hope.

"Mom would love it. She misses you." I hoped that would help push her over.

She still looked torn, but then she smiled at me. I wanted to sing, I was so freaking happy.

"There's just one thing I need to do first." She gave me the sexiest smirk I think I had ever seen. Then, without warning, she straddled me and brought her mouth to mine. This kiss was aggressive and demanding and had me instantly hard. It drove me crazy when Sylvia sucked on my bottom lip before she nipped at it playfully, then smoothed over it with her tongue. She moved along my jaw the same way, suck, nip, lick, suck, nip, lick. When she got to my ear, she traced around the outside with her tongue.

I wanted to take her right there when she whispered, "I need you, Quinn. I need to feel you." Her lips closed over my earlobe and gently sucked on it as she ground against me. I would happily give her whatever she needed. She fisted her hands in my hair and returned to my mouth. I may have moaned as she moved over me, pressing against me. She had on a pair of jeans and I could feel the pressure of the seams as they rubbed together. I wrapped my hands over her hips to slow her down.

Sylvia ran her hands up and down my arms. She slipped her fingers up under the sleeves of my t-shirt, grasped my upper arms, and moaned against my mouth as I thrust up against her. Her hands slid out from under my sleeves and across my chest, down to the hem of my shirt. She tugged it up over my head and began the same torture as before -- suck, nip, and lick -- all over my chest.

I groaned and threw my head back to rest on the couch when I felt her reach for the button on my jeans. She expertly undid them. She tugged at them and I raised my hips, letting her pull them off -- along with my shoes -- as she sank to her knees on the floor in front of me. She trailed her finger nails up the insides of my thighs, sending a shiver through me. When she reached the edge of my boxers, I thought she would continue up under them. But she skimmed over and started to slowly stroke me through the thin layer of cotton. I wanted to feel her skin on mine so I reached for her hand and moved it through the fly.

She giggled. "A little impatient, aren't you?" she teased.

"God, you have no idea how long I've been waiting for this."

"Well, then I shouldn't keep you waiting." She closed her hand around me and moved at a faster pace. It wasn't long before I had to stop her. After sleeping next to her for the past month without more than a few chaste kisses, I was beyond ready for her. I wasn't going to last long if I didn't stop her.

I pulled her up to me and kissed her as I raised her shirt over her head. Her skin was so soft, and I just needed to run my hands over her. I wanted to touch her everywhere and feel that soft skin under my fingers. She let out a small sigh as I tickled along her back while keeping our kisses slow and deep. I unhooked her bra and slid it off. I didn't even look to see what it looked like. I just wanted to feel her bare chest against mine.

I wrapped my arms around her and hugged her tight. I tried to convey that I would always be there to hold her with that hug. I inhaled her scent as I held her to me, and was overcome with the need to taste her. I started at her ear, doing the same thing she had done to me. I moved from her ear down to the sweet spot behind it. I knew the reaction I would get if I sucked there. Sylvia didn't disappoint. She moaned deeply and rubbed her hips against me. The denim was rough against my cock, but I didn't care. I moved from the sweet spot to her throat, and then down to her breasts.

I cupped them in my hands, marveling once again at what a perfect size they were. I massaged them as I took a nipple in my mouth. I loved how it went hard under my tongue as I licked and sucked on it. Her hands were in my hair again pulling lightly as I kissed over to the other one to shower it with attention, too.

"God, Quinn, I need to feel you against me." Her voice was low and husky and had my dick twitching.

I reversed our positions on the couch and quickly moved down to her jeans, undoing them and pulling them off along with her panties. I knelt in front of her, just as she had been in front of me. I looked her over, drinking in the sight of her. She was absolutely breathtaking. Her eyes were heavy with lust, her red swollen lips were parted, and I could just make out the hint of her tongue as it moved along the lower inside of her bottom lip. Her perfect breasts rose and fell with each breath she took. Her pink nipples called to me again and I leaned forward taking one into my mouth as I reached down to feel her warm wet heat.

I had to have a taste. I let go of her nipple with one last flick of my tongue. I pulled her hips to the edge of the couch and brought my lips down to her. Her taste was something I'd craved while we were apart. Now that it was in front of me, I felt like a parched man at a drinking fountain. I took long, slow licks, teasing her as she had teased me. I licked up and circled her clit before licking back down. She arched her hips to me every time I passed her pearl. Finally I gave in and sucked on her. She cried out and pulled my hair, pushing herself against me. I pushed her hips back down and went back to tormenting her. She tasted so good. I just wanted to enjoy every minute I had with my mouth to her.

Soon her little cries and moans had me ready to bring her over the edge. I slipped my hand down and slowly slid a finger in, hooking and pulling back out, only to slide two back in. I pressed my tongue flat against her clit and felt her tighten all around me. She thrust her hips up once again and pressed my head down into her. There was no better feeling on earth than knowing that I could make her body react like that. I held my tongue against her until I felt her slowly relax. I gave her a few more gentle licks as she came down. I couldn't wait any longer, and I pushed my boxers off as I rose up to my knees.

"Sylvia, I don't have a condom, love." I didn't want to stop but I would if she needed me too.

"It's okay; I'm still on the pill. Please Quinn. I need you inside me." That was all the encouragement I needed.

With one swift stroke, I was in her. She was so hot and wet around me. She whimpered as I moaned her name. I couldn't take it slow. I had to have her. I gripped her hips as I slid back out. I thrust into her hard and fast. Her legs wrapped around my waist and she circled her hips, timed with my thrusts. She brought her hands up to her breasts and I watched her pinch and roll her own nipples. It had to be the hottest thing I had ever seen. It wasn't long before she was calling out my name and tightening her legs around me. She pulled me hard against herself with her legs as she went over the edge. I groaned and came, too, shoving myself into her again.

We stayed just like that for several seconds. I reveled in the feeling of her surrounding me. Finally I pulled away and joined her on the couch. She curled up next to me, kissing me sweetly. We enjoyed the slow kisses while we let our bodies calm back down.

"Sylvia, I love you." I whispered between kisses. I felt her lips curve up into a smile. Even though she didn't answer me, I was sure it was just a matter of time before she would.

Chapter 20 - Sylvia

Ifound myself in the window seat in the Lobatos' family room, watching the lights glint on the cold glass. I couldn't sleep, and I knew that my restlessness was keeping Quinn from sleeping well, so I had decided to get up and read. I had wandered down to the Lobatos' family room but once I was there I didn't want to ruin the stillness of the room combined with the faint lights from the tree. I had been childishly breathing on the glass and drawing patterns in it.

I still felt like crying over Dad. Coming to the Lobatos was both a blessing and a curse. It was good to be social again and they let me know I belonged there with them. It was bad because the family setting made the pang from the loss of having none of my own more acute. I tried not to think about what I would have been doing with him throughout the day. Everyone was well aware of my internal struggle, even though they didn't mention it. They kept the conversations light and no one asked me how I was doing.

I drew in a deep breath and released it against the window again. I started over with a new design. I didn't really pay attention to what I was drawing; I just moved my finger along the glass. I thought over the day and smiled. Quinn had come back for me. He hadn't left me again, even though I had given him reason to. The morning with him had been wonderful. It was exactly what both of us needed.

I only hoped that Quinn wasn't upset that I still hadn't told him I loved him. I knew I did, I just couldn't bring myself to say it yet. I knew that whatever my future would bring, Quinn would be in it. That was just what I wanted. I was grateful for all he had done for me, yet there was still a small piece of my heart missing. I knew he wouldn't leave me again. I just didn't understand how he could have left like that in the first place.

I gasped and jumped when an image in white floated in the reflection of the window. I turned, clutching my hand to my heart and looked at

Quinn's grandmother standing beside me. She looked a little ghost like in her long white pajamas.

"I'm sorry dear," she whispered. "I didn't mean to startle you."

I smiled weakly at her. "That's alright. I didn't realize anyone else was awake. You just surprised me." My heart rate was slowing back to normal. I had met Marie's parents in the past. They used to come visit several times a year when the Lobatos lived in Quarry Springs.

I had always liked Mildred and Martin Spencer. They were exactly what I thought grandparents would be like. I barely knew my own. Both sets had died before my twelfth birthday. Mildred always brought cookies when she came, and took tons of pictures. She was always helping out in the kitchen or finding something to do around the house. Martin was just as busy. He would spend his vacation tinkering with all sorts of little projects around the Lobato house. He would fix things like a squeaky door or a broken rain gutter. Neither of them sat still for long. Both absolutely adored Quinn. He was their one and only grandchild and they showered him with attention and praise.

Mildred reached out and placed her hand on my shoulder. "Are you thinking of your dad?" Her voice was sad, but still offered comfort.

"Some. I've come to terms with it, but I still can't seem to stop the tears when he crosses my mind." She squeezed my shoulder.

"It will be a long time before you will. You can never replace someone you love like that. Eventually the memories won't be so hard on you. With time, the memories will make you smile and you will be grateful for having them." Her voice was a little louder as she moved the chair by the wall closer to me and sat down in it. She was still close enough that she picked up my hand and held it.

"I know that will happen. It did with my mom. I just don't want others to have to walk on egg shells around me, worrying over how I'm doing or afraid they will say something wrong. I feel guilty for the way I've been this past month. All of them were so helpful and I just blocked them all out. I still can't believe Quinn stayed by my side with me being as moody as I was." I didn't know how much I should say about Quinn staying with me. I'm pretty sure his grandparents were aware of it, and I was sleeping in his room. But I didn't know how Mildred would feel about it.

"Dear, that boy understands what you're going through. It wasn't so long ago that he spent the summer at our place going through the same thing." I looked at her curiously. "Oh, he wasn't grieving a death, but he was grieving over the loss of someone close." I knew then she was refer-ring to our breakup. "I had never seen Quinn so emotional. He was a mess. We never really knew which Quinn we would see. He was angry, withdrawn, sullen and just all out ill-tempered. Some days he refused to leave his room. He wouldn't even eat. Other times I caught him staring at the phone for an hour. I think he wanted to call someone but never did. Then there were all the letters I found wadded up in the trash. At least I think they were letters, I didn't read them. Some days he wouldn't say anything to us and other days snapped our heads off at any little thing. If I hadn't known what happened, I would have thought he was on drugs. He was so different."

I stared at her wide-eyed. Quinn had said that he never really got over it but if he acted like that it must have been just as heartbreaking for him, too. "You make it sound as if he still loved me. If that were true he wouldn't have left me like he did."

"Have you asked him why he left?"

"Yes, he said it was so I would take the scholarship. I would have had to take out loans for Princeton and he must have been worried about paying them back. He left me so we wouldn't have to do that in our future."

Mildred gave a small dry chuckle. "Oh, child, money was never the issue. I don't know why he did it. You will have to talk to him about that. But I assure you that money doesn't matter to Quinn. If I had to venture a guess, I would say he left you for some altruistic motive. He is so much like Alex that way. The pair of them are always putting the needs of others before themselves. You are like that too."

I pondered her words. Could there have been more to it than what he told me?

"Well, dear, I need to be going back to bed now. Maybe that old buzz saw in there will have quieted down by now." I giggled. It was well known that Quinn's grandpa could wake the house with his snores. I stood with Mildred. She hugged me to her. "You talk to my grandson. The two of you were made for each other. It's not every day you get a second chance." She stood up and I stood with her.

"I will." I surprised myself when I reached out to hug her, yet it just felt right. "Thank you."

I slid her chair back against the wall and we turned together towards the door. That's when I saw Quinn standing there watching us. He looked incredibly sexy, standing there in just a pair of black sleep pants. His eyes

were heavy lidded and his hair was all over the place. He had a very be-
mused look on his face. I'm sure he was wondering just what I was talking
about with his grandmother in the middle of the night.

Mildred squeezed my hand. "Speak of the devil." Quinn walked over
to us.

"Grandma? What are you and Sylvia doing up?" He sounded like such
a confused little boy that I couldn't help but smile.

"Just trying to catch Santa." Mildred dropped my hand and patted his
cheek. He looked at her in utter confusion. She pulled him into a hug and
whispered something in his ear. I'm not sure what she said but he looked
at me with his eyes wide open.

"I'll just leave you two young people to this late hour. I'll see you both
in the morning." With that, she made her way out the door and -- I assumed -- back to her room.

"Sylvia, what are you doing up? I rolled over and you were gone. I was
worried." Quinn reached for my hand as he spoke with me.

"I couldn't sleep." He nodded. "I had an enlightening conversation
with your grandma." He quirked an eyebrow at me, waiting for me to
continue. "I think we need to talk."

He sighed deeply and ran his hand that wasn't holding mine through
his hair, and then rubbed his eyes. I felt guilty for keeping him up on
Christmas Eve talking about this, but I thought this was the perfect time.
He led me over to the small love seat that faced the Christmas tree and sat
down pulling me on to his lap.

I snuggled in against his chest and ran my fingers up it, feeling his
silky hair slide between my fingers. Neither of us said anything for a few
minutes. I didn't know how to start and I'm sure he was waiting for me to
begin. I watched the lights from the tree change colors against his chest,
giving it a blue tint before morphing into green then yellow then white
and back to blue. I loved the fiber-optic lights on that tree. Marie had said
this was the first year they didn't get a real tree. She wasn't sure if she was
happy with it or not. I thought it was beautiful. Even more beautiful was
the way the light played against Quinn's skin.

I finally gathered up the courage to ask him. "Quinn, did you still love
me when you left?"

He squeezed me tighter to him and I felt his lips brush the top of my
head. "Yes, always." He whispered it.

I continued to stare at his chest, watching my fingers play with his chest hair, afraid to look up at him. "Why did you leave then? I know you said so I would take the scholarship but your grandma said money wasn't an issue for you. I'm confused." I whispered it, but I knew he'd heard me.

He let out a big breath, and I felt him pull away from me slightly. I glanced up and watched him. His head was thrown back against the couch and he was pinching the bridge of his nose. I knew he probably wasn't expecting this, but I had to know. Once he'd gathered his thoughts, he raised his head and looked down at me. His dark eyes were clouded with hurt and remorse.

"Sylvia, one of the things about you that I love and hate is how independent you are. I admire your desire to accomplish things on your own without the help of anyone else. You never expect things of people and never expect things to just be handed to you. It's also frustrating because you never let anyone give you anything. It doesn't matter if we want to, if giving you something to make your life better or making you happier is, in return, our gift."

I was definitely confused now. I wasn't sure where he was going with all of this. I started to say something but he stopped me by placing his fingers over my open mouth.

"Shh. I need to tell you all of this. Please just listen and you can talk when I'm done." His brow was creased and I reached up to rub my thumb along the furrow, smoothing it out. I nodded and stayed silent.

"I'll start from the beginning, then. I wanted nothing more than to have you at Princeton. Yet from the time we started talking about it I always felt that you applied there just because that was where I was expected to go. Honestly, if I hadn't been a legacy and if Grandpa Lobato was more understanding I would have chosen the University of Minnesota to start with. That was never a choice for me. You knew that. You knew that we went back three generations at Princeton and it was just another one of those things that came with being a Lobato. Dad told me I didn't need to go there, but I saw the disappointment in his eyes and knew that would never be an option."

I shifted in his lap and reached up so I could wrap my arm around his neck. I knew the pressure he had on him, not so much from Alex but from his Grandpa Lobato. I never once resented his decision to go to Princeton. I wanted to reassure him of that.

"Do you remember the day I offered to help you pay for Princeton so you wouldn't have to take out loans, or at least not have to work once you were there?"

I nodded. That was one of the biggest arguments we'd had. I didn't want Quinn to feel like he had to pay for anything for me. I was perfectly capable of working and paying my own way. We argued and I pushed him out the door before slamming it in his face. Of course I opened it back up right away and we worked it out.

"Well, when you got that scholarship I was afraid that if you didn't take it you would begin to resent me for taking away that option from you."

"I..." He shushed me before I could tell him that I would never resent him.

"You would have. As soon as I paid for something, you would have thought about that scholarship. Maybe you would have let it go, or maybe it would have been in the back of your mind, eating away at you. I just couldn't live with the risk that one day you would wake up and hate me for taking that away from you. I see now that I was wrong on it."

I had never thought about it that way before. I still didn't think I would have ever resented him for it.

"Why didn't you just tell me this in the first place?"

He pulled me in against him, and I could feel the hardness of his chest against my cheek. "Sylvia, I tried. You wouldn't hear of it. I was about to give up. Then during the graduation ceremony, it hit me. If we broke up, you would take the scholarship. At the time it seemed so simple. I would break up with you. You would go off to the U of M and I would go to Princeton. You would get settled in and start your classes and see that it was a good idea that you were there. You would meet some friends and be happy. I figured then I could come home for summer break and make it up to you. That we could work it out and hopefully get back together. By then you would be established at here and would return in the fall but we could still keep our relationship going. I figured we were meant to be and everything would work out just fine." His voice was so sad and wistful that it tugged at my heart.

"Why didn't you come back?" I could lie to myself but I knew that, had Quinn came back that summer, I would have been back in his arms in a heartbeat.

"At Christmas I saw you walking down the street with Jason."

I sat up straight and looked at him. The expression on his face was heartbreaking. "It was never like that with Jason. You should have come to see me."

Quinn pushed me down against him again. He started playing with my hair, running his fingers through it and twirling the ends around his fingers. "I know that now. I didn't then. It looked like you had moved on. I had been so miserable and angry without you, and I knew you had a hard time at first. But then I saw you with him and I thought you were happy. Sylvia, I would do anything to make you happy. If that meant leaving so you could be with another guy, then I would do that." His voice was hoarse, and I imagined he had the same lump forming in his throat that I had in mine.

"I went back early after that, and refused to come home. I just couldn't bear to be in the same town as you and not go to you. Mom encouraged Dad to take the job here. I think she knew how hard it was for me. I still hated coming back, and rarely ever did. I focused my whole life on school. I didn't make many friends at first. I didn't do anything. The second year, I made a real effort to join in. But I never really enjoyed it. I know Mom was worried, and she begged me to come home. Finally, when I was done with my undergraduate stuff, Dad talked me into coming back. Mom was thrilled and she set out to find the apartment. That's when she found you and decided to play matchmaker."

"Have I told you how much I love your mom?" I felt Quinn chuckle against me. "So it wasn't about the money?"

"It was never about the money. It was about your happiness. That's all I ever want, is for you to be happy."

We sat in silence after that for several minutes. I played over what he'd told me as I trailed my fingers over the hard muscles of his upper chest and over his shoulder. I understood now why he chose to leave. It still stung that he didn't have faith in me, but I could see why that was. I had given him little to have faith in. We could never know if I would have resented him for that, but now I needed to not resent him for taking that option away from me, for taking himself away from me. It was over, and the only thing I could do was go on from here.

I raised my head to tell him I loved him. I looked deep into his eyes. I wanted to see them as I told him.

"Quinn, I love you." I whispered as he bent forward as if to kiss me. He slowly brushed his nose against mine. I could feel his warm breath against my parted lips as he slowly grazed his nose along mine. My eyes fluttered closed as I felt him inhale deeply, breathing me in. I tilted my head slightly to reach for his lips, but he continued with the idle nuzzling.

Just as I thought the anticipation of his lips against mine was going to kill me, I felt the tip of his tongue on my lower lip. He nonchalantly swept up over my lips with just the very tip of his tongue. It was just a hint of what was to come.

The second pass was slightly faster and firmer. I felt the warm, wet, satiny texture of the broad part of his tongue slide up over my parted, ready mouth. I licked my lips, tasting him on them. It was a heady mixture of Quinn, the mint of his toothpaste and a slight hint of the hot chocolate we'd had just before bed. It was intoxicating. I wanted more.

When Quinn came in a third time I was ready for him. He started the same as before, his tongue slid out running all across my lower lip. I felt the strength of it massaging my full lower lip. I slipped mine out to greet his, to invite him in, but he resisted. Instead he licked the tip over and briefly tested the corner of my mouth before circling up over my top lip. As he rounded the opposite corner and came back to my bottom lip, I captured his tongue and drew it in before he could tease me further.

His hand strayed up my shirt. His finger left tingles up my side as he glided over my ribs. He stopped and just grazed his fingertips around the outer edges of my breast, barely touching me, making me ache for more. I felt his chest move against me and my nipples hardened under my thin shirt as my body consumed his heat.

He gradually slid his sweet tongue out of my mouth, only to lick my bottom lip one more time. Again he traced the outline of my welcoming mouth, leaving no part untouched. His full lips momentarily moved against mine, making me long for more. I followed his lead, loving the smooth feel of the inside of my lips as I chased his tongue finally snaring it with my lips.

His slow, sensuous kiss was warming my entire body, awakening every part of me, making me yearn for more. I needed to have more of him but he continued to taunt me with his tongue, almost bringing his mouth to mine but never quite closing the distance. I played along with him as our tongues spiraled around each other, savoring each other. We each pulled back, tempting the other to follow, only to join together once again.

Quinn's hand curved around the swell on my breast, cupping the weight of it in his hand. Softly he kneaded the flesh, tormenting me. I arched into his hand silently begging him to take more of me. I sucked his tongue into my mouth every chance I got, trying to relay my need, pleading with him to give me more. He continued to sample my lips, with just his tongue taking leisurely trips around the inside, yet never fully bringing his mouth to mine. Just as I thought he was going to give in and deepen the kiss he pulled back, enticing me once again with just the tip of his tongue as he left me with quick slight licks at my lips and tongue.

Our noses once again brushed as we moved back slightly to catch our breath. I tilted up, touching my lips to the tip of his nose before moving on to his mouth. I reciprocated his teasing with my own. I felt his lips part as I flicked just the tip of my tongue over them. I concentrated on the feel of his fingers circling up to my nipple as I swiped at the corner of his mouth. I relished the softness of his lips with my tongue, particularly the middle of his upper lip.

Quinn let me control the pace of the kiss. He held steady as I came in time and time again with gentle pleasure-seeking licks. His breath cooled my wet skin, sending little shivers out around me. I felt myself growing damp in another place and as I stroked Quinn's tongue with my own I thought about him tasting me there, too. I wanted the same languid licks lower as he had given my lips. I moaned into his mouth and he once again began to memorize my mouth with his tongue.

His magic fingers pinched and flicked at my nipple as he began to deepen the kiss. He pressed me to him tighter, and I felt his hardness pressing against my thigh. I brought my hand down his side to his hip as I turned into him, trying to get closer. I took his tongue into my mouth, urging him to take more. At last, he caved and brought his lips fully against mine. By then my need for him nearly consumed me. I moaned again as I felt more than heard him do the same.

We greedily absorbed one another, our mouths wet and strong, taking and giving, each leaving the other breathless. His fingers only stopped playing with my nipple long enough to move on to the other one. Just when I thought I couldn't take any more and I desperately needed to feel him against me, in me, he stopped devouring me. He left soft little kisses on my swollen, parted lips before pulling away completely.

He took his hand away from my breast, leaving me longing for its warmth. He wrapped his arms around me and pulled me into a tight embrace. I felt his lips curve up into a smile as he rested his forehead against my temple. That's when I noticed the wetness against his cheeks. I moved my head away, and in the incandescent lights of the Christmas tree the tears on Quinn's cheeks glistened.

"I love you, too."

Chapter 21 - Quinn

S YLVIA LOVES ME. SYLVIA LOVES me. It was my first thought when I
woke up in the morning, cuddled up to the most perfect girl in the
world. It was on my mind as we kissed good morning. She said it aloud
after the kiss. It was the only thing I could think about while she was in
the shower.

I thought about it when she answered the phone, first with Kai and
then with Kerri. I knew what they were calling to tell her and I was so
happy that we were able to share in the excitement of their engagements.
Sloane and Reed had it planned out to propose to each of the girls on
Christmas Eve. They decided if they proposed at the same time, then neither girl would be upset that the other was asked first.

I was just as happy as if I had proposed myself. It wouldn't be long
before I did. I remembered what Grandma whispered in my ear the night
before. "You tell that girl the truth and in the morning come get my ring."
I knew Sylvia wasn't ready for that yet. I wasn't ready either, but we would
be someday. For the moment I reveled in the fact that she loved me.

I wore the goofiest grin all day. Nothing wiped it away. It didn't go unnoticed by my parents and grandparents, either. Dad teased me mercilessly
all morning about the gift that put a smile like that on my face. Sylvia
blushed madly and Mom walked around with a self-satisfied smirk on
her face. Yet whenever a comment was made, I smiled wider and thought
Sylvia loves me.

We all gathered in the family room and opened gifts. First were the
stocking gifts. Mom had never gotten over the idea that I didn't believe in
Santa and still insisted that she didn't fill the stockings with little gifts and
treats. This year she added an additional stocking for Sylvia and it looked
good there hanging with the rest. It balanced out the family.

Sylvia had been embarrassed with the amount of attention and gifts she
received. She shot me a few angry glares as she apologized profusely for

not having brought anything. I should have thought to take her shopping before we came the other day but my brain had been rattled by the events of the morning. Mom assured Sylvia that she had brought them the best gift: the smile she put on my face. That made the pair of us blush.

The rest of the weekend went by quickly. We stayed at Mom and Dad's until Grandma and Grandpa left. I love my grandparents, but I couldn't wait until they were gone. I really wanted to get Sylvia alone. During that time, every member of my family pulled me aside and had a heart to heart with me. Mom wanted to tell me how happy she was for us and that I needed to bring Sylvia over more often. Dad reminded me that she was still grieving and not to push her. Grandma made sure we talked about why I left. I assured her everything was fine with that. She then gave me her ring, telling me that she knew it would be beautiful on Sylvia and that I would know the perfect time to give it to her.

Grandpa's advice was something I could have done without. It started out innocently enough.

"Quinn, son, come talk to your grandpa." He was sitting in the study alone. I think he was laying in wait for me.

"Sure, Grandpa. What did you want to talk about?"

"You and Sylvia." I figured that was it. It was what everyone wanted to talk to me about. "I know your grandma gave you her ring. She has been waiting years to give that to you. She always said she knew you would give it to Sylvia one day."

I smiled thinking of how much my family loved Sylvia.

"When I gave that ring to your grandmother my grandfather gave me some advice. I'm going to pass it on to you. Learn to answer 'yes dear' and mean it. Always listen to her. What she says is important, and you never know when your life may depend on it. Make sure you kiss her good morning every day and good night every night. Then you will never have to wonder whose bed she's in. Never go to bed mad at each other. You do and it guarantees you won't be getting any that night." Grandpa smiled conspiratorially at me. I couldn't believe he was talking to me about sex.

"Make her happy first and she will make you happy. Your grandma likes it when I use..." He was holding up his pinky finger. I couldn't listen to anymore and jumped up. I stumbled over the chair in my haste to get to the door.

"Thanks for the advice, Grandpa. I think I'm good on the rest." I stuttered out quickly. I looked back to see him smirking before I headed out the door. I didn't think I ever wanted advice from my grandpa again.

Finally we said our goodbyes and I was able to take Sylvia home. We still had five whole days to ourselves before the others came back from their family visits. We even had New Year's Eve alone together. I already started forming a plan for it.

We were in my car driving back and Sylvia was very cuddly, even more than she had been all weekend. I wasn't complaining. I just wanted to get us back to her place that much quicker. She rubbed her hand up my thigh and over me. I sucked a breath in, half hoping she would go farther and the other half hoping she would stop until we got home.

I felt her hot breath against my ear. "Let's go to your place when we get back." I stepped on the gas a little harder when she bit my earlobe as she squeezed the growing bulge in my pants. I had wanted to get Sylvia back to my place at some point. I smiled, happy with the knowledge that she wanted that as well. The rest of the ride home I battled images of Sylvia in various states of undress and in various positions all over my apartment. It didn't help that Sylvia continued to massage me all the way home.

We left our bags in the car when we got back. I told her I would go get them later. For now I just wanted her in my bed. The sooner that happened, the better. We made our way upstairs, holding hands and exchanging kisses, giggling like teenagers. Once we were inside, we went straight to the bedroom. Clothes were shed, with kisses and touches being given on the way.

As much as I would have liked to have taken it slow and worship her body, I knew that wasn't going to happen. After a long weekend of having her close with nothing but stolen kisses and quick caresses, I had to have her. A naked Sylvia standing before me was my undoing. I leaned down taking her nipple into my mouth while I teased the other one. She had perfect breasts. I couldn't get enough of them. She moaned and pulled away from me.

"Quinn, I can't wait. I need you." The combination of her husky voice with her moving onto her hands and knees on the bed in front of me had me even harder. Then she looked over her shoulder at me with her eyes half closed as she wiggled her ass at me. "Please," she begged. I pulled her hips to me and was in her in one thrust.

God, it was good. So perfect. Ugh. I could have just died happy, right there in Sylvia. She groaned and I began to move. It wasn't slow or easy, yet she urged me on. "Harder and faster". I'd never heard Sylvia so vocal before. She begged for more and told me how good it felt as she moaned and cried out. It turned me on more than anything had before. I was completely focused on Sylvia, the feel of her heat massaging my cock as I slipped in and the slight pull as I slid out.

It was hardly any time before I felt her clench around me holding me in tight. She called out my name followed by a scream. I held on to her hips stroking along them as she came down. She dropped down to her elbows, changing the angle, allowing me to go deeper.

"Please come for me, Quinn." She pleaded breathlessly as she reached back below us and took my balls in her hand. She rolled them and tugged them. It felt amazing. I felt my own release building as all my muscles tightened up. With my own unintelligible groan of her name I came hard. I stayed in her like that for a few seconds as my body slowly relaxed.

After I pulled out and collapsed next to her, I felt like my limbs had turned to jelly. We both laid there catching our breath, basking in the heat that was between us. I felt Sylvia shift around until her body was curled up next to mine. She lightly ran her hand over my chest as she sighed.

"It's never been like this before," She whispered to me. "Never like it is with you."

I smiled smugly. It was good to know that I could make Sylvia feel that way. When she called out my name and begged me for more, I felt like a god. I laid there savoring the feel of her naked body against mine as I listened to her breathing calm back down. We were lost in our own bliss, each silently thinking of the other. At least that's what I thought until Sylvia asked, "how many others have there been for you?"

I groaned. "Is this really something you want to talk about right now?" I felt her head nod against my chest. I sighed. I didn't have any secrets, and really there wasn't anyone else. I just knew she'd had other guys in the past. One, I didn't really want to talk about them and two, I didn't want her to feel bad about that.

"Please, Quinn. You know about mine." I didn't know any specifics except for Beau and I would rather not know any.

"There were no others," I answered her quietly.

She sat up and looked at me. "What do you mean?" She looked at me like I hadn't understood her question.

"I mean I have never been with any girl other than you." I reached up and caressed her check. She pulled away from me. With a confused look she glanced at the side table then back at me.

"What about the condoms in your drawer?"

I couldn't help but chuckle. "Sylvia, I'm a 22 year old guy. Why wouldn't I have condoms on hand?" She continued to appraise me with distrustful eyes. "What?" I was starting to feel self-conscious.

"Did you plan to get me back into your bed?"

"Oh, Jesus, Sylvia. You're kidding right? I didn't even know you were here. We've been over this. Please, please let this go. I had no idea when I moved here and then once I did I never thought we could be more than friends. Not until the weekend you stayed here did I even hope there could be more between us. Seriously I just had them in case I ever needed them." I brought my hand up and ran it through my hair. Of all the things she had to be worried about, I couldn't believe this was it.

I glanced back over at her and she was biting her bottom lip. I knew she was thinking over what I had just told her. I smiled when she dropped her head back down to my chest and snuggled in.

"So you didn't date anyone after me?" I felt her lips curve up into a smile and could hear the smug tone in her question.

"No. I dated a couple a girls, but that's all they were. Just dates. There was never anything more."

"Oh," her voice lowered and I felt her smile fade.

"None of them were you. I know now that no one could ever replace you." I wrapped my arms around her and pulled her tightly to me. We laid there quietly for some time, lost in our thoughts. Soon our hands began to roam over each other and our lips soon followed. Before I knew it we were well into round two.

Our days alone together were like that. It seemed we spent them naked or at least mostly naked. We occasionally came up for air and food. Time meant nothing to us. We ate when we were hungry and slept when we were tired. We moved from my place to hers and back again, it just depended on what we wanted or needed at the time. The whole time my heart sang out joyfully. *Sylvia loves me.* The grin seemed to be a permanent fixture. We spent hours talking, catching up on what we missed in the other's lives and just reacquainted ourselves with each other. We also talked about the future. We made no concrete plans but I knew we would be together from now on.

Then there was the sex. It didn't matter what we were doing, there would be a look exchanged or something said and we would be all over each other. This must be what newlyweds are like. We'd never had this much alone time before. We couldn't keep our hands or mouths off each other. We christened every room in my apartment and hers as well. There were showers shared and food left uncooked or burned. There was hot, passionate sex and slow lovemaking. There were hours of just exploring each other's bodies. We may have known each other's bodies and likes in the past, but it was all new again. We tried things I would never have thought of in high school. It was all good and it was ours.

New Year's Eve rolled around and I knew we needed to leave our little bubble of paradise. Sylvia still had to buy gifts for our friends, who would be home in two days. We would have our own little Christmas party when they were all back. I knew the girls had talked to Sylvia a few times while they were gone, but I was sure they would all be happy to see the change in her. She still had moments of sadness, but they were fewer and farther between. She had started talking about going back to work, too. I didn't want her to push herself too hard, but she felt the obligation to return with the new semester starting soon.

I suggested we go out in the late afternoon and do some shopping. After that, I had reservations for a nice quiet dinner for the two of us, and then I wanted to take her back home and ring in the New Year together. Fortunately, Sylvia agreed to go. I told her about the reservation so she wouldn't be surprised and so she could dress appropriately. She was beautiful in a deep green sweater that was so soft I couldn't help but rub my hands over her. Of course the deep v of the neck line didn't hurt either; it gave me a fantastic view of her cleavage.

As we pulled out of the parking lot, I checked my right for traffic before checking my left. The hair on the back of my neck stood up and my stomach tightened. I swear I saw Beau's pickup out of the corner of my eye. When I looked again it was gone. I didn't say anything to Sylvia but I found myself looking around all afternoon. Sylvia noticed of course.

"What is going on with you? You're so jumpy." She playfully punched my arm.

I debated on whether or not to tell her. In the end I figured it was best that she knew. "I think I saw Beau's truck outside the apartment." Her eyes went wide and I think fear flashed in her eyes before she drew herself up as she sucked a deep breath in. I didn't want to alarm her so I hurriedly continued, "I'm not sure it was him. I just can't shake the feeling that it was."

Sylvia closed her eyes and took another breath. When she opened them she looked me in the eyes and grabbed my hands. "I swear I haven't heard from him since Thanksgiving. I doubt it was him." At my incredulous look she quickly added, "that doesn't mean I won't be careful or on the lookout too. I promise if he does try to contact me you will be the first to know." I squeezed her hands to reassure her that I trusted her. I nodded and tried to let it go. I didn't want her to worry needlessly or pull back into herself.

"Let's just finish shopping. What do you need to get yet?" I knew she had gifts for Sloane and Reed. She planned to get the girls gift certificates to a spa. I thought I would get her one, too, so she could go with them. I knew she would protest but a little pampering and some girl time would be good for her.

"Hmmm. I just need to get a couple things. Can we meet back here in an hour?" I didn't really want to let her out of my sight. "I have my cell phone with me and we're in a crowded mall. Nothing is going to happen to me. Really, I need to go my own way for a bit." She was challenging me with her eyes.

I huffed. "I suppose. But don't be gone too long, and pay attention to your surroundings."

She rolled her eyes. "Yes, dad." As soon as she said it I saw the hurt pass over her face. I pulled her in for a hug. She sniffed against my shoulder. When I felt like she was okay I stepped back and looked into her eyes. The sadness was there, but not as prominent as it had been.

"It's okay. I'm going to be okay." She said it to herself as much as to me. I reluctantly let her go after that. I wouldn't have, but I wanted to get something for her, too. In addition to the spa I had thought I would get her a new soft blanket to replace her old one. I set off in search of one.

Sylvia and I met back where we agreed. I only noticed her carrying one big bag. I tried to subtly check and see where it was from but she caught me.

"Nuh-uh, Lobato," she chided as she jerked it from my view, "No peeking."

I had slipped the blanket in with Reed and Sloane's gifts so she wouldn't be able to see it. It didn't stop her from trying.

"The same for you, O'Mara." I joked as I kissed her.

We made our way out to the car and I had the eerie feeling that we were being watched. I surreptitiously looked around. I didn't want to alarm Sylvia. I didn't see anything. I tried to chalk it up to paranoia, yet there was a tiny seed of dread growing within me. Maybe I was just worried that everything was going so well between us and I was waiting for the pendulum to swing back the other way.

We were still too early for our reservations, so we drove around and looked at the Christmas lights that were still up until the end of the season. Sylvia sat next to me, quiet for most of the drive. Occasionally she would comment on the odd choice of blow up cartoon characters decked out in full holiday regalia or the strangeness of nativity scenes that included reindeer and Santa. I would steal glances at her face as we would slowly drive past the often overly festive displays. She had a contemplative look on her face and I wondered what she was thinking about. At one subtly decorated cottage I saw her smile.

"What brought that delightful smile to your face?"

"This is exactly how I picture our place someday," she answered wistfully.

I took another look at the small gingerbread house with the simple white icicle lights dangling from the roof. From the virgin snow covered yard to the brightly glowing Christmas tree predominately placed in the bay window, everything about it resembled something out of a Thomas Kinkade painting. It was charming and homey and completely as enchanting as Sylvia herself. I reached over and squeezed her hand. I didn't say anything but I could see us there too.

Dinner was a quiet event. I had reservations at a tiny French restaurant simply called Le Chateau. The place was dimly lit with just candles. The music was soft, romantic classical pieces. Sylvia sat across the table from me and we barely talked as we enjoyed our delicious meal. I knew I tasted the food. In fact I knew we had both remarked on how good it was. Yet I still couldn't recall what I ate. I could recall how the soft curls of her hair looked as they gracefully lay against her breasts or the way her lips parted as she daintily took a bite. I was entranced with the sparkling emerald of her eyes. I saw the look I remembered and longed for in them. I smiled again. *Sylvia loves me.*

We didn't go out for a big New Year's Eve blast off. Instead we opted for a quiet night together. Just Sylvia and me with a bottle of fine champagne -- a gift from Mom -- to ring in the New Year. We had the TV muted but on, ready for the ball to drop in Times Square. Our midnight kiss was slow and passionate, everything I ever wanted.

The TV was left forgotten as we moved to her bedroom. We made love, as slow and passionate as our kiss, I saw the love, the smile. I saw each little detail I noticed earlier, but it was more intense now, even more personal and significant, because here, together in her bed, our bodies joined, we could fully express ourselves.

Everything had been so perfect that night that I was more than a little concerned when Sylvia began thrashing around and crying out close to morning. I couldn't make out her words at first but she was very distressed. I placed my hand along her check to comfort her and felt the tears. I immediately assumed she was dreaming of Kelly. I tried calling her name to wake her. When that didn't work I leaned over to gently shake her. That's when I heard her cry, "No more raptors!" What the fuck? I listened a little more and sure enough again she cried out, "There are too many raptors. No more. No more."

I bit back a smile and shook her shoulders. "Wake up, Sylvia. You're just dreaming. Wake up."

She bolted upright and grabbed at her chest, breathing hard. I was a little shaken myself, seeing her like that. I reached over and ran my hand over her hair. "Sylvia, love, it's okay. You were dreaming."

She looked over at me a little unfocused and blinked several times before sleepily mumbling, "The raptors were everywhere and you kept saying we needed more raptors. We didn't need more. There were too many." She must have still been partially asleep.

I bit down on my lip to stop the chuckle and took her into my arms. "Shhh, sweetie. There are no raptors. It's okay." I pulled her back down with me. We curled into each other. I stroked my hands along her back as I whispered reassuringly that everything was fine.

She murmured a few things to me that I didn't really understand with her face pressed against my chest. I continued to soothe her as I hummed to her softly. Soon her breathing was even and I knew she was back to sleep. I smiled contentedly. I may not be able to keep all the bad things out of her life but I could at least save her from raptors.

Chapter 22 - Sylvia

MMM, THE WARMTH WAS SO nice. I snuggled closer to Quinn, spooning up against him. There is nothing like cuddling up to a body that's all nice and warm. The sun peeked in through the curtains. I felt as if the sun on New Year's Day was a good omen that this year was starting off right. Maybe it was a sign that the year itself was going to be one of sunshine. After the years of gloom I'd had, I could certainly use one of sun.

I smiled and pressed myself even closer to Quinn. He was still asleep. I ran my hand along his abs. I couldn't get enough of the feel of them. I grazed my fingertips over the ridges, silently moaning as I thrust my hips forward. I could feel the heat radiating off him and I wanted to feel that heat raging within me. I kissed and nibbled along his shoulder, hoping it would wake him. Finally I felt him shift and heard him groan. He shifted his hips and pushed back against me. I slid my hands down and cupped him in my hand before closing my hand around him. *God, he was so hard already. I love morning wood.* I smirked as I squeezed my fist tighter and began to move it.

Quinn had yet to acknowledge me, he just went along with my hand, thrusting into it. His breathing increased, as did his moans. I loved being able to do that to him. I hooked my leg over him to bring myself against him. I just started to shift my hips and rub against him when my phone sounded a text message. I groaned and moved away.

"God damn Kai."

"Don't check it," came a husky reply.

"If I don't she's just going to continue to send messages or call. Don't lose that," I said giving him a squeeze to let him know what I was referring to, "I'll be right back."

I rolled out of bed and walked over to my pants lying on the floor. I would need to plug my phone in. After forgetting for the night I was surprised it still had a charge. I looked over at Quinn lying in the bed. He had turned onto his back. His eyes were still closed; his lips were slanted in a sexy smirk. His hair was all over the place, even more chaotic than usual. But it wasn't any of that that had me catching my breath and debating on just tossing the phone back to the floor and climbing back in bed with him. It was the motion of his hand under the covers. I knew he was stroking himself and it had me hot. I wanted to watch that. I sighed and sucked in a breath and flipped open my phone I wanted to get this text over with so I could join him back in bed. I kept my eyes on him watching the motion of the blanket as I imagined his hand moving over his cock. I didn't even look at the phone as I pressed the buttons to open the text. Finally I glanced down and my body went cold with fear.

`Happy New Year Sylvia. That kiss should have been mine. - B`

I gasped as I looked at the text. I flicked my glance over to Quinn. He was sitting up starring at me.

"What's wrong Sylvia?" His voice was laced with worry, his face full of concern.

I didn't know what else to do, so I silently handed the phone over to him. He took it from me and cursed before closing it.

I met his eyes which flashed dark in anger. I knew my own held fear. What was Beau doing texting me? It had been over a month since I'd last heard from him.

"Sylvia, we need to do something about this." His voice was flat as he closed my phone and eyed me expectantly.

"What am I supposed to do?" I snapped at him more than I meant to, but I was frustrated. I became self conscious as I stood there naked with Quinn staring at me so intensely. I fidgeted a bit before grabbing his shirt from the night before off the floor and slipping it on. I watched as Quinn ran his hands through his hair, actually taming it some from its previous disarray. He met my gaze with his own. I felt as if I were being accused of something. I knew he was thinking, but his silence was irritating me. We continued to eye each other for several seconds before I huffed and threw my hands up. I headed to the bathroom to take a shower and think things through. I didn't make it to the door before Quinn called out to me.

"Sylvia. Please don't be like that. I just want to keep you safe." I stopped and kept my back to him, listening to him. "I don't want to lose you again." His voice was tinged with despair.

My heart ached hearing him sound like that. I turned around and walked over to him. He was studying the sheet he had wrapped around him. When he glanced up at me I wanted to kick myself for making him look so sad. I leaned forward and kissed his forehead. I pulled away and cupped his cheek. We gazed into each other's eyes and I tried to convey to him that I was sorry and I knew that he was just thinking of me.

"We'll figure something out. I'm just going to go shower. We can talk when I get out." I left a quick kiss on his lips and went to shower.

The shower did nothing to help. Often I do all my best thinking standing under the hot spray, yet today I just couldn't get anywhere. My mind kept going back to the night before and how perfect it was. In fact, the past week with Quinn was wonderful. It was everything I always thought it would be when we were out on our own. It was just a pity it took us four years longer than it should have. Better late than never, though. Maybe we needed that time apart. I knew I had changed and there were obvious changes with Quinn, too. Yet no matter how we changed or how far apart we were, we'd still found our way back to each other. I smiled and finished my shower quickly. I just wanted to go out and snuggle up with Quinn and enjoy our last day together before the others returned.

I slipped on some comfy clothes and pulled my hair back and went out to find Quinn. I could see him on the couch with his laptop open. I stopped in the kitchen for my morning caffeine and asked if he needed anything. He said he didn't, but his words were short and had an edge to them. I wondered if he was mad at me about this morning.

After grabbing a pop I hesitated in the doorway of the kitchen, just watching him. He sat there shirtless, in just his boxers. His legs were stretched out in front of him with his feet crossed. The laptop had to be getting hot, balanced on his tense, bare thighs. His brow was creased and he appeared to be annoyed. I wondered what he was looking at that had bothered him so. Even though he was visibly upset, he still took my breath away. His chestnut wayward hair always made me smile. He had his glasses on, too. I loved it when he wore his glasses; it always took me back to high school when I saw him in them. His lips were pursed as he scowled at the screen. He let out a little huff and his long fingers flew over the keyboard for a second. I thought about those fingers and just what they could do to me. I must have sighed out loud because Quinn called me over.

"Quit watching me and come over here and look at this." His tone was harsh and crisp.

I rolled my eyes. "Who said I was watching you?"

He just looked at me knowingly. I grinned at him but his expression didn't change. I walked over filled with trepidation. I stood behind the couch and looked over his shoulder. He had the screen filled with open tabs. They had things like: Women's Law, Protection Orders, Minnesota State, and Minnesota Courts on the tabs. It took me a second before I figured he was looking into a restraining order. I read over the page that was open and it was how to go about getting an anti-harassment order.

I glanced at Quinn. He had his head back resting on the back of the couch watching me.

"There's a problem, Sylvia." The frustration he felt was clear in his voice. I looked at him; sure the confusion was clear all over my face. He patted the seat next to him and I came around the couch and sat down next to him.

"What's the problem?"

"I don't think he has really done anything that will allow you to file for an order."

"Well that's a good thing isn't it?" I wasn't sure why I thought that was good. It creeped me out that Beau could possibly be following me, but really I hadn't felt threatened. He had threatened Quinn, not me. "Wait, what about you? I mean he did make a threat against you."

Quinn shook his head. "He said it to you and we can't really prove it. I don't think that would work. Plus he hasn't made any move against me. Slimy bastard. He's done just enough to worry me but not enough to get the police involved." Quinn pinched the bridge of his nose.

"What about the background check my dad ran?" I swallowed and tried not to think of what that check caused. "Couldn't we turn him in?"

"We could if we knew where he lived. I'm sure they know who he works for, but they haven't been able to get him there."

We both sat there quietly, each thinking through the situation. My phone sounded again and I reached in my pocket for it. It was from Beau again.

"Quinn, he sent another one. Should I just delete it?" I was nervous about opening it.

"No, we need to see what he says. Maybe he'll slip up and give us something we can use."

He can't replace me Sylvia. I'm what you need. - B

I snorted when I read it and handed it over to Quinn. He rolled his eyes. As if Beau had anything I needed or wanted. He could in no way ever compare to Quinn.

Quinn closed my phone, laid it on the table in front of him, and picked up the remote. He sat back and closed the laptop, placing it on the floor next to the couch. He threw his arm around my shoulder and pulled me next to him. I breathed in deeply. I loved the smell of Quinn. It was uniquely him and I could never get enough of it. He placed a kiss on the top of my head and I felt him draw in a deep breath and knew he was taking me in, too.

"Sylvia it will all be okay. Don't worry. I will never let anything happen to you." He whispered it, and I wasn't sure if he was reassuring himself or me. He turned the TV on then and we sat together like that and flipped through the channels, each trying to put Beau from our minds.

Quinn and I spent the lazy day I had looked forward to. It would have been perfect if Beau hadn't continued to text throughout the day. In the end, we were both on edge and started to snip at each other over little things. I would have liked some time apart but I knew there was no way he was going to let me out of his sight any time soon. Finally I grabbed some of the work I had yet to turn in from last semester and worked on that.

I didn't pay any attention to the time. When Quinn asked me what I wanted for supper I realized the sun was gone and it was already dark out. I stood up to make something.

Before I could Quinn suggested. "Let's just order delivery. I feel like some Chinese tonight." He smiled at me and I knew it was an attempt to lighten the tension.

"That sounds perfect. I think I have some menus somewhere around here." I started for the kitchen to look in the junk drawer but Quinn stopped me. He pulled me into a big hug.

"I know where they are. I'll get them. You keep working and I'll call the order in."

I smiled and thanked him, telling him what I wanted. I went back and worked on my paper until the food arrived. We ate in the living room, sitting on the floor in front of the coffee table. Quinn turned on The Princess Bride and we laughed as we watched, both of us quoting along with the movie. It was relaxing, even though Beau texted once more. I didn't open it. I would worry about it later.

We were both up fairly early the next morning. We needed to go to the grocery store and it was going to be a busy day. Sloane and Kai were due in just after 2pm and Reed and Kerri at 7pm. Quinn had promised to pick them up, which meant two trips to the airport.

I was looking forward to seeing them all again. I really missed them. It had been less than two weeks, but for me it was really closer to six. I hadn't really been myself after the accident and didn't actually interact much with them since before Thanksgiving. I was ready for some girl time. I couldn't wait to hear all about the proposals. They both called to tell me they were engaged, but both wanted to wait and share the stories when we were all together. I was excited for them but I also knew that it was going to send them both into planning mode. I hoped they would talk to each other about it more than me. I hated that stuff, but I would go along with whatever they wanted or needed because I loved them. They were, for all intents and purposes, my family. Although after Christmas I realized I also had the Lobatos. It felt good knowing that I belonged with all of them.

On the way back into the apartment from the grocery store, I shivered. I had the eerie feeling that I was being watched. I looked around, but didn't see anything suspicious. I scanned the parking lot and street, expecting to see Beau's truck or motorcycle. I didn't see either one but I still couldn't shake the feeling. The hair on the back of my neck stood up and my stomach was queasy. Quinn stopped and turned back to me when he realized I wasn't behind him.

"Sylvia?"

"Sorry. I'm coming."

"Is everything alright? You look pale." He was examining my face trying to detect what was wrong.

"Yeah it's alright. I just had a strange feeling. I'm being paranoid is all?" I was sure that was all there was to it. The texts obviously still had me on edge.

Quinn looked around, too, carefully taking in our surroundings. "Let's just go in, okay?" I nodded and he pulled me tight to him.

Once we were on the third floor, he started towards my apartment. I had a sudden surge of panic. Even though I choked it down I still couldn't bring myself to want to go in.

"Can we put this stuff in your apartment?"

He looked at me with confusion. "Sure." The word was drawn out and I knew it was more of a question than an answer. I felt like I needed to explain myself.

"I just have a strange feeling and just don't want to be in my apartment right now." I tried to shrug it off as no big deal but I knew Quinn knew better.

"That's fine. We can put it in mine. My cupboards are bare anyway." He tried to sound reassuring, but I could hear a hint of suspicion in his tone.

I was so relieved that he didn't make a bigger deal out of it. While we were putting away the groceries I got another text. I knew it wasn't Kai or Kerri because they were supposed to be in the air about then.

`Beautiful Sylvia I miss u please call me I need to hear ur voice - B`

This time I was angry. I tossed my phone down and went into a rant. "Seriously, does he think I'm really going to call him back? Why does he keep texting me? Why won't he get the hint? I don't want anything to do with him. Ugh." I yelled it at no one, but I knew Quinn heard every word.

He came up behind me and pressed against my back. He placed his hand on my thigh, effectively stopping me from kicking the cupboard in front of me.

"Sylvia, he's getting a rise out of you. It's exactly what he wants. He wants you to be thinking about him. Don't let him. Why don't you go watch some TV or something to take your mind off it and I'll finish putting away the groceries?"

I knew Quinn was right. Beau was just trying to get to me.

"I want to get started on a few things for tomorrow's party. I'll just stay in here and work on that." I planned to make a big meal for all of us and even a few treats. I had put it off all week and now I was down to crunch time.

"That sounds like a good idea. I'll turn some music on and finish with the groceries then I can help you out."

I cringed a little. Sometimes Quinn in the kitchen was a bigger hindrance than a help, but I was far enough behind that he could be useful with little tasks like chopping or stirring.

We worked together in the kitchen until it was time to go get Kai and Sloane. I sent him over to my apartment several times to get things I needed. We decided to have the party at my place since it was the only one between the two of ours that was decorated. Which I suspected Kai had done sometime before she left. I didn't recall her doing it but everything before Christmas was a haze. After getting Kai and Sloane we worked some more until it was time to get Kerri and Reed.

It had been Kerri's first time going to Reed's and the way home from the airport was filled with laughter as she told us the craziest stories about his family. Even though I had yet to hear about the proposals, I did get to ooh and ah at their rings. Kerri's was the classic big rock. I didn't understand carats and cuts, but from the way she went on it must have been a big deal. Kai's was smaller but circled with brightly colored stones.

We left Reed and Kerri in their apartment and stopped off at mine to pick up their presents. We took them back to Quinn's and wrapped them. By the time we were done I was ready for bed. I was exhausted and needed to be up in the morning to start the ham I planned to make for lunch. Before I went to bed I checked my phone, only to see that the battery had died. Quinn ran over to my apartment and grabbed the cord so I could recharge it. Once that was set up, I went to sleep.

I slept restlessly, even though I was in Quinn's arms. My dreams always started out good. In one I was walking down the aisle towards Quinn, but once I was there I looked up expecting Quinn's brown eyes only to be met with Beau's steely blue ones. In another I walked through a large house, possibly a castle, and I was looking for Quinn. Yet every door I opened was empty. I was about to give up but I tried one more only to step in and have the door close behind me. I tried opening it but it wouldn't budge. I heard laughter and turned to find the source of it, it was Beau standing in front of me. He said, "*You are mine now, Sylvia. You will never leave me again.*" I woke up screaming from that one.

Quinn calmed me down, holding me and humming to me. I fell asleep once again and this time I dreamed that I was in the hospital. I was holding a baby in my arms and arguing with someone over the name. We were arguing about girls' names, so I assumed the child was a girl. Something inside of me told me that I was arguing with Beau yet when I looked up, it was Quinn smiling back at me. I didn't recall anything after that.

I awoke later than I intended to the next morning. Quinn was still sleeping peacefully beside me. I slipped out of bed quietly, hoping I wouldn't disturb him. I went over to my apartment to start the ham. I figured there was no sense to making it at his place if we were only going to end up at mine for the day anyway. While I was there, I straightened up the place and took a shower. After I was done, I went to my room to get dressed.

I was standing in front of my vanity when I realized something was missing. The pendant I had hanging on the mirror wasn't there. It was the pendant my dad had given my mother when I was born. It had been his mother's and his grandmother's. It was passed down whenever the first child was born. After my mother's death Dad gave it to me. I never wore it but hung it from my mirror where I could always see it. I looked around the top of the vanity but didn't see it. I figured the vanity was probably bumped into and it fell off. I just got down on my hands and knees to look for it when I heard my door open and Kai call out to me. Sighing I stood up to go see what she wanted. I would just have to look for it later.

"Sylvia?"

"Don't you ever knock?" I scowled at her then started giggling. I was just happy to see her.

"I thought you might be in the shower. I came up to see if you needed any help."

"Like you would know what to do in the kitchen. I'm good with it all. Quinn and I started most of it yesterday. Just come talk to me. I want to hear all about your Christmas." I pulled her with me over to the couch and we both sat down.

"So you and Quinn were cooking huh? I see that things are going well between the two of you." Her eyes were currently sapphire and twinkled knowingly at me.

I bit my bottom lip and then grinned, as visions of Quinn and me all over the apartment played through my head. "Very good. In fact, I think it may be going even better than it had before."

"Oh, Sylvia. I am so happy for you," she squealed and hugged me. After she pulled back, her face was serious. "And how is everything else?" Kai held on to my hands and squeezed them, gently letting me know she cared and was concerned.

I sighed. "What exactly are you referring too?" I wasn't sure if she wanted to know how I was dealing with the grief or if she somehow knew Beau was back in the picture.

"All of it. I want to know how you're feeling. The glow of love is over-shadowing everything, but I can see there is something more going on in your head."

I nodded and told her all about my breakdown, how I yelled at Quinn and sent him away and how he came back. I talked about staying at the Lobatos' and how great it felt. I explained why Quinn broke it off and how even though I still don't agree that it was the right decision; I at least understood why he made it. I blushed as I briefly revealed parts of our blissful week alone. We giggled together and she teased me that if I wasn't careful I would turn into Kerri.

Once the laughter died down the mood become sober as I filled her in on Beau's texts and how Quinn thought he'd seen him on the street. I held back about feeling like I was being watched. I never was able to confirm it and I didn't want to concern anyone or make them think I was going crazy. She asked why I hadn't gone to the police, and I explained to her how we looked it up and didn't think he had done enough for them to do anything. We sat silently for a few seconds after I was done. I suspected she knew I was leaving something out but she didn't press me on it.

"What about you? I want to hear all about your vacation. How was the fam?" For just a moment, she had a far away dreamy look in her eyes. I could only imagine what she was thinking about. She snapped out of it and proceeded to give me a play by play of her holiday. She still wouldn't tell me about how Sloane proposed. She just got that same starry eyed look and smiled softly and shook her head. By the time she was done it was time to start the rest of the lunch.

"I wonder where Quinn is. I figured he would have been over here the moment he realized I wasn't at his place."

Kai was moving decorations around on the tree. She didn't break from her task as she answered "Oh, Sloane wanted to talk to him about a couple things. He knew that I wanted some time with you." She stepped back and looked at her work and frowned a little before switching a couple things around and smiling, obviously pleased with the results. I watched her and shook my head, she was such a perfectionist.

Kai helped me go over to Quinn's and get all the food I had over there. Quinn and Sloane helped us carry it all over. Then Kai and Sloane went home to get their gifts and check on Reed and Kerri. Quinn helped me finish up the meal as we waited for the others to come over.

Once they were there I spread the food out on the table and we all filled our plates and ate in the living room. We ate while we talked about our Christmases. It was great having everyone together again. It felt right. While our group had been together so long, something had just been missing, but now that Quinn was with us and we were together, our group was whole. I realized that was the same feeling I couldn't name the few times we were all together for games nights or bowling. I smiled as I watched my friends laugh and joke with each other.

"So, Kerri, how did Reed end up popping the question?" Quinn asked.

All eyes turned to Kerri. She rolled her eyes and Reed had the goofiest grin ever. I knew this was going to be good.

"It was Christmas Eve, and Reed's parents' house was packed. I have no idea how they could fit that many people in a house that small. There had to be at least 50 there." She shook her head and continued. "They had all been drinking all day and it was noisy and chaotic. There were kids running everywhere. Someone had given all the kids those little fireworks poppers that you throw on the ground and they pop." Reed wore a guilty yet pleased look.

"Baby, I warned you it was going to be like that. It always is." Reed was grinning.

I smirked, thinking of a house filled with drunken Reeds. I could only imagine how entertaining that would be. Then again, I imagined Kerri was out of her element with all that going on.

"If you think that was packed, just wait until the wedding." Reed wiggled his eyebrows at her.

Kerri groaned. "Oh, God, what have I gotten myself into?" We all laughed and Kerri continued. "So Reed's uncle and...who was the other one?" She asked Reed.

"Cousin Ray-Ray," Reed filled in as he took a big bite of mashed potatoes.

We all looked at Reed to see if he was joking. Kerri answered for us.

"Seriously, he has a cousin named Ray-Ray. In fact Ray-Ray has a son. Ray-Ray Jr. So anyway, his uncle and Ray-Ray had just gotten into a fist fight and broken his mom's NASCAR display case. After they were dragged outside to cool down, this moron here decides to break the tension by turning on Beyonce. He starts dancing around the house singing along to Single Ladies."

Laughter broke all around the room. We've all heard Reed singing that and it truly was one of the silliest things ever.

"I just wanted to go hide but nooooo, he pulled me up and made me dance with him. He was spinning me all around the living room. At one point we knocked into the tree, almost tipping it. He about dropped me when he dipped me."

"I'd never drop you, baby." Reed was beaming.

"Whatever," Kerri tried to sound annoyed but the love was written all over her face. "After he about dropped me, I thought he was done because he let go of me. I was looking for an escape and I realized he was down on one knee in front of me, holding out a ring."

That was so Reed. We were all laughing.

"I about told him no just for having put on that little spectacle. What would you have done then?" She cocked an eyebrow at Reed.

"Oh, baby, there is no way you would have said no. No one can say no to the Reed charm."

We all dissolved in laughter again. When the room quieted down I turned to Kai.

"It's your turn. How did Sloane ask?"

Kai met Sloane's eyes and they shared a long loving look. It was so personal I fidgeted and glanced away. I met Quinn's gaze and smiled. I expected Kai to go all out on her retelling. She surprised me.

"He just slipped the ring on my finger." She practically whispered it.

"He didn't ask?" Kerri asked.

Kai shook her head. "He didn't need to. I knew what he wanted." She was still watching Sloane, her eyes full of love, and he reflected that love back at her.

"Yeah, well what were you doing?" Reed asked his mouth full.

Kai and Sloane both smiled, but didn't say anything. The room was quiet for a few beats before Reed yelled, "Dude, you asked her while you were banging her?" He reached over to give Sloane a fist bump, but Sloane leaned forward and punched him playfully instead.

"No! Jesus, you doofus that's something crass that only you would do. I'm surprised you didn't do that." Sloane scoffed at him.

"Hey, that was my original plan but I went with the moment." Reed shrugged.

"Well I just went with the moment, too." Sloane drawled out and sat back wrapping his arm around Kai.

We were all quiet for a few minutes while we ate, until Reed started complaining that we needed to hurry up and get on with the gift opening. The Titans were playing the Vikings at two and he wanted to watch the game.

"Hey, I have money riding on it. Jason is going to owe me big after this."

"Where is the dork anyway?" Kerri asked. "I would have thought he would have been here."

"He's on his way back today. He partied all weekend back home." Jason checked in with me every couple days. He still wasn't Quinn's biggest fan and I figured that was part of why he was keeping his distance. I really hoped that once he saw that Quinn and I were definitely back together that he would come around.

We all pitched in and had lunch cleaned up in no time. Kai and Reed were practically bouncing off the walls with child-like anticipation. We gathered in the living room and Kai donned a Santa hat and handed out gifts to everyone. We all took turns opening a present until all the gifts were opened. Reed gave us all engraved flasks filled with some of his "Tennessee Tiger Sweat." Sloane gave me an Amazon gift card, which Kai claimed wasn't right cause I didn't even have to go to a store to use it. Kerri gave me an assortment of barely-there lingerie, which made me blush and Quinn grin. Quinn gave me the same spa gift card that I had given to the girls. Telling me I needed a day out with them. He also gave me a new comfy blanket to cuddle under. Kai's gift brought tears to my eyes. She gave me a Christmas ornament with a mother of pearl finish and had it hand painted with the date and "When the heart spoke, love answered." I didn't even question her as to how she knew. She always just seemed to know that stuff.

We finished just in time for kickoff. The guys settled in to watch the game as I was stuck going through bridal magazines with Kerri and Kai. Both had brought a stack with them. After a while I made my escape to the kitchen to get leftovers out for supper. Once the game was over, everyone made a hasty retreat. Reed grumbled the whole way about the stupid Titans and how much he had to pay Jason. Sloane laughed at him and told him it was his fault for betting on a worthless team. I could hear them arguing all the way down the stairs.

I closed the door and leaned against it. Quinn came over to me and took me into his arms, pulling me tightly against him. I breathed him in and relaxed against him.

"Sylvia, my love." Quinn held me as he gently swayed us side to side. "How are you doing? Did you have a good day?"

I nodded as I murmured yes into his chest. He chuckled and I let the vibrations from it course through me. He released me and stepped back.

"Are you ready for tomorrow?" He carefully scrutinized my expression. He was looking for any trace of apprehension. Admittedly I had it and it was showing.

"Yes and no. I've been gone long enough I need to get back to work sometime and tomorrow is just as good as any. Besides, it's just a short shift to ease me back into it." I sighed and started to pick up around the apartment. Quinn joined me.

"You can always call in if you're not up to it yet."

"No. I want to go back. It's time that I start living in the real world again. The new semester starts in a week and I want to be sure that they have enough help."

"You don't need to work, you know. I can help..." I placed my finger over his lips, stopping him from finishing that.

"No. I know that you can and I know that you want to. It's not that I don't appreciate the offer. I just feel that it's more than the money for me. This is just another step in the process for me. I know you understand that."

Quinn nodded and before I removed my finger he playfully bit it. "I know. I just don't want you pushing yourself too soon."

"I'll be okay. I promise." I called out as I walked into the kitchen to get a glass of water. "On the bright, side I didn't get any texts today." I smiled at him over the rim of my water glass.

"Did you remember to get your phone from my place when you left this morning?"

I groaned and let my shoulders and head drop. "No. Damn it."

"Well do you want to go back to my place or do you want me to go get it for you?"

"Go grab it for me. I want to stay here tonight."

"Do you want me to check it for you?" Quinn grabbed his keys off the table by the door and waited for my answer with his hand on the knob.

"Yes please. I don't want to know what he said."

"Okay. I'll be back in a few minutes."

After he left I took my gifts into my bedroom and set them on the vanity. I looked again around the top to see if I could spot the pendant. When I was sure it wasn't there I got down on the floor and looked for it. I heard the door open while I was looking and Quinn called out to me.

"There were eleven texts, Sylvia." I heard his voice grow closer as he moved down the hall. "I'm going to call my dad in the morning and get the number for the family attorney. There has to be something we can... What are you doing?" I looked over my shoulder at him. He was standing in the doorway staring at my ass which was in the air as I had been looking under the vanity.

"Don't get me wrong. I like the view and all, but you don't normally go crawling around on the floor."

"I'm looking for the pendant I had on the mirror." I returned to scanning the carpet for it.

"The one from your mom?"

"Yes, that one. Have you seen it? It was off the mirror and I thought maybe it fell on the floor."

"Here, I'll pull the dresser out and you can look behind it." I moved back so Quinn could move it. It wasn't behind it either. I knew it was ridiculous, but that bad feeling started creeping up on me again. It had to be around somewhere. Quinn picked up on my foreboding and hugged me again.

"It'll turn up. It probably got snagged on the clothes I had setting on here. Tomorrow while you're at work I'll go through my stuff and see if I can't find it." He was nuzzling my neck along my sweet spot, and I forgot all about it for the time being. "Why don't you try on one of your gifts from Kerri?" His voice had gone husky and low, and it sent shivers darting straight between my legs. I moaned an agreement and grabbed one off the vanity where I had set them down and took it in to the bathroom to change. I may have been embarrassed opening them in front of everyone but I had secretly been waiting to put them on for Quinn. Tonight was going to end well.

WORK HAD GONE much better than I had been expecting. It was only a four hour shift and it was almost over. The time had flown by. I worked with Bobbie and Corrina. I had missed both of them and it was nice to catch up with them again. In fact I did more talking with them than I did working. I had to tear myself away from them and get some work done.

I was stocking books on the back corner shelf when I heard someone say my name. My body froze. I didn't know what I should do. I dropped my hand to my pocket and felt my phone in there. I debated on calling Quinn although I didn't know what that would accomplish. In the end I turned to face him. As I did I glanced around to see if anyone was nearby. I figured at least I was in a public place everything would be okay. I needed to get this over with eventually.

"Beau."

He stood before me in his ripped jeans and leather jacket. I once thought he was so hot, now he just looked dirty and unkempt. He stared back at me, moving his eyes across my body in a way that made me feel violated. I couldn't stop the shudder that ripped through me. He didn't speak. He just continued to look at me, increasing my nervousness.

"What do you want?" I tried to keep my tone even and not give away my fear.

"You. I want you, Sylvia. I miss you." He stepped closer to me and I stepped back. My back hit the shelves behind me and I realized I had no place to go to. I put my hand in my pocket and wrapped it around my phone.

"Beau, it's done. I've tried to tell you that. Don't you get the hint when I don't respond to your messages? What do I have to do to make you understand that I don't want you in my life?" There was a slight tremble to my voice and my heart was racing. He stepped closer and was right up against me. He swept a lock of hair behind my ear and leaned in close to me. I felt his breath against my cheek. I could smell the alcohol on his breath and it made me sick. I swallowed hard, trying to keep the fear choked down.

"Please, Sylvia. We were so good together. I've never felt this way about anyone. I need you, Sylvia." His voice was was low and guttural. He ran his hand over my shoulder and down my arm. I cringed and tried to pull myself away. He grabbed my arm tighter so I couldn't move. "I know you feel it too, Sylvia. You can't deny it. I felt how wet you'd get for me. I've heard you moan my name." He pushed himself up against me and his other hand came to rest against my hip. I tried to push him away but he held me too tightly. I let out a little cry.

"Please, just let me go. I don't feel that way. In fact I never did. Please, Beau, just let me go. I won't scream, and you can just walk away from here." His eyes were so cold, piercing into me, stabbing me with fear.

"Is it him?" I heard the hatred drip off his tongue. I knew he was referring to Quinn.

"No, it's you and me. I will not be treated like this."

"Don't lie to me, bitch." His fingers on my arm and my hip dug into me. I knew they were going to leave bruises. "Do you love him?"

"Yes." I whispered it. I was afraid for Quinn, but I couldn't lie either. I didn't want to give Beau any false hope.

He shoved away from me roughly, causing me to fall back against the shelves and knocking the books off. He grumbled something about ending the bastard as he turned and stalked away from me.

"Stop. Beau, don't." I tried calling out to him, but he didn't turn back around. I got to my feet and tried to catch up with him. I reached out and grabbed his arm. He threw me back.

"I'll be back for you." He snapped at me coldly, and disappeared out the door.

I could see the others I worked with heading over to me. I reached into my pocket and pulled out my phone and called Quinn. It rang until it went to voice mail. I tried again. When that didn't work I panicked. I called out to no one in-particular that I had to go and I ran from the building. I slowed down long enough to call Reed on my way. He was out shopping with Kerri but he said they would leave and head straight home. He assured me that he would call Sloane, that he thought he was home. I thanked him and started running again. I didn't know if I would get there in time, but I had to try.

Chapter 23 - Quinn

I WAS RELIEVED HAVING EVERYONE back. I was becoming even more concerned about Sylvia's safety daily and I needed their help. The numbers of Beau's texts were increasing, and the tone was becoming more and more desperate. Even though Sylvia never responded to them, I knew he wasn't going to give up. On some level I could understand his pull towards Sylvia. I wouldn't let her go again without a fight either, but I wouldn't go about trying to get her back the same way as he was. I couldn't prove it, but I was sure he had been hanging around watching her, too. Other than New Year's Eve when I thought I saw his truck I hadn't seen him. But I had the feeling of being watched whenever I was out in the parking lot. I had Sloane and Reed looking for him too since they'd gotten back, but so far they were unable to see him.

The morning of the Christmas get-together I became even more concerned. I woke up to find Sylvia out of bed already. I didn't think anything of it. I knew she planned to get up early and start cooking. I figured she would just do it at my place since that was where the food was. I was surprised when she wasn't in the kitchen. I went over to check on her at her place and heard the shower running. I wanted to go in and see what in the hell she was thinking leaving her door unlocked but I didn't want to start the day out with an argument.

I figured since she was busy it would be a good time to talk to Sloane and Reed. I didn't want to alarm Sylvia, but I really needed to talk it out with someone. I texted Sloane and told him I would wait in the hall for him. I didn't want Sylvia to find me waiting in her apartment for Sloane. I locked the door behind me on my way out but then Sloane and Kai showed up together. So I unlocked the door and let Kai in.

Sloane and I went over to my place to wait for Reed. We talked about our holidays as we waited. Sloane commented on how much better he thought Sylvia was doing since they'd left for break. I told him about her outburst and how after that she just improved more every day. He said Kai had been happy to hear her sound so lively on the phone while they were gone.

Once Reed showed up, I turned to the matter at hand.

"I need your help."

"What's going on man?" Reed asked.

"Beau is trying to contact Sylvia again. And I'm not sure, but I think he's been hanging around watching her, too." I told them what was in the various texts and how I thought I'd seen him. "Sylvia hasn't responded to any of them, but I just have a feeling that he's not going to give up."

Sloane was sitting on the couch and a knowing look crossed his face and he nodded. "That could be the explanation for the way Kai was feeling last night."

I looked at him confused. "What do you mean?"

"She was complaining about something being wrong. She couldn't put her finger on it but she was just off all night."

I had heard enough stories of Kai's premonitions that I couldn't discount it. If anything, it solidified my worries. I explained to them that I looked into getting an anti-harassment order but it didn't seem like we had enough evidence to get one.

"Do you have any suggestions for what should be done?" I turned first to Sloane, because he always had sound advice. This time, though, he was just sitting quietly on the couch with his arms crossed in front of him. I could see he was deep in thought. He was staring at his feet, which were kicked out in front of him. It didn't seem like he was actually seeing them. One glance at his eyes and I could see the strategizing taking place in his mind.

Reed drew my attention back to him when he smacked his fist into his other hand.

"We just need to go hunt the motherfucker down and beat his ass. You know he won't go to the cops about it. We'll teach him a lesson and then he'll stay the fuck away." Reed's voice was heated and his eyes were alight with the thought of pounding on Beau. I knew that wouldn't be the right approach, but it was sure as hell tempting.

I shook my head. "I don't think that's the best way to go about it. I don't trust that asshat. Unless we killed him..."

"We could do that," Reed interrupted me.

"I won't say it never crossed my mind, but no. We can't do that. We're not killers. As I was saying, unless we killed him..." Reed raised one eyebrow and I shook my head and rolled my eyes but continued on. "He would just want revenge for us giving him a beat down."

"We could injure him bad enough that he wouldn't be able to hurt anyone again," Reed replied.

Before I could respond Sloane spoke up. "What if we lure him out using Sylvia as bait?"

"What the fuck, Sloane? We are not getting Sylvia involved in anything," I roared at him. He stared back at me with calculating eyes. The anger in me continued to boil. "How can you even think of putting her in any danger? Would you do that to Kai if it were her being stalked?"

The bastard sat there calmly, watching me rant.

"Quinn, calm down and just listen to what I have to say." Sloane had his hands held up in front of him, motioning for me to just calm down.

I didn't want to hear what he had to say, but I huffed and agreed. I sat back down and Sloane straightened up.

"When Reed mentioned that he wouldn't go to the cops, it made me think that maybe we could set him up. We know from the background check that Kelly ran that he's wanted. What if we contacted the police and let them know that we can help them get him?"

"Like calling in a tip to America's Most Wanted?" Only Reed would see it that way.

"Yes, Reed, kind of like that." Sloane humored him. "We could work with them to help bring him in. If we could get them to come to the apartment we could have Sylvia call Beau and tell him she's ready to talk. From what you've said he'll jump at the chance. Once he shows up at the apartment we'll just sit back and let the cops handle it." Sloane sat back with a self satisfied smirk on his face. I had to admit, it was a solid plan.

Reed leaned over and gave him a fist bump.

I grinned at the two of them. "I like it. I still want to speak with my dad's attorney too but your idea's pretty good. We can't do anything today since its Sunday. Don't say anything to the girls and I'll talk to the attorney in the morning and we can hopefully call the police after that and get this taken care of." I just wanted it over, I'd had enough of seeing the fear in Sylvia's eyes every time she heard from him.

We agreed to let it go until the next day and then take it from there.

The rest of the day was good. We ate and heard about the different proposals. It made me think about how I would ask Sylvia. So far I didn't have any solid plans. I just knew that when the time was right I would ask her. After we ate, we opened gifts and watched football. I didn't really care about the game, but it was interesting to watch Reed. He really got into the game. I held back from laughing several times when Sloane would taunt him just to get a rise out of him. I never had brothers, but this is what I always imagined having them would be like.

Somewhere around halftime, I lost interest in the game. I caught my mind drifting to picturing Sylvia in the stuff Kerri gave her. She was so embarrassed when she'd opened it. She wouldn't hold anything up, but I looked over her shoulder into the box. I didn't get a good look at anything in particular. It was just a lot of lace and silk in mostly red and black. The black caught my attention and made me think back to how she looked passed out on the bed at Halloween before I dressed her. I had to actively push those thoughts away. The last thing I needed was for Reed to look over and see me sporting wood while I watched football. I'd never hear the end of it.

I kept stealing glances at Sylvia. She was being a good sport going through the wedding shit with Kerri and Kai. I pitied her when they got going into full-on wedding planning. Thank God guys don't have to worry about that crap. Tell me where to be and what time and that's all I needed to worry about. Okay, that and the bachelor party. I was sure Reed's was going to be a riot, especially if his family was involved.

I was slightly concerned with how Sylvia was doing. It was her first time with them all back together since she started coming back to her old self. She seemed to be fine, but Sylvia could put on a pretty brave face. Finally, everyone left and I was able to just hold her for a little bit. When I asked how she was, she answered. Her face was pressed up against my chest and it tickled slightly.

I questioned her about her decision to go back to work in the morning. I scrutinized her face as she answered me. I could see the trepidation in her eyes and in the little worry line on her brow. At least she admitted to it. I was proud of her for wanting to get back into the swing of things, yet at the same time I didn't want her to push herself too quickly. I knew when I suggested to her that she didn't need to work, that she would turn me down. That was just who Sylvia was.

I was ready to let the worry go but then she brought up Beau's texts. We both realized she forgot her phone at my place and it was probably still turned off. She wanted to stay the night at her place so I went over to my place to get it. I turned it on to find eleven texts from Beau. I clenched my jaw and was tempted to just throw the phone against the wall. She needed to get a new number. I didn't want to look at them, but I knew I needed to. I would need to tell the attorney in the morning.

He sent a new text about every two hours starting with the previous night when her phone was dead.

```
Come back to me we can make it right - B

Doesnt he ever leave - B

Hes just a pussy u need a real man - B

I have what ur looking 4 - B

I miss ur boobs and how they felt n my hands and
mouth - B

Im here...waiting when you decide Im the better
man - B

Im sorry...please let me make it up 2 u - B

I can make it better I promise - B
```

The others were just the generic "I miss you and call me" texts. I hoped the one about missing her boobs would be enough to get some sort of protection order. The thought of him touching Sylvia pissed me off something fierce. For a brief moment I was ready to go get Reed and go through with killing him.

I gave myself a few minutes to calm down. I didn't need Sylvia to see me that upset. When I felt in control of myself again, I headed back over to her place for the night. I started to tell her about the texts and that I was going to call the attorney, but as I walked into the bedroom the sight in front of me made every thought in my head disappear. Sylvia was on her hands and knees with her ass pointed right at me. She had such a sweet ass, too. The jeans she had on were tight to begin with, but they were pulled even tighter with the slight pull on them from being on her knees. I just wanted to go up to her run my hands over her or, better yet, rub up against her. The thought of that black lacy thing popped into my mind again, and I wondered just what I could do to get her into it.

I realized she was watching me so I quickly asked her why she was on the floor.

"I'm looking for the pendant I had on the mirror," she answered simply. She turned back to start looking again.

"The one from your mom?" I pictured the little cameo done in blue with the picture of a mother holding her baby. I didn't know if that was it but I knew she always kept that one around. She never wore it but it was important to her.

"Yes, that one. Have you seen it? It was off the mirror and I thought maybe it fell on the floor." She answered without looking back at me.

I offered to move the dresser for her and she moved so I could. We both looked behind it and didn't find it. I noticed the black thing that had been prominent in my most current fantasy on top of the dresser when I moved it back. I was really hoping she would try it on for me. I wrapped her in my arms and muttered something to her about looking for it in the morning. She smelled so good, the flowery stuff she used still lingered but it was mostly masked with the scent of her. My dick had been mostly hard already after having the view of her ass wiggling around while she looked around the floor. The smell combined with the feel of her body against mine had it rock solid.

I brushed my face against her neck just up under her ear. I knew this drove her crazy, and I loved to drive her crazy.

"Why don't you try on one of your gifts from Kerri?" I whispered to her as I continued to move along her neck. I felt her tremble in my arms. Then she let out the sexiest little moan and I knew soon I'd be taking that black thing off her.

Sylvia and I slept in after the late night we had. I questioned her again about going to work, but she insisted that she wanted to. It was only 10am to 2pm. It wasn't that long. I reluctantly walked her to work. It just felt off to me. I told myself it was just because I didn't want her to go so I was finding excuses to keep her home. I never did tell her how I felt about it. I didn't want her to needlessly worry about something while she already had so much she was dealing with just being there.

I met Kerri and Reed on the steps of the apartment as I was walking up. They were going out shopping. Kerri wanted to exchange some of the gifts she got at Christmas and they needed to go get groceries. I told them to have a good time and reminded Reed to call me when he got back. I figured he told Kerri what was going on when she didn't question why I wanted him to call.

I stopped by Sloane's just to let him know that I was going to call the attorney and I would come see him after I had some advice. I had thought over his plan this morning while Sylvia was getting ready and came to the conclusion that it really was the best route to go. Before I did that, I wanted to be assured that there was no way he would be getting out any time soon. I wasn't about to do anything that could potentially cause him to be even more irrational and vindictive.

Sloane said he would check in with me later. He and Kai were going to do some laundry and he would come up when they were done. I teased him about it. Reed had told me all about Sloane and Kai's laundry adventures in the basement laundry room. It seemed Kai had a thing for the washing machine.

I decided to go to Sylvia's instead of my place when I got upstairs. I told her I would look around for the pendant today while she was at work. First, I needed to call Dad to get the number for the attorney. Both he and mom knew what was going on. I filled them in when I talked to them on New Year's Day. They were both concerned. Mom, of course, wanted both of us to stay with them. I refused. I didn't want to lead Beau anywhere near my parents place. I hoped he hadn't already been around there.

After a lengthy conversation with Dad I was finally able to call the attorney. Of course, he was in a meeting and would have to call me back later. Sometimes it seemed like all I did was wait for things. I went into the bedroom and pulled the dresser out again and looked all around the floor, running my hands along the carpet in hopes that it was just sunk in a little and my hand would catch it. No luck with that. I moved it back and looked through all the drawers. When I didn't find it in there, I checked the dirty clothes in the hamper. It wasn't in there, either. It had to be around somewhere.

I started to look around the room but noticed that it was already 1:30. I still needed to shower before I went to get Sylvia. I would probably end up driving over to get her. That would give me a little extra time. I threw my shirt and socks in the hamper in her bedroom and headed into the bathroom to shower. I was still thinking about the lost pendant when I stepped under the hot spray. I stood there a few minutes and just let the hot water cascade over me. I was absentmindedly watching a trickle of water run down the shower wall when one of Beau's texts came to mind. *I have what ur looking for. I have what ur looking for.* It played on repeat in my head until the light bulb flashed on. At the time I figured it was just alluding to the fact that he thought he was right for her. Now I was fairly certain it was about the pendant. If that was the case, and it had to be, that meant he had broken into her apartment.

That now gave us something to go on to get that anti-harassment order. I would have smiled if it weren't so damn creepy knowing that he had been in her apartment. I wondered how many times he had done that and what else could be missing. I hurried and soaped off and washed my hair. I did a quick rinse off and shut the water off. I was going to take Sylvia straight to the Clerk of Courts office after I picked her up so she could fill out the paperwork, and then to the police. I grabbed the towel and started to dry off when I heard a knock at the door. It was about time Sloane showed up. I needed to tell him about the new development. I just grabbed my jeans off the floor and pulled them on quick. I could come back in and change after I let him in. I didn't want him to leave thinking that I already left to get Sylvia.

I walked to the door running my hands through my hair. I hadn't dried it off very well and it was still dripping on me. The pounding on the door continued and it was loud enough that I changed my mind. It sounded more like Reed. I was surprised he was back already. I would have thought Kerri would have kept him out all day.

"Yeah, yeah, I'm coming." As soon as I called it out I groaned recalling the first time I answered the door for Reed. I turned the knob, expecting a lame "that's what she said" comment. I opened the door partway only to have it kicked wide open, swinging back against the wall and bouncing off it. I stood, slightly stunned for a fraction of a heartbeat, staring at an enraged Beau.

He swung at me once, missed, then followed through with the other fist. I didn't even have time to think about it. When his left fist lashed out, I pivoted back on my right foot, pushing his attack aside and letting his momentum take him away from me.

He recovered quickly, and tried to throw an elbow behind him to catch me where he thought I'd be. I wasn't.

I slid my left foot across the floor to his other side, sweeping hard with my right leg into the back of his knees. I realized a fraction of a second too late that he wasn't going to hit the ground like I'd thought he would. He turned and lunged at me, his left hand grabbing my throat.

I staggered back. I was surprised at how powerful he was, like a wild animal. I hunched my back so it was my shoulders that slammed into the wall rather than the back of my head. He brought his other fist around in a roundhouse towards my cheekbone. I got my hand up in time to grab his wrist. I wasn't strong enough to stop the punch, but I was able to direct it up, connecting him with the crown of my head. I winced. It still hurt like hell. The pressure of the punch pushing against his other hand at my neck made my world go white for a moment. I'd narrowly saved myself from being knocked out. For a brief moment, we stood there at an impasse. His hand held my neck, and my hand held his other fist. Our eyes met, and I saw his rage change to something else.

That's when it dawned on me: For all his bullying and bravado, he wasn't actually a very good fighter. He'd never had to be. He depended on being a mean sonofabitch, and on people either running or going down after his initial onslaught. He didn't have a second move. The look in his eyes was uncertainty. If I'd had time to smile, I would have.

It occurred to him just then to try to drive a knee into my groin. I caught it with my own knee, then followed through by viciously planting my heel in the soft muscle above the knee he was standing on. He stumbled back, letting go of my neck. He bumped into the bookshelf Sylvia had against the wall near the door, knocking off several items. I heard the sound of breaking glass, but I didn't check to see what it was.

This was my chance. It was time to go to work.

I'd kept my right leg up, and as soon as I got the separation I needed, I pivoted my hips and drove a kick into his midsection. He tried to grab the leg, but I managed to awkwardly swing my right hand sidelong into his jaw, and he let go. I swiveled around into a round kick, digging the ball of my left foot into the side of his already damaged right knee. Arm followed leg. I followed through with a left upper cut, then a solid right cross to the nose. I heard the crack, and it started gushing blood. Continuing my spinning motion, I kicked with my right foot at the free-floating ribs below the left arm, which he'd started to pull back for a punch. As he brought his arm down instinctively, I planted my right foot and spun around on it. Keeping my left leg straight, I catapulted it around, heel first, towards his head. I'd underestimated Beau. He'd stepped into the kick, so instead of catching his face with my heel, I smacked into it with my calf. He wrapped an arm up to catch the kick. Off-balance and highly vulnerable, I windmilled my arms slightly as I tried to get back the advantage.

Luckily, that's when the damage I'd done on his knee paid off. As he moved to twist me off my feet, his right leg buckled under him. He had to let go of my ankle to keep his balance, and I knew it was nearly over. Planting my left foot in front of him, I stepped forward. I led with my left upper-cut again -- not very creative, I thought absently, but he wasn't arguing. The punch to the underside of his chin stood him up straight, and I settled back into a wide-footed back stance my instructor would have been proud of. I briefly flashed back to a board-breaking clinic, taking a split second to compose myself and picturing that board laid across Beau's chest. I shifted my weight from my back leg to my front and rotated ankles, hips, shoulders, and wrists. I pushed every ounce of force my body could muster through the square inch of my first two knuckles, and struck directly into his sternum.

He was already on his heels, and my punch sent him reeling backwards, arms flailing, into the doorway. He hit the door frame unevenly, head first, and bounced off it out into the hall. I heard a thud as he hit the floor.

I'd never punched a human being that hard in my life. But instead of being filled with revulsion, I found that all I wanted was to hit him again. I knew I couldn't give him time to recover. I stepped forward, preparing myself for the worst.

I heard Sloane call my name from the stairs, but I didn't take my eyes off the bloody mess that was Beau. He would be sneaky enough to pull a fake-out until my attention was elsewhere and then rise up and came at me again. Then again, a punch with that much force probably did some major damage to his lungs and ribs, possibly even his heart. I couldn't find it in me to be care.

I kept watching him as I ordered, "Sloane, call the cops." I was breathing rapidly the adrenalin coursing through my veins. The whole altercation only lasted a couple minutes, but it had me pumped as if it were an entire workout.

"I already did, man. They're on the way. What the hell happened?" I flicked a glance over to him and saw that he was standing on the landing trying to keep Kai behind him. She was peeking out from behind his back.

"Did you kill him?" She asked in alarm. "He's not moving."

"No, he's still breathing." Sloane assured her.

He cautiously stepped forward and leaned over Beau. I was ready to attack if he tried anything. When he didn't move, I became slightly alarmed. Sloane kicked at him and he still didn't move.

"Kai, you better call for an ambulance too," I said in a harsh tone.

Kai pulled out her cell phone and dialed. She moved to the second floor as she talked.

Sloane looked up at me. "How hard did you hit him?" His voice was full of awe.

"Pretty damn hard, but I don't think that's what did it. He hit his head on the door frame as he went down."

Sloane was still looking me over. "Are you okay? You're covered in blood."

I looked down at my naked chest for the first time and noticed the blood spattered across it. It made me conscious of the sticky mess. "Yeah. It's not mine." I smirked at Sloane. It felt fucking awesome to know I'd made that bastard bleed.

"So what the hell happened?" Sloane asked as he straightened up and looked around me into the apartment.

I turned and surveyed the mess for the first time. There were some books, picture frames and other broken knick-knacks on the floor. I cringed and hoped that it was nothing special to Sylvia. I would replace anything that was broken.

"I heard a knock at the door and thought it was you or Reed, so I went to open it and Beau kicked it open and swung at me. It just went from there." I shrugged, not really knowing how to describe what happened.

Sloane nodded as he looked between Beau and myself with slight disbelief. "I missed a call from Reed while we were in the laundry room. He told me to call the cops and get them to the apartment. Beau had been to see Sylvia and left her and she was worried about you. We heard the crashing sounds as I was checking the voice mail. Kai called the cops on her cell."

I heard the sirens at the same time Kai appeared at the top of the steps. She threw something at me and I felt something warm and wet hit me in the chest. I grabbed at it with my hands and looked down to see the wash cloth.

"You need to clean up the blood before Sylvia sees you. She's on her way." Thank God Kai thinks of everything. Sylvia would freak if she saw the blood on me.

I thanked her and washed it off before tossing it behind me into the apartment.

The cops came rushing up the stairs and we all moved aside to let them through. The EMTs were right behind them and they went to work on

Beau while the cops pulled the rest of us off to the side. I cooperated with them, answering all their questions. I told him about Beau kicking in the door and what had happened after that. I explained to him how he had dated Sylvia and she broke it off with him but he kept texting her and my suspicions that he was in her apartment. I watched Sloane and Kai being questioned. Every once in a while I would glance at the EMTs working on Beau. I didn't hear what they said but I knew it wasn't good. It wasn't long before they had him on the gurney and took him away.

The whole time I was being questioned, I thought of Sylvia. I wanted this over with. If Sylvia was on her way I just wanted to hold her in my arms and know that she was fine. Sloane said that Beau had been to see her. He didn't tell me if she had been hurt or not. I was worried about her. I could only assume that she was at work that others were around and that would keep her safe. Still I would be on edge until I saw her for myself.

The officer told me to wait there while he talked with the one that had been interviewing Sloane and Kai. While I was waiting something caught my eye on the floor where Beau had been. I walked over to investigate. It was Sylvia's pendant. I knew that asshole had taken it. I picked it up and brought it over to the officers. I told them this was on the floor where Beau had been and it belonged to Sylvia. They took it from me and turned back to each other.

After a few minutes, the officer I was talking to said that due to Beau being unconscious and unable to make a statement, I would have to come with them down to the station. He led me down the stairs and outside to his car. It was freaking cold and I stopped as we got to the car and asked if I could go grab my shirt and shoes. Just as I asked, Kai came out holding both. The officer let me pull the shirt on before I got into the car. I heard my name called as I was sliding in the back. I turned and saw Sylvia across the parking lot.

"Kai, there's Sylvia. Take care of her for me and meet me at the station. Call my dad. My phone's in the bedroom," I called out to Kai before the door was shut on me. I watched Sylvia through the window for as long as I could. I was still pissed about the whole thing, and I was coming down off the adrenalin high. I should have been concerned with what was going to happen at the station, but I knew I was in the right and I would do whatever they needed from me so I could get back to Sylvia. I took a deep breath in and slumped back against the seat. For the moment, I knew she was safe. That was all I cared about.

Chapter 24 - Sylvia

R UNNING WAS NOT THE BEST idea. Any time running would have saved I spent picking myself up off the ground. After my fourth stumble I gave up and walked quickly. It was normally a ten to fifteen minute walk, and it seemed to be taking twice as long. I rounded the corner onto the street that would lead me home. I was still several blocks away, but at least I was getting closer. I heard the sirens. I froze, peering down the street trying to make out what it was and where it was coming from. My gut told me that it was indeed coming from my apartment building, but my brain was trying to keep the rest of my body calm. The wail of the siren steadily built to a crescendo as the ambulance approached. I remained stuck to the sidewalk as I watched it for a few heartbeats. My fear for Quinn was crippling, yet all I felt was hollow as the ambulance passed by and continued towards the hospital.

I envisioned the guy from the bar, all bloody and laying on the floor. His face transformed into Quinn's. The sick feeling I had in my stomach was creeping up. I swallowed hard, wincing at the thought of losing it here where anyone could see me. I was so lost in my fears that I jumped when my phone sang out to me. It was Reed's tone. I was nervous as I answered it and my hand shook, causing me to fumble it for a couple seconds before I could push the answer button.

"Sylvia, are you home? What's going on? Sloane won't answer." Reed was clearly distressed. His normally loud voice was turned up a notch as he yelled into the phone. I could hear Kerri trying to quiet him in the background.

I took a big breath as fear coursed through me. *Sloane won't answer,* ran through my mind, sending shivers up my spine. My voice trembled as I answered him back. "I don't know. I'm not there yet, but an ambulance just passed me coming from that way."

"A what?" Reed hollered, making me flinch and hold the phone away.

266

"What's going on there?"

"I don't know. I can't see." I couldn't hold back anymore and started to cry, the frustration overwhelming me.

I heard a little scuffle and Kerri came on the line. "We're on our way, Sylvia. Don't go to the apartment alone. Call Jason and wait for him somewhere else. If you can't get a hold of him, call us and we'll pick you up. You need to keep yourself safe right now, and I don't think home is safe for you. We'll see you soon." Then she hung up.

I knew her advice was probably the best, but I couldn't take it. I had to know what was going on. I needed to know if that ambulance held Quinn. I started back down the street, clutching my phone tightly. I would at least have it ready if I needed it. Every step I took brought me closer to the chaos that awaited me in the parking lot. The first thing I noticed were the flashing lights still there. I was finally able to determine them to be police cars. That reassured me of my own safety, but struck the terror back into me full force.

I picked up my pace but stopped dead once I reached the edge of the parking lot. I breathed a sigh of relief as I watched Quinn walk out of the apartment. He was safe and he appeared to be unharmed. I couldn't tear my eyes from him. He was like an apparition of a god, walking out all shirtless with his muscles tense and hard. He was like Zeus coming down from Olympus. Once he stepped out of the shadow the sun hit his hair, reflecting the deep bronze highlights and casting a halo-like effect. In that moment he transformed from a god into an avenging angel. His face was a barely-contained mask of rage and aggravation. His jaw was tight and his hands were clenched into fists. As he continued to move, I watched the way he stalked forward. He seemed to be so self-assured and in control of himself, even though his face told me different. The jeans rode low on his hips, revealing the deep v of muscles that I considered mine alone to look at. I moved my gaze lower to reassure myself that he was indeed unharmed. I couldn't understand why he was walking outside without his shoes on. For that matter, why wasn't he wearing a shirt?

It was then I noticed the officer next to him opening the door to the cruiser. He turned and said something to the officer as Kai ran up and handed him a bundle. He pulled a shirt on and I realized he was about to get into the car.

"Quinn!" His name tore from my throat.

He turned and looked at me. His eyes locked to mine as he slid into the backseat. He said something again but he didn't tear his eyes from mine. I was aware of the officer getting in the front, and I began to panic as the car started to pull away. *No, they have the wrong guy. Quinn is the good guy. They are supposed to be taking Beau, not Quinn.* I turned my eyes, following the car as it left the lot and made its way down the street. Quinn turned and watched me the whole way. I reached out as if I could stop him from being taken away. When the car was out of sight, I felt arms around me and heard Kai reassuring me that all was going to be fine.

I whirled on her. "How is it going to be alright? Quinn was just taken by the police. Wait, why was Quinn taken? What is going on here?" My words were tumbling together as my hysteria rose. I was looking around wildly, as if something somewhere held all my answers. I noticed the residents of the complex all standing around watching the spectacle that had been taking place in the parking lot.

Kai calmly reached for my thrashing hands, effectively stilling them. "Sylvia, look at me." Her voice was authoritative, and I turned my attention to her. "Quinn will be fine. They just need to ask him about what happened."

"What did happen?" I was worried, yet relieved.

"Beau showed up and kicked in your door." Her words hit me like cold water. I flinched.

"But Quinn..."

"Quinn took care of it. He is fine." She was talking to me as if I were a child in the midst of throwing a fit. I guess, in a way, I was.

"The ambulance?" I knew the answer but I needed to ask anyway.

Kai nodded, confirming my thoughts. "It was Beau. We don't know how bad it is, but he was unconscious when they left with him."

"Unconscious, but breathing right?" The ice water seeped into my veins, causing me to tremble. I wasn't concerned with Beau. I was worried about Quinn. If he killed Beau, would the police let him go?

"Yes, he was breathing. We need to go get Sloane and I need to call Quinn's dad. Then we'll go to the station to wait for him."

Kai let go of one hand and pulled me along with her by the other. She continued telling me about the voicemail from Reed and the commotion they heard coming from my apartment. Kai insisted it all happened so fast that by the time they got there it was over. We started up the steps, but she stopped in front of me on the second landing.

"Sylvia, don't freak out when you see your apartment. I promise,

Quinn was not hurt." Kai was all serious, and it made me wonder what I was walking into. Visions of war zones danced before my eyes. I imagined broken furniture, holes in the wall and the door hanging by the hinges.

The reality was nothing. Just a few broken trinkets and picture frames. I looked over everything as Kai went to retrieve Quinn's phone. I was so relieved. Of course there was a hole in the wall where the doorknob hit it and a boot print on the door from Beau. I was about to laugh at Kai and her worry over my reaction until I spotted the bloody cloth lying on the floor. I felt immediately sick.

"Sylvia, are you alright?" Sloane came out of the kitchen with the broom and dust pan.

I just pointed to the cloth. *Please let that not be from Quinn.*

Sloane's gaze followed my finger and he strode over and picked it up. "Don't worry. It's Beau's blood. Quinn just needed to wipe it off him."

I nodded, not really knowing what to say. Quinn had told me not to worry, that he could handle himself. But I had never really believed that he could. I had been wrong. I was trying to process that as Kai came from the bedroom, hurriedly speaking on Quinn's phone.

"...I assume that's where he will be. He told me to call you." Her eyes fluttered to mine. "No, she's fine, just a little shook up." She smiled at me. "Yes. We're on our way."

Kai took the phone from her ear and stuffed it in her pocket.

"Okay, let's head to the station." Sloane reached for her and hugged her for a brief second. I was momentarily envious. I wanted Quinn's arms wrapped around me like that. I wanted to feel his comforting embrace, letting me know that everything was indeed just fine.

"Sylvia, do you need to get anything before we go?" Sloane turned and asked me before pulling me in for a hug too. It was slightly reassuring but it wasn't Quinn.

"No. Wait, we need to call Reed and Kerri. They are on their way here." I didn't want them to come and find all of us gone and not know where we'd gone.

"I'll do it from the car. Kai, you drive." Sloane ushered us both out the door and shut it tightly behind him.

We made our way to Kai's little blue car and got in. They both talked all the way there, but I didn't listen to them. The guilt was worming its way in. I should have broken up with Beau before all this started. I should have never let him back into my life after that first weekend I stayed with

Quinn. I should have gone to the police, I should have told my dad. All of the should haves kept piling up. By the time we reached the station, I felt the weight of the world on my shoulders.

We walked into the brightly lit room through a set of metal detectors. There weren't many in the front waiting area. Kai motioned for Sloane and I to go sit down as she walked over to a high front desk encased in what I assumed was bullet proof glass. Sloane and I sat on the hard blue plastic chairs and waited. I glanced around and noticed that Alex and Marie weren't there yet. Not that I expected they would be. They lived on the other side of town and Alex had more than likely been at work. Kai approached us and took a seat on my other side.

"They aren't telling me anything. Something about privacy laws. Don't worry; Alex is coming with an attorney. We'll get answers then." She patted my back reassuringly.

A young blond haired man in a gray suit, carrying a briefcase walked in and headed straight for the desk. He spoke quietly and confidently. I heard Quinn's name and snapped my head in his direction. I studied him as he reached into his pocket and showed the person behind the desk what I thought was probably identification. I was hoping he was the attorney we were waiting for. I continued to watch him as he waited patiently for someone to come and lead him back behind the closed doors where Quinn must be held.

After he was led back, I hopped back on the guilt train. What had I dragged Quinn and his family into? What if he was charged with something? Would it hurt his career? Oh my God, did I destroy all he's worked for? I was so not worth all that. My foot began to bounce frantically as more and more worries and scenarios played out in my head. Sloane reached over and put his hand on my leg to still it.

"Sylvia, you need to calm down. Look at me." I looked into his tranquil green eyes. They implored me to calm down. He spoke quietly to me and only me. "Worrying isn't going to help anything right now. Quinn knew exactly what he was doing. Beau deserved it, all of it. You know that, right?" I swallowed and nodded. I felt my eyes fill with tears and tried to blink them away. He rubbed comfortingly along my knee as he continued his voice still low and soothing. "You're worrying about all the wrong things, Sylvia. Trust me on this -- no one is in jeopardy. You are under too much strain as it is. Don't add to it with totally unnecessary worries." He pulled me to him, his strong arms wrapping themselves around me, sharing his strength and optimism with me. He whispered in my ear, "You are worth it."

I smiled at him the best I could. His words had the intended effect. I leaned against Kai as I waited. I tried to block out all unnecessary thoughts and worries. I just focused on tiles on the floor and counted them. I was on sixty-four when Reed burst into the room, followed by Kerri.

"Have you heard anything? How's Quinn? Did someone make him their bitch yet?" All our eyes flew to Reed. As Kerri flicked his ear. "Jesus, baby. That hurts." He whined as he rubbed his ear.

"We don't know anything yet. Have a seat and wait with us." Sloane motioned to the chairs across from us.

Kai stood. "I need to use the restroom. Sylvia, would you like to come with?"

I didn't know what else to do so I followed her. I didn't have to go but I did splash cool water on my face and wipe it off with the rough paper towel. I looked horrible. My eyes were bloodshot and puffy from crying. I had a crease across my brow that I knew wouldn't disappear until I saw Quinn again. I turned from the mirror and my self-examination as I heard Kai flush. She stepped out and washed her hands before enveloping me into a hug. Her tiny little arms could hug something fierce.

"Thanks, Sylvia. I needed that." It was more like she knew I needed that. "Marie and Alex should be here by now. Let's go see if they can find out anything."

We walked back out and I overheard Sloane saying, "He messed him up real bad. I don't think it's going to be good."

Kerri hissed and jerked her head in my direction. They all stared at me and I remained frozen. Before I could do anything, the door to the back opened and a young, blond officer stepped out.

"Sylvia O'Mara?" he called out loud and clear.

All eyes were on me. I swallowed and stepped forward. "That's me," I whispered.

He smiled at me warmly. "Miss O'Mara, I need to talk to you. Will you please come with me?"

I nodded and followed him beyond the doors, which closed behind me. I wondered what he needed to talk to me about. I looked around as I tagged along behind him. I was looking for Quinn. I knew he had to be here somewhere. I didn't see him before the officer stopped and motioned to an open door. I entered the little room, which I knew from having grown up a cop's daughter was an interrogation room. I never feared the police, and I wasn't afraid of them now. I was just worried about Quinn and wanted to know what was going on with him.

I sat down on the chair he motioned towards. I waited patiently for him to take his seat and get started.

"Miss O'Mara, I'm Officer Francis." He reached over and held out his hand. I tentatively shook it.

"Sylvia, please," I corrected him. He nodded.

He was young. He couldn't have been much older than I was. He was blond, with sharp angular features. Yet he was pretty. Almost feminine in his features. His eyes were pale blue and kind, yet cautious.

I settled back in my chair, crossing my arms in front of me as I waited for him to begin.

"Miss...Sylvia, I need to record this." I nodded as he pressed the button on the recorder. "Do you know Beau Dalton?"

"Yes."

"How do you know Mr. Dalton?"

I bit my lip, not wanting to admit it. "I dated him briefly."

"What can you tell me about your relationship with him?"

I told him how I'd met Beau, and how he became increasingly possessive towards me. I told him of how he'd grabbed me that Monday after I had stayed with Quinn and threatened to end Quinn. I relived Halloween and all that he had said to me.

He asked me some questions about Beau's activities and if I ever saw him do anything illegal. I told him about the beating he gave the man at the bar, but that I hadn't witnessed any illegal activity. He asked about the few friends of Beau's that I had met, and if I knew where any of them could be found. I wasn't much help with that, since I didn't even know where Beau lived.

After I told him about Thanksgiving, Officer Francis asked me some questions about that and if I knew my dad had run a background check on him. I told him I did. He asked why I didn't contact the police when I knew that he was wanted. I became concerned that I was in trouble for not having done that. I explained about my father's death and he seemed to understand. He asked me if I'd had any contact with Beau since then. I pulled out my phone and showed him the texts he sent. Lastly, I told him about Beau showing up at work that day, and how he'd hurt my arm and what we'd talked about.

He had me show him the bruises and then went out the door. He came back in with a female officer, who was holding a camera.

"Sylvia, we need to take some pictures of the bruises." I held out my arm and let them get what they needed.

When the pictures were done, the other officer left and Officer Francis sat down across from me again.

"How do you know Quinn Lobato?"

"I've known Quinn for years. We dated in high school and this fall he moved across the hall from me. We recently started dating again."

He asked me more questions about Quinn. How Beau and Quinn acted towards each other and if Quinn had ever acted violently before.

By the end, I was frustrated with the questions. Quinn wasn't the bad guy in all of this.

"I don't understand why you need to know all of this. Beau is the one who has been harassing me. He's the one who kicked in the door and started all of this. Why are you questioning me about Quinn? Quinn was only protecting himself." I snapped my jaw shut and waited for an answer as I tried not to grind my teeth.

Officer Francis just nodded his head and smiled sympathetically. "I know, Sylvia. We just need to make sure we cross all our t's here. We want to put that scum Dalton away for a very long time, and we want nothing coming back to potentially hurt Mr. Lobato." I was relieved that at least they seemed to see that. "One last question, Sylvia. Do you recognize this?" He held out a little evidence bag with what appeared to be my pendant in it.

I picked it up and looked it over carefully. "This is my pendant. I've been looking for it." I looked back at him in confusion. "Where did you get it?"

"It was found on the floor in the hall of the apartment complex. It's believed that Mr. Dalton had it in his possession. Did you ever at any point give this to him?"

"No," I gasped. "I never gave this to him. I noticed just a couple days ago that it was missing. I've been looking all over the apartment for it. It belonged to my mother. Can I have it back?"

"Yes, but not right away. Right now it's evidence. We think that Mr. Dalton may have broken into your apartment and taken it. Has there been anything else missing?"

"Oh my God. He was in my apartment?" A shiver of fear passed through me, leaving me cold all over. "How many times?"

"We don't know. We were hoping you could help us with that."

I had nothing to add. It could have been at any time. I spent a great deal of time at Quinn's recently, and at his parents' house. I thought back to the day we'd picked Kai and Sloane up from the airport, and how I had the strangest feeling when we came back from the grocery store. He must have been in my apartment that day.

He held out his hand to me again and I shook it. "I think that is all we need here, Sylvia. Either the police or an Assistant District Attorney will be in touch with you regarding this case. Here is my card. If you think of anything else or notice anything else missing, call me. I'm sorry for the circumstances of our meeting, but it was nice to meet you." He got up and walked to the door. I followed, but stopped just outside of it.

"What about Quinn? Is he done? Will he be coming home with me?" I was still afraid that they were going to keep him.

"I don't know, but I'm sure someone will be able to tell you something soon. I wouldn't worry too much, though. It looks like he did all of us a favor taking Beau Dalton off the street."

He led me back to the waiting room. Everyone was there, joined by Alex and Marie. Marie rushed up to me and pulled me into her arms as she rocked us sideways. When she pulled away, she reached down and captured my hand, pulling me over to the chair next to her.

I looked around at all of them. "Anything yet?" I didn't know why I even bothered asking. The bleak looks I was given in return were all the answer I needed.

"We were hoping you would be able to tell us something," Alex said. "What did they talk to you about?"

I filled them in on the questions that Officer Francis had asked. I also told them that he didn't seem like they were going to keep Quinn. We waited a little longer. Finally, the door opened and I heard one of the sweetest sounds in the world to me - Quinn laughing.

I jumped up and headed towards the door, and there he was. His head was thrown back and he was laughing a real laugh -- not a fake, just-to-be-polite laugh. It made me simultaneously happy and relieved, yet it pissed me off, too. We were all out here worried sick over him, and he was standing there laughing with the officers. I cleared my throat and he turned to me. Whatever anger I held evaporated instantly from the heat of his gaze. Those eyes penetrated me and I melted. I threw myself at him. He caught me and staggered back just a bit.

The officer next to him made some comment and everyone laughed. I didn't hear what it was, and I didn't care. I had Quinn safe in my arms. His hard chest was pressed against mine, and his arms tightened around me. It was heaven. I didn't want to let go. But when he relaxed his hold on me, I let my arms loosen as well. I couldn't bear to release him completely, though. I looked up at him and he smiled down at me.

That's when I noticed the bruises along his neck. My eyes went wide in shock. Kai and Sloane had both said he wasn't hurt, yet he had marks on him. I reached up and gently touched them.

"What..." I whispered, but Quinn cut me off.

"Don't worry about it. I will tell you later. Let's just get out of here." He looked around at everyone then. "Dad, thank you for sending Randy in." He let go of me and reached over to Alex and Marie, hugging them both.

"Son," Alex returned the hug. "What is going on?" His concern prominent in his voice.

"I'll tell you all about it at home. Let's just get out of here."

"Reed and I will pick something up for supper and meet you all at your place." Kerri suggested.

"That sounds great. Thank you, Kerri." Quinn gave her an appreciative grin. "Dad, can we ride with you?" I was happy that he included me in that. There was no way I was letting him out of my sight anywhere in the near future.

The ride home was much shorter than the ride there. I stayed in Quinn's arms the entire car ride back. We each shared our stories of what had happened with Beau. I felt Quinn tense up as I told them about Beau showing up at work and what he had said. Quinn muttered something under his breath that I didn't quite catch, but it was something about breaking his neck when he had the chance. I felt the same when Quinn told about Beau kicking in the door and taking a swing at Quinn. I asked about the bruises on his throat and he explained that Beau had choked him. Both Marie and I gasped, realizing that we could have lost him.

We went to Quinn's place instead of mine. I didn't want to go there yet, and Quinn was just fine with that. Kai and Sloane followed after us. I retold my time with Officer Francis to Quinn. The others listened patiently. Soon Reed and Kerri showed up with pizza. Marie and Kai got out plates and drinks from the fridge and everyone grabbed a slice and settled in, waiting for Quinn to begin.

I couldn't eat. I still felt uneasy and slightly sick over all of it. I sat next to Quinn and sipped at my beer, anxiously waiting to hear about his time at the police station. Quinn, on the other hand, didn't have a problem with eating. He was relaxed and joked with Reed and Sloane while he ate. His easy manner should have helped put me at ease, but I just couldn't calm down until I knew for sure that everything was alright.

Finally, Alex asked. Quinn's eyes flashed something as he looked at me, but the look was gone as quickly as it had appeared. He put his plate on the floor and kicked his legs out in front of him, crossing them at the ankles. He already had his arm draped over me, but he pulled me closer to his side as he sighed. I got the feeling that he just wanted to put it all behind him.

"First, let me reassure you all that it should be just fine. The police or the Assistant District Attorney may contact some of you just to find out how Beau acted around Sylvia and me." Everyone nodded. They had expected as much. "They basically asked me what happened today and I told them. He kicked the door in and took a couple swings at me, which I avoided. I tried to sweep his legs out from under him. It didn't work, and he choked me and got a punch in that I deflected. I'm not sure what all else happened. It just went so quickly. I got a couple kicks to his knee, the punch to his nose and then one to the sternum and that's when he went down."

Quinn calmly relayed it all like he was talking about something he had watched on TV more than something he had been involved in. He shrugged and took a drink of his beer, and then continued.

"I told them about Beau harassing Sylvia, and how we were looking at getting some form of protection order. They took pictures of my bruises and the ADA came in and I had to retell it all again. While I was talking to the ADA, there was word from the hospital that Beau was conscious and was going to recover. He has some broken ribs and his nose was broken. There was some severe damage to the ligaments in his knee. Aside from that, there was the nasty concussion he got when his head hit the door frame. All in all he will recover. So no worries that I killed him, Reed."

Reed had a guilty look on his face, and I wondered what that was about.

"What about charges? What are they going to charge him with?" Kerri got to the matter we were waiting for.

"Well, he was already wanted for a whole slew of things. He will probably be extradited back to Texas, where he's wanted for smuggling drugs across the border. There was some other stuff that they were looking for him for, too. He probably won't be charged with anything in connection with today unless I decide to press charges, which I'm not going to do because he can counter them. They are looking into the possible break-in into Sylvia's apartment." He squeezed me tighter and looked at me to see if I knew about that.

"They showed me the pendant. I don't know how else he would have gotten it other than breaking in for it," I answered Quinn.

"Well, he'll be charged for that then. They were also going to take another look into Kelly's accident. They had the reports faxed in and Officer John said that it looked like an accident, but that they would follow up on it. Other than that there really isn't anything to tell."

"Can they charge you with anything? I know it was self-defense, but I don't know how it works." I was still worried about him. We'd just gotten him back. I didn't want to lose him again.

"No. Because he choked me I had reason to believe that my life was in danger. I didn't use deadly force on him, either. I just did what I needed to defend myself. You have nothing to worry about, Sylvia. Believe me, it's over. Beau could go after me in civil court, but the ADA and my attorney, Randy said I would have nothing to worry about. It would likely get thrown out but they didn't think Beau would even try for it. He has enough legal stuff going on."

I was finally able to breathe easily. Quinn wasn't going anywhere and Beau wouldn't be coming back. I looked around at everyone in the room and was thankful for each of them. There was some more questions and Reed and Sloane teased Quinn some more about his ass-kicking skills. Finally, everyone was ready to leave. I made Marie leave the dishes, telling her that I would do them in the morning. I just wanted to get Quinn alone.

I hugged each of them as they left. I made tentative plans with Marie and Kai to go to lunch with them soon. Once they were all gone, I turned to Quinn. Neither of us moved. We just looked at each other, all our love and desire for each other shining in our eyes, flowing freely between us. We both started towards each other at the same time. Each of us realized it and chuckled lightly. We reached for the other and pulled in close. It was just what I'd needed. My arms were filled with him, as was my heart. I sighed against him and just absorbed the feel of him in my arms

"Sylvia, love, I was so worried about you. You were all I could think of. I didn't know if he had hurt you or if he would go back to find you if he managed to get away. All I could think about was you." Quinn's voice was thick with emotion. "I just couldn't live without you again." He kissed the top of my head and continued down to my check and onto my lips.

I met his kiss eagerly. Our kiss shared everything our words couldn't. At some point during the kiss, my thoughts shifted from relief to desire. The picture of him as he walked out of the apartment appeared in my mind. The image turned me on and caused me to groan against his lips. I visualized him all tense and cat-like as he strode out into the sunlight, the pure maleness of him as his muscles moved with each step. Then I remembered that I never asked why he was shirtless. I pulled away and looked up at him.

"Why didn't you have a shirt on or shoes before you left? You looked like you should have been on an episode of Cops."

Quinn stepped back as he laughed at that. He walked over and locked the door and turned back to me.

"I had just gotten out of the shower when he knocked on the door. I thought it was Sloane, so I just pulled my jeans on before I went to answer it." He walked over to me and took my hand, leading me to the bedroom, turning the lights off as we went.

"That's why you didn't answer when I called." I said it more to myself than to him. I knew there had to be a good reason he didn't have his phone on him.

"Yeah, I left it lying on the dresser. I was just going to shower quick and come to pick you up."

We reached the bedroom and he pulled his shirt off and tossed it in the laundry basket. I got another look at his muscles rippling as he moved in the moonlight. He wrapped an arm around me and pulled me with him towards the bed.

I ran my hand up his back and over his shoulder and back down again. As soon as I reached for the zipper on his jeans, it hit me. He said he just pulled his jeans on and went to answer the door.

"So you don't have anything on under these?" I raised my eyebrow.

"Nope," he answered as he began to nibble along my neck.

"Mmmmm," I liked the visual that popped into my head. I tugged the zipper down and pushed the jeans off his hips before pushing him down onto the bed,

He pulled me with him and rolled us so I was on my back. His kiss was long and deep. I was truly alone with Quinn in my happy place, and it was all so very real.

Chapter 25 - Quinn

I T HAD BEEN A HELL of a week. We'd finally gotten confirmation after three long months that everything with Beau was indeed over with. Sylvia's pendant was returned and she was finally able to put it all behind her. She never really came out and admitted that she still worried about him, but I noticed she often looked around carefully whenever we left the apartment. She would hesitate before opening text messages, too. I never said anything to her about it. She never really wanted to stay at her apartment. She had more or less moved into mine. I knew it was just something she needed to work through. I hoped now she would be able to get over that fear.

They also put Kelly's accident to rest, too. There was absolutely nothing to tie it to Beau. I still had a seed of doubt in my mind about that, but I guess I just needed to let that go. From all accounts it was just ice and speed and just a tragic accident. Sylvia accepted that, and was really trying to let it all go. With Mom's help, she finally put his house on the market. She still had his ashes to spread on the lake, but she was waiting for it to get warmer and go out on the boat with Jason's dad to do it.

To top off the week, Sylvia had been sick with a sinus infection. I never did get her to go the doctor. She kept insisting she was fine, that it was just a cold. I kept asking her to go, and finally she relented and let my dad look her over. The antibiotic helped, and she was doing better by the end of the week.

It was spring break and Easter weekend, but no one left town. Kerri and Kai had taken a couple day trips shopping for wedding stuff, but Sylvia stayed behind because she wasn't feeling well. Mom had gone with them one day and she was excited to have us all over to their place for a big Easter dinner. Mom and Dad had taken to all of my new friends. Even Jason came around some. I didn't have the type of friendship with him that I had with Sloane and Reed, but we could be in the same room without it turning into a pissing contest. I think he finally accepted that I wasn't going to leave Sylvia again, and that she loved me.

I put down the textbook I was pretending to study and picked up the remote. Sylvia was due back any minute. I couldn't wait. I missed her whenever we were apart for a whole day. She'd gone to the spa with Kerri and Kai and then they were going shopping. They'd finally made use of the gift certificates from Christmas. Sylvia hadn't really wanted to go, but with a little coaxing she gave in. I was worried about what mood she would be in when she got home. She would probably be tired after having to follow Kai's pace all day. If I'd known when she was going to be home I would have ordered supper or something, but I had no idea when she would return.

I flipped mindlessly through the channels, hoping that Sylvia would feel up to something that night. We hadn't really done anything since she got sick, and I was about at my breaking point with wanting her. After the morning at the spa she would be all soft-skinned and would smell so good. I didn't even think about what I was doing. I was too lost in my thoughts on Sylvia and what I would like to do to her that night. I heard the key in the lock and froze, realizing I had my cock out and in my hand.

I quickly tried to get it back in and zip up before she opened the door. I felt my cheeks get warm and knew I was blushing at almost getting caught by her. It wasn't that she didn't know I jerked off. In fact, she'd even watched me. It was more getting caught doing it in the afternoon on the living room couch that had me flustered. Hell, I wasn't even watching porn to justify it. What was on TV? I glanced over and groaned. I had Discovery Health on. They were showing some random surgery.

All thoughts left when the door opened and I got my first glimpse of post-spa/shopping Sylvia. I knew it was all Kai's doings, but I could have kissed that girl right then and there for what she'd done to Sylvia. Sylvia was standing in the doorway, biting her lip, looking the picture of innocence. Her strawberry blond hair hung in loose curls down her back with a few tendrils over her shoulder in front. She had just a light touch of make up on. Nothing over the top, just enough that it drew my attention to it. I continued my perusal. She had some white button-up sweater looking thing on with a pink and brown argyle pattern on the front. It was slightly tight and cut low enough that it gave a nice view of the milky skin of her collarbone and a hint of the roundness of the top of her breasts. Fuck, she was even wearing a pearl necklace. I had no idea how Kai managed to talk her into the skirt she had on. It was pink and appeared to be denim. It was short as hell, leaving her legs bare and tempting.

"You look so good, Sylvia. How was your day out with the girls?"

I met her eyes after taking her all in, and knew that she was aware of my thoughts as I looked her over. Her eyes grew dark and a light blush rose up from under that revealing sweater and continued to climb up her throat and over her cheeks. That was a blush I knew well, and I knew Sylvia's thoughts weren't too far from my own. It wasn't embarrassment that caused the blood to rush through her. It was lust. Her gaze turned predatory as she stalked towards me. The phrase '*something wicked this way comes*' flitted through my mind. It may have been something wicked, but it was going to be oh-so-good.

She slipped out of her shoes before she got to me, leaving them lying in the middle of the floor. She licked her lips as she stood before me.

"My day was good, but it's about to get much better." Her voice was husky and low and my dick stood up and took notice.

I shifted a bit and she peeked down at my lap and smirked. Without warning she straddled my lap, her tight skirt was pushed up around her hips. I could feel the heat from her as she ground down onto me, simultaneously tormenting and pleasing me. She was all sorts of hot as she lunged forward with a little growl and attacked my throat just under my ear. The little nips and licks sent torrents of electricity shooting through me. She made a little groaning sound and I moaned in return and threw my head back on the couch, letting her have her way with me. I thrust my hips up to her and she pushed back down on me harder.

Sylvia was demanding and seductive and hot as fuck. It was such a contrast to the angelic visage she had on. Her fingers threaded into my hair, digging in slightly before she pulled my head to her. She licked the shell of my ear and sucked on my earlobe, pulling on it with her teeth before she let it go. Her hot breath caressed my ear as she whispered, "You were all I could think about today. I couldn't wait to get home to feel you against me." She slowly rotated her hips as she rubbed against me, eliciting a moan from me. "And in my mouth," she ran her tongue over me again, "and in me." With each word her voice became lower with wanton need. She grabbed my hands as she hummed in my ear, "I need to feel your hands on me." She brought my hands up to her waist.

She leaned back and arched her back and took a deep breath in. I was captivated by her movement, watching her chest rise in front of me. She circled her hips again before unbuttoning her sweater. I was torn between watching her eyes as they promised me delicious things to come, and the unveiling of the pale pink lace bra that was hidden under the sweater. Once the sweater was completely unbuttoned she slid it off her shoulders and let it drop to the floor behind her. She brought her hands back to her sides and slid them up until they were cupping her breasts. She didn't remove the bra but it didn't exactly hide anything, either. Her dark pink nipples were hard and just begging to be taken between my lips. She rubbed her thumbs over them before moaning and letting go. She grabbed my hair again and pulled my mouth to her breasts.

I traced my tongue over the lace from one to the other and back again. Sylvia kept her back arched and her hands in my hair not letting me up. I brought my hands up to her breasts and pushed them together, sucking on the exposed skin that pushed out the top. She let go of my hair and reached down to pull my t-shirt off. I briefly broke contact with her soft, warm skin as she pulled it over my head. Once it was removed, I went back to the delight in my hands. I pulled on the bit of lace and satin with my teeth, scraping her tender skin along the way. She shivered and I smirked, knowing she liked it.

Her hand slipped between us and the heat from her body momen-tarily disappeared. It was replaced with her hand rubbing roughly over my denim-clad hardness. I pushed up against her hand and she pulled it away. I whimpered and she brought it back, stroking up from the base to the top of the waistband. She unbuttoned and unzipped it and slipped her hand in and down around me. She teased me by gently sliding her hand over me, barely touching me. I was still massaging her breasts and licking over her nipples, but my mind was on the feeling of her hand over my cock. I just wanted to thrust up against her and get the friction I craved.

Sylvia shifted to the side and slightly off me and I wanted to pull her back until I realized she was just moving to tug my jeans down. I raised my hips and she pulled them to my knees and resumed her position be-fore tangling her fingers in my hair. She rubbed against me again and I could feel the silk of her panties slide over my dick causing it to twitch in anticipation.

"God, Quinn. You're so hard and it feels so good." She yanked me by my hair up to meet her hungry mouth. There was nothing sweet or innocent about the kiss we shared. It was full of fire and power. Sylvia in charge blew my mind. She was like I had never seen her before, and I'd seen her many different ways. She rubbed herself on me harder with each rotation. I could feel her getting wetter and wetter and her legs started to tense around me.

I slipped my hand down between us and pushed the little patch of material covering my heaven aside. I just wanted Sylvia, no matter what. Her little moans and whimpers against my mouth were driving me crazy. God, she was wet. I easily slid my middle finger along her, probing into her heat. I circled my thumb up to her clit, circling it but not touching it.

"What do you want, Sylvia? Tell me. I want to give you what you want, but you need to tell me." I growled it in her ear before I brought my mouth down to her sweet spot just below her ear.

"I want you to make me come. Please, Quinn. Please make me come." Her words were low and breathy as she begged me.

I hooked my finger, rubbing where I knew she wanted it and pushed against her pearl with my thumb, alternating the pressure between them. It wasn't long before I felt her entire body go rigid and she drew her breath in, holding it, keeping herself from crying out.

I slowed my movements, waiting for her to calm down. It wasn't long before her body relaxed around me and she pushed my hand away. She grabbed my aching cock and brought it to her, rubbing the head along her wetness, teasing us both. As she positioned me where she wanted me, I brought my fingers up to my lips and licked her off them. I loved the taste of her sweetness and, as far as I was concerned, this was just an appetizer.

Her eyes were wild as she sank down. Her warmth enclosed around me, squeezing me as she slid down. She arched back again giving me access to her beautiful breasts as she shifted her hips up and around on me. The sight of her with hungry eyes and her hair cascading down her back with nothing on but a lacy pink bra and a pearl necklace was an image I never wanted to forget. I kept one hand on her hip, massaging it, and brought the other to her still-covered chest. I slipped her breasts out of the cups and took a nipple into my mouth. She cried out and rocked harder onto me. Her nipple puckered tighter as I swirled my tongue over it. I clamped my lips hard around the little bud and grazed it with my teeth.

Sylvia ran her hands up my arms and shoulder sending sparks, deep into the muscles as she passed over them on her way to the back of my neck. She pulled me to her breasts tighter, urging me on with carnal sounds. My hips thrust up to her, matching her movements. She was not slow or tender as she rode me. She took what she needed and it was so very erotic.

I dropped my other hand to hold on to her waist so I could hold her as I thrust up into her. After I let go of her breasts she returned her hands to them, cupping them in an offering to me. I moved to the other one, giving it the attention I had given the first. I was faintly aware of her fingers on her other hand tweaking the other nipple. It was more than I could take, and I raised my mouth to her once again.

It wasn't long before her cries became louder and incoherent. When she tightened around me I didn't even think I could move. She held me in place as her inner muscles massaged my cock, begging for me to come with her. I felt the tightness and pressure rising from my center and I was gone, lost in her as she pulled me over the edge with her into a bliss that I can't even begin to describe.

Sylvia collapsed against my shoulder and we stayed like that for a few minutes as we came out of the fevered haze. I placed soft kisses on her head and took a big breath, drawing her essence in. There was nothing on earth that smelled as wonderful as a recently fucked Sylvia.

Finally, she slid up off me and sat next to me on the couch, where she snuggled up against me.

"God, I needed that after the week I had," She sighed.

I leaned down and kissed her slowly. "I did too." For now I was content, but I was already looking forward to later.

It was an unusually warm day for the end of May. I thought about seeing if everyone was up for going to the park or just doing something outside later. I didn't know what they all had going on since, I had been in class all day. The rest were done for the semester. Mine just went longer, the disadvantage of being in med school. I cut across the street towards the parking lot, gazing at the building ahead of me. When I'd moved in just months ago, I'd never expected my life to change as much as it had. I never would have guessed that this building held everything I'd ever wanted. Once again, my mother knew what was best. Even if I didn't.

I thought back over the time since I'd moved in. How worried I had been waiting for Sylvia to know I was there. How disappointed I was when I found out she was dating Beau, and then how concerned I was once I saw him for who he was. I pushed thoughts of him and that time from my mind. He wasn't worth the seconds my brain wasted on him. Sylvia was happy now, and she was mine and that was all that really mattered.

As I got closer to the door I saw a person sitting on the front steps of our building. I smiled when I realized it was Sylvia. She had been sick quite a bit lately, and I had started to really worry about her. Every time I brought it up she insisted she was fine, that it was just nerves about finals or that she had just eaten something that didn't agree with her. After the episode this morning, I'd been ready to call my dad and have him come talk to her. I figured if she still wasn't feeling well that night I would suggest they come over.

My smile faltered as I approached. Sylvia looked really upset. My first thought was to get her to smile. I did a silly little dance as I walked up and hoped that would help. When her expression didn't even waver, I began to worry. Something was obviously wrong. My first thought was that Beau was out. I knew that was irrational. There was no way he was getting out of a federal drug trafficking charge, and added to that was the gun they found in his pickup the day he came to the apartment plus some other little charges. He was facing over 30 years. There was something else wrong. My thoughts raced: my parents, one of our friends. I realized it could be about anything.

"Sylvia, what's wrong, love?"

She didn't answer me, just stood up and took my hand and pulled me towards the door. I followed her, but I continued to question her. She never said a word all the way up the steps just kept gripping my hand tighter. We got to the door to my apartment and she opened it, leading me inside. She still didn't say anything as she led me down the hall to the bathroom. I was extremely puzzled. The light was left on in there, and Sylvia walked over to the counter and picked something up. I didn't see what it was until she handed it to me. I looked down in confusion at the little white plastic stick in my hand.

Then it hit me. I was holding a pregnancy test. I didn't even need to know what the two pink lines meant. That was obvious from Sylvia's reaction. She was having a baby. No, we were having a baby. My first reaction was fear. My eyes widened and I looked at Sylvia as if to confirm it.

"Are you...is it..." I couldn't even get the question out. Sylvia nodded in confirmation.

I dropped the stick and opened my arms and Sylvia fell into them. She clung to me there in the middle of the bathroom as I held her and rocked her slowly side to side. I didn't know what to say. I had so many emotions coursing through me. I was terrified and yet some part of me was thrilled. I was worried about Sylvia and her health, and then questioned why I hadn't thought of pregnancy as a possibility for her symptoms lately. She was on the pill and this shouldn't have been a problem.

Sylvia sniffled in my shoulder and I realized she was crying. I leaned back and pushed the hair covering her face behind her ear. I swiped my thumb over her cheek to wipe away the tears.

"Sylvia, it's okay. Please don't cry. We can get through this together. It will all turn out." I tried to soothe her.

"But we haven't finished school and we aren't married and we don't have a job and..." She was almost incoherent with her sobs.

"Sylvia, I love you and it's going to be fine. We will work it out. We're together and we can handle this. Come on, let's get you some water and we can talk about it."

I led her back to the couch and went to get her some ice water. I was still in a state of shock, but had to hide that. I needed to be solid for Sylvia right now. She'd had so many life altering things happen to her in such a short time, I didn't want her to hit a breaking point. As much as I was nervous about it, we could do it.

We spent the rest of the afternoon and evening talking about it and making plans for the future. We decided to wait to tell anyone. I'm sure Kai would know soon enough, if she didn't already. Both of us were mentally and physically drained as we lay in bed that night. I smiled as I thought of us and how last year at this time I was alone and now I had Sylvia and we were having a child together. I had my arms wrapped around Sylvia and I knew as long as I had her here next to me everything was alright. She had been quiet for awhile, but I knew she wasn't asleep yet.

"What are you thinking about, love?" I asked her as I snuggled closer to her.

"Just wondering if it's a boy or a girl, and then what to name it." I felt her shoulders move in a shrug. "It's just a huge responsibility, and I want to do it right." I kissed the top of her head and rested my head on hers.

I held her and listened to her heart beat just thinking over her words. "I think Kelly is a nice name."

Epilogue - Sylvia

I FOUGHT MY HEAVY EYES as the gentle rocking motion and stillness of the room threatened to pull me under. I looked down at the peacefully sleeping Spencer. Only ten months old, and he looked so much like Quinn. His soft little tufts of brown hair stuck up at odd angles. His delicate eyelids were closed, hiding the clear curious eyes that were so dark. His long lashes brushed his sweet chubby cheeks. Tiny cherub lips sucked on an invisible nipple in a self-comforting manner.

I hated to get up and put him in his crib, but my arms were getting stiff and I really needed to stretch my back and move around before I too fell asleep. I held him a little tighter with my left arm as I pushed myself up from the rocking chair with my right hand. The little guy had been gaining weight well. He was starting to get heavy when held with just one arm. Once I was up I snuggled him closer with both arms. I prayed with each step that he wouldn't wake up. I kissed his forehead -- loving the feel of the soft skin there -- before laying him down gently. I bundled the cozy, butter-colored fleece blanket around him. I gazed at him for a few seconds longer, just to make sure he was well and truly asleep before I walked away from the crib.

I yawned and stretched as I left the room. I leaned first to the left then the right as I worked to remove the kinks from my low back. *This is why people have kids when they're young.* I wondered what Quinn and Anne were up to as I walked through the house. I heard a high pitched giggle come from the direction of the living room and headed that way. I smiled as I rounded the corner and came to a stop. I stood there at the edge of the room and happily watched my husband and the cutest little princess in the world. They were snuggled close together on the couch giggling. Across their laps was the huge photo album I kept on the shelf near the fireplace.

Anne's curly light red pigtail kept brushing along the underside of Quinn's jaw as he leaned over the little girl to peer at the book with her.

288

He swatted at it and rubbed the spot it tickled, only to have it tickle him again as she bounced with laughter.

"What are you two troublemakers up to now?" I asked and returned Quinn's grin with a wink.

"Papa and I are looking at your funny picture book." Anne announced with a giggle.

"You are?"

She nodded furiously, tickling Quinn again as she did.

"We don't have pictures like this in books at home. Will you come look too, Grammy?"

Her big green puppy eyes pleaded with me. How could I say no to that?

I joined them on the couch and wrapped an arm around Anne as I sat close to her. The arm around Anne pressed against Quinn's side and he reached over with his free hand to trail his finger tips over it. I took part of the book placing the middle of it directly onto Anne's lap. I gave her a little kiss on the top of her head as I settled in.

"Now where are you?"

"We're looking at the pictures of you when you were a princess." She stated with the fascination and awes that only a five year old can have.

Curious to see just when I was a princess, I looked down to see her dainty little finger pointing to a picture of Quinn and I at our senior prom. I laughed and told her that night I felt like a princess.

We flipped through a few more pages of pictures of Quinn and I from high school. We came to the graduation pictures and my eyes involuntarily filled with tears. It wasn't the fact that I knew there should have been more pages following this of the years Quinn and I had missed. I was long over that. It was my dad's image staring back at me that did it. Even after all this time, I still teared up when I saw his picture. There were several pictures of everyone from that day. Both Quinn and I alone, together, with our respective parents and even a group shot of both families combined. I choked back the sadness that threatened to over whelm me. I sniffed and lightly touched the picture of Quinn's parents along with Dad standing with Quinn and me in the middle of the big, happy group. I couldn't help but think that there should have been more like that. I felt cheated of a group photo like this from Kelly's birth, our wedding, holidays and all the other occasions when both families gathered.

Quinn squeezed my arm in comfort and understanding. I bit my lip and then felt a little finger brush over it in the same gesture we used to get her to stop biting her lip all the time.

"Don't do that, Grammy. You'll make it hurt."

Anne had inherited my bad habit of chewing on her bottom lip. Her mother, Kelly, had been trying to break her of the habit because she often had chapped lips.

I gazed into her serious green eyes and didn't see them as my daughter's or my own, as they were so often remarked upon. Instead I saw them as my dad's. Little Anne was similar to him in so many ways. She tended to be a serious little girl who, even though she spoke clearly and well for her age, often remained silent unless there was something that needed to be said. She had his curls, which were slowly darkening to the same auburn shade as both mine and dad's had been. I often felt that she was a little piece of him come back to me.

I gave her a shaky smile and said, "You're right, baby. Thank you for reminding me."

We all turned back to the book and flipped through the next page of the graduation pictures. We continued on through the book. The next few pages held a few with Jason and the rest of the guys I knew through him. After that there were some with Kai, Sloane, Kerri and Reed.

I began to notice that Anne was flipping through the pages more and more quickly with every turn. I assumed she was getting bored, until she peeked up at me with an odd look and a crease on her brow. I glanced at Quinn questioningly to see if he noticed her behavior. He just shrugged and looked back at the book.

I let it go and enjoyed seeing my friends as we were so many years ago. I would have liked to look at the pages longer but Anne turned the pages after just a quick glance. Finally, she stopped and looked from Quinn to myself, still with a look of confusion wrinkling her forehead and scrunching her nose. She freed her bottom lip from between her teeth as she asked, "Where did Papa go?"

"What do you mean sweetie?" I wasn't sure what she was asking.

"He isn't in any of the pictures anymore."

I shifted from Quinn's sad eyes into those of our granddaughter's.

"Papa went to college at Princeton and I was at the University of Minnesota." I answered simply, thinking that was all the answer she would need. Of course that wasn't enough.

"Why didn't you go with him?"

"Well, I still had some growing up to do." I flashed a smug grin at

Quinn, only to have him wink at me in return. "If I had gone with your Papa I never would have met your Aunties Kai and Kerri or your Uncles Sloane and Reed. Then what would you do without your Uncle Reed to toss you around?" I tickled her side, and she grinned before peering up at Quinn. I firmly believed that we were living out the fate meant for us. I looked at our time apart for those few short years as worth it to have brought the others into our lives.

"Keep looking, short stuff. There will be more with me coming soon." The happiness I heard in his voice warmed me. It reminded me that it really was only for a short time in our lives that we were apart.

Sure enough, Quinn appeared on the next page. It was of Quinn and me with the others at one of the many games nights we used to have. I didn't recall which one it was. I could tell from the distance Quinn and I were sitting apart that it had to have been before we were together. While everyone else was looking at the camera, I was looking at Quinn. From the look of sheer longing on my face there wasn't any wonder just how much I had wanted him back in my life. From then on, in the photos that both Quinn and I were in, we were always close together, often touching one another.

A couple of pages chronicled the months I was pregnant with Kelly. My favorite one in that set was the one Quinn took of the two of us on the day he proposed. I closed my eyes and let the vision in my mind replace the picture.

Quinn took me on a drive early one Saturday morning, not long after we found out I was pregnant. We still hadn't told anyone but we planned to do that on Sunday when we would all be going to the Lobatos' place to celebrate the Fourth of July. It didn't take me long to realize that we were headed towards Quarry Springs. I tried everything to get him to tell me why we were going there. He remained silent, just smiling at me smugly. I had just given up when my last threat only got him to wiggle his eyebrows at me and ask if I would do that anyway. I turned and looked out the passenger side window and realized we were near the turn-off for the farm. I turned to him and asked if that was it and he nodded.

Quinn had slipped down to Kai's place that morning, before he'd woke me up, and put a picnic basket together. After a show of my appreciation for planning it, we had a simple lunch that Quinn had made. Later Kai told me she tried to get Quinn to just order something made but he insisted on doing it himself. We feasted on fresh fruit, deli meat sandwiches and Reese's Peanut Butter Cups. It was perfect. After lunch, we spent a lazy day out in the sun just enjoying each other. It was getting near twilight and I jokingly asked if we were staying out there all night or going back. Quinn said we would go back but there was one thing he had to do first.

There in the fading light, he took my hands and told me when he'd let me go before he'd lost a part of himself but finding me again had made him whole. He pulled a ring from his pocket and my breath hitched as I stared at it. I recognized it as his grandmother's and knew he had to have it since Christmas because that was the last time he had seen her. When I turned my attention off the ring that was catching the fading light and throwing sparkles back onto Quinn's face, he smiled at me. "Sylvia, this ring is a symbol of my promise to you that I will never leave you again. Even when we aren't physically together you will always have this reminder with you that I am yours now and always."

He said more and I'm sure it was very beautiful, but my focus was entirely on his eyes and the sincerity and love that was in them. There was never really a question of what my answer would be. It did become a question of when it was going to take place.

I looked up into Quinn's eyes then and saw the same expression in them as there was thirty one years before. I melted at that look now as I did on that day.

We also had pictures from a very quiet, very private wedding for Kai and Sloane. It surprised us all when Kai announced that her wedding was going to be limited to just their close friends and immediate family. Of course it was an extremely beautiful and absolutely perfect Christmas wedding, except I was also about thirty-two weeks along. It didn't seem to matter to Kai since she found me "the perfect dress" anyway.

Anne was thrilled with the next group of pictures. She giggled at seeing her mom so small, "just like baby Spencer." We had pictures of Kelly with everyone, but my favorite was the one of her, Quinn and I. I was holding her, gazing into her beautiful little face with wonder, while Quinn was beaming with pride down on us. Quinn pointed to his favorite. It was of me asleep with Kelly tucked in my arms both of looking both peaceful yet completely wore out.

There were several more pages of baby Kelly. She was everyone's darling and we all took pictures of her frequently. After that followed our wedding. By sheer coincidence it took place exactly one year to the day of us finding out I was pregnant. We had a lovely outdoor service in Alex and

Marie's backyard. Quinn picked a spot in the yard near his mom's flower beds and said the spot had special meaning to him. He didn't elaborate.

I briefly took in the first of the pictures. It was Quinn standing at the end of the isle waiting for me. I turned my gaze off the book and onto him. That line you hear in too many movies and books was true. He was just as handsome now as he was that day. His hair was still dark but silver was in a fully fledged takeover, especially in the last few years. His laugh lines were deeper and the crinkle around his eyes had expanded. Both of which were more pronounced as he smiled down at his first grandchild. His brow also had a couple permanent furrows. None of it bothered me. I knew each worry and each smile that helped bring them about, and each one had been shared with me.

I heard the pages being turned but I didn't look down at them I continued to study Quinn lovingly. I knew the pictures of our wedding well. There were the standard wedding pictures of me with Quinn and I, Quinn with his parents and all of us together. There were the ones of the wedding party and Jason giving me away. I wasn't sure if he would because I knew he wasn't the biggest supporter of Quinn and I. He was the closest thing I had to a family member. Jase had been thrilled I'd asked him to do it.

Then there were the candid pictures from that day. Ones of Kai and Kerri helping me get ready, some of the guys decorating Quinn's car and the one and only proof we have of why Reed should not be trusted to take care of things.

"Grammy, why is Uncle Reed crawling on the grass in his dress up clothes?"

I elbowed Quinn and asked sarcastically, "Yeah, why is he crawling around?"

Quinn chuckled as he told Anne, "Look at Grammy's pretty rings. See the one without the shiny stone on it?" She nodded and pointed to my plain gold band. "That is the ring I gave your grandma on the day I married her, but before I did I had Reed pick it up at the store where I had a man write a special message to your grandma in it. Uncle Reed was handing it to Uncle Sloane to hold until I needed to give it to your grandma."

Quinn had simply had *"yours forever"* etched inside my ring.

"Reed dropped it in the grass and we almost didn't find it. I almost didn't get to marry your grandma and that would have been sad." Quinn teased the girl. Nothing, not even a lost ring, would have kept us from marrying that day.

Anne knew the teasing tone her grandpa had and played along with him. "That would have been real bad. Who would have made you cookies?" She said, shaking her head.

I giggled at the two of them and took over turning the pages for the moment. We flipped past pages of the day we moved into our first house. Marie's parents had given us a small house for our wedding. It wasn't the cottage I had admired that New Year's Eve with Quinn so long ago, but it was still in the same neighborhood and was very similar. It had been a picturesque little place. I hated leaving it after just five short years but we outgrew it with the birth of our son, Billy.

Quinn and I laughed at the pictures from Kerri and Reed's wedding. After a nasty argument with her mother over a reception venue, Kerri spitefully turned all wedding planning over to Reed's mom. The ceremony itself was a very upscale traditional catholic wedding, with one exception. A few minutes before she was to walk down the aisle, Kerri had had it with her mother's constant complaining. The question of whether or not a shotgun would be involved pushed Kerri over the edge. She sweetly replied, "No, but the bride is going to be barefoot." She then kicked off her overpriced heels and did indeed walk down the aisle barefoot.

The reception, which had been the source of contention between Kerri and her mother, ended up being at the local VFW in Reed's hometown. Mrs. Walker wanted there to be a "touch of class" to show Kerri's parents that they, too, were "cultured." The reception was followed by a dance on a farm in one of Reed's uncle's sheds, which his younger brothers complained about having to "spiffy up" for the newlyweds.

It was the best wedding I have ever been to, other than my own of course. I believe a good time was had by all. Even Kerri's mother had fun -- after a few glasses of champagne.

The years chronicled in the album flew by as quickly as the pages turned. The book was filled with images of birthday parties, holidays, family reunions, vacations and just everyday life, all had really only been just a blink in time. They were frozen images of moments that would forever evoke warm, loving memories.

As the images proceeded by I paused a little longer at some than others. The births of each of our children were certainly ones that caught Anne's attention. With each child all our little families grew right along with each other. The year that Kelly turned three we added Kai and Sloane's daughter MaryBeth and Kerri and Reed's daughter Violet.

Two years later we all "drank the water" on a shared vacation and all ended up due within weeks of each other. Reed and Kerri were unfortunately the first to greet their new addition. Little Lily was born at thirty two weeks. She was tiny but a fighter. She was still the spunkiest one of the bunch.

I had our son, Billy, nine days before Kai and Sloane's son Mark. Both Kai and I were done after that. We had one of each and thought that was enough. Kerri and Reed tried again and again and again. Kerri gave up when they had their own basketball team. Each daughter bore the name of a flower. Reed named them all saying each one was as beautiful as their mother and deserved to be named after a beautiful thing. In addition to Violet and Lily there was Dahlia, Jasmine and Zarah. Nineteen years after Violet's and ten years after Zarah's birth Reed got his son. We were all shocked. Poor little Robby was mothered not only by Kerri but his sisters as well.

Robby was only a little older than Anne and she idolized him. He wasn't always thrilled to be in that position as he ended up spending a lot of time having to play with her when we were altogether. At least he had Reed and Kerri's first grandchild, Patrick, a boy just four years younger than Robby. Patrick and Robby were the best of friends. Whatever they got up to Anne wanted to join in.

We came to the end of the book with the pictures of baby Spencer's birth. I needed to add some pages to fit the pictures from the past few months in. I tended to get behind on that.

"That was a great book, Grammy."

I hugged Anne tight but gazed into Quinn's eyes as I did so. "Yes it was, baby." Quinn's dark depths spoke volumes of love and happiness back at me. We were truly blessed with good things. His parents were still living in Minneapolis. Our friends were nearby. Reed and Kerri stayed in Minneapolis, too, but Sloane and Kai moved to Chicago, which really wasn't all that far. We were still able to get together often.

I closed the book and asked, "Who's ready for some cookies?"

Anne bounced on the couch and happily sang, "Me, me, me!"

Both Quinn and I chuckled at the little darling's enthusiasm. I moved towards the bookcase to put the album away. I would have to take it out again sometime soon and add the other pictures in. Maybe then I would sit longer and take the time to truly enjoy each memory. Anne and Quinn had gotten off the couch and I figured they would beat me to the kitchen.

Instead Anne called out to me.

"You dropped one." I held out my hand for the photograph that Anne picked up. Before she handed it to me she looked at it quizzically. "Grammy, why are you outside with your shirt off?"

Confused to see what she could be talking about I looked down to see the picture in her hand. It was the one of me from way back in high school out at our abandoned farm. I shot a chiding look at Quinn as soon as I realized what it was. He just shrugged nonchalantly but there was nothing innocent about the gleam in his eye or the sexy smirk he flashed back at me.

- The End -

ABOUT THE AUTHOR

NM Facile is the youngest of a large Midwestern family. She grew up in a small town before going on to college at the University of South Dakota. Her works are contemporary romances that can deal with controversial social topics. When not writing, she spends her time with her family and friends.